EUROPA
AWAKENS

Jim Fairchild

Jim Fairchild

available through Amazon.com

Jim Fairchild

Published by
James H. Fairchild
P.O. Box 7485
Missoula, MT 59807-7485

ISBN 9781976893377
Library of Congress data pending

For
Dave Scheiding
(1946 – 2014):

Merchant Mariner, mountaineer, carpenter, barber, Antarctic heavy equipment operator *extraordinaire*. Grandfather. Orphan. Not to mention a *mean* harmonica player—he taught the penguins to dance, and filled our hearts (human *and* penguin) with joy.

Jim Fairchild

All I want is the truth. Just gimme some truth.
--John Lennon, "Gimme Some Truth"

The truth will set you free. But not until it is finished with you.
--David Foster Wallace, *Infinite Jest*

FOREWORD

I t has been a daunting challenge to research the odd life and equally odd disappearance of Arroyo Bronson. Arroyo was a very private person and kept no journals. He rarely joined the incessant chatter and hum of the human hive via iMind. He had no friends (or so he thought). Despite repeated requests, I never received a scintilla of cooperation from the National Science Welfare Foundation, which ran the Europa program for three decades before the agency was recently abolished. The agency's archives, which should have been preserved in the public domain, seem to have vanished. My research leads me to the inevitable conclusion that vast troves of documentation about the early years of Europa's habitation have disappeared into the ether.

I have relied heavily on interviews with dozens of co-workers from Arroyo's long years on Europa. To speak with them, I have travelled to the rime-encrusted rusting relics of oil rigs in Antarctica's wind-whipped Ross Sea, to the starkly shadowed ice mines of Luna, to the glitzy neon-lit Strip of Ganymede's Kardashia, and to the ambitious new city of Arroyoville currently under construction on Europa. Arroyo's co-workers tend to be interplanetary gypsies who do contract work and then move on; they can be hard to track down.

Jim Fairchild

I received considerable help from the kind library staff at the Edward H. White Space Museum in Kardashia. While its archives were never meant to provide an exhaustive history of the settlement of Europa, its displays include many priceless relics from the ill-fated U.S.S. Pegasus mission to the Jovian moon. I fell in love with the venerable but shiny old U.S. Navy Challenger tractor on display, which is a sister to Arroyo's beloved old Drag Queen.

I have relied heavily on the remembrances of Brooke Applegard and her riveting unpublished memoir, *Arroyo Shrugged: The Man Who Bore Europa on His Shoulders.* Some passages from her memoir are used with her permission. I cannot thank her enough and pray for her continued safety. As will be explained later, Ms. Applegard is currently in hiding.

My greatest gratitude goes to Annie Pfleger, currently the first elected mayor of Europa's newly renamed McMurdo City. She was the last human to see Arroyo as he fled upward onto Europa's Polar Plateau three days before Christmas 2297. Annie, above all others, knew Arroyo—or at least as well as one might hope to know a reticent, even anti-social person—and wants his story to be remembered: free of rumors, free of tales, free of half-truths.

J.F.
Lava Hot Springs, Idaho, Earth
9/13/2304

PART ONE:

FLAT LIGHT

Arroyo couldn't remember much. He'd be the first person to say so, and most of his co-workers would heartily concur. This morning was even worse than usual. His head hurt so badly after a month of R&R on Ganymede that he barely knew where he was. All he knew for sure was that this was the first day of his new contract on Europa. He could have taken the standard year off back on Earth between contracts (on top of nearly two years of travel time back and forth in stasis at quarter-pay). But Arroyo had been gone from Earth so long he'd forgotten much about it. The idea of returning was strangely repulsive to him.

After a day-long psych test to verify his ability to handle back-to-back contracts—he'd memorized the answers years ago—he'd headed off for the paid month on Europa's larger and comparatively urban sister moon. Ganymede: Bright Lights, Big City. He'd been on another colossal Trank bender the whole time on Ganymede, and now it was the first few minutes of the first day of his sixth three-year contract as Heavy Equipment Operator with Europa Traverse Operations. He would turn 47 before he finished the new contract. He assumed he'd die on Europa some day. Monday morning meetings were bad enough without feeling as if you'd just been dragged a thousand kilometers behind a tractor across Europa's hideous Chaos Terrain.

The meeting was in the delapidated orange and white shack officially known in McMurdo Station as Building 17. Like the rest of Mactown, Building 17—known as Stalag 17 to its congregants, in deference to a pre-Crash movie nobody but Arroyo had heard of—was deep within the ice of Jupiter's moon. The cavernous, frost-caked station had been built almost 75 years earlier by the U.S. Navy, a hundred meters beneath the ice to shield its occupants from the radiation above. A human without protection would receive a lethal dose on Europa's surface in a single day. The names of McMurdo, Stalag 17, and countless other features on Europa had been borrowed by the Navy from Antarctic lore in homage to its legendary VXE-6 Squadron, which had done so much pioneering on Earth's frozen continent more than a third of a millenium earlier.

When an inner solar system treaty penned three decades ago prohibited (in theory) the militarization of the solar system beyond the asteroid belt, the Navy turned over the station's keys to the National Science Welfare Foundation. Stalag 17, like the rest of Mactown, showed its age and the appalling apathy of generations of bureaucrats and politicians toward maintaining infrastructure.

The station had been hastily blasted into the granite-hard ice of Europa by a Navy crew on a one-way mission in search of a Mars Peoplemover that had been hijacked by a middle-aged commercial pilot turned Thumper fanatic. No trace of Mars Flight 370 was ever found; the religionist behind the controls likely plunged it nose-first into Jupiter's swirling atmosphere, taking all 2,911 mostly Chinese would-be Mars colonists (hermetically sealed in stasis like comatose canned sardines) down with him. The crew of the Navy cruiser hastily diverted to search for Flight 370, the U.S.S. Pegasus, had left Earth orbit knowing it had insufficient fuel to return. No human had yet set foot on Ganymede or Europa; there were no fueling stations yet in the Jovian system. So Europa was the end of the line. They had the dubious distinction of being the first humans to make landfall on the fractured iceball. Temperatures at the equator averaged minus 160 degrees Centigrade. When the crew hurriedly built McMurdo, it was with the understanding that they might die there before a rescue ship could arrive. The crew's Seabee contingent gave the job the best efforts Navy tradition, their meager construction materials and their spirits allowed, but they apparently misplaced their tape measures and levels. The current landlord, the NSWF, had never found infrastructure upkeep a sexy line item in its annual budget requests. So, as the Traverse Ops manager droned on about new NSWF and Company policies, Arroyo could gaze out through a yawning crack in the bowed plascrete walls and glimpse the rime-caked ice of the station's huge grotto. He imagined squeezing his aching head through the crack and pressing it against the opaline blue ice.

Apparently the Europa science program—known simply as The Program to the 750-ish support workers and eighty or ninety researchers ("grantees" in NSWF parlance) who called Europa home—was in yet another budget crisis. The Program was a two-headed monster: the NSWF was responsible for its administration, but the actual work was farmed out to what Arroyo simply called The Company: whichever massive defense contractor happened to currently have the contract. Arroyo and the other support personnel were on The Company's payroll, not the NSWF's. Of course, the money came from the NSWF, and the NSWF in turn relied on Congress for its funding. According to the Traverse Ops manager, yet another government shutdown was being threatened by squabbling Senators. Government agencies had been instructed to begin planning to shutter their operations if the impasse couldn't be resolved. The Traverse Ops manager—a careerist with full benefits, as opposed to the contract peons who received fat salaries but little else—assured the assemblage that Traverse Ops was considered "mission-critical," and would continue to function until the last fiscal plug was pulled. Fuel, food and cargo still needed to be dragged to the Pole Station and the dozen or so smaller field camps as long as they were staffed. Hauling loads to the field with tractors would always be far more cost-effective than using flitters or heavy-lift ships; Traverse Ops was the darling of NSWF's bean-counters. Traverse Ops operators were jealously derided by other workers because their jobs were almost shutdown-proof.

If the Senate couldn't resolve its differences, other departments on station would begin the shutdown process. The shutdown threats had happened several times before, in this age of perpetual, purposeful, political chaos, so everyone knew the drill. Grantees would start to power down research projects that had been in development for decades and on which academic careers hinged; they would try to preserve all the data gathered so far and plan (without much hope) to deal with the blank spaces in their data logs that a shutdown would cause. Plumbers, electricians, lab techs, weather observers, IT geeks, supply clerks, bakers and janitors and the station's solitary barber/beautician would start to tidy up their work areas, pack their duffels, and face the possibility of a stint in stasis until the next resupply vessel could pick up their palletized hibernation chambers for the year-long trip back to Earth. Their contracts were written to absolve The Company of financial responsibility if the whims of governance required a premature return—they wouldn't even draw stasis quarter-pay if sent back to Earth early.

The NSWF station manager, Barry Wilton, was introduced. Barry had started on Europa as a contract worker an amazing 28 years earlier, just after The Program was turned over to civilian hands. He had worked as a contract peon for many years before being hired by the NSWF's Office of Off-Earth Programs (known as OFFOFFPRO to the jaded and cynical, which was almost anyone who had been in The Program more than a year or two). Barry was a quiet, gentle man, but he certainly *looked* like someone who had spent almost three decades on a frozen slushball from which the Sun is just a bright star. As an NSWF manager, he was entitled to rotate back to Earth every other year via the exclusive Slingshot Express to work in a corner office suite with a cramped view of the Potomac at headquarters in Arlington. The Express runs took a mere 45 days, didn't require a stint in stasis, consumed enough energy to light New New York for a month and were reserved for high Program muckety-mucks or the obscenely rich with a bucket list including a First-Class flyby of a Jovian moon. But Europa was in Barry's blood; he, too, had forgotten much about Earth (or couldn't trust the memories he had), so he almost always declined the chance to rotate back. There were rules restricting how many years someone could work on Europa—to protect an individual's health and sanity, and to protect The Program from liability.   But if a person was considered indispensable (like Barry) or hopelessly addicted to life on Europa (and hence likely to self-destruct if forcibly returned to Earth, as Arroyo predicted about himself), waivers to the rules could be requested, so long as cumulative radiation exposure was carefully documented and fell within certain fuzzy parameters.

Even though the heat in Stalag 17 was as stifling as a locker room, Barry wore his oversized red parka, the hood pulled up over his grey, scraggly ponytail. The ponytail had probably looked dashing thirty years earlier. He rubbed at his long, grey, egg-yolk-encrusted mustache and beard. "I assure you operators you'll be the last to go into stasis if the Senate drops the ball. Until then, I know you'll pull your loads out to the field as efficiently and as safely as ever. I was one of you folks once. I'm not just The Man, you know."

Barry was, indeed, The Man on Europa. In addition to his humdrum administrative duties, he was a U.S. Marshal (certified via online correspondence course), allowing him to make an arrest and lock someone up in the supply room of the station Chapel if criminality above the usual Saturday night overindulgences occurred. This was the extent of law enforcement on Europa; while Ganymede had a police force as huge (and as ornery) as pre-Crash Los Angeles, Europa was a tiny science outpost with no industry or cities. Barry *was* The Law. It was rumored that in order to cope with any potential employee insurrection Barry had snuck onto Europa a four-centuries-old Colt .45 revolver (a classic but forbidden antique in the year 2297) and a box of mouldering ammo, and that the pistol was disassembled into several parts, each stashed in a different hiding place on station. Barry only smiled knowingly, eyes twinkling, twirling the ends of his mustache sinisterly, whenever Fuckin' New Guys asked him about the Colt. Of course, *if* such a pistol existed, and was stored in pieces all over the station, it would be useless in an insurrection. But that didn't stop the rumor. McMurdo was full of hundreds of similar rumors and tales and half-truths, and the old-timers did nothing to dispel them. They were usually far more alluring than the lowly truth. Arroyo had forgotten enough of them—half-truthful and otherwise—to fill a book.

The latest rumor buzzing through the galley at mealtimes was that the newly finished rebuild of the ice runway just outside Mactown had been constructed directly over the icy unmarked grave of the last survivor of the Pegasus crew that was stranded and perished on Europa. Rumor had it that the NSWF knew about the grave and decided it was a bit of historical unpleasantry best buried without a trace. Arroyo was constantly amazed by the audacity of new rumors, even though he'd been on Europa longer than most and thought he had heard them all. For all he knew the story about the grave could be true—the NSWF had an unwritten but obvious policy of making distasteful history disappear. Although it was an obscure little government agency that many taxpayers didn't even know existed any more, it was marvelously adept at the science of spin.

Arroyo could remember that when he first came to Europa

Jim Fairchild

there was a McMurdo Historical Society on station. Originally founded by Navy personnel, the society consisted of a half-dozen volunteers who maintained a dusty corner office in a delapidated Quonset. The floor of the office was so off-kilter a Trank bottle laid on its side would roll from one wall to the other (Arroyo could attest to this). The office's shelves were filled floor to ceiling with rare editions of books documenting decades of both Navy and civilian exploration of the outer solar system. Vastly more were stored on the society's hard drives. Cabinets were filled with yellowing photos of the early expeditions—both the spectacular successes and the spectacular failures. Much of history wasn't pretty; many lessons among the outer planets had been hard-won. The most hallowed part of the office was the softly lit glass cabinet containing personal journals, photos and mementos from that original stranded Pegasus crew: a pair of hopelessly frayed boot socks that some sailor had repaired dozens of times with mismatched yarn, ornaments from the doomed crew's last Christmas together before the deaths started, a photo of the rime-caked cemetery just after it was discovered by the next Navy crew to arrive. A visiting NSWF manager from Arlington felt that the office space could be better used as a pottery workshop. The books, photos, hard drives and mementos were crated up until a new location for the collection was decided upon. No decision ever came. The crates vanished. The volunteer head of the Historical Society asked for an accounting of the missing items from station management. After repeated inquiries his contract was voided for poor performance. He was in stasis within 24 hours and forklifted onto the next resupply vessel headed back to Earth.

Arroyo had spent considerable off-time when not hammered on Trank searching old online Navy archives for an account of the Pegasus crew's demise. It seemed those records no longer existed. The best he could gather from civilian news

14

archives was that the crew perished within five years of landing on Europa, succumbing to radiation, despair and suicide. The final survivor apparently gussied up his companions' neatly marked graves, then sat back on the top of a high penitente with a commanding view of the icy chaos of Europa and took his own life by hooking a helium bottle to his suit's oxygen inlet.

The belated Navy rescue mission that arrived on Europa a year after that final death found the silent, frozen rudiments of subsurface Mactown, the neatly ordered graveyard, and the radiation-fried remains of the last man on the icy rise. Appalled, the rescue crew hastily dragged the lone corpse like a satchel of crispy dog treats down to the flats and slid it into a shallow hole scratched in the ice several hundred meters from his companions. Eager to leave the forlorn moon, mortified by what they had found, the rescue crew neglected to properly mark that final grave, assuming that a third Navy mission would build a proper memorial to the lost Pegasus crew. That next mission didn't arrive for decades. By then the location of the last survivor's grave had been lost to history.

At least that was what Arroyo had gleaned from his research. Yet as he searched fruitlessly for the original Navy duty logs and journals that should have still existed somewhere, he sensed a deliberate effort to make the past go away. He didn't know where truth ended, where rumor and deliberate misinformation began. When he was sober enough to give it thought, his suspicions infuriated him. Which was enough to drive him to drink.

* * *

Despite his hangover, Arroyo grinned at Barry. Only one other operator had worked on Europa as long as Arroyo, and nobody knew Barry better than Arroyo. Which wasn't saying

Jim Fairchild

much. After fifteen years on Europa, declining to take the usual breaks on Earth that are offered between contracts, Arroyo's interpersonal skills had atrophied. Barry had been on Europa almost *twice* as long. Barry could be seen walking around the sub-surface station between buildings with his parka hood pulled up— even though the temperature was a comfortable minus 10 degrees Centigrade in the common areas—one hand buried in a parka pocket, the other stroking his long beard, eyes glued downward, as if searching the ground at the tips of his scuffed low-g boots for leprechaun treasure. He didn't touch Trank, but FNGs assumed he was ripped out of his gourd most of the time. He had seen thousands of contract workers rotate in and out in his time; FNGs would smile and say hello but rarely get a response. Arroyo was the only person on station who could walk past Barry and say hello and *always* get a smile or a wave. Barry and Arroyo had an unspoken understanding about what each other had occasionally seen and endured. Smart people came to Europa once, worked hard, saved their money and then went back to Earth wealthy. If you stayed too long, like Barry and Arroyo, it was a one-way career cul-de-sac. Money was irrelevant. There was no going back.

Barry had also spent his early years working in the deep field, far from the comforts (and close science-ghetto confines) of Mactown. Barry knew that Arroyo had spent the entirety of his Europan career as far out in the deep field as he could go. They both detested Mactown; Barry was stuck there because he had to man the NSWF office, but Arroyo volunteered for every slot available on resupply traverses or on the staff at field camps in order to get out to the Back Forty. They had both seen things that an Earth-bound human would never comprehend. Arroyo never bothered to describe the deep field to new operators before their first traverse, even if they were crusty veterans of the ice mines on Luna or Mars. Words failed to describe what it was like to look

16

upward at the monstrous, dimly lit, swirling globe of Jupiter hanging just over your head, blotting out half the universe, as if you were trapped in a huge black hydraulic press poised to crush you. Europa is tidally locked to Jupiter, with one side of the moon always facing the gas giant. That side was always cloaked in almost complete darkness. Many FNG operators making their first traverses to the Pole Station located there freaked out. Arroyo had seen people climb out of their tractors at the Pole after the grueling sixteen-day run from Mactown, stretch their tired muscles, then accidentally glance upward at the swirling mass of dark gases hanging just over their head, and fall flat out on the ice, insensible, the inside of their helmet visors sprayed with vomit. Arroyo had sedated more than one operator over the years and each time, following SOP, radioed Mactown for a flitter to fly out a replacement operator to make the retro run back to town. He would pass on a message for the replacement operator: When you get here, be prepared before you look up.

* * *

Barry finished his chat with the crew, buried his veiny hands in his parka pockets and shuffled out of Stalag 17 into the coolness of the station grotto. The Traverse Ops manager was trying to program a live feed from the NSWF Ganymede office on the large-screen monitor; face turning splotchy purple, he sputtered and cursed under his breath, fumbling with the remote, until a twenty-something operator jumped up from a couch to help him. As he rose, a miasma of dust billowed up from the couch. The miasma reeked of decades of poorly-washed middle-aged men's asses. Arroyo always thought that the aromas emanating from the office couches told one important aspect of the history of Europa for those strong enough to stomach the tale.

Abbie Hoffman, Arroyo remembered. The department's

Jim Fairchild

resident Neo-Hippie. Ginger dreadlocks, freckles, *tres* expensive faux bad-teeth implants, an aversion to bathing, the perpetual stench of patchouli oil. An irritating, know-it-all, rich kid on a paid three-year lark to the outer solar system. He was on Europa for shits and giggles, not to work. The hippie thing was into a full-on reboot more than 300 years after Hippie 1.0 had been released.

The kid's name wasn't Abbie Hoffman, of course. Arroyo had named him that. Right now Arroyo couldn't remember who the real Abbie Hoffman was, but he was sure he'd learned the name from his father—one of the world's leading authorities on the final century of pop culture before the Crash. His father was by day a prominent New Minneapolis neurosurgeon, but in his free time studied the absurd things humans obsessed about as they profligately bred and consumed their way up to and over the population precipice in the second half of the 21st century. Human numbers had plunged from an insanely unsustainable nine billion down to slightly more than a billion in less than a century. The refusal of pre-Crash humans to acknowledge that they were just as susceptible to the laws of population biology as gazelles and cockroaches (one species now extinct, the other more populous than ever) seemed quaint and endearing now to the artistic and hipsterish. Arroyo found nothing quaint about human idiocy. His mother, the head librarian at the University of Minnesota, was perhap's the world's last non-computerized authority on Jonathan Swift.   In a world in which almost every square inch of many people's bodies was festooned with a garish mishmash of clashing tattoos (another nod to pre-Crash pop culture), Arroyo had only one, discretely inked across his shoulders. It was from *Gulliver's Travels*, a book his mother had given him on his tenth birthday:

I CANNOT BUT CONCLUDE THE
BULK OF YOUR NATIVES TO BE
THE MOST PERNICIOUS RACE

OF LITTLE ODIOUS VERMIN
THAT NATURE EVER
SUFFERED TO CRAWL UPON
THE SURFACE OF THE EARTH.

The meeting quickly lost focus during the live-feed snafu; a dozen simultaneous conversations broke out. The din was too much for Arroyo; years of operating equipment had ruined his hearing despite the most high-tech of protection, and all of the voices blended into a painful cacophony of white noise. He wanted desperately to slink out the door behind Barry. Instead, he slid farther down into the plastic chair in the back row, amongst other old hands. They had seen and heard it all before, and sat silently, some with stubbled chins in hands, greasy baseball caps and slouch hats pulled low over their bleary eyes, nursing hangovers not quite so epic as Arroyo's, lost somewhere in their iMind inbox or dreaming of a favorite childhood swimming hole on a Terran river or the tender curves of a lover they hadn't seen in years—if they could in fact *really* remember that swimming hole or those tender curves, and if those things even really existed any more. In fact, once you forgot those things completely, surviving a contract and inking yet another became much easier. The old hands sat near the filthy sink and coffee machine at the back of the room. The counter and the floor around Arroyo's low-g boots were littered with crushed plastic cups. Operators, especially the veteran men, proudly refused to clean up after themselves—they felt it was below their pay grade. Arroyo was an exception. He had worked at Traverse Ops for so long he considered the office part of his home; he arrived early before the start of his shifts to do housecleaning before his less-tidy co-workers arrived. He did not resent this at all; it was simply the right thing to do.

Something suddenly burned intensely across Arroyo's back. He sat upright with a jolt. He reached rearward and winced

19

when he touched his back. At first he thought someone had spilled scalding coffee on him. But his back was dry. He had no clue what he had done to himself on Ganymede, but would have to check himself for damage right after the meeting.

A crushed coffee cup ricocheted off the back of his head. He turned around.

"Hey, turdball. Welcome back." It was Derrick Sanders, Arroyo's foreman. Derrick grinned, sticking the tip of his tongue out impishly. He wore wire-rimmed glasses that brought the name *John Denver* to Arroyo's hazy mind—another ancient cultural reference he must have absorbed from his father. Derrick wore the glasses even though the lenses were non-corrective. Nobody had needed glasses in a couple of centuries unless they *chose* to be blind. Glasses—as well as blindness and bad teeth—were retro fads. Derrick was a zealous lady's man, and he calculated that the glasses had gotten him laid enough times to justify having them shipped to Europa from an antique shop on New Zealand's South Island. The cost of shipping them to Europa was probably a year's salary, but Derrick had started on Europa a year after Arroyo, and after so many years money had little meaning.

"Catch me after the meeting," Derrick whispered. The live feed from Ganymede was ready to start. "I'll get you up to speed after your groovy R&R."

"Cool," Arroyo rasped. He sat upright and reached back through his layers of clothing. His shirt was stuck to his back—he had no clue what sort of bodily fluid (or whose) was responsible.

The room grew quiet. The live feed was from NSWF's Office of Jovian System Operations—OFFJOVSYSOPS. Almost everything in The Program was known by an acronym. As in all bureaucracies, knowledge was power. Acronyms served to obfuscate both the important and the mundane and force newcomers to constantly ask their meaning—an effective and humiliating way of reminding them of their place in the pecking order. Arroyo, keenly aware of the relatively opulent lifestyle on Ganymede compared to the rugged realities of Europa, called OFFJOVSYSOPS "Sissy Ops." He had to be careful with whom he shared the appellation, however. Shaming was a hate crime, so like many (if not most) thoughts that lurched through his addled brain, he kept it to himself.

The first speaker was Sally Train. She was one of two co-directors at OFFJOVSYSOPS. Skinny, weighing perhaps forty-five kilos dripping wet, caved chest and hunched shoulders, not yet thirty years old. Hair looking like she hadn't bathed in a week, although on Ganymede you could take all the showers you wanted (on Europa it was one three-minute spritz a week). She began to intone her encouragement to the Europan workers facing the potential shutdown. She stumbled over the notes she was reading verbatim off her Darkberry, coughed repeatedly, muttered *um* and *like* far too many times. *Real leadership material*, Arroyo thought. But then he had never really encountered leaders in The Program—just a revolving turnstile of careerist managers.

And then he remembered that he had met her. It was years ago at a field camp—Upstream Delta? Midstream Charlie? Siple Dome? He had hauled loads to—or worked at—almost all of them, many of which hadn't existed for years. She had flitted out for a surprise inspection from Mactown on one of the whirlwind visits high Program muckety-mucks reluctantly make to the boonies from time to time. She swaggered into the galley Jamesway like a conquering general, the flitter pilot behind her, and threw her helmet and suit onto a table on which the camp cook had been carefully filling sugar shakers. Shakers and sugar flew everywhere. Arroyo, the cook and the camp Fuelie were the only camp staff in the galley, and they shielded their eyes from the flying debris.

"What's a woman got to do to get laid around here?" she asked. "Daylight's burning." She set down a half-empty bottle of

21

antique whiskey in the midst of the sugary carnage. Arroyo had heard the same tone of voice when other DVs (Distinguished Visitors) had arrived, but usually they just wanted to know where they could find a restroom *pronto*.

Arroyo had passed on the opportunity. The Fuelie and the cook hadn't. The next morning, Arroyo had to cook breakfast for the rest of the camp and fill the camp's generator tanks, as the other two were too exhausted to work. They later apologized to Arroyo, who told them that a few centuries ago they could have honestly said they'd been up all night "pulling a train." Neither knew what a train was, so Arroyo had to explain the obsolete public conveyance, eventually resorting to drawing a picture complete with a chugging steam engine.

Sally stepped away from the podium. Her co-director stepped up next and introduced himself: Bryon Sturm. He sported a camel-colored leisure suit that must have been as old as Derrick Sanders's glasses and might have come from the same New Zealand antique shop. Arroyo remembered when Bryon had started with The Company as a lowly shuttle van driver at one of the domestic spaceports on Ganymede. Bryon had done one unhappy contract and then disappeared back to Earth.

Several years later Arroyo saw Bryon's name on an NSWF organizational chart—he had a mid-level management job with OFFOFFPRO at Arlington headquarters. His father—a corporate oligarch from the New Confederate States and a reknowned bankroller of secessionist and religionist groups—had Senator friends, and they had found a cush job for the kid. Certainly one contract as a shuttle driver on Ganymede gave Bryon more firsthand knowledge of The Program than most of the Arlington political appointees around him—many of whom had never even made it to Earth orbit, nor wished to do so—so Arroyo held no ill will toward him.

Although the same couldn't be said for everyone on

Europa: Bryon Sturm routinely came up with wildly complicated and impractical ideas about the most mundane tasks from the comfort of his office suite. His proposals, always vigorously applauded by Europa mid-level managers actually possessing some knowledge of hands-on work, were also always discreetly ignored shortly thereafter by the same mid-level managers once Sturm's attention fixated elsewhere. The ideas were called "Bryonstorms," and one mid-level manager with a sense of humor cataloged 214 of them and posted them on his iMind blogsite until Bryon found them and promptly reassigned the offender to Europa's wastewater treatment plant, where he spent the rest of his deployment inventorying sludge cakes.

Bryon had Bryonstormed countless pieces of equipment for the Europa program—Rube-Goldbergesque ice road planers, ice runway groomers and compaction carts, a fifty-meter-long people mover that was too gargantuan to make the turns on the ice roads around Mactown and therefore required a massive road rebuilding project—evidently all sketched out on the backs of *very* damp cocktail napkins before being put into production in no-bid deals with the Kregg Corporation, where it was assumed his brother-in-law must be lead sales agent.

It seemed a matter of pride with Bryon not to ask the workers who actually used and knew equipment if his visionary (those less sycophantic would say hallucinatory) designs had any merit—or were even *needed*. Apparently he felt his time as a Ganymede shuttle van driver gave him sufficient expertise to spend hundreds of millions of taxpayer's credits on his cocktail napkin fantasies. Many required drivetrain or hydraulic connections that didn't exist on the Europa heavy equipment fleet. Some ran on fuel blends unavailable anywhere beyond the asteroid belt. Every time a resupply vessel arrived on Europa, mid-level managers and operators pensively peered into the dark depths of the cargo holds to see what shiny new unrequested Bryonstorm

Jim Fairchild

would be craned out next, and then scratched their heads trying to figure out its purpose once lifted onto the ice pier. The end users never knew about arriving Bryonstorms until they received the manifests of vessels already halfway to Europa. Some of the equipment needed complete redesigns and rebuilds in order to be usable, often with parts unavailable on Europa or Ganymede, so that parts had to be Slingshot-Expressed from Earth, easily doubling or tripling the original cost to taxpayers.

Much of it was so useless it was permanently parked in the Retro Yard and served only to catch ice drifts. The Retro Yard was hidden from sight from Mactown behind a mountain-sized ice dome affectionately known as Mt. Erebus, created by a perpetual water plume erupting from the sea beneath. The Retro Yard held endless cargo lines of waste and broken-down, unrepairable equipment waiting for final disposition. In the Navy days, it was all just bulldozed into a bottomless crevasse and allowed to plummet into the sea beneath; the NSWF now made some effort to recycle what it could or ship usable items at an absurd expense to Ganymede. An entire row of the Retro Yard was dedicated to Bryonstorms, the once-shiny paint jobs on multi-million-credit oddities quickly eaten away by radiation.

The rah-rah session with the managers on Ganymede concluded. The Traverse Ops manager began to discuss work assignments for the week. "I almost forgot," he said, slapping himself on the knee. "We've got some new faces today. A bunch of folks came in on the resupply vessel last Friday. Stand up and introduce yourselves."

Arroyo had already spotted them. The FNGs, all sporting blindingly clean, stiff, newly issued cold weather gear, had been sitting politely and listening to every word spoken in the meeting. Or at least it *seemed* they had been listening. Some of them wore external iMinds—the gold-rimmed monacle and earbud that kept them connected to the human hive. Arroyo could spot a few iMind

24

4.0s and 5.0s and 6.0s amongst the FNGs, but it was obvious that some of them had the new 7.0 implants. The implants left no scars—many parents were having them installed in their offspring as soon as they could read (in fact, starting with the 4.0, the devices could *teach* a child to read more efficiently than most schools and parents). Arroyo had been amused during the meeting to watch zombie-faced FNGs tapping a finger on their thigh, or even more distractingly, in the air—as if grasping for floating feathers—depending on how they'd set up their iMinds to scroll through menus.

In their defense, the FNGs might not have been checking personal messages during the meeting. The Company conducted job orientation via iMind while employees were in stasis on the way from Earth. Nobody remembered everything that had been piped into their cranium while enroute, but it often took several weeks after arrival to stop spontaneously blabbering out-of-the-blue about how not to create a hostile workplace, The Company's dedication to workplace diversity, The Company's mission statement, and further career opportunities with The Company. Arroyo had watched FNGs in the galley suddenly snap out of it several weeks after arrival. He had witnessed one recent arrival spit out a mouthful of chicken-fried chicken onto his tray and slap himself on the forehead, panic etched on his face. It was an eye-opener to realize you'd been brainwashed in stasis, that some corporate entity had been *way* up inside your head, and even those most resistant to the process (Arroyo liked to think he was one) could never be sure what "knowledge" had been imparted to them enroute—and how much of it still lurked hidden in the folds of their grey matter months or even years later.

Derrick Sanders, who was up on all things high-tech, had the iMind 6.0 (the last of the external offerings) built into his high-priced antique wire-rimmed glasses. He had been window-shopping online recently, and was planning to buy the latest 7.0

25

and have the outpatient surgery done next time he was on Ganymede.

Arroyo, on the other hand, still had a 2.0. His father would probably have called it the flip-phone of iMinds—hopelessly outdated. The Company insisted he have an iMind—it was written into the employment contract's Terms of Agreement (paragraph 87b)—but the contract didn't specify which version he had to have. And the contract didn't specify that he had to keep it *turned on*. Arroyo didn't like having other people—especially The Company—inside his head. While in Mactown he wore his old 2.0; if he didn't, he'd get a friendly reminder from the HR representative, Darla Hovenweep. It was her first contract off-Earth, she took her job *very* seriously, and at first she didn't know much about Arroyo. She would see him shambling from Stalag 17 to the motorpool to fire up his tractor at the start of shift and notice he wore no iMind. "Good morning," she would trill, then point to her ear and ask, "Forget something?" Arroyo would just wave vigorously, smile dumbly and keep walking. At first she would get back to her cubicle and text Arroyo to make sure he was using his iMind—which was a a waste of time, because of course he wasn't using it and therefore wouldn't read her cheery query. Later, she contacted Derrick, who as Arroyo's boss was asked to pass on the cheery reminder.

"Hey, Chief," Derrick would say, coyly sticking out the tip of his tongue. Arroyo wondered if the tongue tip charmed women. "Don't go Luddite on me. At least when in Mactown plug your head into the hive." Arroyo taught himself to wear his obsolete iMind while in Mactown, but he still only rarely turned it on. He figured if someone truly had something meaningful to tell him, they knew where to find him. McMurdo wasn't a huge place. He was either in his closet-sized dorm room, at Stalag 17, in the galley or in his tractor. Such was his life.

He wondered what it was like to live with your mind *completely* to yourself, unconnected to the rest of the two-legged fratricidal insects laughably called humanity. He dreamed of a time before iMinds. His father had once told him about a time when workplace information was disseminated by something called an Interoffice Memo. There were things called manual typewriters and carbon paper, and brute force was required to type enough copies for all concerned. He imagined that those tasked with typing Interoffice Memos must have had massively developed forearms, much like a centuries-old cartoon sailor his father had once shown him who gathered his strength downing barrel-sized cans of spinach.

The FNG introductions were done. Chairs screeched across the warped plascrete floor as people began to stand up. "*Pipe down*," the manager shouted. "One last announcement, folks. I want to welcome back one of our veteran operators, Arroyo Bronson. He's been on R&R on Ganymede between contracts. He's only been gone a month, but I know for the rest of us it feels like much more than that. Sorry, Arroyo, I guess you can take that a couple of different ways."

Suddenly everyone in the room—even the FNGs, who didn't know Arroyo from Adam but had clearly been instructed on what to do—formed around him in a tight circle. They all reached into their pockets and pulled out a variety of children's party noisemakers. Some were spun by hand and something inside ratcheted harshly, sounding to Arroyo like his tractor throwing a bogey wheel on steep ice. Others were shrill kazoos, their shrieks reminding him of the time he blew his turbocharger 250 kilometers from nowhere high on the Pole traverse route during impossible flat light while making an unwise solo run without a survival bag in his tractor.

Arroyo jumped up, nearly tripping over his chair. He wanted to run. But something told him that a normal person

27

should smile and say "Thank you," so he did. Cold sweat began to pour down his face. His stomach churned. His throat tasted like bile. His back was on fire. He needed fresh air.

"Welcome back, Drag Queen!" one of the old hands yelled, raising a sloshing cup of bitter coffee in salute. Drag Queen was the name of Arroyo's half-century-old ex-Navy tractor, but he was often called by that name, too. He considered the nickname an honor, not an insult, because he treasured the tractor's rich history. He was eager to get to the motorpool soon to check on his old workhorse.

"Yeah," one of the grumpier older operators said. "Welcome back, *Drug* Queen." This nickname Arroyo wasn't so fond of. But he knew he had earned it.

* * *

Arroyo stumbled outside into the station grotto behind the rest of the operators. He was quickly left alone, bent over, hands on knees, sucking in the cool air. He began to feel a bit better, although he needed to check on his burning back.

The door to a milvan slammed behind him. He jumped and turned. It was the milvan that Traverse Ops operators used to store excess personal gear. Derrick Sanders locked the milvan's door and turned. "Hey, Bucko," he said, winking. "Just the simulacrum of a human being I was seeking." He strolled over, carrying a couple of empty storage boxes. He set the boxes on the groomed ice beside him. "I take it you survived your first Monday morning meeting back at work."

"It was rough, but I'm feeling a little better."

"Did Ganymede kick your hairless ass again?"

"It's not Ganymede's fault," Arroyo said. "I know what I'm getting into whenever I go there. Maybe I shouldn't stay in Kardashia next time. It's equal parts Babylon, Sodom and

Gomorrah. But at least I get the thirty percent Program discount everywhere."

"How's your tallywhacker, you old stud? You need to swing by Medical for antibiotics?" Derrick stuck out his tongue twice this time and poked Arroyo hard in one shoulder.

"I'm an old man," Arroyo said. "I confined my recreational pursuits to supporting the Ganymede distillery industry. Do you want to get together after work and abuse a bottle of Trank?"

"Sorry, Sport. I gave up the hooch while you were gone. I'm studying for the priesthood. I'm going to have a little more problem with that celibacy thing."

"Wow," Arroyo said. "Congratulations. I guess." Mactown had been known for years as "a drinking town with a science problem." Certain NSWF managers wanted to change that, but so far the changes had been modest. Even most NSWF managers enjoyed getting schnockered from time to time. Derrick had been one of the station's most notorious Trankheads ever since he and Arroyo had first worked together fourteen years ago. Mactown had two tiny bars—holdovers from the Navy days—in filthy, delapidated Quonsets threatened by huge hanging icicles at the far end of the grotto. One bar was named *The Asteroid Belt*; the other was *Insane in the Membrane*. Arroyo was a quiet drinker, content to sit alone at an end of the bar away from the light. Derrick, on the other hand, was a crazed ball of energy once he had a few stiff ones under his belt. Arroyo suspected that Derrick was actually a shy person, but after a few sips he was ready to sweet-talk every woman in the bar. He occasionally got a drink poured over his carefully blow-dried hair, but it often got him an invitation back to someone's room, too. Arroyo didn't have that touch—nor the interest to develop it—but he found Derrick hopped up on Trank extremely amusing. Derrick's laughter made Arroyo feel good; he would go to bed after the two of them had closed down the bar and his jaw and abdominal muscles would ache from laughing so much.

Derrick liked to bar-surf: sliding the length of the bar on his belly while belting out snippets from "La Traviata" or "Barber of Seville." He was fluent in Italian—or at least to those who weren't it sounded authentic. Drinks would fly everywhere, but he always tipped the bartender handsomely and always cleaned up his own messes. He only got punched occasionally when he bar-surfed, and rarely in the face, because everyone on station had heard how priceless his antique glasses were, and because he bought two replacement drinks for each one he knocked off the bar. For many years on Monday mornings Derrick would stroll directly to Barry Wilton's office before coming to work at Stalag 17. They would chat about the weather and about ice conditions on the Pole traverse route, and then Barry would give Derrick the usual gentle Monday morning dressing-down for his Trank-fueled antics. Some Mondays Derrick would then stop by the Firehouse and have firefighter friends hook him up to a saline drip. They needed the venipuncture practice, and he needed the quick rehydration.

"You look better," Arroyo said. "Do you feel better?"

"Oh, *yeah*, Hoss," Derrick said. Derrick knew pre-Crash pop culture, too. "I only quit just after you left, but already my hands shake a little less. I've also been sporting the most amazing morning wood. Once the shaking completely goes away maybe I'll be able to grip it."

Arroyo could remember the Trank-induced spider veins in Derrick's cheeks. Already, they seemed almost gone. He was amazed that Derrick looked so much better in just a few weeks.

"What about you, Bud?" Derrick asked. "You giving any thought to slowing down? It's going to cost The Program a pretty penny if it has to freight you out a new liver on the Slingshot Express."

"We'll see," Arroyo said. It was something he thought about every conscious moment—and of course he realized he'd have more conscious moments if he hit the Trank less. "While I've got you here, I wanted to ask if I'd be heading out on this week's Pole run. I need to get out to the Back Forty."

"*Yeah*," Derrick said, "*about that*. I had a talk with the head honcho. He'd like you to stay in town for a few weeks. You could head out every day with the crew filling crevasses in the Shear Zone. The last outbound traverse said some of the ice bridges were sinking. We could use our most experienced hand on it. You could take Drag Queen, give her a shakedown each day, then sleep in your tidy little dorm room each night."

"Wow," Arroyo muttered. "You know how I feel about being stuck in Mactown."

"I know, Bubbalouie. It's not my call. You've been gone awhile, and the Powers-That-Be want to make sure you're comfortable in the saddle before hitting the lonesome trail."

"Alright," Arroyo said after a moment. "I'm nothing if not a Company Man."

"That's my Laddie," Derrick said, patting him on the shoulder. "I'm guessing we'll get you out of Mactown in less than a month." Derrick glanced down at the empty boxes beside his boot. "There've been some changes since you left. I've been offered a career gig at the Ganymede office. *Huge* payraise and full benefits. I'd be an office pogue, but I can be on the Strip in Kardashia every night doing research on sexually transmitted diseases. I put myself pretty deeply in hock when I was back on Earth, and I'd like to pay down my debts before I go back."

Derrick had bought the town of Ten Sleep, Wyoming a couple of years back while on a drunken road trip. He'd taken time off between Europa contracts and with two other Traverse Ops old-timers had signed up as civilian contractors in the seemingly endless Australian Campaign of the Thumper Wars. Their plan was to get rich and never come back to Europa.

It hadn't worked so well. In Derrick's case, back in the States after Australia and seemingly rich, he'd purchased a town and amassed a new mountain of debt. He already had his free forty-acre allotment available to every citizen of both the Progressive States of America and the New Confederate States (the regions centuries ago referred to as the Blue States and Red States and now demi-governments with limited joint control of mutual defense and the space program). Apparently forty acres wasn't enough for him, so he bought the entire near-vacant town. Arroyo, on the other hand, had never filed for his forty acres. He couldn't understand the desire to stay rooted to one piece of geography. Then again, he realized he had done exactly that on Europa.

Arroyo offered his hand in congratulations; they shook warmly. "I'll miss you," Arroyo said. "Thanks for everything. You've pulled Drag Queen and me out of our share of crevasses."

"Don't I know it, Sweetcheeks. But you've done the same for me and my own faithful steed." Derrick looked at the boxes a moment. "I've got to pack my things today. I'm headed for Ganymede tomorrow. There are a few more things I need to fill you in on."

"Shoot," Arroyo said.

"Darla Hovenweep at HR texted me. She'd like you to drop by her office to sign some contract paperwork. And she'd like you to drop by Medical to chat with the doctor. Just a routine visit after your R&R. I hate to say it, but you are one of our department's Grand Old Geezers. Everyone wants to make sure you're hunky-dory before you head out on the Ice again."

"Fair enough."

"And Lazarus is gone. His father fell gravely ill while you were away. Lazarus hopped the Slingshot Express, so we all hope he'll get home before his father has a downturn. The Program picked up the tab. Lazarus asked me to tell you he's sorry he won't see you."

"Sorry about his Dad," Arroyo said. "I'll catch Lazarus when he gets back."

"Sure, Wild Thing. But he might be gone a *long* time. We'll see."

Lazarus was the nickname of the only other operator who had been on Europa as long as Arroyo. His real name was Herbert Pinkton. They had, in fact, arrived on the same resupply vessel. They awoke from stasis at the same time, and Lazarus was the first thing Arroyo saw when he opened his encrusted eyes. Lazarus had his naked, hunched, tattooed back to Arroyo, dripping with purple stasis fluids, and was stumbling like a zombie toward the bench where their new cold weather clothing was laid out for them. *Death walking*, Arroyo thought, and the first word that croaked out of his mouth was *Lazarus*. It stuck.

When Lazarus turned, Arroyo realized that Queequeg would have been a better nickname, because his face was covered with an elaborate tribal tattoo. Lazarus had been through a bitter, expensive divorce before coming to Europa. After paying the settlement, he made a vow to spend every penny of what he had remaining. At some point during that process, he had gotten twisted on absinthe (vintage stuff with wormwood) and staggered into a tattoo parlor. He vaguely recalled asking for a temporary henna facial design. But perhaps his mouth wasn't working properly; when he woke up the next morning with his face glued to the pillow by blood-caked bandages, he realized that there'd been a most unfortunate communication breakdown.

Lazarus was prone to days of silence and fasting, so the facial tattoo didn't exactly impact his already minimal social life. He had a brilliant mind and could have excelled in the hard sciences or mathematics if he had gone the academic route.

Instead, like many on Europa, he was a rootless vagabond, working on Alaskan oil rigs and fishing vessels and on the oil platforms of Antarctica's Ross Sea before getting the itch to leave Earth. Like Derrick and Arroyo, he had done a stint in the Luna ice mines before climbing into a stasis chamber on a Europa-bound vessel. He spent a great deal of time alone on his iMind, researching tattoos, trying to decipher the elaborate pattern on his face. Like Queequeg, he'd had no luck.

Lazarus had gone with Derrick to get rich in the latter years of the Australian Campaign. They'd both initially operated equipment, putting in fireline around the towns and cities that had been set aflame repeatedly by marauding religionists of every denomination. Almost a million of the vermin had flocked to sparsely populated Australia in a wild scheme to escape the population growth limits mandated by the United Nations. They wanted to turn Australia into a sanctuary for all Believers where they could breed like Spirit-filled wharf rats and thump their various holy books in unison. They felt it was their divine duty to repopulate the world to pre-Crash levels, and quickly. It was easy to overwhelm the tiny Australian military and police forces. Australia, like many smaller nations after the dark post-Crash reconstruction decades, had disbanded much of its military when it seemed that humanity had at last begun to regain its senses. On a good day Australia could barely muster enough troops to fill a primly manicured parade field. The crazed religionists, armed with antique pre-Crash weapons and garden tools, landed in waves on Australia's beaches in hijacked cargo and fishing and pleasure vessels, set fire to everything burnable and quickly carved out zones for each denomination. Australia had to request military assistance from around the world. Mercenaries and contractors did much of the dirty work. The generals thought it would be a quick campaign, but the religionists, routed from the cities and towns in less than two years, had gone to ground in the bush like drug-fueled Aborigines. The conflict had now dragged on for almost a quarter-century.

Lazarus, with his concise, analytical mind, was soon pulled out of the cab of equipment and put to work managing major reconstruction projects, meeting with generals from various nations to assess their needs for new roads, dams and power plants destroyed by the marauding Thumpers. He banked millions of credits. But it wasn't enough. So he formed a joint venture with a Scripture-quoting Bulgarian contractor he'd met and they put in bids on several construction projects. The Bulgarian felt they should pool their cash in a joint account to prove their solvency to the contract officers. It was the last Lazarus saw of the millions he'd made in the war zone. All Lazarus had to show for his time in Australia was a new tattoo across the back of his neck, a quote from *Moby Dick*: "Better sleep with a sober cannibal than a drunken Christian."

He finished his contract in Australia and came back to Europa to start all over. While passing through Kardashia he gave in to his one true vice. He engaged the services of an escort who texted him a couple of months after he was back in Mactown. She claimed to be pregnant with his child. Based on that single iMind message, Lazarus began sending the woman a large cut of his salary each month to support the child. Derrick and others had ridiculed him for being so gullible.

"I *know* it's not mine," Lazarus had replied. "I got myself fixed right after the divorce. But everything in this universe is a circle; everything comes and goes and comes again. I'll have more money than I'll know what to do with again someday. I'll put this kid through the best college on Earth once he's old enough, as long as he has the grades to get accepted. I'll be able to say I did *one* decent thing in this lifetime."

But what if she didn't even have a child? he would be asked. *What if she borrowed a neighbor's infant for the photo she*

35

sent you?

"What does it matter?" he would ask, and go back to perusing college websites on his iMind.

*   *   *

"There's one last thing I have to tell you, Kemo sabe." Derrick clenched his teeth and inhaled. There was no impish tongue tip this time. "Nicholas is dead."

Arroyo felt as if someone had just punched him in the solar plexus. *"What happened?"*

"Too much flat light."

"Fuck. We all warned him about that game of his."

"I know," Derrick said. "He was always too flippant about the risks. That know-it-all art school attitude. He told me once to give this to you in case the game went south." Derrick looked around to make sure nobody was watching, then slipped something small and black out of his parka pocket and handed it to Arroyo.

Arroyo recognized it: the small three-prong plug-in module that Nicholas had programmed to override the safety lockouts on the window radiation shields of his tractor cab. He quickly tucked it into an inner parka pocket.

"He thought you might be the only person strong enough—or *stupid* enough—to take the game to its logical conclusion," Derrick said. "I trust your judgment. Use it carefully for a mind-blowing experience—or better yet, run over it with your tractor and toss it into the deepest crevasse you can find. I'm Management as soon as I buckle up for that shuttle to Ganymede tomorrow. I know nothing about that bulge in your pocket, unless it's because you're happy to see me."

"Understood," Arroyo said.

Derrick buried his hands in his parka pockets. "Dude, I'm really glad you're back safe and sound and apparently in one piece.

I wish I could tell you more." They hugged awkwardly. Derrick pointed at his ear. "Forget something?" he asked, then stuck out his tongue and winked. Arroyo dug into his pocket for his iMind. Derrick picked up his boxes and walked away.

*　*　*

There had been a third operator who went to Australia to get rich off the Thumper Wars: Nicholas Bradshaw. Nicholas had started on Europa the same year as Derrick. He was another one of the Merry Tranksters. He had a phenomenal tolerance for the watered-down-alcohol-and-sedative elixir. The concoction—manufactured without the need for aging—had been popular on Earth right after the Crash when the distillery industry, like most others, collapsed. But it had been outlawed on Earth for more than a century and was now only found beyond the asteroid belt. In the outer solar system things were still full-on Wild West. Big Brother wasn't always around to protect you from yourself, as on Earth, Luna and Mars. Trank was openly sold in Mactown's tiny company store at an exorbitant mark-up. The production of Trank on Ganymede was one of that moon's more profitable industries, although dwarfed by its primary industry, the ugly, endless sprawl of spaceport and warehouse facilities.

Nicholas had a quick wit that dripped with sarcasm. Perhaps Sarcasm 101 was required during freshman year of art school. In fact, sometimes the sarcasm was so intense that Arroyo would have to leave the room, even though he loved Nicholas. There were few on station who could drink as much as Arroyo and still function on the job, but Nicholas was one of them. An evening out Tranking with Nicholas left Arroyo just as sore from laughing as an evening with Derrick, and if the *three* of them closed the bar together, the laughter could be too much. One night the three left the bar an hour before closing and broke into the food warehouse.

Jim Fairchild

They pulled a Lateral Property Transfer on a frozen whole Martian Berkshire hog saved for holiday banquets and snuck it into the bed of a foreman who was still at the bar. They laid the pig on its side with its head on the pillow and tucked the sheet and blankets up neatly beneath its frozen, whiskered, smiling face. Nicholas, like Lazarus, was generous to a fault, and would give his warmest parka to a stranger in need. In fourteen years Arroyo had never seen Nicholas without a bright smile on his face. Now Arroyo wondered if that had been an act.

Nicholas maintained a well-written and outrageously humorous iMind blog, "Big Dead Space," which mercilessly lambasted the Europa science program. The Program's high muckety-mucks had Nicholas in their gunsights, and while he had not been disciplined yet for the blog, it blatantly violated his contract's Terms of Agreement. Posting unapproved commentary that reflected poorly on The Program was strictly *verboten*; Nicholas knew that some day the curtain might drop.

Nicholas didn't have a background in equipment operation before coming to Europa. He had started as a lowly supply clerk, sorting alternators and head gaskets and nuts and bolts at the Heavy Shop. He OJTed on his off-time with Traverse Ops, though, because he wanted to get out of the claustrophobic confines of the station grotto and out onto Europa's surface. He was a natural in a tractor cab. As Arroyo would tell anybody, *any* monkey can learn to pull levers. The operators who took their jobs too seriously (like the one who called Arroyo "Drug Queen" at the end of the meeting) despised Arroyo for that.

Nicholas seemed to follow Derrick and Lazarus to Australia because it would be one more lark, more grist for his blog. That was perhaps five years ago. When he announced that he was cutting short his Europa contract to join the other two back on Earth, Arroyo wondered if Nicholas grasped the gravity of working in a combat zone. They'd all heard about the antics of others who'd ditched their jobs on Europa to make it rich in Australia. When you weren't working your terrified ass off, it sounded like one big party.

Arroyo wanted to warn Nicholas that he might experience things that would haunt him forever, and to consider if the money was worth spending the rest of your life trying to stay one step ahead of your memories. Arroyo knew something about this, but as much as he *wanted* to warn Nicholas, he couldn't talk about it.

Arroyo had a padlocked closet in a dark corner of his mind where he hid his *own* memories of Australia. He had joined the Army at the age of nineteen after a blow-up with his parents which was now too hazy to recall. His few friends thought he had lost his mind. In the world of The Forever War, most considered serving one's country in uniform a foolish career path reserved for hard-luck cases and sociopathic mercenary mentalities. Arroyo felt alone in the world and needed a purpose. Within a year he had completed Basic, AIT, Airborne and Air Assault schools and had been assigned as an Eleven-Bravo infantryman with the Ranger battalion at Fort Lewis.

And then the Australian Campaign broke out. His unit fast-roped into the outskirts of Perth to establish security for firefighters trying to battle the flames of the burning city. His platoon never saw the worst of the combat. But there were ambushes and skirmishes and things that Arroyo had locked away in that hidden closet. One memory had somehow snuck out from behind the padlocked door recently, and although he'd tried to stuff it back in, it often kept him awake at night. He could remember a crazed kangaroo that raced out of the flames, its fur ablaze. Arroyo loved animals more than humans and clenched his fists tightly until the nails cut the skin, too afraid to remember what he did next. He kept a bottle of Trank by the bed for nights like that. He wasn't sure if the memory was even *real*—it made no sense. He never delivered the warning to Nicholas. He'd never even told anyone

Jim Fairchild

on Europa that he'd been in the first American wave to land in Australia, or that he was a veteran at all. There were countless veterans who had experienced *far* worse trauma than an encounter with a flaming kangaroo. He would be mortified to tell anyone about it.

A year or two after Nicholas went to Australia Arroyo booted up his iMind on one of the rare occasions he bothered to check his bank account. His inbox was flooded with thousands of texts and e-mails, and as usual, he was about to delete them all. As he did a quick scroll down through them before hitting DELETE, wagging a finger impatiently in the air, one message's subject line jumped out at him:

CUM TO CANBERRA AND
FROLIC ON THE SHORES OF
LAKE BURLEY GRIFFIN WITH
ME

It was a message from Nicholas. He was working 120 hours a week in an office as a scheduler for reconstruction projects and needed an assistant. He wondered if Arroyo could bail on his Europa contract and buy a ticket on the Slingshot Express to Earth. Nicholas assured him that with all the opportunities for wartime graft and corruption he could make back the cost of the ticket in the first year. He wrote:

> The job will entail endless hours of meetings
> with unimaginative clowns in brass-encrusted
> uniforms. You will have to pretend to enjoy
> the company of other human beings, an art at
> which I know you are adept. You will be
> remunerated beyond your wildest dreams.
> Imagine mind-numbing boredom punctuated

40

every few weeks by the quaint concussion of
another Thumper blowing himself up a block
away. RSVP ASAP. Nicholas.

Arroyo fumbled with his iMind and sent a short reply. He
thanked Nicholas for the offer but declined the opportunity. He
wrote simply that he already had more money than he knew what
to do with and had no debts, so would do his frolicking on Europa.

When Nicholas finished his hitch in Australia he bummed
around a year but then came back to Europa. Despite his sarcastic
blog about The Program, his new contract sailed through HR. He
felt like he needed a purpose and missed his co-workers. To
Arroyo, he seemed a changed man. He was bloated from far too
much booze; his face was splotchy. And although he still smiled a
lot, Arroyo detected a nervousness behind the smile. Derrick, who
had returned about the same time, confided to Arroyo that
Nicholas had been living in a steel shipping container at an airfield
far to the rear of the fighting. One night Thumper sappers hit the
perimeter, backed by well-aimed pre-Crash 81-millimeter mortars.
A mortar round had hit the roof of the shipping container next to
his. Two acquaintances were blown to shreds. Nicholas had
helped bag the remains. He never talked about his Australian
experience with anybody. Arroyo wanted to help him, but was
grappling with his own demons—or more precisely, a bizarre
blazing kangaroo.

Shortly after Nicholas and Derrick returned, they joined
Arroyo for a quick four-day resupply run to a nearby field camp.
Nicholas' tractor was having a spate of electrical gremlins, and
he'd had to stop several times to jiggle wires and control modules.
When they made it to the field camp the second evening and had
collapsed, exhausted, over bowls of steaming chili in the back of
the galley Jamesway, Nicholas grinned.

"Funny thing happened on the way out here," he said.

"We saw," Derrick said. "You'd think that a tractor with less than a thousand hours on it wouldn't have so many gremlins. Glad you figured it all out and were able to keep on truckin'."

"One of those gremlins made the radiation shield on my left canopy window rise up," Nicholas said, grinning.

"You should have said something," Derrick said, grabbing a pack of twenty-year-old crackers for his chili. "We get enough background rads as it is that I could nuke a burrito in my bunghole."

"*Mon ami*," Nicholas said, "by the looks of this chili I think you just did. I was able to get the screen down after about a half an hour by jiggling its control module. According to my dosimeter I should be okay—maybe a week's exposure in half an hour. BFD. But something *really* weird happened."

The only reason the tractors had windows was that they were originally designed for agricultural work on Earth. They had been massively modified with pressurized cabs, fuel systems compatible with the blends tankered over from the vast refineries on Saturn's moon Titan, thick radiation shielding and comms that could beam a clean signal to an operator's bookie in Kardashia. But beneath the surface the wire-mesh-tracked tractors would have been at home in a North Dakota wheat field. The Traverse Ops tractors always operated with heavy radiation shields lowered in place over the glass. A control module assured that the shields stayed locked down once GPS data told the tractor's computer that the tractor had exited the station. Operators scanned the terrain around them on banks of monitors fed by cameras mounted all around the tractor's exterior. The signals were scrubbed by a computer that corrected for the terrible lighting. An operator never directly laid eyes on the surrounding terrain once he was rolling. On this run, a gremlin in Nicholas' cab sent an errant signal to one of the shields. It rose up, startling Nicholas. He thought about radioing the others and telling them he had to stop once more to fix the problem. But he thought that if he jiggled enough wires and modules inside the cab he'd find the problem and not delay the run again.

They had been hauling their loads at dusk, just as the bright star that is the Sun was slipping low on Europa's horizon. Sometimes the thin atmosphere was rich in a haze of suspended ice crystals drifting from nearby ice plumes. If the low-angle light of the Sun or a transitting moon struck the cloud of ice, it was common to suddenly lose all ground definition. It was something *far* more dangerous than the blackness of starlit night. Sky and ground became one murky grey curtain, the horizon completely undetectable. An operator might not see a piano-sized crater in the ice a meter in front of his tractor. It could be so disorienting that an operator couldn't tell up from down. "I had the tractor on autopilot," Nicholas said, stirring crushed crackers into his chili. "So for half an hour, while jiggling connections, I looked outside the window. *Complete* flat light. The whole world around me was a grey piece of canvas. I started to use my imagination like a set of brushes and oil paint. I covered the entire canvas with the most amazing paintings. I wish I could remember them. The experience blew my mind."

"Wow," Derrick said. "Good thing these traverses are dry. Otherwise I'd think you'd been drinking and driving."

Arroyo flinched at that. He'd kept a bottle of Trank in his cab for emergencies for years, but so far had never broken the seal. Somehow he could stay sober out on the trail. Maybe the hours were so long and the work so grueling that he didn't even have time to *think* about drinking. Maybe it was the only time he could find peace. Maybe that was why he was always eager to hit the trail.

* * *

Jim Fairchild

Nicholas had made his living as a programmer at one point in his life before Europa. Back in Mactown he studied wiring schematics for his tractor and quickly designed a module that allowed him to circumvent the safety lockout on the shields. One night over a long holiday weekend he snuck into the Comms Shop and built his module, which he called the Dali Box. Whenever he was out on the surface in his tractor he took it with him. Despite the concerns of Derrick and Arroyo, he often set his tractor on autopilot and plugged in the module. It was a given that if the light was flat Nicholas had one of his shields up. Later, back in his tiny dorm room in Mactown, he stayed up all night, feverishly sketching on his iMind what little he could remember of the panorama of otherworldly art he had seen around him.

Someone at NSWF—perhaps Bryon Sturm, but others suspected Sally Train—got wind that Nicholas had been re-hired by The Company. Neither had much sense of humor about "Big Dead Space." Whoever it was, The Company's HR office was contacted, and Nicholas was called in to chat with Darla Hovenweep. He was notified that his contract was under review and might be cancelled for breaching the Terms of Agreement. He was on pins and needles awaiting the decision. Europa was his home. His only friends were there. He had nowhere else to go.

On his final resupply run, Nicholas was apparently overwhelmed by the beauty—*or perhaps the horror*—of what he had seen painted on the canvas spread all around him. He put on his helmet and gloves and pressurized his suit, dropped the tractor into low gear, opened the hatch and climbed down the ladder of the slowly creeping tractor. He strode briskly to the front, knelt down and laid his head in front of the oncoming tracks. The tractor and its sled carrying a hundred thousand kilos of fuel turned the artist into a crimson splotch on the rock-hard ice canvas.

* * *

Arroyo would swing by Darla Hovenweep's cubicle and Medical soon enough. His back was on fire and he needed to figure out why. He crossed the ice of Derelict Junction, the station's largest common area, and headed for his dorm room in Building 209.

As he stood in the hallway outside his room, fumbling in his parka pockets for the door key, a hand lightly touched his arm. He flinched and turned. It was a young woman in fuel-stained Carhartts. She had auburn hair cut in a practical Pixie style and opaline eyes that reminded Arroyo of the elusive, evanescent color he had seen in backlit sastrugi and the depths of crevasses while training in Antarctica for his first trip to Europa. It was a color he had seen countless times out of the corner of his eye; whenever he turned, it was always gone. She couldn't be much more than half his age.

"Arroyo," she said, smiling. "Welcome back. Glad to see you in one piece."

Arroyo stared at her so distractedly he dropped his key. He knew her. But *how* he knew her he couldn't fathom. He struggled for a name.

She took her hand from his arm. "It's okay," she said. "I know you probably don't remember me. I'm Annie Pfleger, from Fuels. We met out at the Discovery Bay field camp a year ago."

"I'm so sorry," Arroyo said, reaching out a hand. She took it and they shook lightly. "I just got back from a month of intemperance on Ganymede. I'm not at my best."

"I fully understand," Annie said. "It's great to have you back. Do you have any bags you need a hand with?"

Arroyo couldn't even remember at first if he'd brought any luggage with him from Ganymede. Then he remembered that he'd gotten back late the night before, and that his solitary daypack was already thrown in the room, where he'd only had a catnap before going to the morning meeting.

"I'm good," he said. "But I could use a hand. I've hurt my back somehow. Please don't be offended, but would you kindly take a peek at it and see if I need to go to Medical?"

Arroyo had to push the door hard to get it swung into the windowless room; the floor was cluttered with grease-caked cold weather clothing and boots and a bag of rancid laundry. Dust rose from the threadbare carpet as they both entered.

Annie told him that he'd just missed a wonderful Thanksgiving banquet in the galley while he peeled off his parka and several lighter layers. Arroyo had forgotten what month it was. He sat on the edge of his sagging bunk and turned his back toward her.

"*Oh, Lordie,*" Annie gasped. "Don't try to lift your shirt. Somebody visited the tattoo parlor while he was on R&R. Your shirt is caked with dried blood." She went to the corner sink and rummaged for a clean towel. The search was fruitless. She dug into the bag of rancid laundry, lifted out a crumpled towel and sniffed it doubtfully. She rinsed it in the sink.

"I'm going to soak your shirt a bit to loosen it. We don't want to rush this."

Arroyo glanced over his shoulder. "I really appreciate your help." He could see her reading the Jonathan Swift quote across his shoulders. His mind was racing, trying to figure out how he knew Annie. He felt horrible that she was being so kind and he couldn't remember their connection. He tried to recall so hard that sweat dripped down his forehead.

"*Gulliver's Travels,*" Annie said, smiling, dabbing gently at the shirt.

"It's my favorite book," Arroyo said, wincing.

"I know. Mine, too. We talked about it for hours at Discovery Bay."

Arroyo was horrified. He realized that he was losing what was left of his mind. A fellow human being was showing him compassion and tenderness, they apparently knew each other well, and he couldn't even remember her.

He was done with Trank. The world had been awash in pain and grief ever since the first gadget-loving killer hominids had risen onto two legs on the African plains and started their migration across the continents and then across the solar system, killing, maiming or destroying everything they encountered. Arroyo didn't want to cause any of that pain and grief for other living beings. And it was obvious he had hurt Annie.

It was time for him to wake up and remember what he had done with his life.

"I don't expect you to forgive me for not remembering you," he said.

Arroyo jumped. There was a ripping noise and it felt like part of his back had been torn off.

"Relax," Annie said, tossing the bloody shirt across the tiny room. It splatted into the sink, leaving a trail of watered-down blood on the floor and wall. She dabbed at a remaining layer of gauze. "I know you pretty well. I knew what to expect when you got back." She seemed to dab a bit more briskly now.

"Discovery Bay," Arroyo said. "I was the camp's equipment operator for awhile. A grantee group was doing research on the Tetras out there."

"Gordon Angstrom's people," Annie said. "I was the camp Fuelie. We had some nice times at Discovery Bay. This is going to hurt." There was another loud ripping noise; Arroyo almost screamed.

Annie tossed the wadded gauze into the sink and stood back. "Well," she said. "Interesting artwork."

Jim Fairchild

Arroyo tried to look over his shoulder but couldn't see the tattoo. "What is it?" he asked, scrambling to the smudged wall mirror over the sink and looking behind him.

"*The Scream*," Annie said. She handed Arroyo a hand mirror from a nearby shelf. "By a fellow named Munch. It's really quite beautiful, in an absolutely horrifying sort of way."

Arroyo gazed into the hand mirror so he could see his back. The tattoo covered his back from just below the Jonathan Swift quote to his belt line. A sky that seemed drenched with blood hung low over the head of a terrified figure, its hands pressed to its face. *The distillation of pure horror*, Arroyo thought. His own blood weeped out of the figure's eyes. "I must have been completely hammered," he muttered.

"It's a timeless piece of art," Annie said. "I've certainly seen less tasteful ink." She plopped down onto the bunk with her back to the wall and pulled her knees to her chest. "You know the drill. Keep it clean, use antibiotic ointment, yada yada."

Arroyo found a clean shirt and gingerly pulled it over his head. He sat down on the old grey plastic government-issue chair—the only one in the room—a polite distance from Annie. "Thank you for helping me. And I promise that you'll never see me this messed up again."

"That's *your* business. I've heard it before. I really don't care. But in lucid moments you must realize that you are killing yourself. Do you *really* even remember my name?"

Arroyo was filled with shame. "It's Annie. You told me when we met in the hallway."

"You're a good person," Annie said. "I learned that at Discovery Bay. There *are* people in the world who care about you, even though you don't believe that. And when you do this to yourself it's like you're shitting on our hearts. You've got one boot in the grave and you've been kicking yourself in the ass with the other. *But again*, we all make our own choices."

"Tell me about Discovery Bay," Arroyo said.

* * *

Discovery Bay was the site of a field camp a bone-jarring three days' journey by tractor from Mactown. It sat on a relatively flat and peaceful expanse of clean ice a couple of kilometers in diameter, surrounded to the horizon by endless stress fractures, pressure ridges and razor-sharp penitentes up to a dozen meters high melted into the ice by eons of feeble sunlight and radiation. The flagged route required passage through the ever-changing Shear Zone, where two ice plates fought against each other and created crevasses broad enough to swallow Mactown. The constant ice changes meant that the route had to be surveyed by the lead tractor with ground-penetrating radar even if it had been traversed safely just days prior. New crevasses had to be filled by bladed tractors or spanned with plascrete bridges; endless stretches of penitentes had to be knocked down and leveled to make a path. It was a slow and exhausting process. Those lucky enough to fly to the camp from Mactown could be there in a couple of hours if the flitter had a tailwind.

The subsurface camp was just large enough to support about twenty people. The camp staff consisted of a camp manager, comms operator, weather observer, cook and cook's helper, mechanic, Fuelie and equipment operator. Grantee groups would flit out for a month or two at a time to conduct research in the area. For years, the camp had often supported Gordon Angstrom's exobiology group.

Angstrom and his young assistants were at the vanguard of research into the Tetras, one of only two animal species so far found on Europa. Serious science on Europa had only been conducted for the last couple of decades. During the Navy's tenure, a few observatories were built and mapping surveys were

Jim Fairchild

conducted, but science was in reality a sham in those years—an excuse to maintain an armed military presence on Europa. The civilian scientists who came to Europa during those years had the best of intentions but science had only been window-dressing. The real reason Congress funded the effort was astropolitics—making sure that the Asian Bloc space program or renegade religionists didn't lay claim to the remote iceball.

The Tetras were a bizarre, roughly tetrahedron-shaped, obsidian-black life-form (although some would quickly amend that to *apparent* life-form). Every specimen encountered so far was about a meter tall; nothing resembling juveniles had yet been observed. They seemed to spend most of their time in the mysterious sea hidden beneath as much as ten kilometers of ice. The sea consisted of salty water similar to the oceans of Earth. This had been deduced by scientists long before the Crash, and it had always been conjectured that Europa was probably the solar system's best candidate to support life aside from Earth. The Tetras' underwater behavior had received only limited study with cameras glued to released Tetras that were quickly dislodged by the creatures. Small, remotely controlled submersibles had also been employed to study the Tetras in the sea, but the vehicles frequently became trapped when winching them up through the jagged ice and several had been lost. Some simply disappeared mid-mission. What little had been gleaned so far under the ice indicated that the Tetras made slow, gentle descents far down into the black sea—alone and in groups—seemingly impervious to pressure. The Tetras climbed up through cracks in the ice—singly, in pairs and in larger groups—for occasional inquisitive sojourns on the ice, where they had attracted a great deal of attention from humans.

Tetras had been glimpsed by the Pegasus crew after its stranding, and the snippets remaining from journals of those sailors mentioned initially spotting distant clusters of black triangles waddling amongst the ice penitentes far outside their camp, almost on the horizon. Slowly, over the course of many weeks, the Tetras closed the distance, until they were wandering close about the laboring crew, seemingly curious. Sailors gave individual Tetras nicknames, and for much of the crew the Tetras were the only thing they encountered on Europa that lightened their hearts and gave them hope.

A yellowed photograph (Arroyo had seen a copy in the old McMurdo Historical Society's collection before it disappeared) showed a Petty Officer Third Class Bowers in his EVA suit and helmet with his arm around a Tetra he had adopted. Or perhaps the Tetra had adopted Bowers. The Tetra, nicknamed Socks by Bowers, followed Bowers everywhere. It allowed Bowers to place a Tam O'Shanter on what—for convenience—might be called its head. It often waddled down into the new grotto to watch Bowers work. Bowers was an accomplished mouth organist, and once the grotto was pressurized and he could work without a suit and helmet, he would play old pre-Crash blues and folk standards on his harmonica for the Tetra. Socks would come close and gyrate gently as if in a trance, seeming to approach a state of ecstasy when Bowers teased with his excellent vibrato. Bowers regularly tried to feed the Tetra—although he could find no mouth—until he was ordered not to squander food on the creature. Bowers never witnessed the animal take *any* form of nourishment; it was assumed that, like Earth's penguins, the Tetras must feed while swimming in the sea far below the ice.

· The sole exobiologist onboard the Pegasus, Lieutenant Bresnahan, was not holding up well under the mental strain of their situation, and spent the first few months either in his bunk or endlessly editing his logs in his cabin. Finally, urged by the commander to man up and help the rest of crew, he decided to get out of the ship and do some science. So he commandeered Socks from Bowers.

Jim Fairchild

His initial observations: a tough yet pliable, jet-black exterior that made oxhide look like tissue paper; a lack of skin pores, hair, feathers or scales; four roughly identical triangular aspects; no apparent mouth or cloaca; no apparent external sense organs; no apparent external sex organs; and striated hardenings at the three bottom corners that provided traction on the ice. When moving casually, the Tetras alternated their weight amongst the three corners of their base and were able to pivot forward awkwardly. When alarmed—which with Socks was any time Bresnahan approached its pen—it could flop forward onto the leading aspect and push itself along quite efficiently. This means of locomotion was another similarity to Earth's penguin, which can zip along efficiently on its belly.

Bresnahan was not finished. One day while Bowers was busy below the surface helping to blast out the station grotto, Bresnahan reached into the pen with a hypodermic gun. His intent was to euthanize Socks prior to dissection. Bresnahan instantly made another important observation: Tetras would defend themselves when threatened with harm. In an instant, the Tetra reared back on two hind corners and lashed out with the forward corner. The striated hardenings retracted, revealing a single razor-sharp ivory talon that slashed at Bresnahan. The hypodermic gun—and Bresnahan's hand clutching it—dropped onto the ice in an arcing gout of blood. A sailor raced forward and clubbed Socks to death with a Navy-issue pipe wrench.

Socks' remains were eventually dissected by a one-handed Bresnahan after his recovery. He nearly broke his scalpel blade cutting through the outer hide. When he finally succeeded, there was a loud explosion: the body cavity seemed to be pressurized by some unknown process to protect inner organs while on the surface. A viscous green substance—apparently the creature's arterial fluid—sprayed everywhere, covering the grimly determined Bresnahan. He found only a rudimentary alimentary canal with both ends—mouth and anus—so vestigial that they were almost imperceptible from the exterior. The canal yielded no traces of food ingestion. It was a complete mystery as to how the Tetras took nutrition. An extremely flexible, unjointed, chitinous skeleton radiated directly from a short central spine outward to the four points of the tetrahedral body. The flexibility of the material—much like that of the clear spine of Earth's squid—in conjunction with a thick, non-striated musculature—seemed to provide the undulations needed for mobility on ice and in water. All three corners of the bottom facet had the retractable talons, which no doubt aided the Tetras in negotiating their climbs upward from the sea. A three-chambered heart pumped the green fluid thoughout the body. The nervous system was highly developed, including a thick central axon and a brain without any folds of sulci and gyri. The brain far exceeded, by a percentage of both total body weight and volume, that which is found in Homo Sapiens.

Bowers was heartbroken as he witnessed Socks' final days. He had grown strangely close to the odd creature, and felt he had lost his best friend. And yet Bowers, who had been one of the most mentally fragile of the crew when they had first landed and realized their possible fate, grew into an indomitable force on the crew, always lifting the spirits of those around. Though a little fireplug of a man, he eventually did the work of two or three.

It was, in fact, Petty Officer Third Class Bowers whose remains were found atop an ice penitente in a suit with a helium bottle attached, gazing toward the horizon. He had persevered to the last.

* * *

Gordon Angstrom had been coming to Europa for almost twenty years. As a child, he had read what little he could find about the Pegasus crew and Bresnahan's study of Socks. He had submitted his first grant proposal to the NSWF's Europa program before even being awarded his doctorate degree. He had been coming to Europa ever since graduating.

He concentrated his Tetra studies in the Discovery Bay area. The smooth, relatively newly formed ice was thinner than the surrounding chaos terrain, and the Tetras apparently found it easier here to climb up through fissures to the surface to conduct their odd perambulations. Angstrom set up a study area a couple of kilometers away from the field camp. It was dubbed The Penguin Ranch. It was set up near cracks from which Tetras regularly emerged. A series of plascrete fences—like a stockyard on Earth—funneled the emerging Tetras into an ever-narrower chute. Finally, seemingly unalarmed, the Tetras would cross a scale that automatically weighed them as they passed. Most of the Tetras had been "tagged" with electronic chips during previous studies; those Tetras new to the Penguin Ranch were tagged for the first time. Mindful of the explosion of Socks, Angstrom's group used a tracking chip that could be glued and didn't require piercing. The weight of each Tetra crossing the scale was recorded. All interactions with the Tetras were done at a safe working distance, in light of Lieutenant Bresnahan's offhand experience.

The Tetras were kept in the pens for a few days at a time before being released. Single and group behavior were observed. While often seen travelling in pairs, these pairs displayed no mating rituals. Larger groups exhibited complex cooperation toward shared needs, virtually no hint of aggression toward others of their own species, and extreme concern when one of their kind was in distress. This often occurred when individuals were lassoed with wire cables and winched off the ground, then prodded with a boom while hanging to see if any food emerged from either end of their decadent digestive tracts. The longer they hung, the tighter the cable became. But no food was ever forthcoming.

Angstrom's group never euthanized Tetras for dissection. The NSWF had issued its *Protocols on Flora and Fauna* that suggested kinder and gentler methods of studying exospecies than those employed by Lieutenant Bresnahan. However, a few Tetras had died during captivity, in a few cases due to unfortunate entanglements in the cable. In more cases, captive creatures had simply seemed to lose the will to live. Angstrom's group had a permit from the NSWF to dissect those individuals. Just as Bresnahan had done, Angstrom's group concluded that the Tetras didn't seem to eat. Repeated trips across the scale showed no changes in body mass. No fecal expulsion was ever observed.

Labwork on the green fluid left Angstrom's group scratching its heads. It was 99.4 percent ethylene glycol—except for a few traces of odd organic compounds, it was chemically identical to the antifreeze a pre-Crash truck owner would have put in his Jimmy to make it through the winter in Fargo. The fluid contained no compounds or structures akin to the hemoglobin and red blood cells of terrestrial animals. Also, confirming Bresnahan's anatomical study, there were no detectable respiratory organs—not the vaguest hint of even vestigial lungs or gills. Oxygen *is* the primary component of Europa's thin atmosphere, but if it played a part in the Tetras' physiological processes, it was not obvious how. At the microscopic level, the creatures had some cellular components similar to terrestrial animals: cell membrane, nucleus, nucleolus, vacuoles, ribosomes. And yet no known cellular-level system of energy uptake and transfer could be discerned.

Angstrom's further examination revealed a *quadruple*-helix deoxyribonucleic acid in the nucleus and mitochondria that was nearly identical to terrestrial DNA save for the number of helices. Finally, the most shocking discovery came when the Tetra DNA

Jim Fairchild

was sequenced: while the Tetra had more than three times as many genes as humans, *97.9 percent of the human genome was buried within that of the tetrahedral creature.*

"I just came back from Discovery Bay," Annie said. "Your friend Pegleg is still hunkered down way outside camp, amongst the penitentes, almost beyond eyesight, watching for your return."

Arroyo was flooded with a tsunami of crystal-clear memories. It made him feel dizzy. He could remember the Tetra who had adopted him: Arroyo had named him Pegleg, because one of the creature's three lower "feet" had been crushed in the wire cable used to lift Tetras when brusquely probing them for the contents of their digestive tracts. Arroyo had been helping the grantees at the Penguin Ranch—it must have been more than a year ago, before last Christmas. A huge ruckus broke out, and when Arroyo looked over, a Tetra was swaying upsidedown in the cable, which had cinched tightly around one of its ridged corners. The cable was biting through the seemingly impervious hide, and thick green fluid was staining the ice beneath the hapless creature. One of Angstrom's assistants frantically worked the winch controls trying to lower the creature, but the cable was snarled in the drum. Another assistant approached with a boom, trying to grab the loop around the creature's foot. The assistant got too close; the tough covering on another of the creature's feet retracted. In a flash the Tetra had swung close to the assistant and slashed at him. The assistant's suit was only nicked in the sleeve; Arroyo could hear the hiss of the suit's self-repair sealant.

Arroyo had seen enough. He climbed up onto Drag Queen and reached into the cab. He fished around a moment, then jumped down with a set of bolt cutters. He ran over to the hanging Tetra, oblivious to the fact he was close enough to be slashed, and reached high. The cable parted with a loud *twang*; the Tetra fell unceremoniously to the ice "head"-first. It righted itself, seemed to perform some sort of an indignant internal function check, then—

much to Arroyo's amusement—scooted an inch or two toward Arroyo.

"*Fucking beakers*," Arroyo muttered, his helmet mike keyed for all in camp to hear. *Beakers* was the universal term for grantees that was used by The Program's support workers. Sometimes the term was used affectionately; often, as now, it was a term of derision. The NSWF had officially prohibited the use of the term, as it was determined to violate federal anti-shaming laws. Arroyo didn't care who heard it. They had needlessly hurt another (apparently) living creature.

The injured Tetra created a conundrum for the researchers. First, it was bleeding profusely. Second, it had attempted to injure a research assistant. The ivory talon had only nicked the man's arm, but it *had* resulted in a suit puncture, which was a serious safety matter, and would require the filing of several tedious reports and the return of the suit to Supply for recertification. And third, the accident had been caught on iMind camera by a visiting mechanic who had flitted out for the day to service the camp generators. While the entire grantee group huddled in the open discussing how to handle the problem, a flitter touched down just beyond the Penguin Ranch's flagged perimeter. With the engines still screaming, the pilot waved for the generator mechanic to board.

The flitter lifted up and turned away, enveloping those on the ground in a blast of ice crystals. Angstrom, the lead grantee, began to frantically wave to the pilot, but it was too late. The mechanic, bearing evidence of the embarrassing accident on his iMind, was in the air and headed back to Mactown.

Arroyo listened to the Mac Ops channel with growing disgust. Angstrom asked to be patched through to Barry Wilton. It took a few minutes for the crusty old station manager to get to a radio. When he was on the line, Angstrom asked Barry to greet the generator mechanic at the Flitter Ops pad as soon as the flitter

Jim Fairchild

landed in Mactown. Barry was asked to wipe the photo files of the accident from the mechanic's iMind, and to make sure he hadn't already posted them to the hive anywhere. It was the kind of publicity The Program assiduously avoided. Barry said he would take Darla Hovenweep to the flitter pad with him in the event that the request for the iMind files became an HR issue.

One thorn removed, the grantees set their impressive collection of post-graduate-degreed minds to the next. The Tetra would have to be destroyed. None of them had the stomach to perform the deed. Their eyes settled on Arroyo, who still stood near the Tetra, working to remove the cinched cable from its foot.

"Arroyo," Angstrom beseeched, stepping out of the tight circle of grantees. "We have a situation. Can you help?"

Arroyo swung the bolt cutters loosely in his gloved hand, his eyes turning red with rage. "Give me something *humane*," he said, trying not to let his voice betray his loathing. "I'm not going to club it to death with these bolt cutters." One of Angstrom's assistants approached with a small instrument case. "The hypo is already loaded," the assistant said. "We've found that one shot is usually sufficient if administered to the apex. If you could leave the corpse in an open area we can sledge it back later for dissection."

Arroyo looked at the Tetra standing stolidly beside him, its green essence leaking onto the ice. "You and I need to take a little walk," Arroyo said to it. He stepped a few meters toward the Penguin Ranch's perimeter, then stopped and turned. The Tetra took a few hesitant lurches in Arroyo's direction. "That's it," Arroyo whispered. "Follow me." He glanced toward the assembled grantees, wishing a huge crevasse would suddenly open beneath their highly educated feet and spill them into the black sea far below.

The walk seemed to take forever. Arroyo and the Tetra eventually cleared the open expanse of the Penguin Ranch and

58

began to wind amongst the jagged, towering penitentes and tortured pressure ridges. The leaking Tetra followed along faithfully. When Drag Queen and the surface structures of the Penguin Ranch were just dots on the ice far behind him, Arroyo stopped. The Tetra came to an awkward halt behind him.

"This is where we part company," Arroyo said. He opened the instrument case and removed the hypodermic gun. He took off the safety, pointed it downward toward a hump of ice and released the trigger. The euthanizing agent turned to frozen crystals and tinkled onto the ice. "I'm sorry about your foot." He reached into a utility pocket on his suit and pulled out a small trauma kit. He found a compress bandage and tied it awkwardly around the Tetra's injury, although he knew it would soon slip off the stumpy corner of the tetrahedral body. "We humans are a *very* fucked-up, heartless species, if you hadn't learned that already. Especially when science is involved. You'll have to stay out of sight until your wound has healed."

Arroyo had no rational reason to assume the creature understood his words. But he felt a strange connection to the Tetra. As Arroyo left, he turned and waved. The Tetra stood silently, as if watching him go. When he got back to camp, Arroyo handed the expended hypo to Angstrom. Arroyo said he'd take a scootmobile and a cargo sled out to the penitentes in the morning to retrieve the corpse. The next day, Arroyo did, indeed, head in search of the Tetra. All he found was a thin trail of green showing where the Tetra had waddled away into the chaos terrain. When he returned to camp corpse-less, he simply said he couldn't find the right spot. He explained that his footprints from the previous day had left no marks on the rock-hard ice. Of course, there had been a trail of green that he could have followed. But the grantees just seemed relieved to have made the inconvenient "situation" disappear.

Some weeks later Arroyo spied a tiny black triangle far out amongst the penitentes. While there were many Tetras off in the distance, this one seemed to beckon him. Late at night, when most of the staff was asleep back in the Discovery Bay subsurface Jamesways, Arroyo set out on foot. After an hour of walking he stepped around a huge penitente to find the Tetra waiting in the shadows out of the light of Ganymede. Its wound had healed, leaving only a rough scar. It now waddled with a faint limp. *Pegleg*, Arroyo christened the creature at that moment. Arroyo warned it to stay clear of the Penguin Ranch's corrals and weighing station, although he was sure Pegleg already understood.

Arroyo took regular trips out into the penitentes with Drag Queen in the coming days and weeks, keeping an eye on the healed creature. Arroyo had read the 75-year-old accounts of Socks and Petty Officer Third Class Bowers from the Pegasus crew. Arroyo downloaded harmonica music onto his seldom-used iMind back at camp one night. The next night, sitting behind a penitente with Pegleg, he piped it through the external speaker on his suit. The first song was an ancient tune called "Ain't No Sunshine," by someone named Bill Withers. Pegleg sat rock-still for a few moments. Then, hesitantly at first, it began to tap one corner of its base on the ice. Soon it rocked rhythmically back and forth atop its three points of contact. Arroyo laughed with joy.

* * *

"We spent Christmas together," Annie reminded Arroyo. "You, me and Pegleg. After the camp party in the galley. We took a scootmobile out into the penitentes. We stole a bottle of Scotch one of the grantees had left out—none of that horrible Trank that you guzzle. We sat down with Pegleg, and you put out a nice spread of frozen turkey and stuffing on the ground for it on a red-and-white-checkered table cloth. It didn't eat, of course. We sipped Scotch out of an electroflask through our helmet valves and sang Christmas carols. Pegleg rocked back and forth in perfect time. It even let you put an angel ornament on its head."

I remember, Arroyo thought. "Thank you," he told Annie. "You don't know how much that memory means to me." Maybe there *was* hope for him.

"I figured it might help you clear cobwebs," she said. "You and Pegleg were close."

Annie didn't know *how* close. Two decades of research had verified that the seemingly passive Tetras exhibited an uncanny power of empathy with certain humans with whom they apparently chose to bond. When Arroyo was with Pegleg, he remembered for the first time in eons the visceral meaning of the word *joy*. Sitting amongst the towering penitentes of the chaos terrain beside the silent Tetra, Arroyo could suddenly glimpse things and places he thought he'd long ago forgotten—such as the sun-dappled fishing hole on a summer stream when he must have been ten years old, where his father taught him to fish—in particular how to treat the fat yellow perch as fellow living beings. Some of them were carried gratefully home for dinner, but the rest were gently returned to their strange world beneath the shimmering mirror separating depthless dark water and bright blue sky.

Various researchers posited a slew of hypotheses for the "Tetra Effect." Perhaps the Tetras were simply Europa's version of a comforting lapdog. Perhaps they released a pheromone or endorphin that triggered the near-ecstatic wave of emotion-laden memory. Perhaps, warned still others, it was less a pheromone and more a neurotoxin, evolved to disarm prey by overwhelming the target with a flood of distracting memories that are normally hidden away. Arroyo discounted the neurotoxin theory. Pegleg had no discernible mouth, no functioning digestive tract, and Arroyo felt in no danger of becoming an appetizer for the jet-black dancing creature.

* * *

"I've got to get back to Discovery Bay," Arroyo told Annie. "I think I'm stuck in Mactown for a few weeks, but maybe after that."

Annie sat forward on the bunk. "I'm headed back out in a few days to help take out the camp. The threat of a government shutdown seems to be dead-serious this time. Field camps are already shutting down and everyone out there is packing their gear. I heard the staff at the Pole station is packing, too. Beakers are powering down projects and backing up their data. It's scary. We could be out of work soon. The worst part is the idea of going into stasis on short notice. I get panic attacks thinking about lying helplessly while The Company pumps my head full of bromides. Oops. I forgot about the time. I've got to get back to the Fuels Barn." She stood, patted Arroyo on the head like an old dog, and left.

* * *

Arroyo was exhausted. He was worn out from his R&R, his back burned from his new tattoo, and he could smell his own pits and ass. He decided he would grab his weekly shower before going to HR and Medical. He grabbed the bloody towel in the sink and wrung it out. It would have to do. He rummaged through his daypack for his toilet kit. He zipped it open to make sure he had soap and shampoo. A plastic prescription bottle fell out onto the floor. Puzzled, he stooped and picked it up. He read the label:

NSWF OFFJOVSYSOPS Clinic
Kardashia Facility, Ganymede
Dr. Butch Gianforte, MD

RX: 6511391
Fill Date: 10/15/2297
Bronson, Arroyo
TAKE ONE TABLET DAILY FOR
ANXIETY

Arroyo stared at the prescription. He had never seen it before. Perhaps he *was* still losing his mind. He had no recollection of a Dr. Gianforte and didn't recall ever visiting The Program's clinic in Kardashia. The date indicated that the prescription had been filled on Ganymede about the time he was starting his R&R. Normally this sort of confusion would have called for a swig of Trank to clear the cobwebs. Or perhaps he should simply pop two or three of the tablets. But Arroyo had made a solemn vow to clean up his act. He stared at the medication a few more moments, then tossed it into a dresser drawer.

He unlaced his low-g boots and kicked them into a corner. He climbed out of his trousers, bouncing high, as often happened right after taking off the weighted boots. Then he began to peel off his longjohn bottoms. As he did so, both legs began to itch maddeningly. He reached down and scratched like a dog inundated by fleas. When he stood, he glanced in the sink mirror. What he saw made him freeze.

Both legs were covered in welts from his scratching. But even where he hadn't scratched, he could see that both legs from the hips down were bright pink, the color of an infant's skin. When he touched them, purple splotches rose to the surface for a moment before fading. Where once had been the coarse hair of a middle-aged man's legs was a meager growth of downy blond fuzz.

I'm quitting Trank just in the nick of time, he thought. Somehow his excesses must have affected the circulation in his legs. He wrapped the towel around his waist so that it hid most of his soft, pink legs and hobbled down the hallway to the showers.

* * *

Darla Hovenweep's cubicle was one of dozens of identical burlap-covered human pigeonholes in the warehouse-like, windowless Admin building. Most of the cubicles had hand-scribbled nametags of their occupants tacked to their entrances. Many of the cubicle denizens were on temporary assignment to Europa. One gentleman, a Coordinator for Special Projects, had been sent to Europa for six weeks via the Slingshot Express to study the usage of the station's two electric cars. They never functioned properly—their batteries were better suited for a golf course in Arizona than for the metal-cracking cold of Europa. So they had been sitting for years under a tarpaulin behind the Heavy Shop, long forgotten, stripped of parts usable elsewhere. Still, when he could be found, the gentleman was proud of the spreadsheet he'd been laboring over, verifying the obvious fact that nobody ever used the vehicles. Soon he would be Slingshotting back to Earth, where he would spend six months finessing his findings into a Powerpoint before presenting them to a fidgetting committee. The little toy cars were another Bryonstorm, shipped via Slingshot Express at astronomical expense to Europa.

Arroyo found Darla's cubicle. She was gone; he pulled up a creaky chair and waited. Like many of the office workers in Mactown, she was rarely at her desk. Most of the cubicles had notes saying things like "In Finance meeting—catch me tomorrow," or "Got the blues—I'm in my room medicating." Accountability was not something emphasized by Company management on Europa. Asking people to be at their place of work during posted work hours could be seen as harrassment or, even worse, shaming. Formal grievances had been filed for far less.

In a few minutes a rotund woman with immaculately coiffed hair sashayed up and slipped as elegantly as the laws of mechanics allowed behind the desk. She smiled broadly, holding up a steaming mug. "I almost forgot my ten o'clock chai," she sang. She scooted up to the desk. After a sip of chai she folded her hands on her desk. "*Arroyo Bronson*," she said, pleased with her own memory. "Welcome back to the world of the living." She straightened her desk blotter.

"Thank you," Arroyo said, slouched in the chair. "I was told I need to sign some of my new contract paperwork."

"Yes," Darla said. "Let me see." Her right hand lifted swiftly into the air as she began to scroll through the menus on her iMind. Her eyes focused on a projected image only she could see, somewhere in the indefinite distance. Her hand fluttered in a blur, the mark of someone who spent most of the day on her iMind. "Oh yes. We have most of your paperwork already: Contract Offer Letter, Amended Terms of Agreement, Intellectual Property Agreement, Conflict of Interest Certificate, Arbitration Agreement—all properly signed and initialled. We just need a couple of final signatures." She tapped the image of a SEND key that only she could see. "Hmmm." She stared into her projected iMind menu, confused. "I just tried to send two documents to your iMind so you could sign them electronically. I think your inbox might be full."

Arroyo snatched the old iMind off his face. He'd hastily put it on just before coming to visit Darla. "Sorry," he said, fumbling with it. "I forgot to boot it up." He squinted, trying to spot the almost-microscopic power button. He had no luck; he supposed it was time to buy reading glasses. "Maybe the battery is dead," he said, shaking the iMind in frustration. He banged it on the desktop. "Do you have a ball peen hammer?"

Jim Fairchild

"Don't worry," Darla sang. "I've still got a printer. It's Paleolithic but it works." She flitted her hand through the air, scrolling through her iMind files. *There we go.* A printer on a shelf behind her lit up and began to purr. It coughed a cloud of dust, then spat out papers.

She pulled the forms from the printer and carefully slid them across the desk to Arroyo. "How was your trip to Ganymede?" Darla asked. "I miss the big city. What I would do for some good sushi."

"I've never tried the sushi on Ganymede," Arroyo said. "It's mostly bottom-feeders raised in poop-filled tanks. I laid low—I caught up on my sleep, went to church, played some golf and took a museum tour." Arroyo studied the paperwork. "I thought I signed these forms before I left."

"Oh, you know how it goes," she said, beaming. "The home office comes up with revisions every time I blink. It's just a formality. It's the newest Safety Training Acknowledgment and Press Contact Protocols forms."

Arroyo glanced at the safety form. The gist of it was contained in the final paragraph:

> The Company gives you the tools needed to do your job safely. If you are injured while working on Europa, it is not because the job is dangerous, but because you failed to properly use the safety tools entrusted to you. A workplace injury only happens when you fail to meet one or more of your job requirements. If you are hurt while performing your job on Europa, you are a danger to your co-workers and a failure at your job. Your work evaluation will duly reflect that failure.

Arroyo scribbled his signature at the bottom of the form's last page. "Another rousing vote of faith in my abilities from management," he said, chuckling.

"Oh, it's all quite standard," Darla assured him. "I'm sure management has infinite faith in your abilities."

"Sounds like I've still got them hoodwinked, then." Arroyo glanced at the other document needing his attention: the Press Contact Protocols form. Every year the NSWF underwrote visits from various media outlets, most of them from Earth. The all-expenses-paid junkets via the posh Slingshot Express—with stopovers at the best hotels and golf courses on Ganymede—cost taxpayers millions of credits a year. Reporters rarely bit the hand that awarded them the boondoggle. The Program got oodles of earnest, clichéd, skin-deep news coverage that played well with the semi-educated public and even less-educated Congress. Media crews (another ilk of DV) were paraded around Mactown and given flitter trips to all the de rigeur picturesque photo ops on Europa where they could have their hero shots taken. They were taken out to field camps and the Penguin Ranch and the Pole to interview grantees doing very important-looking science work—peering into microscopes, sawing lengths of ice cores, observing clouds on Jupiter. A voiceover should have accompanied the clichéd shots: *SILENCE! SCIENCE IN PROGRESS!* At all times the media crews were chaperoned by hand-picked Program employees who spouted a well-rehearsed profusion of facts and statistics cherry-picked to assure taxpayers they were getting their money's worth from The Program. It was strictly *verboten* for run-of-the-mill employees like Arroyo to step forward and initiate conversation with the media. Permission to communicate with the media—even with a hometown gazzette back on Earth—had to be granted from a functionary in NSWF's Press Relations Office in Arlington. As a general rule nobody ever got a reply to such a request.

Jim Fairchild

"We've got a BBS crew arriving in a month," Darla said. "It's rather exciting." Her cheeks seemed to flush in affirmation. A year into her first contract off-Earth, she still had a FNG's cloying excitement about all facets of The Program. Arroyo had seen media crews come and go over the last fifteen years. He had never seen any true reporting come out of the junkets—just cut-and-paste stories for wide-eyed kids and for adults with no real understanding of science and no bullshit detectors necessary when dealing with spin-savvy science bureaucrats.

Stock footage had been shot of Arroyo operating Drag Queen many years ago by a visiting BBS crew, and he still spotted it edited into new documentaries on Europa. The wildly popular TV and radio political commentator, Tuffie Lindblad, had even used the Drag Queen footage in the first of his rabble-rousing crockumentaries claiming that the entire history of manned space exploration, starting with Yuri Gagarin's 1961 flight in Vostok 1, was an elaborate fabrication by a transnational shadow government run by Jewish and Scandinavian financiers. Lindblad had been a driving force in the formation of the wildly popular New Flat Earth Society. Arroyo had seen Lindblad's first crockumentary when it came out—he was amused to learn from the narrator that the footage of him in Drag Queen climbing over rough ice in Europa's chaos terrain had actually been filmed in a field near the remains of Bismarck, North Dakota. He had no recollection of ever having set foot in the former capital of North Dakota, but he wouldn't want to disagree with the cantankerous Tuffie. Arroyo remembered passing the BBS camera crew that shot the footage. He had dropped his trousers and pressed his buttocks to the tractor's frosty side window after raising the radiation shield. Unfortunately, his icy moon's transit was left on the editing room floor.

"Thank you," Darla said, when Arroyo had signed the forms. She fed them into a scanner, made some bird-like notations in thin air with her iMind, then said, "It must be nice to work on the surface. All I see of Europa is my grey cubicle and the insides of the station grotto. I volunteer whenever I can to help sort waste in the Retro Yard just to get into a suit and go topside. You must see some amazing views."

"It's not too bad," Arroyo said, "*if* you're into that kind of thing."

Darla pushed back a bit from her desk and made herself more comfortable, smoothing her navy blue tunic. "Are you happy to be back at work, Arroyo?"

Arroyo cleared his throat. "Pleased as punch. I'm ready to get back in the saddle and do my small part to help further the jackbooted March of Science across this godforsaken iceball."

"Well. I take that as unqualified enthusiasm. Most commendable. I ask the question because you've been on Europa a *long* time. Fourteen years, isn't it?"

"Fifteen years, one month and three days," Arroyo said. "But who's counting?"

"You could have moved into a management position *years* ago," Darla said wistfully. "You have *so* much experience."

"I prefer to work for a living," Arroyo said.

"I look at your background and you know more about day-to-day operations than most of the managers. Have you ever given any thought to a career position with The Company? I would be remiss if I didn't tell you that with your background you would qualify for almost any slot you applied for."

"Thank you, Darla," Arroyo said. He looked at the photos pinned to her corkboard: a couple of teenaged children in the backyard of a McMansion in the burbs of New San Jose or New Cleveland or New Gaithersburg or New Overland Park or any of the hundreds of cities that had been resurrected after the Crash on a far smaller scale than the originals. A photo of proud, beaming elderly parents. A photo of a nicely groomed and impossibly happy bichon frise. *But no photo of a significant other.* Many people came to Europa the first time because they had just gone through a divorce. Many others came to Europa the first time and soon found themselves going through a divorce. "But I value the freedom that being a contract employee gives me. I'm not tied down in one place to a job that I can never escape from." Of course, he realized, that precisely described his life on Europa.

Darla laughed. "Everyone tells me you never go back to Earth between contracts to take time off. You take a little R&R on Ganymede and come right back."

Arroyo thought a moment. "I guess Europa *is* my home. It's the only life I have."

Darla scooted closer to her desk. "I admire your dedication," she said. "But The Company knows how many years you've spent in the most difficult of situations in the middle of nowhere. The Company values loyalty. I just want to mention one thing in passing: a career position has opened up at the Ganymede office in Kardashia. The salary is at least what you make here, even after your hardship and contract completion bonuses are factored in. You would have full benefits including a posh pension. I could fast-track an application for you, and make sure it goes to the top of the appropriate iMind inbox."

"What's the gig?" Arroyo asked.

"Supervisor of Facility Maintenance."

"*Head janitor.*" Arroyo laughed so hard he had to wipe spittle from Darla's desk.

"It would be *safe*," Darla said, disappointed in his reaction. "You'd be indoors. You would never have to go outside. You would be in charge of a crew of twelve employees and you'd have a real office to yourself—not just a cubicle like mine. You would have a *huge* private apartment paid for by The Company in one of the nicest high-rises in Kardashia. You'd be just a few blocks from hundreds of restaurants, the Kardashia Casino and

Ganymede's biggest shopping mall. I understand a *Bed, Bath and Beyond* has just opened."

"Thank you," Arroyo said, pushing back his chair on the ragged carpet. "But those are all reasons why I belong on Europa. And I've got enough towels."

* * *

Arroyo stepped into Medical. The old plascrete floor creaked underfoot as he approached the receptionist. Many decades ago the building had been a U.S. Navy clinic, and the interior walls were still covered with flaking battleship-grey paint. The receptionist was lost in her iMind somewhere—judging from her giggles, probably looking at cute kitten videos. "Doctor Gianforte will be with you momentarily," she said, seeming to resent the interruption.

He was soon led by a nurse behind a hospital-green curtain, through an examination area that reeked of ether and alcohol and then down a narrow creaking hallway in the back. An office door was open; a thick, balding man with a bristly walrus mustache and arms covered in matted black hair waved him in.

"Arroyo! Come on in. A genuine Europa hero. Sit down."

He introduced himself as Dr. Butch Gianforte. "I just wanted to touch base with you," the doctor said after they shook hands. Arroyo tried to rub the circulation back into his crushed fingers. The doctor leaned back in his rolling chair. A chair wheel dragged, drawing the doctor's ire. "You've been on R&R for a month. How's your liver? Any clap? How about a prostate check? I know you just had one for your rehire physical before you left, but I'm running a special this week."

"I think my prostate is fine," Arroyo said, grimacing.

"Just a little *nyuck-nyuck-nyuck*," Gianforte said.

Arroyo always religiously avoided going to Medical. The

best plan for staying in one piece on Europa was taking care of yourself and never seeing the doctor. Few of the doctors The Company had hired for the Europa clinic would have met the minimal standards required to practice on Earth. Most had graduated in the bottom half of their class, had gone from one job to another, and seemed years out of date with their medical knowledge. Some were well into their retirement years and one had probably been certifiably senile. Two or three were on the lam from malpractice lawsuits back on Earth or Mars. One prior doctor spent most of his contract locked in his dorm room designing what he swore was an apparatus for communicating with aliens on Larissa, one of Neptune's minor moons. The Company didn't pay its doctors on Europa much; The Company got what it paid for. So far, the only thing about Dr. Gianforte that concerned Arroyo was the bearskin-like hair that covered his arms down to the knuckles. Arroyo surmised that the hair might make a prostate exam a ticklish proposition.

"On the serious side," Gianforte said, "I needed to talk to you about your Trank consumption. Has it ever crossed your mind that you have a drinking problem?"

"I never have a problem as long as I can find a drink," Arroyo said. He resented being asked about his drinking, although he knew that as a Company employee in a Company town, there was no such thing as having a private life.

"Don't mind my asking," Gianforte said. "But you have a certain reputation. And I've seen the liver enzyme numbers from your physical before you went on R&R. You passed, but just barely. There's time to stop before you do irreversible damage."

Arroyo didn't explain that he had just vowed to himself to go cold-turkey. "I appreciate your concern," he said. "But I'm just a maintenance drinker."

"Well," Gianforte said. "Feel free to maintain that delusion about your drinking. In the meantime, reality is creeping up on you and will someday deliver a good swift wake-up punch to your sternum." He whipped a furry arm through the air in a Hollywood karate chop, nearly upsetting his mocha latte onto a pile of paperwork.

"Easy, Doc," Arroyo muttered.

"I just want to let you know that as the station physician I have access to medications that can help you wean yourself from any addiction. You don't have to lose time from work. My door is always open. Unless, of course, it *isn't*—in which case knock three times and wait for the rockin' in my office to subside."

"Gotcha. I've got a few questions for you, Doc. First, if I *were* to decide to get off Trank, is cold-turkey a good idea?"

"Most definitely not," Gianforte implored. "Your body has learned to function with its nervous and cardiopulmonary systems awash in Trank. Your physiology has adjusted to function with the presence of those toxins. A precipitous drying-out could lead to cardiac arrest. *Please, please, please*—taper off slowly. Enjoy a few drinks a night, then just one drink, then—maybe several weeks down the road—a cute little Shirley Temple with lots of grenadine and two or—*what the hey*—even *three* maraschino cherries. And maybe one of those cute little paper umbrellas. Nobody likes quitters, but at least you'll still have what remains of your liver."

"Another question," Arroyo said. "I just found a prescription you wrote me back in mid-October. It was filled at The Program clinic in Kardashia. I don't remember seeing you, or picking up the prescription. I was on R&R and pretty preoccupied, but I should remember something like that."

"Well, Arroyo," the doctor said, shuffling papers on his desk. "You were pretty pixilated at the time. I was at the clinic in Kardashia for training before redeploying to Europa. You were a walk-in. You complained that nightmares were keeping you from sleeping."

Arroyo knew his memory was terrible, but something didn't add up. "So you prescribed the drugs for anxiety?"

"Yes," Gianforte said. "I hope you are still taking them. One daily, as I recall."

"Of course," Arroyo said.

"Good." Gianforte glanced into space for a moment, karate-chopping his hairy hand through the air, updating Arroyo's patient records on his iMind. "It's imperative that you maintain that prescribed dose. Come back to see me in a couple of weeks and maybe we'll tweak the dosage. Until then, work and play safely. Remember, the last thing you want is an unplanned visit with The Company doctor. It rarely goes well. It can be worse than, say, a good swift punch to the sternum." He lashed out with a karate chop again. The mocha latte sloshed all over the desk.

Arroyo pushed his chair back to leave. "One last thing, Doc. Can that medication affect my circulation? My legs look pink."

Gianforte frowned. "Yes," he said, after a moment's pause to peruse a list of the drug's side-effects on his iMind. "Peripheral flushing is not uncommon. Capillary dilation and whatnot. Nothing to worry your cute little worker-bee mind about. Remember, come and see me in a couple of weeks, and keep taking the medication." The doctor glanced at the side of Arroyo's face. "Missing anything?" Gianforte asked, pointing to his ear.

Arroyo fumbled in his parka pocket for his iMind. "Sorry," he said, trying to turn it on. "I think it needs a new battery."

"Replace the battery and wear your iMind," the doctor said. "I'm sending you several files of subliminal anti-anxiety therapy. It's even better than meds. You won't even know you are listening to them."

Arroyo thanked the doctor. Outside Medical, he tore the iMind from the side of his face and shoved it back into his parka. Back in his room, he flushed the medication down the toilet.

* * *

After lunch Arroyo strolled to the motorpool. It occupied a cavernous corrugated plascrete archway set back into the ice from the main station grotto. The archway roof, covered by millions of tons of ice that had slowly been sinking downward for decades, was warped and twisted. Ice stalactites hung down through the holes left by rivets that had popped out under the pressure of the ice. The floor was covered with interlocking plascrete panels similar to the perforated steel Marston Mats used on World War II airfields in the Pacific. The floor, like everything else in Mactown, was slightly out of kilter.

Arroyo walked down the long center aisle past dozens of beat-up tractors, loaders, dump trucks and scootmobiles. Another row was reserved for airfield equipment: Hobart power carts and engine heaters used to service the flitter fleet and visiting shuttles. A third of the archway, along one entire wall, was the service bay for the ridiculous fifty-meter-long Kregg people mover. It was Bryon Sturm's ultimate Bryonstorm. A new, broadly curved access tunnel had to be cored down to the motorpool from Europa's surface so that the beast could be brought in for servicing. All of the surface routes near Mactown had to be reworked, too. The roadwork had gone on for two years. It had probably tripled the original cost of the Kregg vehicle, but nobody in The Program seemed interested in accounting.

The Heavy Shop offices were in the rear of the motorpool. Arroyo strolled past perhaps a dozen mechanics—known as Wrenches—their grease-coated coveralls unzipped to the waist, making room for their mostly middle-aged paunches. Arroyo knew them all by name, and waved and called their names as he passed. But to a man they all just peered suspiciously over the tops of their smudged safety glasses at him, wondering what new work

Jim Fairchild

the operator had just created for them. In a workforce in which copping a jaded and cynical attitude was par for the course after a few years, the heavy equipment mechanics set the gold standard for grumpiness. No one group of workers was more irritable and self-pitying than the Wrenches. It was true that the Wrenches were *always* overworked: Europa was a place where brand-new equipment came to die. Thick steel snapped like toothpicks in the cold. Supposedly sealed electronic components went on the fritz from the build-up of internal ice crystals invisible to the naked eye. Half of the equipment in Mactown was broken down on a *good* day. Arroyo thought that some of the problem was the Wrenches themselves: many of them were amongst the station's worst Trankheads, and in their previous lives had bounced from one job to the next, angry at the world that life hadn't been a stroll down Easy Street. Many were divorced before arriving on Europa; most were divorced before leaving. When a cheery, bright-eyed new mechanic arrived at the Heavy Shop from Earth, it was policy to break their spirit ASAP. The Wrenches saved the brunt of their rage-filled *Weltanschauung* for the equipment operators like Arroyo. They were convinced that operators intentionally broke equipment just to make the lives of Wrenches miserable. Arroyo tried to explain to a couple of them that his *life* often depended upon the equipment he operated, and that nothing was farther from his mind than intentionally damaging anything. But the Wrenches he explained this to suffered from the universal human bane of discounting anything that didn't jibe with their preconceived belief system, and they ridiculed his earnest entreaties.

Arroyo stepped into the offices, separated from the service bays by a wall of filthy wire-reinforced glass. As he swung the door shut, the din of air wrenches, compressors and idling engines was left behind. The air in the offices was cool and fresh after the overheated, foul miasma of the service bays. He waved to the office manager, the work scheduler and the Heavy Shop foreman.

They all knew Arroyo well, and unlike the Wrenches were friendly and cheerful. *Welcome back*, each said, waving, as they tried to make heads and tails of work orders.

Collette, the office manager, was in the midst of scrolling through an iMind message, but she managed to smile and wave and silently mouth the word *hi*. Somehow she made the two-letter word seem naughty. Collette was old enough to be retired but considered Europa her home and kept signing new contracts. She stood two meters tall. In her first career she had been a dancer in all the big productions on Kardashia's Strip. She had high-kicked her way into countless gentlemen's hearts for two decades before arthritis made her hang up her pasties. She still had her sly stage smile. No man on Europa stood a chance with her.

Ted, the work scheduler, rose from behind his desk and squeezed past the front counter. "Hey, Arroyo, ol' buddy! It's great to have you back, ol' pal." Ted gave Arroyo a bear hug that made Arroyo melt. Ted had been on Europa too long. He dated to the very beginning of the civilian years, like Barry Wilton. Too many years living in an ice grotto 780 million kilometers from the nearest non-hydroponic blade of grass had made him toasty. Ted sometimes stuttered or went off on digressions. But Arroyo knew that Ted had a heart of gold. The population of Europa was a representative cross-section of so-called humanity: perhaps thirty percent could reliably be counted upon to do the wrong thing in any circumstance, driven entirely by self-interest. Another forty percent were apathetic fence-straddlers, occasionally giving lip service to doing the right thing, but rarely getting off their collective asses to do so. Another thirty percent could be counted on in the worst of pinches to do the right thing. It was in the overworked hands of that last group that the fate of mankind rested; it was near the head of that small phalanx that Ted steadfastly marched, albeit often to his own drummer.

"What can I do for you, buddy?" Ted asked, clutching a pile of grease-smeared work orders to his chest.

"I was looking for Vinnie," Arroyo explained. "I figured I'd better swing by the shop and see how Drag Queen is doing."

"Third service bay from the front, far row," Ted said. "You almost bumped into him on the way in."

Arroyo thanked Ted.

"Hey, buddy," Ted said. "Did I already say it's great to have you back? Be safe out there, buddy." He patted Arroyo vigorously on a shoulder. Arroyo thought he could see a tear in the corner of one of Ted's eyes. Arroyo was touched.

* * *

Arroyo retraced his steps and found Vinnie Kuzawa. His back was to Arroyo; his head was deep inside one of Drag Queen's side engine hatches, searching for a dropped bolt with a flashlight and a magnetic probe. Arroyo recognized him by the long, greasy ponytail and the jouncy, pasty-white saddlebags of fat that protruded from under his t-shirt and hung over his belt.

Hey, Animal," Arroyo said. He had to shout to be heard over the din of air wrenches and revving engines. He called Vinnie by his nickname. Vinnie loved the nickname, and always encouraged others to call him by it, but most of his co-workers snorted with laughter instead. Vinnie was the mechanic permanently assigned to service Drag Queen, so Arroyo faithfully used the nom de guerre.

* * *

Vinnie was well into his second contract. During his first, he had met a young woman named Natalia in an iMind chatroom. She said she lived on Mars in a suburb of New Bradbury. She had

78

a day job as a terraforming microbiologist, she said, but her secret dream was to become a country-western recording star. The ancient musical genre was making a comeback on Mars. She wanted to be the Martian Tammy Wynette or Dolly Parton. She explained that all she lacked was a home recording studio to cut some demo tracks. She discussed what she would need to get started.

Vinnie was soon wiring her huge sums. Some months he wired her every credit he made. She would send him photos of the recording equipment she was purchasing thanks to his generosity. She promised to repay him. He would sit for hours at work, not turning a wrench, zoned out on his iMind, reading her epic missives. He would print them off on the printer at the Heavy Shop, hauling hundreds of pages of hardcopy back to his room for closer perusal.

When the end of his contract neared, Vinnie booked a one-way Slingshot Express trip to Mars. It took the last of his savings—and then some. He and his iMind girlfriend were going to meet at the New Bradbury Interplanetary Arrival terminal, near Baggage Claim. She would be wearing a red rose.

The Heavy Shop threw a big party for Vinnie before he left. He tried on the lavender three-piece suit he'd ordered from a haberdashery in Kardashia for his Martian rendezvous. He beamed like a little child with its first puppy, even though he spilled buffalo wings down the front of the suit and didn't have time to have it cleaned before leaving.

Vinnie's flight to Mars landed precisely on time. He found his luggage at Baggage Claim and waited. And waited. *And waited.* Finally, he spotted a grizzled male dwarf in a black tuxedo standing near the terminal doors. The dwarf was wearing a red rose in his jacket lapel.

Vinnie avoided eye contact for several minutes. Finally, he approached the dwarf. He saw that the dwarf was carrying a small

Jim Fairchild

gift-wrapped box festooned with ribbons.

"Animal Kuzawa?" the dwarf asked.

"Yes," Vinnie said, his heart sinking.

"This is for you." The dwarf handed Vinnie the box and departed. Vinnie nervously tore apart the giftwrap. He ripped the lid off the box. Inside was a lovely multi-colored lollipop from a spaceport gift shop. Beneath it was a note in exquisite gold calligraphy:

My dearest Animal—
Thank you for your bottomless generosity. Enclosed is a token of my appreciation—a delicious sucker for a delicious sucker.
With greatest affection—
Yours truly,
Natalia

Vinnie turned the card over. On the back was a photo of all of the Mactown Wrenches huddled together in a Heavy Shop service bay. They faced the camera, middle fingers extended, laughing. In the middle of the group two greasy men held a mangled piece of cardboard. Crudely spray-painted on it were the words *FUCK YOU, VINNIE*. The entire Heavy Shop crew had taken turns pretending to be the fictitious Natalia on the iMind account they'd created for her. They made Vinnie sweat a few months before they finally wired him back his money—minus what they had paid the dwarf.

* * *

Vinnie jumped when he heard his nickname. He banged the back of his head into the sharp edge of the engine hatch. *"HOLYJESUSFUCKGODDAMMIT,"* Vinnie shrieked, lurching

80

back. Rubbing the back of his head, he stumbled over the toes of Arroyo's low-g boots. They both nearly fell; Arroyo stopped their fall by grabbing a tall tool chest, almost spilling socket wrenches and screwdrivers and test meters everywhere.

"Damn, Arroyo," Vinnie said, turning. "I've told you never to sneak up on me like that. What the fuck do you want? Did you break another piece of perfectly good equipment?"

"No, Animal." Arroyo reached out and patted Vinnie on the shoulder, but Vinnie seemed impervious to the gesture. "I got back from R&R last night and just wanted to see how Drag Queen was doing."

Vinnie wiped his grease-caked hands on a once-red shop rag. "Oh, yeah," Vinnie smiled. "Welcome back, *Drug* Queen. You've been gone a long time. I hope you caught chlamydia."

"Thanks, Animal. I'm stuck in Mactown for a few weeks but if Drag Queen is up and running I'll be taking her out to the Shear Zone each day to help with crevasse remediation."

Vinnie grabbed a clipboard and made some notations, then tossed it onto the top of his tool chest. "Well, for a half-century-old Navy tractor, she's running pretty good. I rebuilt the head while you were gone. The compression is back to spec, and I replaced the turbocharger. I put on a new set of tracks, too, and charged up the nitrogen tension arms. It should be ready for you to take back out and destroy. You operators break 'em, us Wrenches fix 'em."

"Sorry, Animal. I know operators are a pain in your side. That was a lot of work to get done in one month. Thank you." Vinnie began to walk around the tractor; Arrroyo followed.

The tractor had been offloaded from the third Navy vessel to make landfall on Europa. That vessel touched down almost two decades after the rescue vessel that found the remains of Petty Officer Third Class Bowers. The third visit was a landing in force, with the intention of improving the original hastily-built subsurface

Mactown and creating a permanent human presence. A large fleet of heavy equipment trundled down the vessel's cargo ramp onto the ice. Of the dozens of original tractors, dozers, loaders and trucks all painted yellow and bearing U.S. Navy markings, only Drag Queen remained. The rest of that original yellow fleet had been repaired endlessly until at last they hàd been pushed into bottomless crevasses to sink into the sea, dragged to the Retro Yard and stripped for parts or—in a few rare instances—shipped to a salvage yard on Ganymede. Drag Queen was one of four old Caterpillar Challenger X-95 tractors the Navy had brought to Europa. The only other survivor now rested on its laurels in the Edward H. White Space Museum—a popular tourist destination— a couple of blocks from the Kardashia Casino, next to an all-you-can-eat gambler's binge-and-barf buffet.

As they walked around the tractor, Vinnie pointed out parts he had repaired or replaced while Arroyo was gone. The tractor was so old—and so long out of production—that many replacement parts had to be custom-machined in the Heavy Shop. It was an incredible investment in labor time, but shipping parts from Earth for the newer tractors was incredibly expensive, too. "It's running pretty well for a fifty-year-old bucket of rusting bolts," Vinnie said, as affectionately as he was capable of being. "Of course, now you're back, and you'll fuck it up again." They passed the elaborately painted words *Drag Queen* on the rear battery compartment door. NSWF policy prohibited the painting of nicknames on equipment. But the first lettering had been done by a Navy mechanic half a century ago; the Navy Seabees had a long tradition of christening their equipment. Arroyo came to the Heavy Shop on his own time every couple of years to take paint and touch up the lettering. He felt he had an obligation to preserve history.

Vinnie and Arroyo both climbed up the ladder and catwalk to the cab. Vinnie swung the airlock door open awkwardly, almost knocking them both off the catwalk. "I re-sealed all of the window gaskets," Vinnie said. "The cab maintains perfect pressure now."

"Thanks, Animal." Arroyo peered into the cab. The controls were so much more simple than the newer models the rest of the operators preferred. Arroyo loved Drag Queen's vastly less-complicated computer system. Arroyo could lock out many automatic programmed features and operate manually. He believed that he had a more responsive touch with the controls than a software program—written by programmers in an office in New Long Beach who had never operated a tractor—when suddenly encountering bottomless pits of sugar ice, or when massive penitentes or yawning crevasses suddenly loomed out of nowhere in flat light. He was absolutely convinced that it was safer to operate manually. Many of the younger traverse operators would flip on all the automatic maneuvering features, pop a movie into their cab's entertainment system, close the window shades and cruise all day, oblivious to the feels and the sounds of their tractor, the terrain or the load they were pulling. Drag Queen had a longer chassis and track length than the newer models, too. This gave it better traction and load-pulling ability, especially on icy grades. Drag Queen could also cross wider crevasses. While most of the newer operators considered Drag Queen a laughable rusting relic, Arroyo found it an incredible honor and a pleasure to be assigned the old workhorse.

Arroyo looked with dismay at the cab floor. It was ankle-deep with crushed coffee cups, candy wrappers, crumpled black-and-white porn printed off the Heavy Shop printer, wads of tissue paper glued together with various bodily fluids. An old sock was crammed into a broken air vent to keep it from blowing in the operator's face. A pile of broken runway markers, the poles bent and nylon flags faded from radiation, were tossed into a corner, blocking access to the decelerator pedal. Someone had operated Drag Queen kicked back on cruise control with their feet propped up against the windshield; ice had melted from their boots and run down the glass, making such a mess that Arroyo couldn't see out to check his tracks and suspension on the move.

But the worst of it was the smell: Drag Queen's cab reeked of man-ass. Not just man-ass, but *operator-ass*: the ass of some lethargic pig who had spent too many years working off-Earth, had no personal life, and in contempt of his co-workers never bathed until Darla Hovenweep from HR had to call him into her cubicle to tell him there had been complaints (just to be fair, Arroyo discreetly sniffed the operator's seat to make sure he wasn't smelling his *own* scent). Arroyo was too pissed to check the logbook to see who'd been operating Drag Queen in his absence. He was shocked that such a gargantuan mess could be made in only a month.

"Wow," he muttered. He always took pride in keeping a clean cab. It was a matter of safety as well as aesthetics. "Looks like someone had a real party while I was gone."

Vinnie turned indignantly toward him. "Hell, Arroyo. You've been gone a *long* time. Life on Europa didn't stop while you were away. I've been taking it out for test runs. And some of your fellow operators used it from time to time when they needed Drag Queen's pulling power."

They stepped around the rear of the tractor. Arroyo stopped in his tracks when he got to the winch. The drum held 1750 meters of pencil-thin Olympus Mons cable, capable of safely lifting a tractor and its load from the depths of the deepest of crevasses. It was the original half-century-old cable that came with the tractor when it was first unloaded on Europa. It had its share of kinks and rust. Arroyo had requested a new cable dozens of times, but the factory in New Bradbury had been shuttered for decades, and finding another source was never a high priority for the Heavy Shop high muckety-mucks.

A large yellow plastic tag had been locked to the end of the cable. Arroyo read the tag:

SAFETY LOCKOUT
TO BE REMOVED ONLY BY
AUTHORIZED PERSONNEL
DATE: 10/17/2297
REASON: Winch cable worn and kinked—potentially unfriendly to human beings and their body parts
AUTHORIZED BY: Animal Kuzawa

Arroyo held the tag in his hand a moment, then let go. "I use that winch all the time," he said. "I've pulled tractors out of crevasses dozens of times with it. It's really saved my bacon.'"

"Whoever used it last was hard on it," Vinnie said.

"That would have been *me*."

Vinnie stepped back to get a better focus on the winch through his greasy reading glasses. He cleared his throat. "Take it up with station management," he said. "Barry Wilton came through here after you left. He said the winch was unsafe and to deadline it. I checked it out after he left. He was right. The controls in the cab are fine, but the remote handheld control has a short. The winch motor doesn't always stop when you want it to if you operate it too fast. It's amazing you haven't gotten hurt using it." Vinnie looked at Arroyo over his reading glasses.

"Can it be fixed?" Arroyo asked.

"The handheld control unit hasn't been manufactured for thirty years," Vinnie said, laughing. "Maybe if you're good with wiring schematics and a soldering gun you can figure something out. Personally, I'd leave it the heck alone. It's just dead weight, like most of the broken-down equipment on this turdpile of a moon."

Jim Fairchild

Arroyo tossed restlessly the night before his first day back in his tractor. He got up early, pulled on the same dirty Carhartts he'd left in a corner of his room before he left on R&R, ran through the galley to grab a muffin and a tall mug of black coffee strong enough to strip paint, then hoofed it to Stalag 17. He detoured enroute, stopping at the motorpool. He found Drag Queen parked outside the archway on a plug-in line. Equipment pulled out of the service bay was staged here, where it could stay warm. A spaghetti-like snarl of electrical cords ran to built-in heaters that kept engine oil, hydraulic fluid and batteries toasty-warm. He checked Drag Queen's fluid levels, even though Vinnie had just serviced the tractor. It wouldn't be the first time a mechanic had drained a fluid and forgotten to refill it. He reached into the jump seat for the logbook so he could fill out the Daily Operator's Inspection Checklist. He was also curious about who had been using the tractor lately. Oddly, though he knew he always put away the logbook there, it was missing. He searched around the cab, kicking the mountain of rubbish out the door. The logbook was nowhere to be found. He would have to get a new one from Ted at the Heavy Shop office.

At Stalag 17 he was introduced to the the new foreman replacing Derrick. His name was Tom Tillerman. He was midway through his second contract. There were many other more experienced operators, but none wanted the added responsibilities of being foreman given the negligible extra salary. Like many operators on Europa, his career path had been eclectic. Tillerman had spent two decades managing a county road crew in northern Minnesota—as remote a patch of land post-Crash as the Yukon Territories—before getting the travelling itch and leaving Earth. As a young man, he had run away from home and worked on a

Great Lakes ore carrier as a merchant mariner. He later graduated from barber college and had run a barber shop for years. His tonsorial services were much in demand in Mactown. He always refused payment; he just enjoyed the chance to meet new people and chat. And he was a master on the harmonica, with which he serenaded customers before cutting their hair. Arroyo hoped that he could take Tillerman to the Penguin Ranch some day to serenade Pegleg.

After the morning meeting Arroyo, Tillerman and three other crusty old operators walked to their idling tractors and suited up. Once in their cabs, they ran pre-ops diagnostics, calibrated their GPS units, double-checked their cab pressure, did comms checks with each other. Finally, all five gave a thumbs-up. Radiation shields were locked down. They shifted into gear; the huge tractors lurched. The shrieking, smoke-belching rigs trundled slowly up the broadly curving ice ramp to the heavy equipment airlock, then, one-by-one, out onto the surface of Europa.

*   *   *

The Shear Zone was a two-hour trip by tractor from Mactown. When not on traverses or at field camps, the Traverse Ops crew usually worked ten hours a day. That meant four hours would be burned up running the equipment out and back. Being assigned to duty in and around Mactown was cush compared to traversing, when work days lasted until the work was done (eighteen-hour days weren't uncommon), and when there was no such thing as a day off until you had reached your destination and had first offloaded your cargo and checked your tractor for wear and tear. Many operators, like Tillerman, loved to work in town: regular shift hours, a tiny but private dorm room, ample grub in the galley, a steady stream of holidays (most of which didn't actually include time off, unless you were in senior management), and a

Jim Fairchild

broad array of theme parties that hadn't changed in decades: *Mad Max Night, '70s Disco Night, Cross-Dresser's Ball, Goth Night* and *Hipster Night*. All of the theme parties were an impressionistic take on pre-Crash America. Historical accuracy was irrelevant; the parties were an excuse to guzzle Trank and break things. The parties were mandatory for FNGs and hopeless social butterflies. Few things seemed more pathetic than middle-aged men and women dressing up and going to *'70s Disco Night*. Arroyo had avoided the theme parties for years.

The trip to the Shear Zone was relaxing. Ganymede was setting behind them, and its orb seemed to swell larger as it sank and melted behind the jagged horizon. It would return on the opposite horizon in two Europa days. When they reached their work area, Tillerman got on the radio and told everyone to turn off their headlights. Ganymede had now set, and the Sun was not yet above the horizon.

"Look up, ladies and gentlemen," Tillerman said. *"The show begins."* Arroyo turned off the instrument lighting in his cab. The operators looked upward via the cameras on their cab exteriors.

Above them, delicate green and red curtains and threads of aurora danced and shimmered and intertwined with each other across the star-filled sky. The eery diaphanous displays were caused by the same physics as Earth's Northern and Southern Lights: the excitation of atmospheric molecules by impinging electrons from solar plasma as they interact with Europa's magnetic field. But because Europa's atmosphere was many magnitudes thinner than Earth's its own version was less frequently spotted. With the tractor engines shut off Arroyo often thought he heard a surreal tinkling noise in the sky during auroras, like shards of ice or glass falling slowly and gently to the ground. His hearing was terrible, but others swore they'd heard it, too.

And then the sun climbed over the horizon. Although Europa was five times farther from the Sun than Earth, and therefore received 1/25th the solar radiation, sunrise was almost always abrupt and overwhelming. Suddenly, the broad, jumbled expanse of the Shear Zone could be seen, the chaos a patchwork of brilliantly lit ice and blackest shadow, and through it the serpentine flagged route that was followed when leaving Mactown for most of the field camps and the Pole Station. Two broad, tilted ice plates many kilometers thick fought against each other in the zone. The plates were created by tectonic fracturing, in turn caused by tidal upheaval in the sea below. Countless monstrous crevasses lay in the zone, and it was a constant project to keep the zone passable for cargo-pulling traverses headed into the Back Forty. Open crevasses had to be filled by blade-equipped tractors or bridged with plascrete spans; hidden crevasses had to be detected with ground-penetrating radar, blasted open with explosives, then likewise filled or spanned. Tattered flags had to be replaced; remote sensing stations that measured ice shift had to be checked and serviced.

Arroyo spent his first week back in the Shear Zone. He enjoyed the little crew—all relatively geriatric. There was none of the *rush-rush-rush*, testosterone-driven "Cowboy Up" attitude of many of the younger operators, who saw every task as a test of manhood. The older operators got the work done, but at a pace that could be kept up all day, and with less chance of damage to equipment or humans. Tillerman played his harmonica each morning over the radio when they paused before work to enjoy the auroras and during their lunch breaks.

There was also Wyatt: almost as old as Tillerman, i.e., old enough to retire. "Old enough to know better," Wyatt would add. Wyatt's wife, Coretta, was Mactown's postmaster; they shared two tiny dorm rooms with an adjoining door—one room a cramped bedroom, the other a tiny living room—and did their best to live some semblance of normalcy in a community in which outrageous behavior was the norm. They often invited fellow older couples over for popcorn and lemonade. Wyatt and his wife had bought the nearly-unpopulated Bon Homme County in South Dakota on their last visit to Earth, and as soon as it was paid off they would say good-bye to Europa. They had a solid "exit strategy," as Wyatt would say. They had both grown up on farms in Minnesota. Wyatt—tall, laconic and well-spoken when he chose to break his silences—had worked in Antarctica before coming to Europa, on a crew helping to remove the hundreds of rusting abandoned oil platforms and grounded tankers and coal barges in the Ross Sea. After a hundred years of clean-up the results of the collapse of the Antarctic Treaty and the following Antarctic Black Gold Rush still sullied the southern continent.

Before that Wyatt had served in the Army during the South Asian Campaign a decade before Arroyo's time in uniform. The militaries of dozens of nations had made a futile attempt to create a buffer zone between warring Muslim and Hindu factions. The politicians and generals hadn't bothered to read much history. Both legions of religionists quickly turned on the foreigners wedged in the middle. Entire garrisons of peacekeepers were slaughtered, their corpses desecrated, video of the stomach-turning atrocities live-streaming throughout the human hive. Wyatt's wife had confided to Arroyo that her husband had been trapped in the overwhelmed Rawalpindi peacekeeper garrison, and was one of a handful who survived by fleeing on foot toward Kashmir. Wyatt had come back with no visible wounds, and carried himself with dignity and restraint. His hair was always impeccably combed, something at which he spent many spare moments. Arroyo never asked Wyatt about his time in service; Wyatt never asked Arroyo about his.

Strange, Arroyo thought to himself as he sat one morning in his idling tractor watching the auroras. So many of the workers on Europa had come from Minnesota, like himself. A few years ago he had gone on a small traverse to pull out the remains of an abandoned field camp near the Priestley Ice Graben, affectionately known by the acronym PIG. The PIG Traverse crew had *all* been from Minnesota. The last names still rolled off Arroyo's tongue like a mouthful of Grandma's lutefisk: Einerson, Anfinson, Gilbertson, Gunderson, Bronson. They had all fled Minnesota when they were young. Arroyo shook his head trying to remember why. Then he realized the answer was in that padlocked closet in his mind. It was something they all had in common but diligently never spoke about: a bit of history so dark they would simply whistle if one of them mentioned the word *Minnesota*, as if trying to whistle away darkness. As if trying to whistle away *evil*.

* * *

The solar windstorm had passed its peak; in a few more days the morning auroras would probably fade and end. It was Saturday morning, the last day of the usual six-day workweek in Mactown, and the Shear Zone crew sat in their idling tractors, headlights off, watching the shimmering display while Tillerman played his harmonica over the radio. A brilliant flash of light caught Arroyo's attention in the periphery of his vision. It was as if a supernova had just flared up and just as instantly vanished. It was vastly brighter than the aurora—as if Arroyo had just stared into a high-powered spotlight. When he closed his eyes, he could see the outlines of his cab consoles and of the jagged terrain around him. The flash—as if from some massive release of strange energy—seemed to come from the direction of Discovery Bay and the Penguin Ranch.

"Holy buckets," Arroyo said over the radio. "Did you folks see that?"

Tillerman's harmonica had gone silent. "Holy criminy,"

Jim Fairchild

Tillerman said. "That's quite the flash, eh?"

They sat silently, waiting for a reprise, but it didn't come. Wyatt spoke at last: "That's got to be a phosphene flash. My old high school science teacher, Mrs. Rhemann, rest her soul, would tell you that they're usually caused by mechanical, electrical or magnetic stimulation of the retina. It overloads the nervous system. Phosphene flashes have been spotted occasionally out near the Discovery Bay camp, and also at the camp at Marble Point, where the Delta studies are going on."

The Deltas were the second exospecies discovered on Europa: huge triangular jet-black sea creatures that vaguely resembled Earth's manta rays. But, like the Tetras, they had no discernible orifices, sense or sex organs. They had only been discovered a few years ago. So far, the only research done on them was camera footage gleaned by remote submersibles. Most of the submersibles had been quickly destroyed by the highly maneuverable, fast-swimming Deltas. What they fed on—if anything at all—was a complete mystery. No juveniles had ever been glimpsed. Little was known of their behavior, other than that the huge creatures could swim in elaborate, tight packs, perhaps communicating via the patterns they swam. They displayed a social hierarchy. None had ever been captured. No grantee had yet come up with a feasible plan to do so.

"What say you, Arroyo?" Wyatt asked. "You've spent time at *both* of those camps. Have you been zapped by the phosphene flashes before?"

Arroyo strained to remember, but couldn't. "Sorry, Wyatt," he finally answered. "Too much Trank under the bridge." He hadn't told anyone he'd stopped drinking. If he slipped up and started again he didn't want to bear the brunt of their ridicule.

*   *   *

Sunday was a big day in Mactown: it was the one day off a week for most workers. Most slept in late, then had a Bloody Mary and went to brunch. The galley staff always did a magnificent job even though much of the food they served had been in cold storage since the Navy era thirty years before. The galley was packed for Sunday brunch, with people stopping to chat with friends in the serving lines, or to suddenly go zombie and start checking their iMind inboxes, so it often took forever to get a plate of grub. Arroyo usually ran in to get a plate to take back to the privacy of his room.

As he dumped a pile of watery scrambled eggs and coagulating Kielbasa on his plate, someone stepped up beside him. It was Annie, the Fuelie. "Hey," she said. "How's it hanging?"

"In this cold it *never* hangs," Arroyo said. He stepped away from the serving line to wrap his plate for the walk to his room.

Annie followed him, carrying a bowl of Kardashian fruit. "Thanks for the anatomy update. You've probably heard the latest about the shutdown."

Arroyo stopped what he was doing and turned toward her. "No, I haven't. I don't eat in the galley much. I'm not tied into the rumor mill."

Annie grabbed a piece of plastic wrap for her fruit. "A shutdown is looming. Senators from some of the border states have just aligned themselves with the Confederate Senators. They want to disband the mutual military defense pact between North and South. They consider the space program part and parcel of that defense program. They want to shut it *all* down. The last tattered remnants of government-funded science programs like here on Europa are in their crosshairs."

"Unbelievable," Arroyo said. "I'm not excited about going into stasis on short notice."

"You're with Traverse Ops," Annie said. "You'd be one of the *last* to take the Long Nap."

Annie told Arroyo that the NSWF had just ordered all field camp and Pole Station staff to finish packing and prepare for transport back to Mactown ASAP. As many personnel as possible would be transported to Ganymede *if* charter shuttle flights could be arranged; those who made it there *might* escape the need for stasis. But everyone was instructed that they should finalize personal business affairs and be prepared for the increasing probability of a long, dreamless sleep.

* * *

The imminent shutdown had Mactown abuzz with rumors. Panic was beginning to set in even amongst many of the veteran employees. For most the idea of going into stasis was a nightmare. The first time in stasis, at the beginning of their careers on Europa, the months of dreamless sleep seemed just part of the grand adventure. But having done it at least once, most dreaded it— especially knowing that their brains weren't sacrosanct while they slept. Arroyo chose not to panic. It was out of his hands.

That next Monday morning his little group trundled out to the Shear Zone again to resume their project. Near the end of the shift the Sun was setting. A light breeze picked up. A thick fog of ice particles slowly drifted toward the Shear Zone from the Mt. Erebus sea plume. Arroyo remembered the Dali Box. He pulled it out of his parka and plugged it into the control console.

He waited.

The cloud gently drifted around the tractors. Tillerman came over the radio. "Looks like we've lost our light, eh? Let's head back to the barn for some oats."

The tractors lined up for the trip back to Mactown. Arroyo assumed his usual spot, bringing up the rear, gathering stragglers.

The ice cloud settled around them; it dampened noise so effectively that he could no longer hear the tractors ahead of him. The cloud was so thick he couldn't see the taillights ahead.

He hit the controls to raise his left window radiation shield. The shield slid smoothly upward. Arroyo looked out. All he could see was soft white *nothingness*. It was like being wrapped in a soft baby blanket. Arroyo looked away from the window a moment; he set his tractor's cruise controls to follow the tractor ahead of him at a constant distance of 100 meters. Safely on autopilot, he slid back in his seat and again turned his gaze outside.

The fog was so thick Arroyo could see no form to it. It was oddly relaxing. Tension in his back and legs began to release. Arroyo had always assumed that what Nicholas experienced with his Dali Box was hallucinatory. But after a minute or two he had already decided it wasn't that at all—it was just profound calmness. It must have been similar to what people experience in a sensory deprivation tank: an absolute lack of sensory input. In this case it wasn't absolute, but it was still extreme. He turned off his radio speaker to cut out the jovial chatter of the other operators. Now, with his hearing-protective earbuds in place and with the thick fog dampening tractor noise, Arroyo began to feel as if he had fallen backward into a white, formless limbo. *And he was not scared.* It was the safest and most peaceful feeling he could remember.

SHAKESHAKESHAKE. Arroyo jumped in his seat. The shuddering reverberated throughout his body. He thought the tractor's engine was seizing, or that it might be a tectonic icequake. But he looked at his controls, at the paperwork strewn on a console, at his hands. Nothing shook except his hands. He realized it was from adrenaline.

CRUSHCRUSHCRUSH. Arroyo screamed in pain. He grabbed both legs at the hips through his thick EVA suit. It was as if he were trapped in a huge steel vise that was steadily closing,

Jim Fairchild

pinching both legs until he thought they would fall off. The pressure was unbearable; sweat started to pour down his forehead. He began to reach for the Dali Box.

TRAPPEDTRAPPEDTRAPPED. He was suddenly overwhelmed by the sensation of falling headfirst down a tight, winding void—perhaps a tunnel—unable to lift his head, no way to move his arms, no way out, being bashed around mercilessly. He had never known that magnitude of claustrophobia before. It made the crushing sensation seem insignificant.

HEAT. FLAMES. DEAFENING GUNSHOTS. Visuals this time, not just physical sensations. He could see the flaming kangaroo: he was pointing his carbine at it, and in quick succession pumped two rounds into it—one in the chest, one in the head. And then the kangaroo morphed—it was a rabbit. *A stuffed rabbit.* What the fuck? When its chest and head exploded, fuzzy white stuffing, not blood, flew out.

That was enough. Arroyo yanked the three-pronged Dali Box out of its receptacle. He shook with terror as the radiation shield lowered over the window. But he knew that this experience wasn't *really* enough. He would use the Dali Box again tomorrow, and the day after that, and the day after that, too—as long as it took to remember who he was and what he had done with his life. It was as if the Dali Box was helping him to awaken from a long, dreamless slumber. Arroyo understood now why Nicholas had named the control module his Dali Box: it opened the doors of perception to *The Persistence of Memory*. The Dali Box was tugging on that padlocked closet in his mind. Nicholas hadn't been quite strong enough for his own experiment.

Arroyo reached forward and flicked back on his radio speaker. The other operators were laughing about him and his radio silence: "Bringing up the rear, *my patootie*," Tillerman chuckled. "Our boy Arroyo is back there cuffing his carrot."

"Let the kid have some peace and quiet," Wyatt said.

96

"He's an old workhorse. He knows the way back to the barn."

"I'm back up on this channel," Arroyo said. "Sorry about the comms problems." He pulled the old sock out of the broken vent and wiped his sweaty forehead with it.

* * *

At the morning meeting the next day, a volunteer was sought to groom the ice around the Retro Yard, out behind the sea plume known as Mt. Erebus. Arroyo quickly raised his hand. He had done the job hundreds of times. He would hook up a drag—a wide serrated planing blade on skis—and run an intricate overlapping pattern of loops and swirls until he had cleaned up the ice throughout the entire Retro Yard. It was a gloriously mindless way to burn up a day—Wyatt always thought it was like spending a day tending his wheat back when he had his farm in Minnesota.

Arroyo waved good-bye to the rest of the Geriatic Crew, who headed back out to the Shear Zone for the day. He climbed up into Drag Queen, did his usual pre-ops checks, then contacted Mac Ops on the radio to check out for solo surface travel. He and Drag Queen lumbered up the ramp to the heavy equipment airlock, spewing black exhaust that would eventually be sucked through the station's overworked air filtration system.

Arroyo had most of the work done by lunch. After fifteen years on Europa he'd perfected the pattern he followed to clean around the storage berms in the Retro Yard. Instead of going back to the station for lunch, he decided to stay out. He could see that a slight breeze was pushing a bank of ice crystals from the Mt. Erebus sea plume toward the Retro Yard. He parked Drag Queen on the upwind side of the yard and waited.

The dense bank of fog-like ice crept closer. Arroyo turned down his radio speaker; it was lunchtime, and highly unlikely someone would try to contact him. He shut off Drag Queen's engine, leaving on only the heaters for the engine fluids and batteries. It was SOP to never shut down the engine while out of the station, but Arroyo had faith that the tractor would start if the heaters were left on.

The bank of ice crystals wrapped itself around Drag Queen like a white velvet glove. Arroyo could see nothing: not the Retro Yard's cargo, not the hump of Mt. Erebus, not the horizon, not even the ground just outside the cab. He plugged in the Dali Box, then raised the radiation shield on his left window.

Utter calm. Complete relaxation. He breathed deeply and slowly.

SHAKESHAKESHAKE. There it was again. Arroyo steadied himself by clenching the armrests of his seat. *SHAKESHAKESHAKE.* It was if all of Europa were shaking, but Arroyo knew it was just a memory sneaking out. *He knew he could do this.* He removed the padlock from the door in his mind. He opened it a crack.

And then he could remember.

It was his second R&R on Ganymede, nine years ago. The shuttle from Europa had landed at one in the morning Ganymede time. Exhausted, he had checked into the Crowne Plaza, where he got a Program rate. He planned to sleep in late, then go for a walk to peruse his favorite shops, and perhaps have a late lunch at his favorite Thai joint.

But he was too old for sleeping in. Exhausted, he nevertheless woke up at seven. He took a shower—the first time in three years he could use as much water as he wanted—made some coffee in the room, then went out into the gentle morning light to stroll slowly through downtown Kardashia on the plascrete-cobblestone sidewalks. The downtown had been built to resemble a quaint Victorian London (minus the horse dung and coal smoke and Dickensian poverty). Kardashia was a corny tourist trap, the glow of its neon-lit Strip visible with binoculars from Europa. But it was refreshing compared to the rest of Ganymede, covered with countless sprawling warehouse complexes and spaceport facilities. He strolled the grassy banks of the faux Thames that meandered through downtown Kardashia. Arroyo swiped his credit card in a dispenser and got a bagful of breadcrumbs, which he fed to an eagerly awaiting gaggle of bossy geese. He stopped to stare into the windows of tourist shops that hadn't opened yet. In a few hours, throngs of rich Chinese and Martian tourists would be pushing their way through the doors, culturally incapable of forming queues, driving the hapless store clerks into apoplectic seizures. But at the moment foot traffic was light. Although Arroyo wished he could have slept later, he enjoyed the sidewalks in the cool of the morning before the crowds grew.

He strolled the full length of the Strip. He stopped at a favorite market near the Casino and bought a bag of hydroponic fruit to take back to the hotel with him. It had been growing on trees only days before. The fruit flown to Europa on the resupply vessels was often many months old by the time it arrived. Arroyo's mouth watered as he thought about the fresh mandarin oranges, kiwis, cherries and mangoes in his bag.

He stopped to read the menu in the window of a Korean restaurant he had enjoyed during his last stay in Kardashia. It still served bibimbop in fiery-hot stone dolsot bowls. He would have to remember to come back for dinner.

A voice called his name. It was Wyatt. Wyatt and his wife had been in Kardashia for almost a month between contracts and were headed back to Europa in a couple of days. They were staying across the street from Arroyo at Drumpf Tower. They discussed the possibility of linking up later for dinner, but there was no firm plan.

Fruit in hand, Arroyo came to a halt in front of a liquor store. He had toyed with the idea of staying sober this visit.

Jim Fairchild

*Instead, he went inside and bought a pocket-sized bottle of Trank
to start the day. He went back to his hotel room on the sixth floor
and washed down some fruit with half of the bottle of Trank. He
realized he must have been mighty thirsty. It was just past noon,
an odd time of the day to take a nap, but he laid down on the huge
bed. He figured he was on R&R; if he wanted to take a nap in the
middle of the day, that was his prerogative. Exhausted and tipsy,
he immediately fell asleep.*

    SHAKESHAKESHAKE.   SHAKESHAKESHAKE.
*Something had grabbed Arroyo in his sleep and was shaking him
like a rag doll. He struggled to wake up. About the time his eyes
were open and he realized where he was, the violent shaking
pitched him off the bed and onto the carpetted floor. A sustained
deafening roar sounded as if a Slingshot Express had just crashed
into the hotel with engines full-throttle. Loud explosive reports
and the smell of shattering plascrete told Arroyo that an icequake
of phenomenal magnitude was rocking Kardashia. He heard his
window explode; the bed was thrown violently toward the jagged
opening. He had fallen off the bed at an opportune time. Arroyo
staggered toward the door, doing battle with both the violently
swaying floor and his drunkenness.*

    *A particularly vicious lateral movement of the building sent
his bag of fruit flying across the room just in front of him. It burst
against the wall. The half-full Trank bottle catapulted off the desk
and flew into the bathroom, where it hit the shower door in an
explosion of glass. The building swayed wildly; Arroyo, stone-
cold sobered by adrenaline, thought that the building would surely
drop. He lunged for the door.*

    *As he did, a section of ceiling dropped to eye level. If it
had dropped a half-second later it would have come down on his
head. The section of ceiling blocked the door to the hallway.
Arroyo awkwardly lifted the plascrete ceiling section with both
arms—then with strength he didn't know he had, held the ceiling*

100

with one arm while he reached for the doorknob. It was a long stretch but he got ahold of it. He pulled the door inward and used it to prop up the ceiling panel.

The shaking had stopped for a moment. In the hallway the air was thick with plascrete and drywall dust. The hallway was actually a balcony that looked out on a central atrium surrounded by ten stories of glass. Moments ago the restaurant on the atrium's ground floor had been serving lunch to well-heeled tourists and impeccably dressed local business people, echoing with lunch conversations and laughter and the staccato clinking of silverware and glasses. Now it was horribly silent. A man covered in white dust from head to toe staggered toward Arroyo; Arroyo motioned for him to follow. Arroyo had to get to his knees to pass underneath a long stretch of collapsed ceiling. He reached a damaged stairwell and was able to stand again. Before racing down the stairwell, he glanced over the railing. Below, in the remains of the atrium's restaurant, shocked, dust-covered patrons were stumbling over piles of debris and shattered glass, trying to find a way out.

Arroyo emerged onto the street. He glanced back to make sure the man following him had made it. He looked up at the hotel from which he'd just fled. Countless windows were shattered; curtains fluttered in the jagged openings. A floor lamp hung crazily out of one window, apparently held in the air only by its cord, still plugged in. The lamp's bulb was still on. Arroyo could see that the plascrete balconies around the hotel's exterior were warped and buckled; several of the main vertical load-bearing buttresses had huge ugly cracks. Across the street, Drumpf Tower leaned crazily several degrees off vertical. Countless windows were broken there, too, curtains fluttering in the perpetual fake breeze of Kardashia's dome. A stranger with a Kiwi accent warned Arroyo of broken plates of glass hanging from the building directly behind where they stood in the street. Piles of shattered plascrete and glass lay heaped everywhere. Water burst upward through the pavement from broken mains. The pavement of the once-flat street looked like a cobblestone roller-coaster. Dazed survivors walked slowly down the middle of the street, going nowhere in particular, just wanting to get away from the destruction. A huge wall of dust was billowing from the downtown area and settling on everything. Smoke was beginning to pour out of the windows of the Kardashia TV building, where all the stairwells had collapsed and people were being burned alive. Buildings Arroyo had always taken for granted had been reduced to unrecognizable rubble; others still stood but at improbable angles or with facades that had shaken loose and cascaded onto crowded lunchtime sidewalks. Arroyo knew that there were countless people buried beneath that rubble. He had just walked the length and breadth of those sidewalks. If he had been able to sleep late he would probably have been under that rubble, too.

And then Arroyo looked directly ahead of him, perhaps five meters away, on the sidewalk in front of the hotel entrance. His stomach turned.

A huge piece of plate glass from many floors up had apparently fallen. It had plummeted down like a cleaver falling at terminal velocity, striking a woman directly across the top of the head, fore to aft. She sat serenely on the sidewalk in a loose white dress soaked with blood, surrounded by shattered glass, her face the color of the concrete around her. A woman had stopped and had gently wrapped a sweater around the woman's head, trying to stop the bleeding. But Arroyo thought the woman had already almostly completely bled out.

Arroyo realized that he had thoroughly locked away the memory of the icequake. Now he had only one question: had he helped anybody? Or had he only looked out for himself?

He could remember walking many kilometers through the debris of what had until moments before been a vibrant, happy, touristy city. He remembered passing local business people in their smartly tailored suits and tunics, walking like zombies out of the destroyed central business district, pressing bloody towels and rags to nasty head wounds. They walked down the middle of the street because debris hung over the sidewalks, threatening to fall in the gentlest breeze. People jumped at the sound of tinkling glass. Dazed, they tripped over knee-high folds and cracks in the pavement, stopping to help each other up. He remembered the surreal stillness, the utter silence, the amazing courtesy as one injured person stopped to let another pass. Had he helped anybody?

He found his way to The Program's warehouse and offices in the industrial outskirts of Kardashia. Other Program employees who had survived the icequake were congregating there. The walk had taken him three hours. Aftershocks made the street beneath his feet roll like someone pulling a carpet runner out from under him. He constantly glanced upward for anything that might fall on him.

Forty percent of Kardashia's central business district was destroyed outright by the icequake. Another forty percent was so damaged it later had to be demolished. The Crowne Plaza, where Arroyo had been drunkenly napping when the quake hit, was on the demolition list. Wyatt and Coretta had been in the park along the Thames at the time, and had an inkling that something was wrong when the squawking geese suddenly grew silent and hurried out of the water moments before the quake hit. By sheer luck the couple had been in a safe place.

Although 785 people were killed in the Kardashia icequake, miraculously, no Program employees were amongst the fatalities. Some had far worse escapes than Arroyo's. One acquaintance had to leap out of the window of one tilting skyscraper onto the roof of another when he discovered all the stairwells had collapsed. When Kardashia was originally built, engineers only had about fifty years of seismographic records on which to base their design assumptions. The icequake that destroyed Kardashia was probably a once-in-500-years event. When the city was rebuilt far more cautious seismic standards were employed.

The Program had not offered counseling to its employees who had survived the quake. Instead, it offered free "relaxation therapy" that could be downloaded to one's iMind and subliminally enjoyed at one's leisure. Now, just nine years later, nobody ever talked about the icequake—as if it had never happened. Arroyo had, of course, never downloaded the iMind therapy. And yet he had hidden away the memories just as thoroughly as those who had probably been brainwashed by the free relaxation therapy.

He still couldn't remember: had he helped anybody other than himself? With a sinking feeling, he doubted it. He pulled the Dali Box out of the console and fired up Drag Queen.

* * *

Arroyo grabbed a plate of food at the galley and headed back toward his room for a late lunch. As he crossed Derelict Junction someone called his name. It was Dr. Gianforte. He was carrying a galley tray holding several dozen freshly baked cookies.

"Hey there, Arroyo. Got a minute?"

Arroyo walked over and took a cookie off the pile. "Sweet tooth, Doc?"

"I need to keep up my strength," Gianforte said. "All of those prostate exams give a man a fearsome hunger."

"Maybe you need a new hobby," Arroyo said, chewing the butterscotch cookie, crumbs going everywhere.

Gianforte didn't argue. "Say, Arroyo. Could you come by

my office on Saturday before the close of business? I want to touch base with you. And are you still taking those meds as directed?"

"Absolutely," Arroyo said. "I'm nothing if not a compliant patient." He grabbed a chocolate macadamia for the road.

*   *   *

After his quick lunch Arroyo planned to head back out to the Retro Yard with Drag Queen. There was always something to groom with a tractor and a drag. He figured he'd drag the flagged route from Mactown out to the yard and back—four passes would burn up the rest of the afternoon. First, he stepped into the Admin building to turn in receipts from his R&R trip. He was probably the only person on station who didn't submit travel claims via iMind. The folks in Finance always had to dust off their ancient scanner when he came in.

As he walked down the poorly lit corridor, a cheery voice rang out. "Arroyo! Just the gentleman I wanted to see." It was Darla Hovenweep from HR.

She motioned him toward her cubicle. "Sit down." She neatly arranged her tunic, then folded her hands on her grimly tidy desktop. "How does it feel to be back in the swing of things?"

"Outstanding. It's great to be back in the saddle again. Saddlesores and all."

Her eyes twinkled. "I was wondering if you'd given any more thought to that Facility Maintenance position on Ganymede."

"Thanks again. But it's not up my alley."

"Well," Darla said, lowering her voice to a near-whisper. "Just between you and me, I texted Susie Mascarone at the Kardashia office. She's the Senior Human Assets Procurement Generalist. I told her that I've got a superb candidate for the position *right here* on Europa. I asked her to extend the posting a couple of weeks to give you more time to consider. I *know* you say you're not interested. But change is a good thing. Good for you. Good for The Company. Good for The Program."

Arroyo felt as if he'd just been slapped across the face. "Pardon me if I'm wrong, but I get the feeling I'm not really wanted here on Europa any more." He had dedicated fifteen years to The Program and had just started a new contract for three more years. Europa was all he knew. People thought he was joking when he said he assumed he would die on Europa. Why not? He wondered what he had done to get on The Company's wrong side.

Darla laughed as if amused by a silly child. *"Oh, Arroyo.* Don't get that notion in your pretty little head. But we all have to remember that McMurdo is a government worksite, not a home. We're all part of a workforce, not a community. It's important not to get too comfortable here."

Arroyo had no interest in commanding a crack squad of broom-pushers at The Company office complex in Kardashia. A way of life he'd taken for granted suddenly seemed to be in jeopardy. And he didn't know why. "I'll give it some more thought," he finally said. He would rather go back to Earth and file for his forty acres than work on the industrial slagheap that Ganymede had become.

"Please get back to me," Darla said. "I don't want to keep Susie waiting too long. I've already forwarded her your personnel file. One last thing." She rose behind her desk, smoothed her tunic, then motioned slyly for him to follow.

Darla led him out into the dreary hallway. Overhead lights flickered and buzzed; a work order had been filed three years ago, but Mactown's harried electricians were always too busy putting Band-Aids on the station's obsolete, short-circuiting power grid to worry about changing light bulbs. The heels of Darla's footwear—quaint 21st-century Manolo Blahnik alligator boots fitted with low-g soles—clicked sharply against the worn plascrete floor. They

106

took a left down a side corridor, then a right. Darla looked back a few times to make sure Arroyo was still following. She raised a fingertip to her glossy lips, mouthing a soft *shush*. Arroyo found it childish. But he knew Rule Number One for survival in a corporation: don't piss off HR.

They came to a halt in front of a windowless locked storeroom. Arroyo knew what was behind the door long before he could see the sign:

COMPANY STORE
ALCOHOLIC BEVERAGE
STOREROOM
AUTHORIZED PERSONNEL
ONLY
YOU ARE UNDER
SURVEILLANCE

Darla glanced over her shoulder at Arroyo as she entered a code on the lock keypad. She grinned like a fifteen-year-old breaking into her father's liquor cabinet. She swung the door open, looked up and down the corridor for possible witnesses, then motioned for Arroyo to step through the door. She stepped in swiftly behind him, turned on the lights and drew the door closed.

"A little early for a stiff one, don't you think?" Arroyo asked.

"Don't create a hostile work environment," Darla said. The shelves on the right side of the room held a bizarre assortment of liquors and wines: China-China, ancho chile liqueur, arak, Martian spit chicha. Rumor had it that The Company's purchasing agent for Mactown's company store had set up a no-bid contract with his brother-in-law's booze distibutorship in Kardashia. The Company purchased whatever odd cases the brother-in-law couldn't move in his retail outlets. So the selection was a strange mishmash that only those who couldn't stomach Trank purchased. The company store marked it up triple what the brother-in-law was paid. *Someone* was making a tidy profit, although repeated attempts by well-meaning amateur accountants on station had been unable to determine how much profit was actually being made and where that profit was actually going. The NSWF insisted that The Company was holding the profits; The Company insisted the money had gone to the NSWF. It had likely either been swallowed by a black hole or fallen into someone's pocket.

Most beakers who enjoyed a tipple shipped their own hooch to Europa. While it was against NSWF rules to ship alcohol for personal consumption at government expense, many beakers arrived on Europa with massive padlocked instrument cases packed *full* of liquor and wine. Arroyo remembered helping one beaker unload a case marked *DISTILLED WATER— LABORATORY USE ONLY.* Strangely, the case was leaking something that—to Arroyo—smelled and tasted like very expensive tequila. He tasted it strictly in the name of Science.

For contract workers, alcohol was officially prohibited. At least one senior NSWF manager back in Arlington wanted Europa to be a dry moon. The ignoble Saturday night behavior of drunken Europa savages was a particular sore point with visiting NSWF managers of a religious bent. But while the official policy prohibited alcohol sales, the fine print allowed current stocks to be sold rather than destroyed. Somehow, more "current stocks" of alcohol kept being discovered, all arriving on a regular basis from the brother-in-law's warehouse on Ganymede.

"Did you need a hand with something?" Arroyo asked, fidgetting.

Darla motioned to the sagging shelves on the left. They were stacked deep with clear liter bottles bearing the generic Trank label. The Trank was concocted in a Ganymede factory that also made ice core drilling lubricants, industrial solvents and hydroponic fertilizers. She swept one hand grandly toward the shelves; in her other hand she held a folded piece of paper.

Arroyo stared dumbly at her. "I don't get it."

"Take this," Darla insisted, thrusting the paper at him. "It's the code for the door."

"Now I *really* don't get it."

"Oh, Arroyo. There are no secrets in a company town. I've been talking with Dr. Gianforte about your situation."

"Doesn't that violate some sort of privacy law?"

"Don't be absurd, Arroyo. I'm sure you've read your Terms of Agreement. Section 12 of the Addendum states that the employee waives all expectation of privacy while making use of Program medical facilities. HR has a legitimate need to review your medical records so that we can make appropriate work assignments and foresee any possible human asset shortages. So Dr. Gianforte and I have simply been comparing notes on you."

"Did he say anything about a prostate check?"

"Don't be distasteful. The doctor and I agreed that we will assist you with your Trank dependency until a final solution is agreed upon. Please take the door code. You are welcome to take one liter of Trank a day, *gratis*, until Dr. Gianforte determines it is time to modify your consumption."

Arroyo felt blood rush to his ears. He wanted to tell Darla that he hadn't touched a drop in more than a week. "Won't that mess up the bookkeeping for alcohol sales?" he asked.

Darla chortled. "Lordie, Arroyo. Nobody accounts for this stuff. Do you think management actually pays for *its* booze?"

Arroyo looked at Darla. Silently, he took the paper with the door code and shoved it in a parka pocket. He reached to the shelf and took a bottle of Trank, slipping it into another parka pocket. He and Darla stepped back into the corridor and went their separate ways.

Back in his room, Arroyo pulled the bottle from his parka.

Jim Fairchild

He screwed off the cap. His hands shook—not from temptation, but from anger. The Trank made a sloppy *glug-glug-glug* as he poured it down the sink. The smell made his stomach turn. He took the empty bottle out to the end of the hallway and tossed it in a recycling bin. Vinnie from the Heavy Shop was walking down the hallway, headed back to work. He saw Arroyo with the empty bottle.

"Hey, you old lush," he said, grinning like a Kardashian cat. "Now that you're hammered I suppose you're heading out to break some more equipment for me."

Arroyo gave a sheepish thumbs-up.

Alone again, Arroyo stood a moment. Something *serious* was brewing in Mactown. Arroyo was not usually prone to paranoia. But he decided it might be appropriate right now.

He headed back to the motorpool to take Drag Queen out for the rest of the day. As he neared the plug-in line someone in fuel-soaked overalls approached. It was Annie.

"Hey, Arroyo. How's your day going?"

He wanted to say *strangely*. "Okay, I guess. And you?"

The noise of idling equipment masked their voices, but Annie still looked around and then spoke softly. "Listen, Arroyo. Be careful about what you say and what you do. I can't explain the details to you right now. But people are watching you. They might want to make you conveniently go away."

Arroyo tried to grin. "That's a little conspiratorial, would't you say?"

"If anything," Annie said, "I'm not being conspiratorial enough. *Watch yourself.* A lot depends on you. *Europa* depends on you. We'll talk later." She brushed his arm with her hand and walked away.

* * *

Arroyo and Drag Queen headed out to groom the trail to the Retro Yard. After his late lunch he only had a few hours before dinner, but he didn't mind. It was Mexican Night in the galley on Wednesdays, quite popular with the hoi polloi but not with Arroyo's transverse colon. If he ran late and missed dinner he could always grab a sandwich in the Tetra Deli.

The light out on the ice was like soft dawn in the mountains on Earth, if Arroyo's fuzzy memories of family vacations were still accurate. Io was low on the horizon, about ready to disappear. The first pass toward the Retro Yard with the drag took about half an hour. As he approached, he could see a scootmobile parked near a line of heavy equipment high on an ice berm waiting to be shipped back to Ganymede. Two suited individuals were clambering around on the equipment. He parked his tractor a safe distance away, leaving the engine idling.

Arroyo locked his helmet and gloves in place and ran a suit diagnostic before depressurizing the cab and opening the door. He climbed down the ladder and bounced gently to the ground, landing safely in his low-g boots. The soles were weighted to deal with the Europan gravity, which was only one-ninth of Earth's. Mactown had a large workout facility called the Gerbil Gym. Smart Europans worked out religiously to maintain muscle tone. Arroyo had once tried to be a faithful gym gerbil. But as his interest in returning to Earth diminished, so had his desire to maintain muscle tone. He figured that letting his body adapt to Europa's low gravity was just an experiment in evolution.

He waved to the two individuals on the equipment. They were Fuelies: he could see them inspecting fuel tanks with their flashlights and a probe that turned color if fuel was present. One individual looked up and waved, then the other. Arroyo could recognize one as Annie.

"Hi again," she said over the radio. She climbed down off one of six tractors, all identical, parked on the berm. She walked over to Arroyo. "It seems pointless with a shutdown imminent, but Barry Wilton wants us to certify these tractors for shipment back to Ganymede as soon as a retro vessel has available payload weight. They need to be purged of flammables before they're backloaded."

Arroyo stared at the tractors. Most of the equipment in the Retro Yard was ancient rolling stock that had long-outlived its intended lifespan, had been repaired countless times, and had finally been replaced or had been rated manifestly uneconomical or dangerous to use any more. The berm lines were the temporary resting places of dozens of tractors, loaders, trucks, generator carts and scootmobiles waiting to be stripped of usable parts before shipment to the Ganymede salvage yard. But these six tractors looked almost *new*: bright yellow paint not yet eaten up by radiation, crisp, easily-read decals with NSWF property numbers and even the name of the Caterpillar dealership in New Omaha that had sold the tractors to The Program. The nearest one had the name *Misty* painted on it, which was against NSWF rules.

Arroyo thought he had operated every piece of equipment around Mactown. And yet he did not recognize these. They were on a berm near the center of the Retro Yard, surrounded by berms of larger, taller equipment, almost as if they had been hidden. Somehow Arroyo hadn't noticed them before.

The second Fuelie made some notes on a wrist keypad. Then she walked over to Arroyo and Annie.

"Arroyo, this is Consuelo," Annie said. "Consuelo, this is Arroyo. Consuelo is my comfort, my consolation, and my squeeze." Arroyo and Consuelo gave each other a high-five through their thick pressurized gloves.

"Nice to meet you," Arroyo said.

"We've met before," Consuelo said. "At the Discovery Bay camp last February. We talked about H.P. Lovecraft."

Arroyo wanted to crawl into a deep hole and die. "I am *so* sorry," he said. But suddenly he *did* remember her. "We talked about *At the Mountains of Madness*. We both thought it was the most terrifying story we had ever read."

"*Exactamente,*" Consuelo said. She gave Arroyo another high-five. Arroyo could see the smile on her face through her helmet visor, could see the freckles on her mocha skin as her nose crinkled with laughter. "The Old Ones *rocked!*" she said.

Consuelo climbed up onto another tractor while Annie and Arroyo took a stroll. "How are you feeling?" Annie asked.

Arroyo gestured across his mouth as if he were closing a zipper. He reached into a utility pocket on his suit and pulled out an old-fashioned audio cable with three-millimeter jacks on each end. He plugged one into the audio box of his helmet, then plugged the other into Annie's. It was the safest way they could communicate without a chance of someone monitoring them.

"I feel good," he said. "I haven't touched Trank in ten days. I was pretty shaky the first couple of days. Right now I don't have any interest in it. I want to be clear-headed and on my toes. I feel like something strange is brewing in Mactown."

Annie put an arm around Arroyo's shoulder and helped him to turn at the same time as she so the audio cable wouldn't get pulled out. "Do you recognize these tractors?" she asked.

Arroyed stared quizzically at them. They couldn't have been on Europa more than a year. And then he glanced inside the cabs. Where an operator should have sat was a tall stack of instrument cases. They were connected to each other with thick black cables and cannon plugs. "*Robot tractors,*" he said.

"Yes," Annie said. "They came in on a vessel the beginning of the year. They were designed to make autonomous resupply runs out to the field camps and the Pole Station. Without human operators they would be able to run 24 hours a day and cut resupply times in half. They also wouldn't have to pull a heavy living module, because a robot tractor doesn't need to stop to sleep and eat. They were another Bryonstorm. Built, of course, by the

Jim Fairchild

Kregg Corporation."

"Why are they already in the Retro Yard?" Arroyo asked.

"The contract for the tractor software went to the lowest bidder," Annie said. She reached over and put a glove lightly on Arroyo's arm. "There was an accident. You were there."

"*What happened?*" Arroyo's voice broke. For a second he caught a flash of unbearable crushing pain. He'd heard some people say that God never gave a person more than we can handle. That brief flash of memory proved those people to be cretins.

"I'm not sure how much to tell you and how fast," Annie said. "In an ideal world it would be best for you to piece it together at the speed your own mind chooses. Hopefully your mind won't let it all come back *too* quickly. But I need to let you know that time is of the essence. You've been medicated and trauma-flushed for months to drive your memories deep to ground. The doctor has been slowly lifting your memory blocks. But what you end up remembering will be a heavily-edited version of reality. I want you to stay a step ahead of the doctor. A lot of things on Europa depend upon you."

Arroyo had always prided himself at being an exemplary shirker of responsibility. It seemed that Annie had just put the weight of Europa on his shoulders.

"Take some time to try to remember on your own," Annie said. "But not *too* long. I understand you have Nicholas Bradshaw's Dali Box. It could help you open the correct doors in your mind."

"You know about the Dali Box?"

"Nicholas and I were friends. He could never keep a secret."

Arroyo and Annie were startled by an approaching vehicle. It was Barry Wilton's Mattrack. Turning hastily, Arroyo accidentally pulled the cable jack out of his helmet. He grabbed the gently flapping cable, accidentally yanking the other end out of

Annie's helmet.

Barry Wilton sat behind the wheel of the tracked light truck. He slowly wagged a radio mike in his hand, giving Arroyo and Annie the stink-eye. "Hey, yardbirds," he said over the radio. "I've been trying to reach anyone out here on the Mac Ops channel for the last five minutes."

"Sorry," Annie said. Arroyo hastily stuffed the helmet jack back into his utility pocket.

"How are these tractors coming along?" Barry asked. The Mattrack's exhaust hung in a low cloud; Arroyo thought he could hear ice crystals from the fumes tinkle to the ground.

"Great," Annie chimed. "Consuelo and I are double-checking the fuel systems to make sure they were properly purged. We should have them certified to ship by the close of business."

"Thank you, Annie." Barry curled his lips upward and sniffed his mustache for remains of his lunch. "I know it's a hassle to make this a priority right now. But the request came from Bryon Sturm at the Ganymede office. His wish is my command. Annie, have you packed yet in case we get the word to go into stasis?"

Arroyo could hear Annie sigh. "Yes," she said, "although I'm not looking forward to it."

"Well, don't sweat too much. The Senate might work out a deal yet. Unfortunately, we may have to ship a bunch of folks to Ganymede or put them in stasis in the meantime, only to turn around and bring everyone back as soon as the budget deal is resolved. It seems like a tremendous drain of already-tight Program funds."

"Not to mention an emotional drain," Annie said.

"I'm sorry," Barry said. "But I know you're tough. You wouldn't be working as a Fuelie on Europa if you weren't. And I've recommended that all Fuelies and cargo handlers stay to the bitter end along with the Traverse operators. We'll need your help

Jim Fairchild

to shut down the field camps and Pole Station—if things come to that."

Annie smiled, waved to Barry and went back to help Consuelo up on the berm. Arroyo started to turn toward his tractor.

"Hold on, Arroyo," Barry said. "Go to Channel Four." It was a private work channel, used when people didn't want to have their conversations monitored by everyone in Mactown. He punched the work channel into his wrist keypad, then gave Barry a thumbs-up.

"How are you holding up, Bucko?" Barry asked.

"Just like an underwire bra in a lightning storm."

"I heard you were under the weather when you got back from R&R. You still hitting the sauce?"

"Just medicinal imbibation. I like to think of it as a long-term science experiment."

"God bless Science," Barry said with a grin. "It signs our paychecks. I used to hit the sauce myself when I was younger. But I figured I just wanted to die from *one* poison. So I chose radiation. I figure after 28 years on this frozen dung-heap of a moon I'll eventually get my wish."

"The Program wouldn't let you stay this long if you were reaching dangerous cumulative exposure."

"Keep on thinking that," Barry said, snorting through his mustache. He paused to stroke his beard and watch the last of Io slip beneath the horizon. He turned back to Arroyo. "Say. What do you think about those robot tractors?" He pointed at the berm.

"*Funny*," Arroyo said. "I don't remember much about them."

"Another brilliant Bryonstorm," Barry said. "A monumental waste of taxpayer's money. I'll be glad to see them go. *Before* somebody gets hurt by them." He stared out the window at Arroyo a moment. He rapped the fingertips of one hand

116

on the dashboard. Then he shifted the Mattrack into gear. The icy drivetrain clunked into place. *"Play safely,"* Barry said. "Catch you on the flip if not the flop." He pulled away, leaving Arroyo standing alone.

*   *   *

.The Mt. Erebus sea plume was putting on a show like Europa's version of Old Faithful—except that the geyser from Erebus occasionally reached more than 150 kilometers into the atmosphere, while Yellowstone's geyser averaged less than fifty meters—1/3000th of the height of the Erebus plume. The escaping seawater rose so high because of the low gravity. Arroyo dropped the drag from his tractor and headed for Erebus.

The sea plume's top couldn't be seen from the ground. Ice particles slowly drifted down from the sky, catching the light of the dim Sun and refracting into thousands of glittering multi-colored jewels. Arroyo sat in his tractor and marvelled at the coruscating display. As the ice particles slowly drifted downward, they began to settle into a broad fog bank near the ground. Arroyo moved his tractor so that the fog bank was backlit by the Sun. He plugged in the Dali Box, raised a side radiation shield, and lost focus staring into the depthless fog, waiting for his mind to start painting memories across the chill canvas.

He waited. And waited. And then he saw something: flames, and a frantic dog running out of them. Followed by a crazed man. He shook his head. He could not let those memories out of the closet yet. He wanted to remember what he knew about the robot tractors. *One nightmare at a time,* he thought.

The next two days he volunteered to groom the flagged routes near Mactown so he could park near the sea plume every few hours with the Dali Box plugged in. But no memories of the robot tractors surfaced. He ran into Annie several times back in

Jim Fairchild

Mactown. In hushed voices, she asked if anything had come to him, but he glumly said *no*. She reminded him that time was of the essence. It would be healthier if he remembered on his own, but she would help if he asked.

Friday afternoon found him again staring into the fog from the sea plume. He waited. He tried to relax, but nothing. He lowered his radiation shield and chugged in low gear back to the Retro Yard. He parked near the robot tractors, suited up and climbed the berm.

He stopped at the first tractor christened *Misty*. He walked slowly around the tractor, examining every detail. He stopped when he came to the hand-painted woman's name. He traced the five letters with a gloved fingertip. The brushstrokes were so familiar. Who would have christened a piece of equipment and broken NSWF rules by painting the appellation on the battery compartment door? Nobody Arroyo could think of.

Except himself.

He saw vehicle headlights approaching. It was a Mattrack. *Barry Wilton's* Mattrack. It came to a halt fifty meters away, the headlights aimed at Arroyo and the robot tractor. Nobody climbed out of the truck. It sat there idling, a low cloud of exhaust settling around it. Arroyo was being watched.

And then his mind was flooded with a tsunami of memory. His knees almost buckled. He hadn't needed the Dali Box to remember. His mind was flooded with images like a movie played on fast-forward. Shaking, holding back a scream of pain and anger, Arroyo climbed unsteadily down from the berm. He waved fiercely toward the Mattrack. In a moment it shifted into gear, made a slow, broad turn and headed back to town.

He could remember.

Arroyo had been assigned to the Discovery Bay camp as equipment operator the previous winter. It was a three-month gig

118

in the deep field, the kind Arroyo treasured, and it was a disappointment to head back to the Big City in late February. But soon after returning to Mactown he was assigned to an interesting new project. Six shiny new robot tractors had been offloaded at the Ice Pier courtesy of Bryon Sturm and the Kregg Corporation. They would need to go through a rigorous proof-of-concept shakedown. Each of the robot rigs would be paired with a manned tractor. The robot tractors could be programmed to follow another tractor at a precise distance and to run in the same gear and at the same throttle RPMs as the manned tractor that would lead it. It would take all of its cues from the human operator ahead of it. If the human operator locked his differentials, the robot tractor would do likewise. If the human operator suddenly decelerated because a huge dip appeared out of the dark, the robot tractor would make note of the dip's location via GPS and maneuver accordingly. The two tractors would communicate via satellite link in the event they weren't in line-of-sight. There was nothing earth-shaking about the technology—in fact, it was ancient. Even before the Crash, the American military had successfully tested similar technology for its truck convoys in Middle East combat zones.

Arroyo and Drag Queen were assigned to lead one of the robot tractors. The tractor pairs would go out for the day from Mactown, follow some of the easier flagged routes, and be in by dinner each evening. After a few weeks another operator and tractor would probably take the place of Arroyo and Drag Queen, cutting them loose to join a traverse pulling loads to the field.

At the end of one bitter-cold, dark day leading the robot tractor out to the Shear Zone and back, Arroyo parked Drag Queen at the plug-in line near the motorpool. His assigned robot tractor—he had painted the name Misty on it—slowly trundled down the curved ramp from the heavy equipment airlock and pulled up to a perfect stop at a plug-in line ten meters behind Drag

Queen. Arroyo could hear the robot tractor shift into Park. It sat idling, just like Drag Queen, circulating all operating fluids for five minutes before shutting down.

Arroyo climbed down stiffly from Drag Queen. A wiry red-haired young man approached Arroyo. Arroyo waved. It was Frank Pabodie, an engineer from the Kregg Corporation. He had Slingshotted to Europa to oversee the shakedown of the robot tractors. He was carrying a test module the size of a lunchbox. He met the operators each evening as they came back to Mactown; he would link his module to the robot tractors to download data from the day's run. Then he would stay up half the night studying the results.

"How'd it go out there?" Frank asked. He bounced up and down with excitement. Arroyo never failed to be amused at how excited beakers and engineers got about their work. He thought it was very endearing, but must be emotionally exhausting. They stepped to the rear of Drag Queen to chat.

"Smooth as silk," Arroyo said. "The robot rig followed right along in Drag Queen's path, keeping perfect interval and speed."

Abbie Hoffman and his tractor rumbled to a stop beside Drag Queen. The robot tractor following Abbie was not far behind, making a precision turn from the ramp toward the plug-in line behind them.

"I want to thank you for all of your help," Frank said. He leaned back against the winch drum on the rear of Drag Queen. "This is my first trip beyond the asteroid belt. I don't know my head from my keister around here. You've been very patient with me."

Arroyo smiled and patted Frank on the shoulder. "You're very welcome. It's the very least I can do on behalf of Science."

There was a strange grinding noise behind Arroyo. He glanced back. The robot tractor named Misty had lurched back into gear. It was careening toward the rear of Drag Queen.

Frank, his back against Drag Queen, glanced over Arroyo's shoulder and saw the berserk tractor. Arroyo, his back toward danger, could see the terror in Frank's eyes. He put a bearhug around Frank and tried to throw both of them out of the way.

But there wasn't enough time. Six massive steel counterweights were mounted on a bar to keep the front of the tractor from bucking when pulling a heavy load; an outer counterweight pinned Frank to Drag Queen. Arroyo was pinned, too, but by the mounting bar, which didn't protrude to the front as much. Arroyo caught a glimpse of Abbie racing up the steps into the rogue tractor, ginger dreadlocks flying; Arroyo could hear the transmission shift into neutral. And then he heard Abbie start to shift the tractor into reverse.

"STOP!" Arroyo screamed. "Don't move the tractor!" Frank's face had turned grey. Arroyo faced Frank, his arms still awkwardly around him. He heard splashing. Then he looked down. Gouts of blood and feces and urine were pouring out of the cuffs of Frank's coveralls and running onto the ice. The splash slowed to a pitter-patter. Arroyo's low-g boots were slick with Frank's bodily fluids.

"Don't move the tractor until we have Frank stabilized," Arroyo croaked. He knew he was hurt, too. And badly. But adrenaline could have a wonderful pain-deadening side-effect. "Call the Crash Shack. Tell them what we have going. Tell them this is not a drill." Nobody wanted to depend upon the McMurdo Fire Department in a life-and-death situation. Most of the firemen and EMTs had been passed over for jobs at legitimate departments back on Earth or Mars, so had taken contracts on Europa to have something to put on their résumés.

"Frank. Speak to me." Arroyo watched Frank's eyes start to glaze. When Arroyo looked down again, he could see that the

Jim Fairchild

rogue tractor's counterweights were completely flush with the back of Drag Queen. Frank's midsection was crushed as thin as a piece of paper. When the rogue tractor was moved, Frank would die. At the moment, the huge counterweight was pinching off crushed and severed arteries. There was no way Frank was going to survive.

Shrieking alarms and claxon horns began to reverberate throughout the station grotto. Trying to keep his calm, Arroyo glanced away from Frank. He could see overweight, pimple-faced firemen stumbling toward the plug-in line, still trying to get into turn-out pants and jackets and high rubber boots. Two of them carried EMT kits; one carried a backboard. Most were empty-handed and nervous. A gaggle of onlookers began to gather. Vinnie and his Wrench friends had wandered out from the Heavy Shop, some still carrying tools. Supply clerks and lab techs and bakers and janitors started to crowd around.

"ALL OF YOU GET THE FUCK AWAY," Arroyo bellowed hoarsely. "I want one competent EMT front and center. NOW."

The gathering crowd grew silent. Arroyo could tell many were taking photos on their iMinds. The photos would be posted to the hive in seconds.

A tall EMT who seemed to know what he was doing stepped forward. He did a quick check of Frank's vitals and glanced at Arroyo. The look on his face confirmed what was already obvious to Arroyo. Butch Gianforte's predecessor—dodging malpractice lawsuits on three Earth continents and on Mars—ran up, out of breath. Arroyo waved him away.

He took one arm from around Frank and brushed Frank's hair out of his face. "Frank," Arroyo whispered. "This isn't going to end well. When the tractor moves, you are going to bleed out. The rush of blood will be so fast you'll lose consciousness almost instantly. Is there someone back home I can get a message to for you?"

Frank opened his mouth and coughed. Blood sprayed on

122

Arroyo's face.

"Wait," Arroyo said. With a hand shaking so badly he could hardly control it, he reached to his right ear and tapped his iMind. He reached into the air with a trembling finger, frantically scrolling through the projected menus until he could hit RECORD MESSAGE.

Arroyo lowered his hand and got both arms around Frank again. "Okay, Frank. I'm recording."

Frank coughed more blood, clearing his throat. "Send this to my wife, Beverly. I love you, Bev. I should have never come here. You were right."

Then Frank died in Arroyo's arms.

Arroyo looked over his shoulder at Abbie, sitting awkwardly amidst the jumble of instrument boxes in the cab of the rogue tractor. "Okay. Do it."

Abbie gently shifted the tractor into reverse. The tractor inched backward. A pile of wet organs dropped out of Frank's coveralls onto Arroyo's boots. Suddenly free of the tractor, Arroyo collapsed backward onto the ice, still clutching what was left of Frank. Frank felt like a ragdoll in his arms. Arroyo's right femur had shattered into thirteen pieces. The leg was attached to his hip only by a ragged flap of skin, muscle and tendons.

Arroyo could barely remember being medevacked to Ganymede. A resupply vessel that had just launched from Europa on the way to Ganymede was ordered to return for him. It completed a quick orbit and put down. Arroyo was shot up with morphine, but it didn't have much effect on him. Years of abusing Trank had given him amazing tolerance to the drug. He could remember the hushed flight crew on the resupply vessel as his stretcher was carried up the rear cargo ramp; he vaguely remembered being strapped into place like a piece of cargo. He remembered the many small kindnesses of the attending flight nurse. The nurse, a heavy-set man in a snug flightsuit with mirthful eyes like Santa Claus, asked Arroyo where he was from as he checked to make sure the IV was secure for launch.

"Europa," Arroyo remembered saying. He thanked the nurse over and over for his help and apologized for delaying the crew's return to Ganymede. Then he passed out.

When Arroyo woke up after his first round of surgery on Ganymede, the first thing he asked for was his iMind. He sent Frank's final message to Beverly. He never had much interest in using his iMind after that.

Arroyo stood beside the tractor named *Misty* and wept. He quickly overloaded his suit ventilation system; the inside of his visor began to fog. He got control of himself. He ran his gloved finger across the neat lettering he had painted nine months earlier.

Misty. He remembered her. She was his girlfriend back in Minnesota a million years ago. He wondered what ever happened to her.

* * *

Arroyo headed back toward Mactown. He neared a bend in the route where sets of crossed black flags on both sides warned of Big John Crack. This narrow but seemingly bottomless crevasse was named after a Navy Seabee who fell into it forty years earlier and perished. The crevasse was narrow enough to jump across now, but decades ago it had been wide enough to swallow Big John and his bulldozer.

Arroyo suited up and climbed out. He walked a few meters from Drag Queen and carefully approached the lip of the crevasse. He reached into a utility pocket on his suit and dug out the Dali Box. He tossed it into the chasm. He could hear the module ping against ice a couple of times before it plummeted downward with a warbling whistle toward the hidden sea. Arroyo realized that the

Dali Box was a prop, like the pocket watch a hypnotist in a corny movie slowly swings to help a patient concentrate. Staring into the fog with his radiation shield up had no magical power other than to bake him like a potato in a microwave. Staring at a couple of sheets of toilet paper while sitting on the throne *could*, in theory, do the same thing, if one relaxed and concentrated. But the Dali Box had helped him, at first, to remember snippets of his life. For this he would always be thankful to Nicholas.

* * *

Arroyo parked Drag Queen at the plug-in line. He climbed down and untangled a snarl of electrical cords, then plugged in the various heaters that kept the tractor's fluids warm.

He heard a sing-song voice coming his way. It was Darla Hovenweep, greeting everyone she passed, like a religious fanatic handing out tracts. She knew everybody on station—and everything about them.

"Arroyo!" she sang out. "Good timing. I was thinking about you." As she stepped up, her Manolo Blahniks slipped on a slick patch and she almost went ass-over-teakettle. She had paid handsomely to have the alligator boots fitted with low-g soles; she should have coughed up another thousand credits to have lugs attached.

"Hello, Darla. How has your day been?"

"Oh, the usual. Six or seven counseling sessions for sexual harassment. One early trip home for a cook's assistant who went bonkers and attacked a sous chef with a claw hammer. Word to the wise: don't eat the Chili Mac tonight. There might be some sous chef in it."

"Thanks for the head's up. I'll make a sandwich."

Darla wrapped her trenchcoat tightly around her. It would have been a perfect choice for a stroll down Park Avenue in New

New York. She leaned close and whispered. "Have you been availing yourself of the store stockroom?"

"Oh, sure," Arroyo said.

"I took a peek at the inventory and compared it to sales in the store. It didn't look to me like you'd been helping yourself."

"Yeah," Arroyo said. "*About that.* I guess I haven't been thirsty lately. But I appreciate the offer. And the door code is safe with me. In fact, with my memory, it's already forgotten."

A cloud crossed Darla's face. Her upper lip wrinkled, threatening her thick scarlet lipstick. "This was something suggested by Dr. Gianforte."

"I understand. I'll be visiting him tomorrow afternoon, and we'll get it sorted out."

* * *

Arroyo knocked cautiously on Dr. Gianforte's door. He could hear voices inside; they suddenly grew hushed. The door swung inward; the doctor ushered him in.

"Thank you for dropping by," Gianforte said. He pointed to a seat in the middle of the office, across from his desk. "You know Darla Hovenweep from HR. And this is Mike Balzac, The Program's chief safety compliance officer on Europa."

Arroyo waved to Darla, who sat waving her hand in the air, taking notes with her iMind. He shook Balzac's hand. "I thought I was here to have a private appointment with the Doc."

Darla dropped her hand a moment. "I'm here to represent both The Company and The Program," she said. "*Both* have an interest in a healthy resolution to your situation. I assume you don't mind if I take notes." She began waving her hand in the air again, staring off into space as she concentrated on her iMind's projected image.

"And don't mind me," Balzac said. He was a skinny

middle-aged blond man with a nose that could light up a dark closet and hair that looked like it hadn't been washed since he left Earth. "I'm just here to dot some t's and cross some i's on the AIR."

"The *air*?" Arroyo asked.

"The Accident Investigation Report," Balzac explained.

"Whoa, now," Gianforte interjected. "Don't make me reach across the desk and punch you in the sternum, Mike. You're getting ahead of things. This is a delicate process."

Arroyo turned back toward the doctor. "What in the Sam Hill are we talking about, Big Guy?"

Gianforte put his elbows on the desktop and furrowed his eyebrows, staring at Arroyo. "Have you been experiencing severe disturbances with your memory since you returned to Europa? Have there been things that you should remember but can't, or things that you remember but make no sense?"

"Sounds like most of my Monday mornings," Arroyo said.

"*Please*," Darla said. "Let's dispense with the levity and move onward."

"Yes," Arroyo said. "I've occasionally felt like I've been trapped in a bad dream. I can't remember basic things about work, about Mactown, about Europa. I can't remember important events in my own life—things that are at the very core of who I am and what I've done. I've been thinking I might be losing my mind."

"You were involved in an accident early last March," Gianforte said. "It was a *very* bad accident. One man was killed, and you were seriously injured. Have you been getting any intimations—any *flashes*—of this since you got back?"

Arroyo's heart began to race. "*No*," he said. He didn't think he was a good liar, but nobody seemed to blink an eye. "What happened, and why can't I remember?"

"Does the name Frank Pabodie ring a bell?" Gianforte asked.

Jim Fairchild

Arroyo frowned. "Yes. I remember him. A nice young engineer from the Kregg Corporation. We were working together on a project."

"I'm sorry to tell you this, but Frank died in the accident. He was crushed between two tractors."

"*Oh my God,*" Arroyo gasped. He had already remembered the accident on his own, but it wasn't a stretch to feign shock.

Gianforte explained to Arroyo that after the accident Arroyo had been medevacked to Epigeus, the largest city on Ganymede. The hospital there—the best in the Jovian system—couldn't save his legs despite several operations.

"*Legs?*" Arroyo asked. "As in *plural?*" Arroyo's memory of the accident involved only his right leg. But then he knew that both legs looked oddly pink.

"Yes. *Both* legs were crushed beyond repair in the accident."

Arroyo was hard-wired with a very accurate bullshit detector. It started to ring loudly.

"Your legs had to be regenerated," Gianforte said. "Chemically teasing stem cells to replace appendages is old medical technology nowadays. You were put into stasis at the hospital for several months during the regen process to minimize both physical and mental trauma. You were heavily medicated and underwent a deep trauma-flush via iMind. It's a subliminal process that encourages your subconscious mind to identify traumatic memories and compartmentalize them. The regen process—and *all* physical healing—is far faster when the mind is at ease.

"When you were brought out of stasis, you had two shiny new pink legs. They reminded me of little hamster legs. You were moved to a convalescent facility in Kardashia, not far from The Program's complex, to continue healing and to start physical therapy. I came to see you regularly to monitor your progress.

128

That's why you found a prescription from the Kardashia clinic prescribed by me. You were heavily sedated with enough drugs to knock out a rhinoceros and still undergoing trauma-flush. I must say that your new legs are works of art. I wouldn't mind ogling them again when you have the time. A couple of centuries ago you'd be wearing prosthetic legs, or pushing yourself around in a wheelchair. Science is a wonderful thing."

"Yes, it is," Arroyo agreed. "My life for Science."

Gianforte studied Arroyo's face. "You *did* almost give your life for Science."

Darla dropped her hand a moment. "I've got to terminate an employee at five o'clock. Sorry to be a buzzkill, but could we move on?"

Gianforte glanced irritably at Darla. "Arroyo, you've reacted to the news of the accident with flying colors," the doctor said. "Many patients fall completely to pieces when they're brought out of trauma-flush and reacquainted with the details of a bad accident. Some have to go back into stasis for further flushing."

"I think I'm plumb flushed out," Arroyo said. "But I wouldn't mind if the details of the accident were *fleshed* out for me."

Balzac cleared his throat. He lifted a folder from his lap. "I've got the investigation report right here. I sent a copy to your iMind inbox an hour ago. It summarizes what we know from eyewitnesses: that Drag Queen—an old, obsolete tractor that should have been sent to the scrapyard decades ago—slipped into reverse gear, pinning Frank *and* you against the front of the robot tractor parked behind Drag Queen."

Arroyo couldn't stop himself from jerking his head back. "*Wow.*" His bullshit detector was shrieking now. "I had totally blanked out those details. So Drag Queen was at fault."

"Yes," Balzac said, drumming a thumb on his folder. "I've

129

Jim Fairchild

recommended to Bryon Sturm that the tractor be cut up for scrap metal. Or, better yet, pushed into a bottomless crevasse, if we can get away with it. I've been talking with Vinnie Kuzawa. He tells me the tractor is ancient, there are no parts for it, and the only reason it's still running is because *you* insist on operating it."

That fat, greasy douchebag Wrench, Arroyo thought.

"You can read the report if you wish," Balzac continued. "I can leave you this hardcopy if—as I've been told—you don't check your iMind regularly. You'll find all of the signed witness statements."

"You don't need a statement from *me* before you cross all the i's and dot all the t's?"

Balzac chuckled. "I don't know what *you* could contribute. You've had people up inside your brain for several months playing with your memory. And you're one of Mactown's most notorious Trankheads."

"Easy, there, Mike," Gianforte said. "Don't make me swan-dive off my desk and give you a karate chop to your emaciated little sternum."

Balzac looked peevishly at the doctor, then continued: "All I need is your signature, Arroyo. An electronic signature would be fine. Or you can sign the hardcopy."

Arroyo reached over and grabbed the manila folder. He flipped through the pages until he found the place to sign. He grabbed a pen from Gianforte's desk and scribbled his name.

"Thanks," Balzac said, taking back the folder and rising. "I'm done here. Try to stay safe, Arroyo. You make too much paperwork for me." He stepped out of the office and shut the door behind him.

"We're just about done," Darla said, flashing a smile befitting a Komodo dragon. "I just have one form for you to sign." She pulled it off Gianforte's desktop and handed it to Arroyo.

"What's this?" Arroyo asked, taking the form.

"It's an acknowledgment of our meeting today. It states that you were thoroughly apprised of the medical care you received; that both The Company and The Program did everything within their power to aid you in your recovery and that you absolve them of further legal and financial obligation; that you are now fully certified to return to work without restrictions; and that you acknowledge that it is *your* responsibility to maintain a safe workplace environment, since you are provided all the safety methodology and equipment necessary to make that happen."

"Wow," Arroyo said, signing the form. "For a second I thought you were pinning all of this on Drag Queen. I was beginning to feel sorry for her."

Darla smiled coldly. "You *were* Drag Queen's operator in a fatal accident. I wouldn't presume to mete out percentages of responsibility for Frank's death. Let's just go with fifty percent Drag Queen, fifty percent you. Bear in mind that your continued employment with The Company and The Program is predicated upon an accident-free track record from here on in."

"I hear you loud and clear," Arroyo said.

"*Well*," Darla said, her mellifluous voice back. She gathered her things, smoothed her tunic and rose. "I can stuff my *Little Darla Bad-Ass* alter-ego back in the bottle now. HR work isn't always pretty, but someone has to do it. There's a party planned for you tonight at *Insane in the Membrane*. I understand there will be fun, frivolity, and watered-down, overpriced drinks. Music will be provided by a band from the Heavy Shop, *The Foo Quads*. The community wants to formally welcome you back. They've all been playing along with the charade about you only being gone for a month on R&R. You wouldn't believe how many meetings were required to pull it off. It was quite exhausting." She smiled one last time and left the office.

"*Man*," Gianforte groaned after the door closed. He gritted his teeth. "You don't know how much I'd like to give her a good

Jim Fairchild

swift karate chop to the sternum." He told Arroyo he seemed to be doing great, and to stop taking the anxiety medication. Arroyo had disposed of it many days ago. He also told Arroyo it was time to wean himself off Trank. Arroyo was, again, already a step ahead.

*　*　*

The music from *The Foo Quads* rocked the lopsided walls of the ancient Quonset hut. The corrugated grooves in the arched walls pulsated like the ribs of a hyperventilating leviathan. The band's songlist was the typical drunken eclectic amalgam for a Saturday night in Mactown: industrial trance noise, Martian fifth-wave ska, Minnesota death metal, Kardashian Hip Hop, and—to the confusion of many but to the delight of music historians in the crowd—Clash, Sex Pistols and a medley of 1960s bubble-gum pop. Arroyo stood just inside the door, hiding in shadows, in physical pain from the music volume. As he let his eyes adjust, he could see luminous twisting snakes of finger paint on half-naked, deathly-white bodies, many of them middle-aged and showing the less-attractive effects of prolonged life at low-g. Even the darker-complected looked in dire need of sunlight. The Quonset was as hot and as humid as a sauna; it smelled of more than a hundred energetic dancers all in desperate need of their weekly three-minute showers. Arroyo stepped close behind a middle-aged man soaked in patchouli oil to help mask the wrestling match smell. The man's hair was coiled in a teetering man-bun; it seemed to oscillate with the music.

Arroyo's eyes finally adjusted. He could see the banner hanging over the makeshift bandstand:

WELCOME TO ARROYO'S
COMING OUT PARTY

It is one of the blessings of old friends that
you can afford to be stupid with them—R.W.
Emerson

The band kicked into a spirited *Son of a Preacher Man* by Dusty Springfield. The crowd seemed to know the song. Dancers body-slammed, pogoed, spun like dervishes and break-danced to Dusty.

Suddenly the music stopped. One lonely guitar string screeched discordantly. "*Yo,*" the lead singer said. One dim stage light came up; the singer shielded her eyes with a hand and squinted in Arroyo's direction, where he still stood in the cover of darkness. It was Consuelo, Annie's squeeze. "Yo, yo! I see our man, Arroyo. *Arroyo-yo-yo-yo.* Welcome to your Coming Out Party. We can all finally say that there are no secrets between friends."

The crowd turned toward Arroyo, trying to spot him in the shadows. He raised a hand and waved uncomfortably. A chant arose: *Speech! Speech! Speech!* A solitary drunken voice added: "Drinks on Arroyo!" It was Vinnie Kuzawa.

Arroyo climbed onto the bandstand and leaned toward Consuelo's microphone. "Thanks for coming, folks." Feedback made Arroyo wince. "And thanks for taking part in the charade the last couple of weeks until our esteemed medical staff felt I was capable of handling the truth."

A hand waved gaily in a corner. It was Dr. Gianforte. He wore neon-green surgical scrubs. A stethoscope hung from his neck. A zucchini-sized tangerine-colored silicone dildo swayed limply from the end of his nose, held in place by a painful-looking studded leather head harness.

Before Arroyo could say any more, the band kicked into an eardrum-splitting industrial tune called *Sonic Transgression*. The tune didn't require a vocalist; Consuelo and Arroyo jumped off the stand and pushed through the sweating crowd until they reached the front alcove, stacked high with mountains of identical red parkas.

"I was looking for Annie," Arroyo said.

"She ran back to her dorm room to touch up her body paint," Consuelo said. The door opened; cold air rushed in and formed a thick fog. Arroyo could hear Consuelo chuckle; four hands waved the fog away after the door closed. Two of the hands belonged to Consuelo. The other two belonged to Annie. They gave each other a hug; Consuelo returned to the band.

Annie gave Arroyo a hug, careful not to smear the paint on her largely naked body. He could count her ribs. Fuelies had one of the most physically demanding jobs on Europa. "Good to see you," she said.

"I need to talk to somebody." Arroyo spoke as low as the noise would allow.

Annie took Arroyo by the arm and led him toward a janitor's closet. She kicked aside a pile of parkas to get the closet open.

When the door was latched behind them, Arroyo spoke. "I had a meeting this afternoon with the doctor, Darla Hovenweep from HR, and Mike Balzac, the safety dude. They seem to be hanging the motorpool accident on Drag Queen and me. They say they have witnesses. But I remember the accident pretty clearly now. Most of what they say doesn't add up. I've either lost my mind, or I'm a step or two away from *big* trouble."

The closet door throbbed in time with *Sonic Transgression*. "You're already in big trouble," Annie said. The hand on his arm gripped tighter. "And there's more trouble on the way. You need to get out of Mactown ASAP now that you've been cleared to go to the field. Take any assignment that will get you out of this little science burg. The Pole Station and field camp staffs are all packed up and will be boarding flitters Monday morning to come back here. Some of the Senators on the budget committee are now threatening to shut down *all* off-Earth science—especially anything involving exospecies. The subject gives some religionists the heebie-jeebies. They still insist on clinging to an anthropocentric world view—without that linch pin most of their fabulous cosmogonies collapse."

"I don't know much about cosmogonies," Arroyo said. "Or cosmologies. Or cosmetology. I *do* know that a Cosmopolitan is a girl-drink with vodka, triple sec, cranberry and lime juice. Sorry to be flippant, but I feel like trouble is headed my way."

"Trouble is on the way to *everybody* on Europa. I'll be leaving for Discovery Bay Monday morning to shut down the camp generators and put the fuel system to bed. Maybe you can get yourself assigned to the same trip to make back hauls. We'd be able to talk."

The band suddenly ground to a halt mid-*Transgression*. Annie grinned and put a hand to her mouth. She realized she had been shouting in the closet to be heard over the noise. She swung open the closet to see why the band had stopped.

Arroyo blinked when he stepped out into the alcove. The house lights had been turned up. He stumbled over a pile of parkas, then looked around. Barry Wilton stood in the center of the Quonset, his hands buried in his parka pockets, looking for something he couldn't find, immensely uncomfortable with the tight, sweaty crowd and the stifling air.

Then he turned toward Arroyo. "Ah, the man of honor." He offered a veiny, weathered hand; he and Arroyo shook. "I wanted to welcome you back, Bucko. I'm not comfortable with the process of feeding the truth to you in snippets after a serious accident. There's no place harder to keep a secret than a company town. And truth is a tonic vital to the healing process, even if its taste is bitter." Arroyo nodded his thanks.

Then Barry climbed up onto the bandstand. It was a high

step for him, and he had to grab a stiff knee to lift one of his boots. He tapped Consuelo's microphone. "This thing on?" he asked. The shriek of feedback answered him.

"Hi, folks," he said, speaking just above a whisper into the mike. "I'm glad everybody's been having a good time. Like you all, I wanted to drop by and welcome back Arroyo Bronson. You all did your part to pretend that he'd only been gone for a month on R&R. Coming out of a full-bore trauma-flush is a very Byzantine process in the best of circumstances, and doing it in a workplace like Europa makes it doubly so. I'm not a medical person so I won't question the wisdom of it. Anyway, we have our most experienced operator back, which is a good thing. Because we have a lot of work to do."

The crowd grew silent as Barry explained the situation. Warring factions in the Senate had reached a hopeless impasse on the budget. Confederate senators had been joined by border-state senators in denying funds to off-Earth space research. Government-sponsored research programs only existed on Europa and Enceladus. Mars, Ganymede and Titan had been colonized and industrialized (for a century in the first case and half a century in the latter two), already making vast expanses of both uninteresting contaminated wastelands for exobiologists. Enceladus had, so far, yielded no signs of the most minute possible life forms. It was only on Europa that non-terrestrial life forms had been found so far—the Tetras, the Deltas, and a few sulfur-eating bacteria. Some still questioned if the larger two were even living creatures. And those two quasi-species were two too many for those whose cosmos still revolved around man. As a result, Barry said, Europa's science program was directly in the crosshairs. In a sense, The Program was simply collateral damage in the never-ending culture war that had led to the demise of the original United States so long ago.

Barry confirmed to the crowd what Annie had already told

Arroyo: all personnel from the Pole Station and field camps would begin pulling back to Mactown on Monday. The NSWF had no interplanetary cargo vessels of it own, but Barry said a contract had just been signed with the *Kapitan Khlebnikov*, a rustbucket of a Russian freighter that happened to be in port on Ganymede while all but a skeleton crew laid waste to Kardashia's bordello district. The *Khlebnikov* would be arriving at the Pegasus Ice Runway just outside Mactown mid-week; it had berthing for about 350 lucky passengers who would be taken back to Kardashia until a final solution could be ascertained. The remainder of Europa's population—another almost 500 people—would be placed in stasis on Europa awaiting the arrival of the next regularly scheduled resupply vessel from Earth. Unless the Senate miraculously lifted its crosshairs from The Program, those in stasis would be forklifted like other retro cargo into a dark hold for the year-long trip back to Earth.

And, Barry said, those who ended up in Kardashia would likely only have a short reprieve from the same fate. If, after their touchdown on Ganymede, the Senate hadn't arrived at a resolution by the end of the month, they would be freighted back to Earth in stasis as soon as another contract vessel could be found.

"How the heck do you decide who goes into stasis immediately and who gets to party in Kardashia?" a drunken voice yelled out. Arroyo thought it was Vinnie again.

"Check your iMind inboxes," Barry said, sniffing through his crusty mustache. "Everybody in The Program has just received instructions for the stasis lottery."

Nearly a hundred arms lifted frantically, fingers flitting hummingbird-like through iMind menus. Arroyo had to duck to avoid being poked in the eye by a young man evidently with a new 7.0 implant. That, or he was simply having a good-old-fashioned seizure.

Barry continued once most of the crowd had glanced at the

iMind text. "I've tried to make it fair. You'll get no special consideration for the number of years you've been with The Program, for your position on the management totem pole, for your job title, gender orientation, age, nationality or gluten sensitivity. The lowest potato-peeling peon will have the same chances as the most uptight Scotch-swilling Ivy League beaker. By making this lottery absolutely fair I've probably made enemies of many of you here tonight. I'm sorry about that. Being The Man can be a lonely job."

Barry said that equipment operators, cargo handlers and fuelies would begin traverses Monday morning to field camps to pull out whatever sensitive material they could haul back to Mactown for safe storage. They would have no time to traverse to the Pole Station and back, a round-trip journey of five weeks by tractor; shutdown at the Pole Station would be handled by personnel already there, and grantees there would be allowed limited cargo weight to hand-carry data logs and other precious science gear via flitter back to Mactown.

"And if that isn't enough happy horseshit," Barry said into the microphone, "we've got a couple of DVs from OFFJOVSYSOPS arrriving on the *Khlebnikov* to oversee the shutdown. Most of you know them: Bryon Sturm and Sally Train. My bosses. I'm so happy about their visit I'm tempted to climb into stasis right now." The crowd—cooling down now that the dancing had stopped, exposed skin turning to goose bumps— shivered and chuckled.

Barry put the final kibosh on the party. He announced that as of that moment alcohol sales and consumption were being prohibited everywhere on Europa. This time, the ban was for real. It was primarily a matter of safety, he explained: there would be many twenty-hour shifts in the next few days, and nobody wanted alcohol-related injuries. There would be no further days off until everyone was either cooling their heels in the budget motels of

Kardashia or in dreamless stasis on an Earth-bound resupply vessel, or until—and this seemed increasingly like a futile dream— the Senate came to its senses.

* * *

People began to drift toward the doors, searching through piles for their parkas. Some didn't care whose parka they took as long as it was warm and walked out with someone else's nametag on their chest. As the crowd dissipated Arroyo could see Barry climbing down gingerly from the bandstand, his knees gimped up from age, hard work and decades in low-g. Arroyo wasn't sure he had ever seen a human being look so tired and so lonely. He stepped up to Barry.

"I know this is not a good time for questions," Arroyo said.

"It's *always* a good time for questions, if the questions are good."

"I remember the accident pretty clearly," Arroyo said.

"*Which* accident?"

"The motorpool accident. When Frank Pabodie was killed. I feel like I've been set up."

Barry looked at Arroyo, then smiled. The corners of Barry's eyes wrinkled like old boot leather. "I won't let you take the fall for *anything,* my friend. I want you out of town ASAP. You and the rest of the Geriatric Crew scalawags are heading out to Discovery Bay at o'dark-thirty Monday morning. I've cleared it with your bosses. Get your gear and your tractor up to snuff tomorrow. You'll need to haul the living and generator modules and enough grub and consumables for a week just to play it safe. Things have been set into motion that will soon change the face of Europa. The motorpool accident—as much as it is tearing you up inside right now—will fade into insignificance. It will shortly become one of your less-visited nightmares."

139

Jim Fairchild

* * *

PART TWO:

CHAOS TERRAIN

The Geriatric Crew departed early Monday morning while most of Mactown was deep in slumber. Five tractors headed out for Discovery Bay via the Shear Zone. Tom Tillerman led the way. His tractor was outfitted with ground-penetrating radar to check the route for new hidden crevasses. The radar head was mounted beneath an eight-meter alloy boom that flexed and bounced over the rough ice. The booms were notorious for stress fractures in the extreme cold; while they could be field-repaired by anyone with modest welding skills, Tillerman kept two extra booms strapped to the top of his cab just in case. There was no such thing as too much redundancy. The spare booms bounced and flexed wildly on the rough trail. Tillerman kept his tractor on autopilot so he could keep a close watch on the radar monitor bungeed to his console.

Wyatt was second in the travel order. His tractor was equipped with a blade for knocking down penitentes or filling in any new crevasses Tillerman found.

Behind Wyatt came Joy. Her tractor also had a blade. Joy was another operator old enough to retire but who refused to leave Europa. She had started her adult life as a wife on a North Dakota farm. Although rail-thin, farm life had taught her to take hard physical work and endless hours in stride. Once, while trying to get a tractor and its load unstuck from a four-kilometer-deep crevasse, Joy finished hooking up a recovery cable, then grinned through her helmet visor at the other operators standing nearby, all half her age and all exhausted. "Nothing but a little kerfuffle, lads," she said, brushing the ice from the palms of her gloves. "This is a piece of cake compared to calving season." After her divorce, Joy spent many years teaching in a one-room school (they were quite common again in much of America after the Crash); she spent her summers as a wrangler on a ranch in the Black Hills. She had a house on forty acres back in NoDak, but hadn't been there in five years. She had declined time off back on Earth after her last contract, opting for R&R on Ganymede, like Arroyo. She kept saying this was her last contract and she wanted to put away a nest egg. Of course, like many in The Program, she was always saying that this was her last contract—and then she was always signing up for more.

After Joy's tractor came Ellen's. Ellen was in her indeterminate fifties. She looked rough around the edges but had a heart of pure gold. She had inherited money (when the Earth's population imploded from nine billion to one billion, suddenly the economy had a surfeit of capital—even if there wasn't much to buy with it—and the lowliest street person might have a couple of million credits in the bank). She owned a sizable chunk of Telluride, Colorado. It hadn't been a ski town in a couple of centuries, and looked and felt much like the silver mining town it had been 400 years earlier—small, isolated and scruffy. Telluride still had a few part-time residents with deep pockets, who paid handsomely for the cachet of the mailing address, though most of the year-round residents chose a simpler path and lived off the grid on their free forty acres. Unoccupied vacation McMansions owned by rich part-time residents often mysteriously went up in flames shortly after the bars closed on Saturday nights. Some dynamics in a ski town never change.

Ellen had spent much of her life partying, both in Telluride and on Europa, but she had dried out a few years ago when she had problems passing a pre-contract physical. She still smoked like a a flare stack on a Titan refinery. Tobacco consumption had been outlawed on most of Earth two centuries ago. But like most prohibitions, the tobacco ban only made the vice that much more attractive and that much more profitable for dealers. Ellen spent extravagant sums having a kilo of Martian hydroponic brightleaf Slingshot-Expressed to her every other month. On Europa, smoking was allowed, but only in a handful of poorly-heated shipping containers scattered around the grotto that made the smokers feel like lepers.

Big, burly, reeking of hand-rolled brightleaf that she smoked not-so-surreptitiously in her dorm bathroom and in her tractor cab in proud disregard of the rules: woe betide the mechanic who had to climb into her cab to suss out a computer glitch just after she climbed out. When Ellen was still in the cups, Arroyo once watched her deliver a knock-out punch to a plumber fifty kilos heavier than her who had the audacity to make a lewd crack about Joy. The plumber hit his head so hard on the bar floor he had to be medevacked to Ganymede. Darla Hovenweep's predecessor at HR stood behind Ellen. Nobody ever treated the female equipment operators disrespectfully again. Yes, she was tough, but Arroyo had seen Ellen burst into tears when she opened her iMind inbox and found photos of a new litter of puppies that her niece—who was watching her house in Telluride—sent her. If push came to shove, if the chips were down, Arroyo would be proud to have Ellen watching his back.

Arroyo brought up the rear in Drag Queen. His was the only tractor pulling a full load to Discovery Bay. Hooked to Drag Queen's hitch were the living and generator modules, taken on most traverses requiring more than a night away from Mactown. Both modules were converted eight-meter-long shipping containers. They were outfitted with pressurized inserts and crowded airlocks, but it was home on the trail. The living module, directly behind Drag Queen, had a small central galley area with stove, oven, refrigerator, sink and table. Eight operators could cram into the galley for microwaved meals, but it was a godawful-tight fit and a couple of operators usually stood in a corner to eat—the price to pay for being late to a meal. Each end of the living module had a door behind which four bunks were crammed into a space the size of a walk-in closet. Two bunks were on each wall with a narrow aisle between; a few drawers served to store spare socks and toiletries, but not much else. The bunks were similar to what one would have found on a pre-Crash submarine: barely high enough to sit up, the mattresses old beyond the Dawn of Time and full of the smell and dander of operators long forgotten (and some already rotting in their graves), threadbare bunk curtains jury-rigged for privacy, foul-smelling boot socks and long johns hanging from any convenient projection. The heat was always turned up too high for Arroyo's taste, but there was always at least one cold sleeper who insisted on being a heat Nazi. Without earplugs, an operator could almost hear the eyelids flutter of the operator in the bunk across the aisle as he or she read a book on their iMind at the end of a hard day's traverse.

The generator module rode behind the living module. It contained twin powerplants, only one of which ran at any given time. The second was tested twice a day to assure redundancy. The omnivorous generators could burn any hydrocarbon blend that showed up on the tankers from Titan. Lives depended on the generators; on a longer traverse such as to the Pole, a small engine mechanic would be attached to the crew strictly to baby the generators. The generator module also had an electric turd-burning toilet, an ice melter, a tiny washing machine and dryer and a grease-smeared shower. Doing laundry or taking a shower meant making sure the ice melter was packed with ice blocks beforehand; it was terrible traverse etiquette to run the ice melter dry and not refill it. Many traversers quickly grew tired—despite the low-g—of heaving huge ice blocks into the melter. At the end of a twenty-hour day a shower or clean clothes usually seemed less important than a few hours of shut-eye. Arroyo had done countless traverses to the Pole with operators—usually but not always men—who went the entire five weeks without even a single quick whore's bath or a clean change of socks. They would squeeze into a seat at the galley table for breakfast and proudly announce that they were at Day Number 32 and counting without washing their butts.

The back end of the generator module was crammed tight with a tiny work bench and tool chest, the electrolysis system for oxygen generation, the back-up pressurized oxygen tanks, a variety of tanks holding oils and fluids for maintenance on the tractors and generators, and a mountain of spare parts both new and well-used, the purposes of many of them long ago forgotten. Power, water and oxygen lines hung in lazy color-coded parabolas between the two modules. The shells of the two modules were covered with a crazy design of welded patches. The incessant pounding of the sleds across the rock-hard ice led to frequent stress fractures. On a Pole traverse it was not unusual for a mechanic to stay up much of the night while the other operators slept, grumpily welding that day's new cracks before they could compromise the pressurized insert.

The modules behind Drag Queen were mounted to sheets of high-molecular-weight polyethylene. Each sheet, or sled, had a hitch plate attached to the front and back ends for hooking together multiple loads. The HMW sleds were an idea borrowed from Antarctic traverses. It took many generations of HMW to formulate a polymer both slick enough to drag easily under a load *and* resilient enough to deal with Europan temperatures. When Arroyo had first started on Europa the HMW formulation being used was frighteningly prone to stress-fracturing in the cold. Few things were worse for a traverser than to have an HMW sled instantly break into pieces in the middle of the chaos terrain. The load—whether a bladder filled with 10,000 liters of fuel or the extremely heavy generator module—would have to be carefully craned off the destroyed sheet, another sheet had to be slid into place (*if* the crew had the good luck to be hauling empties), and then the load craned back on and strapped down. A half a day could easily be lost. It was exhausting work in an EVA suit. Many of the younger operators worked too fast and overloaded their suit ventilation.

Each succeeding generation of HMW was harder to walk on, too. The plastic was far more slippery and dangerous to walk on than the hard ice upon which it glided. There seemed to be a perpetual disconnect between the Program engineers who ordered the sheets from the comfort of their Arlington cubicles and the operators who had to employ them on the barren ice of Europa four astronomical units away. Many injuries had resulted from operators clambering around on the HMW to secure or check their loads. Ruptured tendons, broken ankles and arms—it had all happened. A broken ankle could become a crisis 500 kilometers from the nearest doctor. SOP stated that operators should avoid walking on the HMW sleds at all costs, but it was impossible not to walk on the HMW and still properly check a load. Arroyo had lost count of the number of times he'd fallen. His policy was to not try to catch himself, but to roll with the fall and try to avoid sharp edges on the way down. He always covered his helmet visor with his gloves. The visor was the weak point in the EVA suit for anyone doing hard labor on Europa's surface. Some day Arroyo expected to see a broken helmet visor after a slip on HMW. The results would be instantly fatal.

Ellen and Joy pulled empty HMW sleds behind their tractors. They would be loaded with any gear at Discovery Bay that needed to go back to Mactown. Ellen's load also included an HMW sled carrying a single 10,000-liter bladder of fuel for the trip to Discovery Bay and back. It was more than twice what the tractors would probably burn, but carrying an abundance of fuel was perhaps the Number One safety rule.

*　*　*

The trip to Discovery Bay normally took three days for tractors pulling full loads. But this trip was different. All the tractors but Drag Queen were rolling light; the crew agreed to get the trip over with as soon as possible, so they planned on two long days, grabbing three or four hours of sleep in between. The Geriatric Crew usually paced itself easier than this, but time was of the essence. Despite its full load, Drag Queen chugged right along and easily kept up. The antiquated Navy Challenger, with its longer track length and wider tracks than newer models, had better traction and pulling capacity. In fact, a couple of times a day other operators bogged down in pits of sugar ice or got hung up in narrow crevasses. It was Arroyo who would unhitch Drag Queen from her load and come to the rescue with a tow strap.

That night, Arroyo laid in his squalid bunk, still reeking of the last unbathed traverser who had occupied it. He locked his hands behind his head on the old government-issue plastifeather pillow. He could hear Wyatt and Ellen snoring in bunks a couple of feet away. Joy and Tillerman were enjoying the rare pleasure of having the other four-person sleeping compartment to themselves. Arroyo stared upward in the darkness. Barring any major new crevasses or mechanical problems, they should arrive at the Discovery Bay camp late the next evening. Annie and a mechanic had flitted out Monday morning; they'd already been busy preparing to bring the camp's generators and fuel systems off-line. Annie had also been busy helping grantees pack up research gear and data logs. Tillerman had gotten an iMind text from her. They'd been having problems with the grantees; some were in full-blown panic. Many had their entire careers riding on research that was now being aborted. The grantees should have flitted back to Mactown that morning, but most were still pulling their hair out at

Discovery Bay. Annie texted Tillerman that she'd be happy to have more muscle available shortly, even if it *was* the Geriatric Crew.

Arroyo was physically exhausted but mentally wired. He could not relax. He listened to the throbbing of the generator from the next module, anxious to hear it miss or sputter. But it purred happily. He looked forward to returning to Discovery Bay, even though he couldn't remember much about it. He looked forward to seeing Annie again. He had a thousand questions for her. And he looked forward to seeing Pegleg again. His recollections of the strange Tetra were fuzzy. But what he could remember filled him with warmth and peace. His parents crossed his mind. He began to relax.

Just as he was about to drift off, a bright flash burst through the closed blind over the sole tiny viewport in the sleeping compartment. The flash was brilliant white, like a silent supernova. Then darkness filled the module once more. When Arroyo closed his eyes, he could still see the clear outline of the bunk and its springs directly above him. When he opened his eyes and held his hand in front of his face, he thought he could see his phalanges and metacarpals. And then the effect faded. He wondered how much of it was imagination. He tossed and turned the rest of the night.

As was his custom, in the morning he snuck quietly out of bed long before the others and got coffee ready for his fellow traversers. He enjoyed that silent hour alone each morning on the trail: no need for conversation, enough room in the galley to relax with a steaming mug of Martian Dusk 'Til Dawn, and a chance to catch up on one of the ancient moldering Louis L'Amour paperbacks a Navy mechanic had hidden in a plastic bag in Drag Queen's belly plate half a century ago as a literary time capsule. Vinnie had found them during routine maintenance and had tossed them in the trash. Arroyo had rescued them and had made it his project to read them all, as long as they didn't turn to dust first. He had just started *High Lonesome*. Some of the pages fell apart as he turned them. According to the back cover, the story followed

> ...the treacherous trail of an outlaw determined to make his big strike and then disappear into a new life. But can a wrong turn be made right and can the heart of a hardened man still be moved by a second chance at happiness? Here's a hard-hitting tale of raw courage, haunting regret, and hope against all odds.

The cover crumbled to pieces as Arroyo read the blurb. The ancient book fell apart in his hands, a victim of Time, its lessons lost forever. Arroyo was overwhelmed by sadness. He had no clue why. A single tear ran down his cheek and came to rest in stubble.

* * *

The traverse convoy crested a jagged rise in the chaos terrain. And then the slope dropped away before them. Ahead of the five tractors a smooth expanse of ice spread out in a broad circle, surrounded on all sides by chaos terrain. The smoothness beckoned Arroyo after two days of hard trail. The ordeal of penitentes and hidden crevasses was behind them. A line of flags wound down toward their welcome destination. The surface structures of the field camp were tiny dots against the smooth ice. Ganymede hung brightly over the far horizon.

Arroyo parked Drag Queen a hundred meters from the stairwell to the subsurface camp. The rest of the Geriatric Crew followed traverse SOP: loads were dropped a safe distance away from the modules with ample room to get rehitched later. Then the tractors slowly ambled to pre-designated parking spots beside the generator module. The old farts suited up in their cabs while the tired tractors idled and cooled. Squeezing through airlocks and clambering down the ladders from their cabs, the operators bounced gently to the ice and plugged a multitude of cables to their tractors. The tractors could then be shut down. The generator powered the tractor heaters that would allow start-up in temperatures cold enough to make forged steel snap at the touch. Once plugged in, the operators clambered around their tractors, looking for leaks, wear to the suspension and bogies, and missing road wheel bolts shaken loose by the horrendous terrain they'd crossed.

Once they were satisfied that the tractors could be put to sleep, they assembled around Tom Tillerman. They gave each other high-fives for arriving safely and on time.

"What the deuce?" Tillerman asked, looking around the Discovery Bay camp. He put both hands on his hips in mock offense. "Where's our welcoming committee? I could go for a big mug of hot grog right now. And a donut cushion. That last five kilometers beat the heck out of my hemmorhoids."

The campsite was littered with haphazard stacks of black plastic coffin-sized instrument cases. Some were piled on the ice, some on small HMW sleds. None of it looked ready to be hauled back to Mactown. Fifty meters away, two grantees leaned over an open case, bickering about its contents. They were oblivious to the arriving Geriatric Crew. The two were so agitated that they didn't realize their argument was coming across the all-hands camp channel. "Goodness me," Tillerman said, chuckling. "Let's all switch to a work channel while the Gods of Science sort out their toys." The Geriatric Crew all reached to their wrist keypads and switched to a private channel.

Two helmets popped out of the hatch to the submerged

151

stairwell. They swivelled until the people wearing them spotted the Geriatric Crew. Gloved hands waved; two people in suits climbed swiftly upward and then jogged toward the newcomers.

Arroyo could recognize Annie by her size and gait. He didn't know the second person. When the two groups met, hugs were exchanged all around. Annie glanced at Tillerman's wrist keypad to see which channel they were using. When she'd switched over, she said, "It's great to have you basty old nastards here." Arroyo could see her broad smile despite the reflection of Ganymede in her visor. "We were watching your progress via your GPS trackers. We wanted to have hot toddies ready and the massage table set up, but things have been crazy here."

Annie introduced her companion. It was the camp manager, Karen. Karen was another person in her fifties who had been coming to Europa almost as long as Arroyo. Arroyo remembered her face; he had worked for her at Discovery Bay the previous winter. He remembered that she was from Denali, Alaska, once a tourist gateway to a national park but now wilderness again. He knew they had chatted over coffee countless mornings. *And she had used cream and two scoops of sugar.* Stray memories kept welling up.

"It's great to have extra hands," Karen said. "It's been absolute chaos here. Trying to get these beakers to make tough decisions in a timely manner is like trying to herd a litter of Kardashian kittens. The beakers should have been out of here this morning when the first flitter landed. I've got to go hold hands with a couple of old men with Ph.D.s and see if I can get them focused on getting the hell out of here. Help yourselves to fresh coffee and scones down in the galley. Dinner may be late but our cook just inventoried the freezer cave. Maine lobster and filet mignon for dinner for anyone with an appetite." The science camps had their own budget for food, and it was usually vastly more palatable than what was served in Mactown. "Oh—despite what Barry Wilton is doing in Mactown—we haven't gone dry yet here. Arroyo, you know where to find the liquor cabinet."

"Thanks," Arroyo muttered. "I'll show the other folks. I'm too tired to hit the sauce."

Karen cocked her helmet and stared at Arroyo a moment. "Well. Will wonders never cease? I've got to run. Welcome to Discovery Bay, and be prepared to work your testicles off—or ovaries, whichever the case may be."

* * *

The rest of the Geriatric Crew, exhausted, climbed down the stairwell to camp. Arroyo, at the rear, glanced over at the pile of instrument cases where the two grantees had been haggling. He saw one storm off, headed to the ice ramp that led down to the scootmobile garage. Arroyo changed his radio back to the camp channel. His helmet speakers were suddenly flooded with a tirade of obscenities; he had to turn down the volume. He walked over to see if he could help the one man remaining by the cases.

Arroyo introduced himself. The grantee looked up from the case in front of him but didn't return the courtesy. Arroyo recognized the face: he knew the researcher had been coming to Europa for years, was an expert in some field or another, and was probably considered a God by his young research assistants who came to Europa as volunteers in hopes of riding his academic coattails. But the assistants had apparently been pushed into the flitter that came out that morning and were probably already back in Mactown playing the stasis lottery. Arroyo knew for certain that this gentleman was not part of the Gordon Angstrom group that studied the Tetras. Angstrom's group had been ready on time and had jumped on the first flitter.

"What can I do to help?" Arroyo asked. He peered into the heavy case. He recognized the instrument: a gravitometer. He

Jim Fairchild
was pleased that he remembered.

"You can help by getting my assistants back out here," the beaker fumed. "They always pack this gear for us. I have no clue how this fits in the case."

"Here," Arroyo said. "Let me help." The gravitometer was supposed to fit snugly into a tight cutout in the case's foam lining. A cable was blocking things. Arroyo began to lift the gravitometer to move the cable.

"*Careful*," the beaker barked. "That instrument is worth more than you make in a three-year contract."

Arroyo paused, the gravitometer in his gloved hands. He was tempted to say something biting. But, looking at the harried grantee, Arroyo could see sweat pouring down the man's whiskered face. He probably hadn't slept in three days. His entire sense of purpose in life was being destroyed by the shutdown.

"*I understand*," Arroyo said. "I'm very sorry this is all happening. I know it's tough on you." He gently moved the offending cable and lowered the instrument into place. Together, Arroyo and the grantee lowered the lid and closed the latches.

"What next?" Arroyo asked.

"You could help me stack these cases on a sled." The grantee had calmed down. "Please accept my apologies. I'm John Torheit from MIT. This was going to be a banner year for our project. We were hoping to finally finish the first comprehensive gravitational study of Europa's iron core. We've discovered so many bizarre anomalies that we're on the verge of throwing out everything we'd taken for granted about what lies beneath the sea. Just when we were on the verge of a whole new understanding of Europa, the Senate chose to play shenanigans. It took me almost a decade to get my grant approved by the NSWF. If I have to return to Earth because of the shutdown it could be another decade before I get back here. By then I might be dead."

"I'm *really* very sorry," Arroyo said. He helped the grantee stack the cases on a nearby sled. Then, while Arroyo waited, the grantee trotted off to find some cargo straps to secure the load. Arroyo busied himself making sure the cases were neatly stacked.

He could faintly hear the crunching of approaching low-g boots. A suited figure stepped beside him. Arroyo turned, smiling, assuming it was Dr.Torheit returning.

"*Who the hell told you to touch these instruments?*" an angry voice asked.

Arroyo, shocked, turned toward the voice. It was Torheit's partner, who had disappeared earlier. "Pardon me?" Arroyo asked.

"Who told you to mess with this equipment?"

"Your partner asked for my help."

"This is priceless equipment. The gravitometer alone probably costs more than you make in a three-year contract."

Arroyo stared through the other man's helmet visor. The man's face was scarlet with rage. Arroyo stepped away, speechless. He suddenly realized how tired he was, and had no energy either to argue or apologize again. He stumbled toward the galley for coffee and scones.

* * *

Late that night two flitters landed just outside the camp. Karen and Annie shepherded the last of the grantees and their carry-on gear into the idling craft. Arroyo and Wyatt crammed a few smaller instrument cases into the tail boom cargo holds. The rest of the cases would be hauled back by tractor. Then, in a blast of engine exhaust and ice crystals, the flitters lifted and headed back to Mactown.

"*Thank you, Jesus,*" Karen said, dropping to her knees in mock prayer. "At last, Discovery Bay is now officially a Science-Free Zone. We can have some peace and quiet again." Ganymede had set; the flitters quickly disappeared in the gloom. She stood up, brushing off the knees of her suit. "Sea cockroaches and grilled ungulate, anyone?" Those remaining in camp shuffled off for the stairwell, the airlock, and a huge midnight feast.

* * *

Fran, the camp cook, had put together an amazing meal in the galley Jamesway. Fran—or *Francois*, as his co-workers called him—had been a chef in five-star hotels in New New York, in Europe, in New Bradbury on Mars, and on Ganymede. He had been sous chef at Drumpf Tower in Kardashia until he had been ordered to make taco bowls. He plopped his toque blanche into a simmering cauldron of taco meat and walked across town to The Program office complex, where he was quickly hired to cook on Europa. That was five years ago. Now, Fran stood under a single bare light over a kitchen table with one short leg prepping breakfast before going to bed for a few hours. Like the rest of the camp, Fran had been up for more than two days with nothing more than catnaps, helping the beakers pack instruments and data logs when he wasn't racing back to the galley to check on his smoking brisket or rising sourdough. "I don't know about you ladies and germs," he said, pushing back his wilted antique St. Louis Cardinals baseball cap so he could wipe the sweat from his forehead. "*This* boy needs to curl up with his thumb in his mouth for a couple of hours of nappy-nap. Help yourselves to whatever you want. Just clean up afterward. When you leave, turn off the lights and don't let the screen door slap you in the fanny."

Everybody thanked Fran. The food had been fabulous, but after the long, bone-jarring trip from Mactown some operators were too tired to finish their plates. All of the Geriatric Crew but Arroyo scraped their plates into a food waste bin, washed their dishes and placed them in a rack to dry. It was gauche at a field camp to leave a mess for the cook. Then, waving wearily, they headed for the living module to catch a few winks.

* * *

Only Annie and Arroyo remained. Annie had already cleaned her plate and clutched a steaming mug of ginger-lemon tea. Arroyo had been too tired to finish his meal, for which he'd apologized to Fran. Now he sat hunched over the meal's remains, staring into a mug of cocoa he'd been stirring for a couple of minutes. No matter how hard he tried, he couldn't break up the lumps. The tiny freeze-dried marshmallows refused to reconstitute. They floated like bits of styrofoam. The cocoa packets could have been in storage since the Navy years.

"You're looking better," Annie said.

"I feel better physically. But I have a lot on my mind."

"Of course," Annie said. She sipped her tea. "You've been blamed for the motorpool accident, and your memory is still foggy after the trauma-flush."

"I've been implicated in Frank Pabodie's *death*."

"That's a charade. Everybody knows the truth."

"But *someone* chose to blame me. It wasn't Darla Hovenweep, Mike Balzac or Dr. Dildo-Nose."

"Of course. They were just following orders."

Arroyo pushed the lumpy cocoa away. *"Bryon Sturm."*

Annie let go of her steaming tea and put a warm hand on Arroyo's. "Yes, Bryon Sturm. He was the driving force behind the robot tractor trials. He's an ambitious man. He couldn't be associated with the unpleasantries of a fatal accident resulting from one of his Bryonstorms."

"Europa is my *home*," Arroyo said. "If I lose my job, I have nowhere else to go."

"I don't think anyone is planning to fire you," Annie said. "But they'll file away their accident report, and if Frank Pabodie's widow—or anyone else—starts to ask questions, the report can be pulled out and dusted off. Then I'd guess you'd be in stasis within 24 hours and forklifted onto the next resupply vessel returning to Earth. Maybe Sturm was hoping you'd bail on your contract and go back to Earth when you felt the pressure, or—better yet—drink yourself to death. Then everything would be wrapped up with a pretty pink bow for him."

"*Fuck.* Fucketyfuck. Excuse my French. All I wanted was to be left alone to drive an old tractor out in the middle of nowhere and watch the moons come and go and the auroras flicker. I feel like my life has been stolen from me."

Annie pushed her tea mug up against Arroyo's cocoa mug. "Are you sleepy?"

"I haven't slept much in a couple of days. I'm too wired."

Annie scooted back her folding chair. It dragged across the seams in the plascrete floor. "Same here. Why don't we take a late-night stroll to look for an old friend of yours?"

They suited up and grabbed a scootmobile.

* * *

Annie kept the throttle low until they were well past the camp perimeter. Then she goosed it. The scootmobile shot forward so abruptly that Arroyo, sitting awkwardly behind Annie with his arms around her and her bulging life support backpack, thought he would fall off.

The scootmobile was nothing more than an ancient snowmobile design upgraded with oxygen injection, a beefed-up suspension, multiple engine preheaters and a fuel system compatible with the less-than reliable blends from Titan. It would have drawn *oohs* and *ahhs* from fellow ice fishermen back in the day when Arroyo and his father zipped out onto Lake Superior on their old Ski-Doo to take their limit of trout, salmon and walleye.

158

Later, his mother would fry up the best, and Arroyo would freeze any fish they couldn't eat and take them to the food bank. Life in Duluth had been good, although sometimes it seemed like winter lasted all year. His father always reminded him the winters had been *far* worse before the oceans rose. The new, much smaller Duluth—really just a village now—was built on hills overlooking the old town—mostly submerged now or soot-streaked heaps of crumbling brick as land reverted to bog. During the brief summers a small but growing number of tourists came to scuba-dive through the submerged lower floors of the ancient Heritage and Arts Center and the Fond-du-Luth Casino.

As he held on to Annie for dear life, Arroyo was filled with joy that those memories had welled up unbidden.

And then it dawned on him: *he had no clue where his parents were.* He couldn't remember the last time he had spoken with them. He wanted to scream. But he was on a work channel with Annie; his scream would have terrified her.

* * *

Annie pulled to a gentle stop when they reached the end of the smooth ice and the start of the chaos terrain. She shut off the ignition and flicked on all the engine heaters so the scootmobile would start easily later. Arroyo climbed stiffly off the back; it was not easy in his EVA suit and he had to grab Annie's arm to keep from falling.

When he had stood up and done a quick suit diagnostic, Annie turned to him. "Look familiar?"

Endless kilometers of tall, teetering penitentes and jumbled ice boulders stretched into the grey distance. The tiny Sun was low over the horizon; the jagged ice cast cleaver-sharp, impenetrable shadows. A faint glow in the distance announced that Io would soon climb over the horizon. Arroyo took it all in,

Jim Fairchild

breathing deeply—as if somehow, despite being encased in the suit and helmet, he might catch a familiar scent.

"Yes. It looks familiar." Arroyo began to walk out into the jumbled ice, oblivious to the fact he had left Annie behind him. She let him get ahead a few paces, then followed.

A couple of old route-marking flags stuck out of the ice a meter apart, the flags faded and tattered by radiation. Arroyo knew this place. He had marked it last winter. This is where he would start his ambles in search of Pegleg.

Arroyo's heart leapt. It felt like a homecoming.

He began to walk faster. He slipped and stumbled occasionally, knowing he should slow down. "*Easy*, Old Man," Annie admonished him. "Don't fall and break a hip. Or tear your diaper."

Arroyo reached a gentle rise amidst the jumbled ice. The glow of Io was getting brighter, the shadows not so impenetrable. Arroyo looked down at the ice around him; he could see the faint scratches left by low-g boots. "I would wait here until I could spot Pegleg, and then I would wave him in."

"That's right," Annie said. "This is where you and I and Pegleg sat together last Christmas. You laid out a tablecloth. We sipped Scotch and sang carols and it seemed like Pegleg was trying to dance."

"Do you think he's still around?"

"I *know* he's still around. Every time I've been out to Discovery Bay since you left, I've come out here at least once to watch. I'll see plenty of Tetras coming and going. But there is one that seems to lurk behind an ice hummock more than a kilometer out. If you're patient, I'll bet another Maine lobster that we'll see a little black triangle rise up from time to time, or stick out from the side of a penitente. I *swear* that it's Pegleg, watching for you."

Arroyo was filled with wonder. He felt like a kid the night

160

before Christmas, waiting for Santa Claus. He lowered himself down so that he could sit with his back against an ice boulder. Annie sat beside him.

"Do we have binoculars in the scootmobile's cargo box?" he asked.

Annie shook her helmet in the negative. "I know you won't care for this suggestion, but if you turn on your iMind you can use the zoom function."

Arroyo, faithfully following a safety SOP, always wore his old iMind while suited up. It was there as a back-up comms system. Of course, Arroyo's was turned off. The newer models had a wireless link with the suit's wrist keypad and could be turned on with the touch of a gloved finger. Arroyo had to bang his old 2.0 against a speaker bracket inside his helmet. Sometimes he could hit the ON button on the first try. Sometimes, like now—shaking with excitement—he had to bang his head several times to find the sweet spot.

"Don't hurt yourself," Annie said. "FYI, Amazon has a great deal on last year's 6.0 right now. You wouldn't have to knock yourself unconscious to turn it on."

Arroyo's right ear was suddenly filled with an annoying squeal, then almost a minute of chirps, cheeps, peeps, chirrups and twitters as the ancient electronics warmed up and re-booted. Suddenly a glaringly ugly pink and fuschia start-up screen appeared suspended against the chaos terrain in front of him. The colors reminded him of the neon signs over any one of a dozen family restaurants with all-you-can-eat botulism buffets on the Kardashia Strip. Arroyo flinched and tried to turn away, but wherever he turned his head, there was the iMind logo and scrolling copyright and trademark information.

A strident buzzer went off in his ear as the iMind reached the main menu. Arroyo frantically waved his right hand in the air, scrolling through endless sub-menus, trying to shut off the buzzer.

161

Jim Fairchild
Finally, he got a visual prompt:

INBOX EXCEEDS STORAGE CAPACITY.
PLEASE DELETE UNNEEDED MESSAGES
OR CONTACT iMIND™ CUSTOMER SERVICE
TO PURCHASE ADDITIONAL STORAGE.
☺HAVE A GREAT DAY!☺

YOU HAVE 1,911 MESSAGES
FLAGGED *URGENT*
☺HAVE A GREAT DAY!☺

Arroyo swept at the projected images to acknowledge his inbox's dire straight. He declined an offer to be immediately linked to iMind Customer Service. He opted to check for software updates later. Finally, he reached the utilities menu. He found the eyepiece zoom function. Just as his sense of joy had turned almost completely to frustration, he got his eyepiece set on ZOOM.

He began to scan the ice hummock that Annie had pointed out. They sat together, leaning against each other for the illusion of shared body heat. They sat for almost half an hour, Annie patient but Arroyo antsy with excitement. They both tapped their wrist keypads from time to time to crank up their suit heat. Sitting still in minus 160 degrees C. asked a lot of even the best of EVA suits, of which the old, beat-up Company suits on Europa were not.

Annie squeezed Arroyo's arm. She whispered into her helmet microphone. "*There.* Just to the left of the highest point. Did you see it?"

"Yes. *Yes.*" Arroyo jumped up despite creaky, cold joints. He began to jump up and down and wave.

"Don't scare it." Annie, still sitting, reached for Arroyo's leg to steady herself, then stood beside him.

The little black point vanished almost as suddenly as it had

162

appeared. Arroyo stopped jumping and waving. He watched. And waited. A minute later, a little black triangle, modestly larger than the first, popped up from above a hummock a hundred meters closer.

Arroyo and Annie waited. Every minute or so the black triangle appeared again briefly, peering over a rise. Then it would vanish again, and appear another hundred meters closer. Arroyo was so excited he held Annie's hand. She didn't seem to mind. He could feel her give him a gentle squeeze through their thick gloves.

Then, no more than twenty meters away, a spot of black began to peek out from the side of a penitente. It was the base of a jet-black equilateral triangle, shimmying awkwardly sideways out from cover, a centimeter at a time.

Io popped gloriously above the horizon like a long-forgotten hope. The shadows amongst the penitentes shrank back and disappeared into their hiding places. For a moment the black triangle seemed alarmed and shimmied back behind the penitente.

And then it emerged into the light.

It was a Tetra. Arroyo moved cautiously forward a step. The Tetra waddled forward the same distance. Annie stayed just behind Arroyo. They played this game—a step forward, a pause, a step forward—until only a couple of meters separated them.

"*Pegleg*," Arroyo whispered over his external helmet speaker.

"Can it even hear you?" Annie asked. "I thought they didn't have sensory organs. Are you sure it's Pegleg?"

Arroyo slowly squatted and studied the lower corners of the Tetra. He could see the scars where the creature had once been snared in a cable. The scars were an ugly reminder of the casual cruelty of Science.

"It's Pegleg," he said, smiling broadly behind his visor. "I'd recognize it anywhere. And not just because of the scars.

163

Jim Fairchild

Have you ever read about people being reunited with a pet that had disappeared years ago and thousands of kilometers away? There's a bond that can't be broken. *You just know.*"

Arroyo and Annie sat down on the ice with Pegleg. Io climbed upward into the sky. For awhile the shadows were gone. "Tell me what you've been up to, old buddy," Arroyo said, laughing, though tears streamed down his cheeks and began to fog his visor.

"The wound looks better since the last time I got a close look," Annie said.

"Yeah. It shows the capacity to heal. I know that the jury is still out as to whether Tetras are life as we define it. *I* think Pegleg is *very* alive."

Arroyo stared at the featureless black hide, trying to spot some vestige of sensory organs. He had no clue how the Tetra found its way about in so brutal an environment. And research had indicated that the Tetras spent the majority of their time *beneath* the ice. That part of their existence—far down in the utterly black sea—was almost a complete mystery.

Annie reached over and patted Arroyo on the shoulder. "I'm glad you two got to see each other again." She glanced at her wrist keypad. "Old Man, it's almost three in the morning. We should get back to camp and catch a few winks. The long days aren't over. Now that the beakers are gone we still need to build loads for the traverse back to Mactown and take all the camp systems off-line."

Arroyo rose up on his knees. He couldn't remember being this happy before. "I promise to be back," he told the creature. Without thinking, he reached over and patted Pegleg good-bye.

Arroyo felt as if he had grabbed a live megawatt cable. An overwhelming jolt coursed through his body. The hair on the back of his neck stood up; his mouth foamed. His body convulsed as if he had leapt into an icy lake. A reflex made him yank his hand

164

away.

It was Christmas in Duluth. He was ten years old. "You're going to have to feed it and water it and clean up the poop," his mother said. He had just brought home his first dog, a collarless stray mixed terrier he named Chrissie. It had been wandering through the icy streets down by the new Lake Walk, hungry and ice-caked and shivering in the merciless wind raging off the lake. "I know, Mom. I know." His mother tousled his hair. "And remember never to take it out on the ice with you."

"Are you okay, Arroyo?"

Arroyo stepped back a moment. He hadn't thought of Chrissie in years. He couldn't remember what happened to the dog.

"Arroyo?"

"I'm okay. When I touched Pegleg I had a clear rush of memory from when I was a kid. I have no clue what just happened." He began to reach toward Pegleg again.

"I wouldn't do that, Arroyo."

Arroyo gently touched Pegleg with the tip of a finger.

The flames leapt skyward through the greasy brush. A relentless wind off the coast pushed the conflagration toward Arroyo and the rest of his patrol. Somewhere on the far side of the wall of flames was supposed to be a squatter camp of Thumper stragglers. Rather than give up, they had set fire to their camp. Mass suicide by immolation. The fire would accomplish the patrol's mission without any weapons being employed. Arroyo turned his head away from the flames, trying to spot the rest of his squad, somewhere ahead in the thick pall of rolling smoke.

Something leapt out of the flames and ran toward Arroyo. He swung the barrel of his carbine toward it. It was a skinny

Jim Fairchild

mongrel dog, panting frantically, its back on fire. It was running straight for Arroyo, its eyes pleading for help. Arroyo's trigger finger had a mind of its own, developed through endless training. He squeezed off two rounds and put down the pathetic animal, still aflame.

Something else leapt out of the flames. A man this time: a rusted machete in one hand, a tarnished crucifix in the other. His roughly woven tunic exploded in flames on his back; he lifted his machete high above his head. Arroyo had never seen so much hate chiselled into a face before. In the fraction of a second it took Arroyo's trigger finger to act, Arroyo could see strips of burned flesh hanging from the man's arms. The tunic was almost gone; the man was naked beneath. Arroyo could see a grapefruit-sized blister where the man's genitals had been. Arroyo's finger efficiently squeezed off two rounds into the center of mass. The man crumpled in a heap to the scorched earth. Arroyo leaned into the heat and pumped one more into the man's cranium. The man lay dead like smouldering roadkill. Arroyo suddenly realized he was out of breath. He had held it while his finger and lower brain stem did their work. He sucked in several lungfuls of thick, acrid smoke. He gagged, then wiped his mouth on the back of his fast-rope gloves.

And then the wall of flames parted again. A flaming kangaroo leapt toward him. He swung the flash suppressor of his carbine and reflexively squeezed two tightly grouped rounds into the kangaroo's chest.

Fiberfill batting drifted to the ground. The toy kangaroo, shredded by the carbine rounds, dropped to the ground. A small girl, perhaps ten years old, stood before him. Her blond hair and flowered dress were engulfed in flames. Two scarlet flowers began to blossom across her chest. She looked down at her destroyed toy, then looked up at Arroyo. Then she collapsed onto her rear end. She sat for a moment like a flaming ragdoll on a shelf. She

166

stared up at Arroyo with a look of hopeless confusion. Her blistered hands fell into her lap. Her soot-covered face was frozen in a permanent silent scream. It was the same scream he now wore tattooed on his back. Her head fell backward and she pitched into a burning bush. Arroyo leaned forward into the heat again and pumped a final gift of savage mercy into her head. He wiped his mouth. He screamed into the smoke and the wind. He screamed, and he screamed, but there was nobody or nothing to answer him.

Arroyo staggered back. He fell to the ice beside Annie. "Oh my God. *What have I done?*"

Annie grabbed Arroyo by his backpack and tried to pull him away from Pegleg. "We need to get you out of here, Old Man." She punched a button on Arroyo's wrist keypad to scan his vitals.

"I'm okay," Arroyo insisted. "It's not Pegleg's fault." He rose to a knee. But as Annie tried to tug him toward the scootmobile, Arroyo stretched out with his free arm. He lightly brushed Pegleg again with a fingertip.

He was with Misty, his girlfriend. It was another Christmas. They were down by the lakefront. They held hands despite the cold. An amazing ice castle rose before them. It was lit from within. The most elusive, gentle opaline light radiated through the ice. Arroyo would later see the same gentle color in sastrugi and crevasses in Antarctica. "It's the most beautiful thing I've ever seen," Misty told Arroyo, squeezing his hand. "I'll never forget this moment. I love you."

Annie helped Arroyo into the galley. She poured him a cup of coffee. They both still had their suits on, leaving their helmets and backpacks and gloves in a heap beside the airlock. Arroyo's hair was matted with sweat.

Annie helped Arroyo into a chair and sat beside him. She rubbed his shoulder. "Can you tell me what happened out there?"

Arroyo clasped his hands around the coffee but they trembled too much to take a drink. "Pegleg has the power to help me remember things. Things I've been wanting to remember. But maybe I also see why they've been hidden from me."

"Are we in danger from the Tetras?"

"*No,*" Arroyo said. "*Anything but.* I think it was trying to heal me."

Fran, bleary-eyed, walked into the galley. "Didn't you two lovebirds ever go to bed? That's exactly where I left you before my nappy-nap." Then he saw the color of Arroyo's face, the matted hair, the trembling hands. "Oh, buddy. Did you get into the Trank last night?"

Joy and Ellen stepped into the galley. They looked at Arroyo. Without saying a word they stepped to the table and gave him hugs.

* * *

After a catnap Annie and Arroyo joined the others. They were building loads on HMW sleds. One sled was stacked high with instrument cases belonging to the Torheit gravity survey group; another held the gear of the Angstrom exobiology group. The most precious items—data logs, hard drives, journals—were tucked into Tillerman's tractor cab for safekeeping during the long, rough ride back to Mactown. There, the items would be turned over to the science groups—if they were even still in Mactown. They might be onboard the *Khlebnikov* bound for Ganymede or in stasis by the time the traverse got back, for all anyone knew. Annie had been in near-constant communication via iMind with Consuelo; Consuelo reported that everyone in Mactown was entering the stasis lottery, but no "winners" had been announced yet.

Fran, helping to load sleds when not running back to the galley to check on lunch preparation, announced his own plan. He had already iMinded his former boss at Drumpf Tower in Kardashia, and had been offered his old job back, provided he didn't mind making taco bowls. He had gladly accepted. He hoped that the job offer would assure him a ride to Ganymede and not to the stasis chambers. "I've got to warn you guys and gals. If you come to Drumpf Tower for lunch, do not—I repeat *do not*—order the taco bowl. I'll be adding my own special ingredient: a fresh Cleveland Steamer."

A flitter had touched down while Annie and Arroyo were napping. It dropped off two cargo handlers, Sonia and Ryan. They were experts at building loads, and the work went quickly with them assisting the Geriatric Crew.

By late morning almost half of the load-building was done. Annie stood nearby, speaking with Consuelo via iMind. The rest of the crew were taking a break, sitting against the cases remaining to be loaded. A bright point of light appeared high above the horizon, then approached on a downward trajectory from orbit. Soon, the light became a flickering arrow of orange and blue flame. It arced directly over Discovery Bay, perhaps twenty kilometers up. A sonic boom—weaker than a sonic boom on Earth, but impressive nonetheless—passed.

Annie pointed up. "The *Khlebnikov*. Coming in hot. A Sturm is on the horizon." She squatted near Arroyo. "Take a look beyond the parked scootmobile," she said.

Arroyo glimpsed the tip of a jet-black triangle peeking over the scootmobile. Within an hour, Pegleg was following Arroyo wherever he went.

* * *

Shortly before noon Fran got on the camp channel. "Testing. Testing. Is this thing on?" Then followed several loud *booms* as Fran banged on the microphone. "Attention Discovery Bay Camp: lunch will be served in fifteen minutes. I repeat, lunch will be served in fifteen minutes. That is all. Carry on." It was a play on an ancient pre-Crash television show called "M*A*S*H" that both Fran and Arroyo enjoyed watching.

Lunch was simple but hearty. Fran had already boxed up most of his cookware and any perishable foods had either been eaten or disposed of in preparation for closing down the camp. The crew leaned over their steaming soup and thick sandwiches— on bread Fran had baked early that morning—too exhausted to chat.

Sonia, one of the cargo handlers, sat next to Arroyo. He had seen her around Mactown; she was perhaps a year into her first contract. "I saw that Tetra following you around," she said. "Very cute."

"That's Pegleg," Arroyo said, taking a huge bite of pastrami and gouda on rye. "He's an old pal of mine."

"During stasis orientation we learned about the NSWF's *Protocols on Flora and Fauna*," Sonia said. She picked a dangling piece of sauerkraut from her sandwich and flicked it onto her plate. "If we are close enough to wildlife to elicit a reaction, we are *too close*. The protocols recommend keeping a minimum distance of one hundred meters. That Tetra follows you like a dog."

Arroyo looked across the table at Wyatt, who rolled his eyes and shrugged. Arroyo put down his sandwich. "I know the protocols. 'That Tetra' is Pegleg. I saved it from a wire snare last winter."

"*That's impossible*," Sonia said. "The protocols expressly prohibit the killing or maiming of native species, or any interaction that might alter their natural behavior patterns. No grantee would harm an animal."

Arroyo looked across at Wyatt, then Ellen, then Joy, then Tom Tillerman, hoping for support. All he got were winks and shrugs. "I've got to talk to a man about a horse," Wyatt said, rising and taking his plate. "See you folks outside." Arroyo had lost his appetite. He grabbed his plate and followed. Suited up again, Arroyo climbed through the airlock and up the stairwell. Outside, Pegleg sat patiently nearby, and waddled along behind Arroyo as he returned to work.

* * *

By late afternoon the loads were assembled. The crew busied itself with odds and ends. The two cargo handlers along with Tillerman, Ellen and Joy were rolling and tucking away cargo strap ends so they wouldn't catch under the sleds on the way back. Wyatt and Arroyo fueled the tractors and did pre-ops checks before the departure planned for the next morning.

Annie walked over to the tractors. Even through her helmet visor Arroyo could see that she was agitated. "Are you okay?" he asked.

"No. Bryon Sturm hit the ground running when he got to Mactown. He's infuriated by the chaos. He isn't satisfied with the stasis lottery Barry Wilton set up. Sturm started walking around with his entourage, singling people out and telling them to report to Darla Hovenweep to be scheduled for the stasis chambers. He walked into a lounge and found a janitor taking a nap. The poor kid had just been up for 36 hours, doing his job as well as packing everything he owns. Sturm kicked the kid in the foot to wake him up, told him he obviously didn't have enough to keep himself busy, and told him to report to HR for immediate stasis scheduling. He's being followed around by Darla, who keeps entering names on her iMind for early stasis."

Jim Fairchild

"It's off to zee chambers mit dir, mein Freund," Wyatt said.

"I'm sorry to tell you this," Annie said to Wyatt, "but Sturm walked past the post office and asked why it hadn't been shut down yet. He said no more personal packages would be arriving on Europa from Ganymede, so there was no need for a postmaster. Your wife Coretta has been told to report for stasis scheduling."

Arroyo could see a dark cloud descend over Wyatt's eyes. "I've had my iMind turned off all day," he said. "If you ladies and gentlemen will excuse me, I need to get ahold of Coretta." He stepped quickly away.

Annie took Arroyo by the arm and lead him a distance from the others. They switched to a private channel. "Consuelo's been ordered to report for stasis scheduling, too," she said. "She was still in town, preparing to head out to Marble Point tomorrow to close down that camp. She was part of a group that greeted Sturm when he got to Mactown. She was wearing a T-shirt that said *Europa for Europans.* He thought it was some sort of political statement, and had Hovenweep add her name to the list for early stasis. I doubt Consuelo even gave the message much thought. She probably thought it was funny. She's got one of those useless interdisciplinary Liberal Arts degrees, for god's sake. It's important for her to be brash and offensive and on the cutting edge of things."

And she's more than a bit naïve, Arroyo thought. Especially when the slogan had a connotation not lost on those few who still read history. "She's a smart, resourceful person," Arroyo said. "There are hidey-holes all over Mactown's grotto. Maybe she can disappear into one."

Annie chuckled bitterly. "The word around the hive is that there isn't enough Z-Gas in stock in Mactown to put 500 people into stasis. Normally only a couple dozen people are put into stasis for any outgoing Earthbound vessel. We've never had to do a mass-evacuation before. There might be a hundred doses total on Europa. Every dose available on Ganymede has been requisitioned, but it could take up to a week to arrive. Fistfights have been breaking out in the galley and outside the HR office. Everyone is arguing about who should be put into stasis first. People have been secretly going to Darla and ratting out neighbors who haven't signed up for the lottery."

Like ratting out your Jewish neighbors to the Gestapo, Arroyo thought.

Annie saved the worst for last. "Sturm brought muscle. He's got six gunslingers from the Ganymede police force with him to 'maintain order.' They're wearing body armor under white camouflage and carry full combat loads of arms and ammo around town. They follow Sturm in a phalanx. When Darla isn't with Sturm, two of the goons provide personal protection for her."

* * *

The glum crew sat in the galley over their dinner of leftover Chili Mac. Most of the food stocks had been packed; Fran apologized for the Chili Mac, but assured everyone he hadn't used any secret ingredient. The news Annie had been getting was getting uglier by the hour. A large brawl had erupted in the galley back in Mactown when Sturm tried to hold a town meeting. A sugar shaker had been thrown at him by someone in the crowd; it narrowly missed his head. The goons from the Ganymede police force waded into the crowd, the majority of whom had been sitting quietly for the presentation. Stun guns and whip batons were used against dozens of innocent people, and blood from split scalps and faces had splattered everywhere.

Sonia broke the silence. "I'm sure Bryon felt threatened. Imagine having a sugar shaker thrown at you. When people get out of control they deserve what they get."

Wyatt, who had been silent ever since getting ahold of Coretta on his iMind earlier, stood and pushed away from the table. He looked across the table and smiled drily at the young cargo handler. "Madame, there is a popular quote often misattributed to both Abraham Lincoln and Mark Twain, the genesis of which is likely Proverbs 17:28. The secularized version is more pithy and humorous than the biblical: *Better to remain silent and be thought a fool than to speak and to remove all doubt.* Sincerest salutations and good evening to all." Wyatt picked up his plate and began to leave.

"I never knew you were a religious man," Arroyo said, pushing back his chair and following.

"Not in the the slightest, my friend. Although I *did* attend seminary for two years before going to war. What I saw there punctured all such delusory pursuits for me. I spent many years afterward trying to purge scriptural quotes from my mind with every intoxicant known to man, but the occasional biblical reference still slips out from a dark, dank hole."

The two men silently scraped their plates clean, then left the Jamesway for the chill of the grotto. They suited up, clambered through the airlock and ascended the stairwell. On the surface, Pegleg was awaiting, and closely followed. The men walked side-by-side to the living module, both too lost in thought to make small talk. At the module, Pegleg waddled to a halt and settled down just outside the airlock as if on guard duty. Once the men climbed into the module and unsuited again, they found they had the place to themselves. Arroyo made himself a cup of cocoa, then began to gingerly flip through another of his crumbling Louis L'Amour novels. Wyatt watched Ganymede through a viewport over the sink stacked high with dirty dishes.

Arroyo gingerly closed his book. "Wyatt, may I ask you a personal question?"

"You may ask, of course. Depending upon how personal it

is, I may or may not elect to respond with complete candor." By the smile Arroyo knew Wyatt was joshing.

"I served in the early days of the Australian Thumper campaign," Arroyo said. "I understand you were one of the survivors of the Lost Garrison of Rawalpindi. You can stop me any time."

Wyatt, still standing, gazed toward Ganymede. "That was another lifetime, my friend. That wasn't really *me* at all." He gripped the edge of the counter with both hands.

"Lately I've been remembering some things I did in Australia," Arroyo said. He spoke as if each word were a shard of glass. "I'm not sure how I've hidden them from myself all these years. And now that I remember, I'm not sure I can live with myself."

Wyatt rocked back and forth. He looked at the pile of dirty dishes in front of him, and began to draw hot water. He squirted detergent into the sink and watched the suds climb.

"I—or that person I used to be—was, indeed, part of the Rawalpindi garrison. I am a very, very, lucky man to be here today with you in this squalid little pressurized box on this squalid little moon. The fact that I'm alive today still fills me with an incredible sense of wonder."

"Do you ever talk about your escape?"

Wyatt stood with his back to Arroyo, scrubbing a plate. "I tried to tell Coretta about it after we had been dating for a time. I felt it important to let her know why I sometimes disappear into a dark place. I wanted her to know that even when the past calls me away for a spell, her love is the most treasured thing in the universe to me."

"Did you ever succeed in telling her?"

"Not in so many words. I didn't want to hurt her. I felt that by speaking about those memories, I wouldn't just relive them myself, but I would make them *real* for anyone who listened. My nightmares would become *their* nightmares. I didn't want to inflict that upon another human, no matter how much I might benefit by talking about it. For years I thought it best to take those memories to the grave with me."

"That had to eat you alive," Arroyo said.

"*Certainement*," Wyatt said, rinsing the plate. "I knew I had to confront the memories. So at first I thought I'd write a horror novel. I would describe the things I did escaping from Rawalpindi under the guise of fiction. I would take the weight of the things I had done off my own shoulders and place that burden on a hapless character in a book few would ever read. And for those who *did* read that book, they would never know which events I had actually experienced, and which were pure fiction. Only I would know. But after several attempts, I realized I was a better farmer than a writer. So I gave up.

"After many years, I've found that I can discuss Rawalpindi and the months afterward if I ascribe my actions to an imaginary friend. I then can tell a tale about the unfortunate things my friend had to do in order to get back to the ones he loved half a world away." Wyatt put down the plate and looked out the viewport. He was silent a moment, as if filled with wonder at the sight of Ganymede, although he had seen it thousands of times.

"We can stop now," Arroyo said. He could see that Wyatt was slipping away into darkness.

"No, Arroyo. It's okay. I haven't told my friend's tale in years. Maybe it's time to tell it again."

The Crash years saw two inevitable nuclear conflagrations. One killed millions of Koreans on both sides of the DMZ and wiped one of the two Koreas off the map. Resurgent Siberian tigers now ruled the northern half of the peninsula. The other conflagration, in South Asia, made what happened on the Korean Peninsula seem like child's play. When India and Pakistan unleashed their nuclear arsenals on each other, perhaps a billion people perished, directly or indirectly. Both governments collapsed, so no reliable records of deaths were compiled; historians can only guess at the toll. The destruction of infrastructure and the collapse of agriculture led to at least as many deaths as the nuclear exchange and fallout. All major urban centers were turned to twisted steel and ash; the percentage of the population lost in both countries was more dramatic than what occurred in Europe during the plagues of the 14th century. In the countryside, tens of millions of survivors wandered aimlessly, looting what they could, eating rats and insects and each other. Pakistan had already been overwhelmed before the war by the frantic influx of hundreds of millions of fellow Muslims from Bangladesh after most of that country disappeared under the rising oceans.

Sadly, the first institutions to reconstitute were religious militias. Muslims to the northwest, Hindus to the southeast: the militias were constantly on the march, like plagues of locusts, commandeering anything edible for their members, leaving the local populations to starve, senselessly torching anything that had been left standing after the nuclear exchange. Soon the two sides were locked in fearsome, hate-fueled battles, torturing, executing and mutilating prisoners by the thousands. They proudly broadcast their grisly handiwork for the rest of the world to watch. Each side blamed the other for the incineration of South Asia. At least they had no nuclear stockpiles left.

The constant images of slaughter turned the stomachs of the rest of the world. Although Europe and the Americas had their own problems re-building after the Crash, Western do-gooders argued for a collective military intervention in South Asia. Politicians—as is generally the case—had little grasp of history. In the first decades of the 22nd century, brigades of Western peacekeepers established beachheads up the coast from the

Jim Fairchild

incinerated remains of Mumbai. As units of the early interventions spread out in all directions,they passed the charred remains of India's once-grand cities. They were now populated by more dogs than people. The people were bone-thin, the dogs fat and happy and not to be trusted. The somber Westerners sought out clusters of survivors, hoping to start the long process of rebuilding infrastructure. In their obsession for revenge, neither Muslims nor Hindus had made more than gestures to restore water, power, roads or hospitals.

The incessant butchery had been going on for almost two hundred years by the time Wyatt turned twenty and answered the perpetual call to arms. Seven generations of Westerners had spilled blood in South Asia and had brought only a few years of enforced peace at a time. After a year of training, Wyatt joined a brigade composed of both American and Brit volunteers. Their mechanized convoy rolled slowly northward as part of the latest intervention, their aim the remains of Rawalpindi, Pakistan. The city's charred and twisted ruins were still uncleared; an impressive star-shaped firebase was built on the flats to the south, overlooking the Indus River.

Gath, Lachish, Constantinople, Tyre, Dien Bien Phu, Kafriya, New Bradbury: the commanding officers had apparently slept through Sieges 101 in military school, and were clueless about the dangers of garrisoned fortifications. They assumed that as peacekeepers they would be met with open arms. Instead, Muslim militias soon formed an arc on high ground to the west; Hindu militias moved into overlook positions to the east. The two warring sides tacitly agreed to eliminate the intruding Westerners before once more attacking each other.

The brutal bombardments from both sides went on for months. Western air forces were tiny compared to before the Crash, most of the world clinging to the delusion that the age of the Forever War would eventually pass like a fever dream. What

178

few resupply flights that could be mustered were harrassed by anti-aircraft fire from the warring factions. Overland resupply was out of the question. Politicians in expensive suits had limited the peacekeepers to light weaponry. Only a handful of armored units had been deployed, and they were already engaged elsewhere to the south. The use of robot soldiers had recently been banned by treaty after some programmed with lowest-bidder software had escaped from Fort Dix and run amok in New Jersey, slaughtering thousands of innocents.

Both sieging factions began to tighten their nooses. Employing techniques proven during World War I, zig-zagging entrenchments were painstakingly dug toward the increasingly hungry garrison. Observers atop the garrison's walls could see vast amounts of freshly excavated soil being moved rearward on all sides. Listening devices and what few drones that weren't shot down indicated that sappers were digging tunnels under the garrison's walls.

The British commanding officer negotiated a meeting with leaders of both factions outside the walls. When he and his aides sallied forth at the agreed-upon time, they were set upon by commandos from both Muslim and Hindu militias. The unarmed Westerners were slaughtered and hacked to pieces. Fighters from both sides fought with each other for gruesome trophies to hang from the twisted wreckage of railroad bridges and power poles.

After 147 days it was apparent the garrison would fall within hours. The new commanding officer wished his men Godspeed and then, in the privacy of his office, pulled the pin on a grenade clutched to his chest.

Wyatt and five others decided to take their fates into their own hands.

That night they squirmed nearly three kilometers through rat- and spider-infested sewer tunnels and culverts and ditches, managing to dodge the Hindu militias to the east. At daylight, they

Jim Fairchild

lost the cover of darkness. Their hope was to flee east to Kashmir, occupied for many years by China. China was a neutral nation, and the men hoped to find refuge there. But much of the terrain between Rawalpindi and the border was open scrubland. They should have gone to ground during the day. Instead, they kept moving. Four of them were picked off by snipers before the heat of midday. Wyatt and his sole companion pressed onward until they found refuge in the pit of an old outhouse. At dark they headed out again.

On the second day, Wyatt's companion collapsed from exhaustion. He told Wyatt to go on. He asked Wyatt if he wanted his New Testament and his final cigarette. But Wyatt had lost God in a foxhole—contrary to an old cliché—and he didn't smoke. After a few awkward words, they parted ways.

Wyatt stayed alive by breaking into farmhouses. He found a cache of rancid goat meat in one house and tucked it into his fatigue pockets. The meat stunk so badly he was afraid it would attract predators—either two-legged or four. He drank putrid water from slime-covered ditches.

On the fourth day the land began to rise ahead. He would have to cross a high line of mountains, their lower slopes already dusted with the first snows of autumn. The highest peaks were capped with permanent ice. He spied a notch that seemed to be the lowest and gentlest saddle. He hoped that Kashmir lay on the other side.

Wyatt climbed for three days. He tried to travel at night but some of the climbing was too dangerous to attempt in the dark. He slept under overhanging boulders and built no fires to avoid drawing attention. His rancid goat meat ran out. Finally, as darkness fell on the third day of climbing, the slope eased. Ahead, Wyatt could see the saddle. He staggered to the top.

A pass is a perilous place; it is almost always under observation by surrounding forces, as it is an obvious potential path for intruders. In an ideal world Wyatt would have skirted the pass somewhere upslope, but he was too exhausted, hungry and dehydrated. But at least he planned to avoid stopping until he had crested the pass and dropped safely down the other side.

Unfortunately, his plan didn't work.

A voice rang out in the darkness: 'Sat sree akaal!'

Wyatt, like the rest of the peacekeeping garrison, had been issued small Punjabi phrasebooks. He often read his during the worst of the siege's shelling; he'd exhausted every other book available early on. 'Sat sree akaal' was a universal greeting used for 'hello' or 'goodbye,' but it literally meant 'God is Truth.' It was the only Punjabi an exhausted Wyatt remembered, so he responded in kind. He knew that the voice in the darkness likely meant one of two imminent outcomes: death or salvation. He was too tired to flee. He staggered toward the voice.

Beside a tall boulder he found a sentry wrapped in blankets. His job was to watch the pass. Beside him was a dishevelled bedroll and a tattered rucksack. Wyatt could see the glow of a cigarette in the sentry's hand. The hand waved briskly, motioning Wyatt in his direction.

'Ki haal hai?' the man wrapped in blankets asked, then took a long drag on his cigarette.

Wyatt realized that these might be the last few minutes of his life. He wished he were back on the farm in Minnesota, buttoning things up before winter. The crisp air smelled of granite and lichens and snow on the way and the occasional foul whiff of stale tobacco smoke. A few flakes drifted gently down. It was the calm Wyatt remembered just before a storm.

He staggered up to the sentry and held his hands loosely in front of him to show he was unarmed. 'I'm sorry,' Wyatt said. 'I don't speak Punjabi. I'm American.'

The sentry blew out a huge cloud of nauseating smoke, then tossed the exhausted butt into the dark. 'American? America never

Jim Fairchild

learns. No worries, my friend. Praise Allah, I am Kyrgyz. I studied civil engineering at Montana State. Where do you hail from?'

'Minnesota.'

'Oh, my brother. Wheat. Corn. Knob and kettle country. Ten thousand lakes. The Humana Colony. God's will be done. Do you have a cigarette?'

Wyatt patted his pockets. They contained his military ID, a photograph of his dead parents, and a hand-written map he had sketched with a stub of charcoal on the third day of his escape when he had tried to remember the border country. 'I'm sorry. No cigarettes.'

'Come now,' the sentry said. In the growing darkness Wyatt could see that his new friend had an ancient M-16 with a mounted bayonet slung across his back. 'No Marlboro? No Winston? No Benson and Hedges? What good is an American without tobacco?'

Wyatt thought that the answer might be 'dead.' 'We outlawed smoking a couple of hundred years ago. Now we just sell it to the rest of the world.'

'God bless capitalism, eh? And where are you off to this fine evening?' The sentry clumsily unslung his M-16; Wyatt ducked as the tip of the old bayonet swung past his face in the dark. For a moment he thought things were reaching the inevitable climax. But the sentry propped the rifle with the butt on the ground, the barrel and bayonet against his hip.

'I'm a mountaineer,' Wyatt said, stalling. 'I got lost. I figured I could find help in Kashmir.'

The sentry pulled back the blankets from around his shoulders and began to dig through his pockets in desperation for a cigarette. 'Bullshit, as I was taught to say in Bozeman. You are fleeing from the garrison in Rawalpindi. I was sent here to watch for you.'

182

'You've got me there, my friend.' Wyatt would not die without a fight. 'How shall we play this out?'

'If you had a cigarette, we could share a smoke and discuss that matter. Perhaps we would smoke and then I would let you walk into the darkness toward Kashmir. I would warn you that it is still a long way.'

Wyatt could make no more small talk. He grabbed for the barrel of the rifle, still propped against the sentry's leg. The sentry flinched. The rifle began to fall toward Wyatt, bayonet tip first. Wyatt jumped out of the way. The sentry lunged for his falling rifle. In the darkness, he missed his target. The tip of the bayonet plunged into the tender inside of the man's wrist with a horrendous tearing sound; even in the darkness, Wyatt could see half of the bayonet's length poke out the outer side of the sentry's wrist.

The sentry yanked back his hand reflexively, pulling the bayonet out of his wrist. The ancient rifle clattered to the rocks. As his wounded arm swung upward, an arcing geyser of blood pumped out. Wyatt was nearly blinded by the warm spray. He could hear the staccato sound of blood splattering onto the rocky ground like water arcing out of a raised garden hose. The blood all over Wyatt's face tasted like copper.

For a fraction of a second Wyatt thought of rendering first aid. In the next fraction of a second he lunged for the rifle again. The Kyrgyz struggled fiercely even as his life pumped out of his wrist. At one point the bayonet whipped past Wyatt's head and slashed across his scalp. His own blood ran down his face and commingled with that of his opponent. The Kyrgyz finally staggered and dropped to his back in the darkness.

'Finish me, brother.'

Wyatt obliged him. He laid the man open like a butterflied tenderloin.

Wyatt caught his breath. When his hands stopped trembling enough to use them, he reached up and found a ragged

Jim Fairchild

flap of flesh the size of a pancake hanging loosely on his scalp. He dug through the dead man's rucksack for a first aid kit, but found none. He found a canteen with the dregs of what might have been spoiling goat milk. He drank it in one gulp. He found a compass and a cell phone. He opened the phone but the battery was dead. In a side pocket of the rucksack he found a single Marlboro in a cellophane wrapper, crumpled but smokable. He tossed it beside the dead man. He removed the man's bootlaces to tie his scalp in place, then took the man's wool hat and gingerly pulled it over his head to hold everything together. He walked another 150 kilometers before encountering a Chinese patrol. A military doctor at the Chinese internment camp reattached his scalp with 47 staples. The doctor picked head lice off Wyatt while he stapled.

The Chinese treated him humanely if not extravagantly. They eventually repatriated him via a flight to Switzerland. He had run low on reading material in the Chinese camp, finally reading Mao Zedong's 'Little Red Book.' He found the man one more in an endless line of insufferably arrogant elitists who were responsible for millions of deaths. But Wyatt agreed with one Mao quote: 'Of course, religion is poison.' When he was handed off to a Red Cross representative at the Geneva airport, his sole possessions were the book and a packet of three Chinese cigarettes that had been rationed to internees. Wyatt left the book in a trash can in Geneva. But he had carried the cigarettes ever since, across half the solar system, in hopes that a chance meeting with a stranger might end on a positive note because he had them.

Wyatt still stood gazing at Ganymede as he finished his tale. He was lost in thought a moment; Arroyo didn't want to disturb him. It was as if Wyatt were gazing unflinchingly back in time, at a young man he had once been, and at something horrible he had once done. He absently reached into a shirt pocket and pulled out his ever-present plastic comb. He ran it carefully

184

through his hair, a ritual he performed so often it was a joke to some. He carefully patted down the results and put the comb away. Arroyo could see only a hint of jagged white scar. The Chinese military doctor had done an outstanding job.

Finally, Wyatt turned around and faced Arroyo. "Did you have a tale of your own you needed to tell me?" Wyatt asked. He smiled like a wise father.

"Ask me again in ten years," Arroyo said. "How did you move on once you got back to Minnesota?"

"At first I was like you. I tried to drink myself to a slow death. I got into fights. I shrank away from everyone I had ever known and everyone who had ever loved me. I kept seeing that bayonet sticking out of that gentleman's arm, and I would wake at night tasting copper.

"And then I woke up one morning after almost a decade of self-induced oblivion. I was done drinking. It was as simple as that. If I continued, I would soon be dead, and I would be causing one more ripple of sorrow in the sea of grief called Life. I had a responsibility—out of sheer decency—to stay alive for the ones who loved me. I found a kind, decent person to love. You can do that, too, Arroyo. Love will help you get outside of your head, my friend. Love will help keep your demons at bay."

"Do you realize that you didn't tell your story as if it were about a friend? You told it about yourself."

"Every day we grow, Young Buck," Wyatt said. "Every day the healing continues, *if* we allow it."

Wyatt sat finally. He reached across the table and tenderly picked up Arroyo's Louis L'Amour novel. "I used to love these when I was a kid." He set the book down carefully. He looked at Arroyo. "Those of us who know you don't know what you did before you came to Europa. Nor do we care. But we know what you've done *here*, and we know it far better than you do at the moment. You're a good man, Sir." Wyatt stood, rapped his knuckles on the table top, and began to step toward the door leading to his bunk.

"How's Coretta?" Arroyo asked.

Wyatt came to a halt. "She's been slated for stasis. There's enough Z-Gas in Mactown for perhaps a hundred folks. Unfortunately she made the list. Doctor Gianforte has been administering the pre-gas oral sedatives to those on the short list. It's been a long time since you've been in stasis, but you probably remember. They keep you stoned for a couple of days on sedatives to reduce anxiety before being gassed. Gianforte and Darla Hovenweep stand and watch while the sedatives are handed out to make sure nobody spits them out. Without the sedatives first, there used to be a certain percentage of panic-induced coronary arrests when the Z-Gas is administered."

"Any timeframe announced for the first folks to go into the chambers?"

"Three days," Wyatt said. "But Coretta says the whole town has descended into bedlam. And Gianforte, with the concurrence of Bryon Sturm, is handing out his precious stocks of sedatives like candy at Halloween, hoping to head off a full-blown insurrection."

"If the tractors head back in the morning, you'll be back to Mactown to see Coretta in time, no matter what happens."

"Roger that, my friend." Wyatt began to open the door to the sleeping compartment, but he remembered something in a pocket of his innermost shirt. He fished around and pulled it out. He tossed something onto the table in front of Arroyo.

Arroyo picked it up. It was a small vacuum-sealed plastic bag. Inside it, crumpled and almost unrecognizable, was a three-pack of cigarettes. Loose tobacco and shreds of cigarette paper partially obscured the package's label. Most of the label was in Chinese. It bore the image of a proud lion. Beneath the lion Arroyo could see some English:

TRUE FLAVOR

"I've carried those long enough," Wyatt said. "They've worn holes in countless shirt pockets. Would you toss them in the trash for me, Sir?"

* * *

Karen, the camp manager, called for a brief get-together in the galley before anyone slipped off to bed. She thanked everyone for their hard work, and told the Geriatric Crew that they were free to head back to Mactown with their loads in the morning. A flitter was scheduled to arrive mid-morning the next day to pick up Fran, Annie, Karen and the cargo handlers. The last things they would need to do would be to turn off the backup generator now powering the camp and to batten down the camp's hatches.

It had been tough getting a flitter lined up. The flitters were operated by a contract company, and it had been under orders to put its fleet to sleep and get its people ready for stasis just like the rest of the Mactown workforce. Most of their flitters had already been winterized and put to bed in their hangars by aviation mechanics who had been working for many days with only catnaps.

Annie spoke up. "I'd like to keep Arroyo here awhile after you leave. I know the generators and can cut the power and secure the hatches. We could do a thorough sweep of the camp for anything we might have forgotten, and then head back in Drag Queen. One of the other tractors could pull the living and generator modules. Without a load we could catch up with the other tractors in a few hours."

Karen paused and looked at Annie. It seemed an odd request, but she had worked with Annie and Arroyo for years.

Jim Fairchild

"Whatever you think best," Karen said. "There will be two of you so nobody will be travelling solo. Just make sure you have good comms with everyone."

Fran hadn't packed the contents of the liquor cabinet. He started to set bottles on a table. "Tonight I'm going to party like it's 2299," he sang. He reached into the air for a projected iMind music menu. He scrolled down with a flitting finger until he found the song he wanted. He synched his iMind to a set of beat-up speakers with at least one bad tweeter. Fran began to mix very dirty martinis to the ancient music of KC and the Sunshine Band:

> Shake Shake Shake
> Shake Shake Shake
> Shake your booty

Arroyo and Wyatt suited up and headed back toward the modules. The rest of the Geriatric Crew agreed to stay long enough for a polite sip. Karen, Annie, Fran and the cargo handlers stayed up late, partying like it was 1974.

* * *

Arroyo and Wyatt sat outside the living module on folding camp chairs, Pegleg between them. The sky was grey; Ganymede had set. Io was still just a faint hint of light on the far horizon, but would soon rise. In the greyness the harshness of the chaos terrain surrounding them dissolved. For the time being they didn't need to think about the two hard days of spine-jarring trail back to Mactown.

"It's been real," Arroyo said.

"And it's been fun," Wyatt said.

"But it hasn't been real fun," they said together. Pegleg waddled a centimeter or two closer to Arroyo's feet.

Tom Tillerman's helmeted head appeared at the top of the stairwell from the submerged camp. He climbed up and walked toward the modules, followed by Joy and Ellen.

"My goodness gracious," Joy said. "There are going to be some hurting puppies down there tomorrow morning."

"*Ah*, to be young again," Ellen said, laughing hoarsely like only a smoker can.

The late arrivals pulled up three more camp chairs and formed a loose circle with Arroyo, Wyatt and Pegleg. "Who has the jug of moonshine?" Ellen asked.

"Pegleg was supposed to bring it, I thought," Tillerman said. "What the deuce, Little Buddy? You're letting us down." He began to reach for Pegleg as if he were reaching to pet a friend's old Labrador retriever.

"I wouldn't do that," Arroyo insisted.

"What's the matter, Mr. Bronson?" Tillerman asked, feigning offense, gloved hands on hips. "You won't share your pet with us? That hound must eat you out of house and home. Music, anyone?"

The others nodded in the affirmative. Tillerman had jury-rigged a harmonica mount inside his helmet. Modifying a Company-issue suit was strictly against SOP, but Tillerman, a talented handyman, had carefully riveted the mount where it was out of the way of his radio microphone and drinking tube. Whenever he had the urge—which was often—he could lean toward his Hohner Marine Band harmonica and play a tune. He knew old blues, bluegrass, R&B, even Martian ska. He could pick up a tune after one hearing. He never infringed on others with his playing. Some operators, especially Arroyo, enjoyed silence. But some—again including Arroyo—had been brought out of deep funks when the going was tough when Tillerman switched on his helmet mike and began blowing an old Otis Redding or Sam Cooke tune.

189

Jim Fairchild

This time, it was an ancient folk number: "I Am a Man of Constant Sorrow." Tillerman made a false start: "Sorry, folks. I just had an Old Geezer moment. Let me try again."

"Turn on your external suit speaker for Pegleg," Arroyo said.

Tillerman wet his lips and tried again. The haunting song of pain and regret poured out of their helmet speakers. Ellen knew the lyrics and began to sing along. Arroyo sat back in awe.

> I am a man of constant sorrow
> I've seen trouble all my day
> I bid farewell to old Kentucky
> The place where I was born and raised
>
> For six long years I've been in
> trouble
> No pleasures here on earth I found
> For in this world I'm bound to
> ramble
> I have no friends to help me now

Tom Tillerman was still working on the chorus. Arroyo watched a tear streak down Ellen's face behind her helmet visor. Even Wyatt swayed gently in his chair. Io leapt above the horizon. In the blink of an eye Arroyo could begin to see a patchwork of light and shadow spread across the distant chaos terrain.

Something caught his eye. Pegleg had waddled closer; it seemed to be gently rocking with the music. Peglegs's scarred corner brushed Arroyo's low-g boot.

It was late March in Duluth, unseasonably warm, and the ice on the lake was getting too thin for fishing. A couple of foolhardy friends from middle school had taken one of their

190

father's Ski-Doos out on the lake anyway, hoping to catch some big ones. Arroyo had been walking Chrissie down by the shore. He and the dog scrambled and played amongst the jumbled blocks of ice that had pushed ashore during the winter. When Arroyo saw his buddies trying to lift the rear of the snowmobile out of a slushy hole fifty meters out, he knew he had to help. He didn't have Chrissie's leash. 'Stay by my side,' he told the dog. 'Be a good girl.' He waved and walked out to his friends, his boots sinking in to the ankles in slush. Chrissie, not happy getting wet and cold, followed along nevertheless. She and Arroyo were inseparable. He helped his friends lift the snowmobile out of the hole. He waved as they revved the engine, spraying him with slush, and left in a cloud of smoke. When he turned, Chrissie was gone. He called her name. He called her name again, and again, louder and louder. He found her pawprints. They veered off and followed a set of deer tracks. She had followed her nose. He stopped before he got to the hole in the ice, where both deer and dog had apparently fallen in. He kept screaming her name. She was gone forever, swallowed by the dark water.

Tillerman had finished his tune. "I need to rivet another mount in my helmet for a sponge. I've got spit everywhere." He looked across at Arroyo. "Are you okay, Old Man? You look like you saw a ghost."

"An old memory," Arroyo simply said. He sat up straight. *But of course that was how Chrissie disappeared. It was my fault.* He had suspected as much.

He wanted more. He gently nudged Pegleg with the toe of his boot.

Chrissie again: the morning she disappeared, like every morning, racing upstairs from her bed in the laundry room, leaping onto a sleeping Arroyo like a canine alarm clock, her tail wagging so fast it was a blur, licking his face like a liver lollipop. Ready for another joyous day with the human she loved.

Arroyo sighed. He forgot that his helmet mike was still on. The others glanced at him. "Thank you," he whispered to Pegleg. He reached over and stroked Pegleg's apex.

Falling. Falling. Falling faster and then even faster. Bouncing off the granite-hard walls of an icy chute, gravity pulling at him, the chute growing narrower. The tight chute twists and turns and Arroyo is bouncing around like a sack of rags. He passes horrible things splattered on the walls of the twisting chute that are so gruesome he must look away. He is falling headfirst now; he tries to slow himself with his gloved hands, but the acceleration is a matter of physics, beyond his will to stop. Something is pulling at his waist, threatening to cut him in two. He is being beaten to a pulp as he falls; he wants to stop the pain, but he must keep going downward. He is needed there. And then, far below him in the impossibly narrow, pitch-black chute, he sees a faint glimmer of light.

Gloved hands were shaking Arroyo's shoulders. He looked up. Ellen and Joy had ahold of him. Tom Tillerman laughed loudly. "Jeez there, Bud. You *really* left the room that time. How many of Francois' dirty martinis did you guzzle?"

Arroyo stood up shakily. "It's been a long day," he said. "I'm going to check on my tractor before bed." He walked back behind the generator module, where Drag Queen was plugged in to stay warm. He climbed into the cab and pressurized it. He took off his helmet and gloves. He had no idea what that last memory was from. Or if it was even a memory at all. Perhaps it was just a good-old-fashioned nightmare. His hands trembled. He unlatched the jump seat beside him and reached into the storage bin. He fished around and pulled out a small tool bag. It had a padlock on it; he punched in the combination. He unzipped the bag and reached in. He pulled out the unopened bottle of Trank he had carried there for years. It had always been there for an emergency. All these years on Europa he had never broken the seal. He held the ice-cold bottle in his hand and stared at it without focusing. His mind was still in that narrowing, icy chute, plummeting downward in the blackness.

He pulled back on his helmet and gloves. He ran a suit diagnostic and then depressurized the cab. He stepped outside the airlock and tossed the bottle upward. It flash-froze instantly and exploded. Tiny shards of glass and icy crystals of Trank drifted upward, catching the light of rising Io like a million sparkling diamonds, and then gently drifted to the ground around him as gravity took hold.

* * *

The morning started early at Discovery Bay. The Geriatric Crew fired up tractors and unplugged them from the generator module long before those in the subsurface camp had arisen. The old folks were eager to get on the trail. Wyatt, in particular, was antsy to get back to Coretta, although he said little about it.

Down in the galley, Fran—a bit rough around the edges from the prior night but eager to head back to Mactown—put out coffee and pastries. Everything else had now been packed away. He had a line of prefab box lunches ready for the operators to take with them on the trail, although they had their own food in the living module. Karen was busy on the radio, doing a final check-in with Mac Ops before the flitter arrived. She passed on lighting and surface conditions so the flitter pilot would know what to expect.

The group assembled in the narrow ice-walled passageway that connected the camp's buried Jamesways, sipping coffee and

Jim Fairchild

chatting. They waited for a morning briefing from Karen. When she was finally done on the radio in her cramped office—stacked high with supplies carefully boxed away for the indefinite future— she looked somber. She squeezed into the tight passageway. "We're still set to leave today," she announced. "No change in our plans. Let's gather in the galley for a chat."

Fran had neatly stacked chairs on top of tables; the crew carefully pulled them down to sit. Karen sat, cleared her throat, and clutched an iTablet to her knees. "I want to thank you all for your hard work the last few days. I'd like to say that when you get back to Mactown you'll have a chance to get some rest. Unfortunately, that won't be the case. I've been told that some of you may have had your names drawn for stasis. I'll leave it up to you to check your iMinds for updates.

"Also, be aware that Mactown is no longer a safe place. A plumber stabbed a carpenter outside HR yesterday afternoon. The plumber's wife was put on the stasis short list, and he thought the carpenter—his neighbor—was responsible. The carpenter has been stitched up and will be medevacked on the *Khlebnikov*. Another brawl broke out in the galley after Bryon Sturm held his second town meeting. This time, the goons from the Ganymede police force pulled handguns and fired shots. Luckily they fired warning shots into the ceiling instead of into people. But next time it could be some of your fellow co-workers they shoot. Mac Ops sent me a feed of what Bryon said last night. I'm assuming some of you may have already heard about it via your iMinds, but I feel obligated to make sure you watch it. Many of us have made this moon our home, and you need to be aware that Europa as we've known it no longer exists."

Karen turned on the wall monitor that normally displayed an enticing slideshow of lush forests, steamy jungles and babbling brooks on Earth, or the 20th-century television sitcoms Fran liked to watch while he was cooking. She synched her iMind to the

194

monitor, waved her hand swiftly through the air to find the video clip, then turned to watch. The video image was inexpertly shot; Bryon Sturm's face was grainy, accentuating the large pores.

I want to thank all of you for attending this evening, he began. *These are trying times at McMurdo Station, across all of Europa, and throughout all of the National Science Welfare Foundation's Office of Off-Earth Programs. You have all been dealt tough challenges on short notice to comply with the government shutdown. Sit down, please. Up front, you must sit down so others can see me! Those of you arriving late, show me the courtesy of finding seats and keeping silent.*

None of us want to see manned research on Europa grind to a halt. I commiserate with those of you who are grantees and have had your life's work thrown into limbo. Just remember that your efforts on behalf of the march of Science across this godforsaken moon have not gone unappreciated. After the budgetary situation is resolved—however many weeks or months or years that might take—and after my staff has had time to review our research priorities, many of your projects will again be funded, and many of you will no doubt return to continue your life's work. I cannot promise that every project will continue when we return to Europa. I will delve into that in a moment. But I can assure you that I am the biggest fan of Science, and will do what I can to help most of you return.

Wyatt reached across the table and tapped Arroyo on the shoulder. "Does your bunghole tickle?" he whispered. "This fellow *really* knows how to blow smoke up an ass."

As for those of you in the audience—sit down! you must sit down, or I will have you removed!—who are contract workers, also rest assured that your efforts have not gone unnoticed. Every

195

time I eat in the galley, I appreciate the unsung work of the lowliest dining attendant. Whenever I use the restroom, I praise God for the efforts of our janitors. You carpenters, you mechanics, you equipment operators, IT specialists, flitter pilots and pastry chefs—all of you unsung little people who work with your hands: God Bless all of you and the daily trials you endure here on Europa.

As you know, we must evacuate all personnel from Europa. Once the process started, there was no turning back. One cargo vessel, the 'Khlebnikov,' is already on-deck at Pegasus Ice Runway. It will upload the first round of those of you who will go into stasis for the trip back to Earth. I am happy to announce that I have just personally signed contracts with two other civilian cargo vessels which will be enroute shortly from Ganymede and should be here within a week. Those vessels will have the capacity to upload the remainder of you who will return to Earth in stasis.

The 'Khlebnikov' will also take on some of you whose final destination is Ganymede; it will rendezvous with shuttles to transfer passengers before leaving the Jovian system. Those going to Ganymede will be spared stasis. Some of you have informed us that Ganymede is your home of record, or that you have jobs waiting for you there. If you have given us sufficient advance notice we will endeavor to place you on the 'Khlebnikov.' And a few of you have made private arrangements for onward travel from Ganymede. Bear in mind that if you opt for private travel onward from Ganymede, it will be at your own expense, and The Program will no longer be liable for your safety and welfare. Please refer to your contract's Terms of Agreement for details.

I'm only going to say this one more time: sit down! I will not tolerate private discussions while I am speaking. My time is valuable. Sergeant McConnell, you have my authorization to use force to maintain order.

Back to what I was saying. When the last of the three

contract vessels lifts off from Europa in—at most—two weeks from now, we will have left the facilities here in McMurdo Station on autopilot. Most infrastructure—heating, plumbing, electrical, equipment and vehicles—will be put to sleep and monitored via uplink from Kardashia. It is my goal to make it as easy and as efficient as possible to re-open the station with a minimum of effort and expense if and when The Program is again funded.

Sergeant McConnell, send some of your men to that back table. The round one, with the four bearded men in dirty coveralls chattering away.

"That describes half of Mactown," Annie muttered.

Yes, that's the table. Eject them! If they won't show me common civility, I will not return the favor. Take them outside and have a discussion with them about proper behavior.

Which brings me to another subject. I know many of you haven't slept for days and still have a great deal of work to do, so thank you for bearing with me. I have been stopped repeatedly around the station by many of you who bemoan the shutdown's impact on what you call 'the community.' I must remind each of you that McMurdo Station is not a 'community.' It is a government worksite. You are all here as either support workers or as researchers at the generous invitation of the National Science Welfare Foundation. Many of you come. Many of you go. This is not your home. Do not expect the privileges of a citizen of a planet or a nation. If you are unclear about your legal status while working or doing research on Europa, once again please refer to the Terms of Agreement appending your contracts. Darla Hovenweep of The Company's Human Resources Office will help clarify these issues for you if she has time. Darla, please stand up and take a bow. Darla has been working tirelessly during this shutdown process. She is my hero. I cannot thank her enough.

Jim Fairchild

For those of you who are self-annointed jailhouse lawyers, I would remind you that by treaty, no planet or nation recognizes territorial claims on Europa. Europa has no sovereign government. We at the NSWF are simply trustees of this frozen ball. Without a sovereign government, there is no citizenship. I will hazard to be blunt, but YOU HAVE NO RIGHTS.

There, in the back again, Sergeant McConnell: that young long-haired man wearing the 'Europa for Europans' T-shirt. I will NOT brook radical political stunts. Yes, the skinny ginger with the dreadlocks. Throw him the hell out of my galley!

Annie gasped. "That's one of your traverse operators. He was out here last summer."

"*Abbie Hoffman*," Arroyo said. "At least that's what I called him."

Wyatt was so mad he was shaking. "I call him *Paul Fucking Revere*."

I need to move on. I have an important telecon with the Senate Science and Technology Committee of the joint North-South central government in Washington in a few minutes. I have mentioned that if and when the Europa program starts up again, there will be new research priorities. This is a critical issue, and I have made suggestions to senators on both sides of the Mason-Dixon line that might lead to a budget solution sooner rather than later. Some of the research that is being conducted on Europa is offensive to people of faith. Many of you are people of faith, I am sure. Show me some hands. How many of you are people of faith?

Sturm paused. The camera did not show the audience. The microphone picked up off-camera chuckling.

Well, that wasn't a spectacular show of hands. I'm

guessing that many of your are so exhausted after your efforts the last few days that your minds are elsewhere and not on your relationships with God. I take no offense. I, myself, must humbly say that I am a man of faith. And I understand why many others who see the universe as an expression of God's handiwork are offended by some of the work that has been done here on Europa. Specifically, I refer to research into the two so-called species found here on Europa: the Tetras and the Deltas.

The Tetras have been studied for a couple of decades now. What do we know about them? That they are large, squat, sedentary gumdrops that fail to exhibit several of the essential characteristics traditional science associates with living beings. We must ask these questions: are they even alive? Are they dangerous to us? Where do they fit into God's Plan, if anywhere at all? I would concur with those researchers who doubt that the Tetras are alive.

And then we come to the Deltas. What do we even know about them? They are elusive. We have only vague images from submersibles. They are just dark, fleeting, frightening shadows in an even darker sea. Are they as inanimate as the Tetras, or perhaps even more so? We have never caught one nor taken a single tissue sample. I do not wish to impugn the reputation of the researchers amongst you who have attempted to study the Deltas at the generous invitation of my agency. But you have provided, so far, little evidence that the Deltas even exist.

Suggesting that these two alleged species have evolved on Europa independently from life on Earth is an affront to people of faith. You must be cognizant that many senators who control The Program's purse strings are troubled by the direction of exobiology projects on Europa. In order to hasten a budget resolution, I have offered to eliminate all exobiology research on Europa if and when The Program starts up again.

Jim Fairchild

A horrendous noise ensued. Chairs could be heard being knocked over. Something flew past Sturm's ear—a stainless steel napkin holder.

Dr. McPherson, I expect better behavior from someone with a Ph.D.! Sergeant McConnell, have your men escort Dr. McPherson from the galley. And teach him the meaning of civility once you have him outside. A postgraduate degree in hard science does not give anybody the right to show intolerance toward those of faith. For those of you in the audience who don't know the miscreant being escorted outside, Fitzroy McPherson is one of the purveyors of fake news about alleged life on Europa. Shame on him. Shame on him. The NSWF very generously brought him to Europa as part of our Visiting Educator Program. I've learned that back at his university, he creates his own facts. His own truth. That is one danger of science. When researchers with an agenda espouse theories that don't comport with what Man knows with certainty about God's Plan, those theories must be exposed for what they are. I believe the good doctor has just placed himself on the stasis short-list.

I am already late for my telecon. And most of you need to get back to work or prepare for the stasis chambers. Be sure to have your personal affairs in order. Two final notes. One: I have been offered the position of director of the National Science Welfare Foundation. The presidents of both United States feel that I may be able to bring a new focus to our work upon which both nations can agree. I have taken the offer under advisement. I assure you that I will finish my duties here on Europa before making a decision.

And two: I have been asked to consider a candidacy for the Confederate Senate from the great state of Alabama. I do not consider myself a politican. But if asked to serve I will not shy from my duty.

Thank you all for your time. With the help of God, let's make Europa great again!

The video ended with hundreds of voices speaking at once, the sound of hundreds of chairs being pushed back. Arguments broke out, followed by the sound of scuffling, and then what must have been a huge free-for-all off-camera. Then came several gunshots. The tape ended abruptly in static.

"*Holy buckets*," Tom Tillerman muttered. "The world has gone nuts, eh?"

Karen reached up and turned off the monitor. "I'm sorry to start your morning with that."

Annie shook her head in disbelief. "Most of what he said about the Tetras and Deltas was pure fabrication."

The ashen-faced crew in the Discovery Bay galley looked at each other. It felt as if the solar system had just entered a zone of the universe that operated under strange new rules of reality. Long-accepted definitions of rationality, of logic, of fact and truth had suddenly dissolved and been replaced by new rules that just a few years before would have been considered sheer insanity by educated people of *any* political stripe. It was as if the very foundations of reality at a quantum level had shifted.

It was as if the *entire universe* had just drifted into its own chaos terrain.

* * *

The Geriatric Crew pulled out with its loads, waving gaily from inside the tractor cabs. The flitter coming for Karen, Fran and the cargo handlers was an hour late; the harried pilot explained that his flitter was the last of the fleet that hadn't already been winterized and put away in hangars. Yet last-minute flight requests kept piling up. Finally, with a blast of exhaust wash and a

Jim Fairchild

blinding cloud of ice crystals, the flitter departed. Karen and Fran waved through the flitter's windows as it rose.

And then Annie and Arroyo were alone.

They sat silently at the galley table, sipping the last of the coffee. When she was done, Annie pushed her mug away and looked at Arroyo.

"It's time for us to have a long talk," she said.

"Have I done something wrong?"

Annie threw her head back and laughed. "Oh God. *No.* You've done everything right. But you still don't remember the most important parts. And you have a lot more to do. Do you remember working at the Marble Point camp last summer?"

Arroyo was thrown for a loop. "I was on Ganymede getting my legs regenerated last summer. I was zonked out from a trauma-flush."

"It's time for you to remember. The accident in the motorpool that killed Frank Pabodie happened in early March. You lost your right leg—*not both*—as a result. You were medevacked to Ganymede, where your leg was regenerated. You *did* undergo a trauma-flush. You came back to us in July. All of Mactown welcomed you as a hero. We all knew you had tried to save a man's life."

"But my other leg has the same pink color."

"You were fully certified to return to work, and, as usual, you requested a field assignment. Barry Wilton arranged for you to be the equipment operator at Marble Point. That camp is where the Delta research has been going on. There was *another* accident."

The blood drained from his face. He could vaguely remember Marble Point: tucked in a sweeping cirque formed by a tectonic battle between two huge plates of ice many kilometers thick. It was one of the most spectacular camps in the field. When the wind blew, though, the cirque cliffs caught the full force of it.

The hurricane-like eddies could scour the area clean of anything not nailed down.

"Was the *second* accident my fault?" Arroyo asked.

"Once again, *God no*. Something horrible happened, and you tried to help. But you got hurt again. Your other leg—the left one—was severed at Marble Point, and you were medevacked again. You underwent leg regeneration and trauma-flush a second time. I'm trying to tell all of this to you in the right order. I need to feed it a bit to you at a time, like bitter medicine. I need to get you up-to-speed, but I don't want to re-traumatize you. I asked Karen if you and I could stay behind here awhile so I could start the process. Because once you remember what happened at Marble Point, you will realize that there is one last task you have left on Europa."

"Why have you taken this on?"

Annie leaned across the table toward Arroyo. "I was at Marble Point when the accident happened. Doctor Gianforte had asked me to be your 'handler' in Mactown when you came back from your second regen: someone to informally keep an eye on you and help you slowly recover your memories—*some* of them. Because the second accident happened so soon after the first, Gianforte felt you might not be able to handle all of the truth at once. The community was asked not to mention either of the accidents; we were asked to pretend they hadn't happened for your own well-being. But that didn't sit well with Barry Wilton. Barry knows that certain people are trying to bury the truth about Europa. He knew you would be needed again, and he thought you would be strong enough to handle all of your memories. Some people think he is an eccentric old goat who has been baked by too much radiation. But he's really a rather bright old goat."

"How do we make all of my memories come back?" Arroyo asked.

"We should start with your iMind. I know you hate it. But

Jim Fairchild

there's someone who has been trying to reach you ever since the second accident at Marble Point. You need to read her messages. I'd like to synch our iMinds. I'm guessing you have thousands of messages you've never looked at. I could sort through them quickly for you and find the relevant ones. We only have a couple of hours to ourselves before things get hectic."

Arroyo reached into his parka for his iMind. He fastened it around his right ear and eye and powered it up. He waited for the obnoxious power-up screens to scroll past, then went to his inbox. He had more than two thousand messages waiting for him. "How do we share?" he asked.

Annie was busy on her own iMind, her hand flitting briskly in the air. "I'm establishing a network for the two of us. I'm sending you an invitation to join. Just open the message from me, then click on the JOIN icon. The rest is automatic."

In a moment Arroyo had his invitation. With a few swipes of his hand, Annie was in his inbox.

She squinted into the distance as she began to scroll down through Arroyo's inbox. "*Wow.* You need to update your anti-virus software. Do you subscribe to Bulgarian porn sites? Do you buy penis potions from Martian pharmacies?"

"No, and no. Delete whatever you need to." Arroyo was watching his inbox race past as he shared it with Annie. It was dizzying.

Annie quickly deleted hundreds of messages. She frowned. "Hmmm. I'm not finding what I'm looking for. *Wait.* Here's one you need to see." She highlighted the message for Arroyo while she continued her search.

> From: Beverly Pabodie
> Subject: Thank you
> Date: Apr 13 2297

204

Dear Mr. Bronson:

I want to thank you from the bottom of my heart for sending me the video message from my husband, Frank, just before he passed away. It must have been a difficult decision to send it. It was horrifying to watch, and I almost deleted it. But as horrible as the truth is, you did the right thing by sharing it with me.

I was informed almost a month ago about my husband's death on Europa via a brief message from the National Science Welfare Foundation. The message expressed the NSWF's regrets and contained the flight info for the return of Frank's remains. I am still in extreme shock; it especially hurts when it happened so far away. Frank's body is somewhere in transit back to Earth right now. I've been told it might take 45 days to reach me. Maybe it will be easier to accept Frank being gone once I have his remains. In the meantime, I have his final message that you kindly sent, although I don't know if I can watch it again. But at least it reminds me that this isn't just a horrendous nightmare. Well, it *is* a nightmare, but it is real.

I have many questions about the accident. After that first brief notification, I didn't hear anything else from the National Science Welfare Foundation until last week. A gentleman named Mr. Sturm sent me a message of condolence and a copy of a press release. It said that Frank 'died valiantly while working to further the March of Science across Europa.' I don't know what was so valiant about being crushed to death in an accident, as I later learned from Mr. Sanders, who kindly sought me out. He asked me not to tell anyone he'd contacted me. Frank was just an engineer—a geek who loved to design things and tinker with them. He had a brilliant mind. I didn't want him to go to Europa, but he insisted. He said it would be a once-in-a-lifetime opportunity.

Mr. Sturm didn't mention you when he finally contacted me. It was Mr. Sanders who informed me how you happened to capture my husband's last words. Mr. Sanders told me about your injury and said you would probably be in either surgical stasis or deep trauma-flush right now. He also said you rarely check your iMind and prefer not to communicate with other people. So I understand if you never read this. But *if* you do, rest assured I am praying for your swift recovery. What *you* did was truly valiant. I hope that you have loved ones somewhere, and that you leave that hideous moon and go home to their warm embraces.

Later, when you have healed, I would appreciate hearing from you. I still have

many questions about what happened to
Frank, and Mr. Sturm has not yet responded
to my many inquiries.

My everlasting thanks and very best wishes—
Beverly Pabodie

Beverly Pabodie's message made Arroyo sick to his
stomach. He flagged it as URGENT, and swore to himself to
answer her as soon as things calmed down.

Annie paused from her search to open a new message in
her own inbox. She read it silently, then looked at Arroyo. "That
was from Consuelo, back in Mactown. A traverse crew left there a
few hours ago on their way to Marble Point. They've been
assigned to close down that camp. And there's something there
they've been told to destroy. We need to speed up your re-
education. It should take them two long days to get to Marble
Point. Our job is going to be to head them off. If we leave in a
couple of hours, we can beat them by a day."

Arroyo's head spun. "I still don't have a clue what's going
on. Keep feeding me messages."

"I've already got dozens highlighted. Keep reading."

From: Brooke Applegard
Subject: Heal Fast
Date: 19 July 2297

Dear Arroyo:

To say that I want to thank you for everything
you did at Marble Point to help our Delta
research team would be one of the greatest
understatements in history. YOU SAVED

MY FUCKING LIFE. I was absolutely certain I was going to die under two kilometers of ice, either when my suit failed or when I found out if Deltas actually eat. I can't even begin to imagine what was going through your head when you decided to come after me. Maybe *nothing*—some of the camp staff had said you were a burned-out old Trankhead. But I know now that you are an angel. Whatever good I bring to this universe from hereon in, I give full credit to you.

I've been trying to contact you constantly since the accident. I've gone through official channels in Mactown and also tried going through Bryon Sturm's office in Kardashia. No responses. Finally I got ahold of Derrick Sanders, your boss in Mactown. He said your mind would be in Zombieland for several months getting trauma-flushed for the second time in a row. Is that some sort of record? He gave me your iMind address but he also warned me that you never check it. If you don't, I'm going to fly back to Europa and kick your decrepit old ass. This is almost the 24th century—get with The Program.

I'm trapped on the Slingshot Express for another five weeks before getting back to Earth. I've tried to contact the grantee coordinator in Mactown to check on the status of all of our data logs, hard drives, laptops, journals and other stuff hastily left at Marble

Point after the accident. It should have all been hauled back to Mactown for safekeeping, but I get the sense it's all still out there. In particular, there is the matter of that 'little specimen' we left in the lab stasis chamber. You'll remember it when you see it—it's in the back of the science Jamesway. I get the sense that the camp was locked down after the accident and currently has no staff present. The specimen chamber has its own backup power source that should run for six months or so. But it is *imperative* that someone get out to Marble Point and make sure the specimen is alive.

I'm hoping that *someone* will be you, if you recover quickly enough. If not you, then someone who can be trusted.

I am growing frustrated with the lack of communication from the NSWF. I've tried to get ahold of the OFFOFFPRO people in Arlington, too, but nobody there will return my messages, either. I am hand-carrying limited tissue samples and my own data logs, external drives, etc. But everything that belonged to Dr. Zellerhaus—Hamilton Zellerhaus, my boss and the project's Primary Investigator—was probably left at Marble Point when his remains were flown back to Mactown with the other three casualties. Doctor Mahovlic can't get a response, either. You won't remember him right now, but he is another of Dr. Zellerhaus's research assistants, and had fortuitously chosen to remain in camp the morning of the accident. He's sitting next to me right now, pulling out what little hair he has left. It's enough to drive a person to drink. Oh wait, I already am. *Glug glug.*

Someday maybe I'll be able to talk about what happened down there where the ice ended and the pitch-black sea began. If I ever reach that point where I *can* talk about it, you will be the human being I'll reach for, because you were there. If you hadn't been, I wouldn't be able to pester you now.

CHECK YOUR FUCKING INBOX (☺).

Cheers—
Brooke Applegard

"Are you okay?" Annie asked, looking away from the projected image of Arroyo's inbox. "You turned white. You're shaking."

"I'm beginning to remember the second accident. I think I slid all the way down a crevasse to the sea. I was looking for survivors."

"It will come back to you, but you have to read fast." Annie kept highlighting messages.

From: Brooke Applegard
Subject: How's it hanging?
Date: 11 Aug 2297

Hey, Arroyo:

I hope you are continuing to heal up. I assume you are still bunghole-deep in the double-downer of your second leg regen and trauma-flush, so you won't be reading this for awhile. But I wanted to let you know where things stand. I know you might not check your iMind even if you *were* conscious, so I'm probably just banging my head against a bulkhead by writing. But I feel like you are the only person in the solar system who would understand. So I am writing anyway.

I'm still trapped on the Slingshot Express. We should enter Earth orbit in another twelve days. I've already booked onward passage for the first shuttle available to get me back to my lab at UC New Santa Cruz. I need to run a genome sequence for the Delta tissue sample I've been carrying. I've got some tricks up my sleeve for some other genome work I want to do. It involves the Tetras. I admit the Tetras are not my area of expertise, but I think I've intuited some connections. More to follow as soon as my feet touch terra firma.

The Earth is growing *huge* ahead of us. I can't believe the cerulean blue of the oceans. If I stare long enough I think I'm going to fall right in. I feel compelled to do a triple gainer into the Indian Ocean from here! The oceans are where life began. We were a lucky species to be given stewardship of such a gloriously beautiful planet. Too bad we never learned to be *responsible* stewards. For millenia we pissed and shat in every corner. Now we are doing it to most of the moons and the outer planets. Europa is one of the few exceptions. From here, with the naked eye, I can see the vast gleaming mountains of tailings from the ice mines on Luna. Didn't you work in those horrid mines before you fled to Europa?

It's been agony to watch Earth grow so slowly: all the people I love, all the memories down there. I want to be there *now*! I've only been gone nine months. You've been gone—what—*fifteen* years? You told me at Marble Point that you don't remember much about Earth any more. I hope you eventually rediscover some good memories.

In addition to being locked up on this ship, it seems obvious now that I've been locked out of the NSWF computer system. Neither Dr. Mahovlic nor myself have had any luck logging in to our government accounts. We've had our access denied to everything we ever saved to the NSWF system—every bit of research data, even personal mail. Luckily I always backed everything up to my own storage devices, which are in a locked case under my bony ass as I write. Neither Dr. Mahovlic nor I have yet succeeded in getting a response from the NSWF about the items we left at Marble Point. It's as if our research never existed. *As if the accident never happened.* As if our dead companions are only figments of our imaginations.

I know it's too soon to get into an in-depth discussion of what happened under the ice at Marble Point. You will be months behind me in dealing with the memories. But when you get to that point, READ THIS E-MAIL AGAIN. Do you remember when you snaked down the last few meters of that crevasse trying to reach me, but your cable wasn't quite long enough? I had gotten totally submerged when I fell into the sea, and my suit's heat exchanger must have been caked in ice, because—of all places in the solar system for it to happen—I was sweating to death in my suit. You tried to reach my hand, but couldn't.

And then the Delta that had been circling beneath me boosted me up to your outstretched hand. It lifted me on its back. I haven't told anybody else about it, because it is simply too hard to believe.

And what the fuck was that *flash*? When the Delta and I made contact there was a huge flash of light, somewhere on the extreme edge

Jim Fairchild

of visibility—almost a near-ultraviolet, although I shouldn't have been able to see it. Did you see that, or was I in such a panic that I hallucinated it? I had a kaleidoscopic flood of memories on contact: too many and too confusing to remember it all. But I *do* remember my mother picking me up when I couldn't sleep. And she started singing "Rock-a-bye Baby" to me. I had been crying uncontrollably, and with that song my mother made the whole world right again. I know it sounds like I'm drunk on Trank. But I swear the Delta triggered that memory somehow to try to calm me.

When I find the occasional courage to think about what happened down there, I now realize there were *two* angels helping me.

I'm not religious, but Godspeed.

Antsy to start sequencing—
Brooke

Arroyo sighed. It was starting to come back fast. *Too* fast.

He had been assigned to the Marble Point camp as its resident equipment operator thanks to the intervention of Barry Wilton. He had only been there a few weeks when it was decided to start a major crevasse remediation project nearby. A spur trail cut from the camp toward the main route to the Pole Station. Arroyo had done a routine check of the spur trail with ground-penetrating radar and had discovered a huge crevasse forming, its depths hidden by a dangerous ice bridge. Arroyo had, in fact, unknowingly crossed it twice in Drag Queen before performing the radar survey. It was amazing that he and Drag Queen hadn't discovered it the hard way. He had contacted Traverse Ops back in Mactown and requested the blast team. Derrick Sanders, his foreman back in town, was a licensed blaster. He would head out with a couple of assistants and an HMW sled loaded with explosives.

Annie had taken a call on her iMind while Arroyo was remembering. When she hung up, she touched Arroyo's arm. "We need to get moving," she said. With a few swipes she closed the inbox she'd been studying. "That was Consuelo. In addition to the traverse crew that left this morning for Marble Point, the Kregg Vehicle has also just left Mactown, headed that way, too."

"Who's on it?" Arroyo asked.

"Barry Wilton is driving. He's carrying Bryon Sturm and two of his armed goons. Darla Hovenweep is along. She's probably still wearing those Manolo Blahnik boots. And they've got Vinnie Kuzawa from the Heavy Shop along for ballast."

"What do they want at Marble Point?"

"Bryon Sturm wants all of the data from the Zellerhaus group. He wants to eradicate any trace of their Delta research. And he wants to destroy that 'little specimen' that's still in stasis out there. It's a juvenile Delta, and its existence proves beyond a doubt that Deltas are living creatures by any definition."

"Why is Darla along?"

"She's looking for *you*," Annie said. "You've just been added to the stasis short-list. You're being terminated for involvement in two fatal accidents. She assumed the Kregg Vehicle would run into the Geriatric Crew coming back from Discovery Bay, and she would escort you back to Mactown. When she and Bryon Sturm realize you stayed here, they'll figure out

215

Jim Fairchild

quickly you might be headed for Marble Point."

"Marble Point is going to be our Old Kindersley Corral," Arroyo said.

"I don't catch the reference. But we need to head there *now*. The Kregg Vehicle moves twice as fast as the tractor traverse headed that way. Barry and crew can be there after one hard day's ride. Grab your stuff and get suited up. We can get there ahead of them in Drag Queen. You taught me how to operate your tractor last winter. 'Any monkey can pull levers'—remember? You can read more of the messages from Brooke Applegard while I drive."

Annie and Arroyo pulled on their suits by the airlock. "How did Consuelo learn all of this?" Arroyo asked.

"Barry Wilton told her," Annie said. "You could say that Barry is leading the resistance."

Arroyo climbed through the back of the suit, tucking his chin down to get his head through the helmet mount. It was always a tight move. As usual, he scraped his face on the lock ring. "What the heck is Vinnie along for?"

Annie locked a glove in place. "He's been brought along to dispose of Drag Queen. Bryon Sturm wants it driven into the deepest crevasse on Europa. Preferrably one that opens into the sea. It's one last link to the truth about Frank Pabodie's death. Besides you."

Disposing of Drag Queen: those are fighting words, Arroyo thought. He locked his helmet in place.

* * *

Outside, Drag Queen sat idling, warm and ready to roll.

Pegleg squatted beside the ladder leading to the hatch.

Arroyo walked up to the creature. "I'm sorry," he said. "Duty lies elsewhere. I'm not sure if I'll see you again. I want to thank you for everything."

Pegleg's apex seemed to tilt back a degree or two, as if the faceless being were looking up at Arroyo. The creature sidled a centimeter or two closer. "You can't go with me," Arroyo said. He reached down and stroked the creature's top point.

A BBS camera crew was visiting Marble Point, eager to shoot the usual hackneyed video of Scientists at Work. Arroyo had always shied away from cameras. He had gone out to the recently discovered crevasse with Derrick Sanders and his helpers. They'd marked the route to the crevasse with flags so they could find their way out and back in bad light. They'd used a hot-water drill to make a series of holes in the ice bridge, then carefully prepared explosive charges to set in the holes. Derrick was fastidious with his preparations. When the charges were linked— and cross-linked—with det cord for redundancy, Derrick and Arroyo and the others stopped for a break, sipping hot cocoa through their helmet tubes while watching Io rise brightly over the horizon. Arroyo could imagine its warmth on his face. It had been so many years since he'd relaxed in the warmth of the Sun on a Terran beach that Io's light sufficed.

Glancing back toward camp, Arroyo could see that four members of the Zellerhaus group had mounted scootmobiles. The BBS crew stood in the back of an open Mattrack, camera trained on the scootmobiles. The researchers cruised slowly back and forth in front of the camera like Shriners parading on go-carts, waving merrily, hamming it up. They began to zip out along the spur road in perfect formation, following the flags, the camera crew following, catching every wave. Catching everything.

Drag Queen had sixteen gears. Normally, running in anything higher than seventh or eighth on the granite-hard ice of Europa would damage the tractor, the operator and the load. But Drag Queen was not pulling a load. Annie grabbed every gear she could find, following the lightly-used cut-across trail toward Marble Point.

All routes outward from Mactown passed first through the Shear Zone. From there, one route led to Discovery Bay. Another route led from the Shear Zone to Marble Point and then eventually to the Pole Station. The Shear Zone, Discovery Bay and Marble Point staked out the vertices of an equilateral triangle. If Annie could push Drag Queen hard enough, they could cut across to Marble Point a few hours before the Kregg Vehicle bearing Bryon Sturm and his goons arrived.

Arroyo, scrunched onto the small jump seat next to the much more comfortable operator's seat occupied by Annie, booted up his iMind again.

> From: Brooke Applegard
> Subject: Back in the (lab) saddle again
> Date: 26 Aug 2297
>
> Arroyo—
>
> I made it back to my lab yesterday. I'd forgotten how wonderful it is to look down from the top of the Santa Cruz Mountains and watch the fog roll in off the Monterey Bay. Every once in a while the fog parts and I see the ghostly shape of some teetering burned-out building rising up from the sea, where Old Santa Cruz sleeps beneath the waves. Then the fog closes in and it is as if that old world never existed. Some say it never did.
>
> I've already got my Delta sample going through a high-throughput sequencing

process. I should have more for you tomorrow. While I hope to have the entire Delta genome sequenced shortly, what I want to focus on first is the possibility that the human genome is lurking intact within the Delta genome somewhere. That was the case with the Tetras, as the work done by the Angstrom group established some years ago. I've contacted their team at MIT and asked them for copies of their Tetra sequences. They've been performing that work regularly for two decades. I'm working on an educated hunch, but I will be looking for certain changes in the Tetra sequence over time. I've even located a preserved tissue sample from Socks, the Tetra that was dissected 75 years ago by Dr. Bresnahan of the ill-fated Pegasus crew. The second Navy vessel that visited Europa had rounded up the personal effects of the Pegasus crew, including some of Bresnahan's lab samples. The samples changed hands several times and lately had been collecting dust on a shelf in a run-down tourist joint called The Aliens and Other Freaks of Nature Museum near the Old Area 51 in Nevada. I am assured by the Navy of their provenance. I wish I had more than the one Delta sample, but it is better than nothing.

It is so strange to walk around a university campus after almost a year in space. The softness of the fog against my cheek, the piercing aroma of eucalyptus. The singing of birds under cover as a gentle rain falls. Students protesting speakers who don't share their Truths. *Ah*, life on Earth. I hope you will try it again some day. I don't miss the Mactown grotto. But I *do* miss the faithful rising and setting of Io and Ganymede, and the way their faithfulness always gave me hope that time would pass and I would some day return to this planet safely again.

I am also sequencing blood samples taken from the camp crew at Marble Point. You won't remember, but we already had some of your vital essence in our lab. Dr. Zellerhaus was monitoring for damage to leukocytes and other blood components due to long-term radiation exposure. It had nothing to do with our Delta research; Dr. Zellerhaus had a personal interest in the matter, having spent much of two decades on Europa. He was beginning to have medical problems that he thought might be radiation-linked, including memory loss. He thought the NSWF's standards for radiation exposure on Europa might not be adequate. I want to take a good look at genomes from you and me in particular.

I hope you are continuing to mend. I assume it will be another couple of months before you return to Europa. I will keep writing even though I know you aren't capable of reading

yet. I've contacted Annie Pfleger, the fuelie
who was out at Marble Point and Discovery
Bay. She is going to keep an eye on you for
me when you get back to work.

Keep the faith—
Brooke

p.s. I still can't get a response from anyone at
the NSWF. Oddly, someone from the
foundation apparently called my department
chairperson yesterday, asking the status of my
work. I find it a bit unsettling.

Drag Queen's radio crackled. It was Tom Tillerman. He
wanted Annie to know that the Geriatric Crew was making good
time. The tractors were doing well with light loads and they
expected to reach Mactown as planned the following day. Then
Tillerman told Annie he was going to to give her a jingle on her
iMind. She and Arroyo looked at each other. Their iMinds were
the most secure form of communication they had.

Annie answered her iMind. "Go ahead, Tom."

"Hello, Miss Annie. Did you happen to overhear the little
radio chat I just had?"

"Sorry," Annie said. "I wasn't picking up the repeater."

"It was an odd chat. A fellow claiming to be Bryon Sturm
raised me on the Mac Ops channel. I wouldn't know Bryon
Sturm's voice from Jiminy Cricket's. Sorry for the ancient
reference. Imagine me in a top hat and tails. Anyway, this rather
impatient fellow claiming to be Bryonstorm told me to stop once
we get through the Shear Zone. He wants me to unload all of the
data logs and hard drives from the Angstrom group—everything
from its Tetra studies. He wants the stuff stacked beside the route

Jim Fairchild

in a well-flagged cache so he can pick it up later."

"Did Sturm give you his location?" Annie asked.

"He said the Kregg Vehicle had just negotiated the Shear Zone and was headed for Marble Point. So we won't be passing each other."

"Don't let those materials leave your sight," Annie said.

"No worries. I've got my feet propped up on them right now."

"Take it straight into Mactown with you," Annie said. "When you get close to town, contact Che Feldman via iMind. He's on the stasis short-list, but he should still be around. He's got a hidey-hole picked out in a corner of the grotto for that stuff. He'll take it off your hands."

"Who the Dickens is Che Feldman?"

"The traverse operator Arroyo always called 'Abbie Hoffman.' Wyatt called him 'Paul Revere.' Che knows what to do. He's one of the good guys."

From: Brooke Applegard
Subject: Delta sequencing results
Date: 29 Aug 2297

Arroyo:

I'll spare you pleasantries this time and get right down to business. I got back the sequencing from the Delta sample yesterday. I have been up all night studying it. Some highlights:

*The Delta's DNA is composed of the same quadruple-helix DNA as found in the Tetras by Angstrom's group.

*The Delta genome is 291% the length of the Tetra genome. The Delta genome is therefore almost *nine* times as long as the human genome.

*97.9% of the human genome is sandwiched within the Delta genome. This is the exact same percentage found hidden within the Tetra genome.

*I have no clue what most of the Delta's genes do. Ferreting out how a previously unseen genotype express itself in phenotypes in an essentially unknown species could take many years just to come up with theories.

*I have compared the complete human genome to the 97.9% that is found in the Tetra and Delta genomes. Some of the 2.1% of human genes missing in the Europan species are quite trivial: they express themselves in complexion, hair color and texture, left- versus right-handedness, etc. In other words, physical attributes that serve to *divide* us.

*Some other missing genes are what we call "trash" genes—vestigial evolutionary genetic remnants that perform no useful function, and which we can live quite merrily without. It is as if some unknown editor has been at work, cleaning up our genetic messes.

*Later today I will have the sequencing back on the old sample from Socks, the Tetra dissected by Dr. Bresnahan. I also have a sequence being run on your friend, Pegleg. When it was injured at Discovery Bay some of its green "blood" was collected from the ground. Angstrom's lab had it in a freezer, still awaiting analysis. I am going to look for genetic shifts in the Tetras over time. Just a hunch.

*And I should have sequencing back on you and me shortly.

Which brings me to another point. I ran a standard work-up on your blood before extracting a sample for sequencing. Your liver enzyme numbers are through the roof. Same with your blood iron numbers. I've never seen them so high. Either our lab equipment is on the fritz or you have done serious damage to yourself. Whatever you've been doing, stop *now* or die soon.

On that pleasant note,
Yours in the Sisterhood of Science—

Brooke

p.s. I've heard snippets of what is happening on Europa via the hive. The NSWF (which is still incommunicado with Dr. Mahovlic and myself) always keeps a tight rein on news coming out of Mactown. For a small government agency none plays the spin game more masterfully. As a fictional FBI agent once said, "Trust no one."

From: Brooke Applegard
Subject: Mind-blowing is an understatement
Date: 30 Aug 2297

Arroyo:

Another day, more DNA results. I have double-checked the results from the last couple of days and feel safe in passing the most mind-boggling of them to you:

*One of the most well-known and extremely controversial human genes is amongst the 2.1% of the human genome that is missing in the Deltas and Tetras. Some stories in the popular press call it the "God gene." Another more pejorative term is the "Thumper gene." Religionists insist its existence is Fake News. But years of work by the world's top geneticists all verify both the gene's location and means of expression. It is intrinsic to the mysticism and spiritual ecstasy that are at the heart of religious experience. Electroencephelograms have shown that most religious experiences are concurrent with synaptic electrical storms. Many argue that a religious experience is simply a brain

Jim Fairchild

malfunction—similar to a seizure or a temporary psychotic break. Almost all species have genes that are deleterious to their survival, and—if we could play God—should be "edited out" of their genome. The "God gene" is a prime candidate for editing if we are to survive as a species. The gene is a dominant allele in humans; it is absent in Europa's species. Why do they have almost the entirety of the human genome but *not* the "God gene"?

*Another well-known human gene is not just present, but has *four copies* in the genomes of both Europan species. This is the so-called "empathy gene." In humans, it expresses itself in highly developed social skills: specifically, an unselfish regard for the welfare and needs of other humans. It is a recessive allele and only expresses itself in a minority of humans. Some argue that if the "empathy gene" were dominant, human behavior would be so altruistic that the survival rates of individuals would plummet. For whatever possible evolutionary reason, not one but *four* copies of the "empathy gene" are in the Europan genomes. Three of them have amino acid "blockers" on either side of them so they lie dormant.

*In the two Tetras with known long-term interaction with humans—Socks and Pegleg—those three dormant "empathy

---

genes" are missing their blockers. Socks and Pegleg both therefore have four fully functional empathy genes. One would assume the three extras are only back-ups. But we don't know much about how the Tetra genotype expresses itself in phenotypes. It is a mistake to presume that the mechanisms of allele expression through phenotype are the same on Europa as on Earth.

*Something has tinkered with you and me. Our DNA sequences contain three extra sets of the "empathy gene." I wish I had a blood sample from Petty Officer Bowers, the sailor who befriended Socks 75 years ago. I understand his corpse may be buried under the Pegasus Ice Runway and lost to history. Both he and you had repeated physical contact with a Tetra. I have stood on the back of a Delta. I had an intense wave of emotional memories as a result. Annie Pfleger has written me that you've had similar experiences with Pegleg. Are these two species somehow capable of modifying our genes? Are they helping us to become more empathetic?

*Food for thought: at first I assumed the ability of a species to elicit a flood of emotional memories in another species was a method of predatory immobilization—a way to paralyze victims before killing them. But what if the Tetras and Deltas are simply trying to *help us* by boosting our ability to empathize? What if they want to help not just individual humans they encounter, but *all* humans?

*More food for thought: the Europan food chain is, well, *non-existent*. We have two large creatures at the top, and nothing more than a few sulphur-eating microbes found near ocean-floor heat vents at the bottom. The many Tetras that have been examined over the last two decades seem to eat *nothing*. The juvenile Delta still in stasis (I hope) at Marble Point also showed no signs of food ingestion. The two species exist, they meet my definition of life, and yet they do not sit near the top of a pyramid of lifeforms that get physically smaller, more prolific and less complicated as you near the bottom of the pyramid. There is no broad pyramid of supporting biomass.

*So one must ask: What the hell is going on with the Tetras and Deltas on Europa? Is Europa home to a strange genetic experiment? What does Europa do to our ideas about evolution? Is Europa a gene depository? If so, *what* manages it? What other species potentially await discovery deep in the hidden sea?

*And   my   preliminary   hypothesis: Instantaneous mutual mutation induced to enhance empathy? That and five credits get you a mocha frappuccino at Astrobuck's. Are those phosphene flashes part of a mutating mechanism? Or is the hand of God involved, for fuck's sake? *Who the fuck knows?*

There are more things in heaven and earth, Arroyo, than are dreamt of in our philosophy.

Neither Dr. Mahovlic nor I have heard a peep from the NSWF. We are awaiting the remains of Dr. Zellerhaus and our other two companions. We thought the remains were in the cargo hold on the Slingshot Express that brought us back to Earth. But a cargo trace shows the three caskets may have taken a wrong turn at a spaceport warehouse in Kardashia. Three families are patiently waiting.

I hope you are continuing to heal. It is almost September. Are you starting physical therapy in Kardashia yet? I know you are still zonked out from the second trauma-flush. Did you get that tattoo you'd talked about?

Exhausted but filled with amazement—

Brooke

p.s. My department chairperson called me into her office yesterday. She asked for a spreadsheet showing how I was using my time since returning. She's also asked that I save all Europa-connected work to the university computer system. I, of course, TRUST NO ONE. I save everything to my own drive and take it home with me every night.

From: Brooke Applegard
Subject: Heebie-Jeebies
Date: 4 Sep 2297

Arroyo:

Things are getting odd here in New Santa Cruz. I've been notified by my department chairperson that due to Dr. Zellerhaus's death, my status at the university is "under review." Dr. Zellerhaus was a tenured full professor; I was one of his lowly research assistants. I have a Ph.D. but seem to have the status of a janitor. I do not teach and am not on the university payroll. My stipend comes from the grant the NSWF gave Dr. Zellerhaus for his Europa work. Now that he is dead, the project is in limbo, and funds from the NSWF seem to be frozen. I already live from month to month; I don't know where money for rent and ramen will come from.

More disturbingly, I am getting troublesome voicemail messages on my iMind. Lots of heavy breathing followed by a hang-up—how original. The messages saying *Godless cunt* are definitely more disturbing. "Sometimes paranoia's just having all the facts," a fellow named Burroughs once said. I'm cognizant of my surroundings at all times and vary my routes around town. Doctor Mahovlic has been getting the same sort of calls. Although I can't attest to what sort of genitalia he is called.

I've cleared out all of my Europa-related materials from my university office. I have things in safekeeping elsewhere. I can't assume that my iMind is secure, so won't say exactly where.

I'll keep you advised.

Brooke

From: Brooke Applegard
Subject: Going to ground
Date: 13 Sep 2017

Arroyo:

I was asked to vacate my office at the university yesterday, as the project I was working on is now officially terminated. Apparently my department chairperson was contacted by someone at NSWF. She wouldn't give me a name. She simply said that Dr. Zellerhaus's project was now officially cancelled due to his death and that further funds would not be forthcoming.

The creepy iMind messages continue. I attempt to block them but they keep coming from new, apparently randomly-generated numbers. Doctor Mahovlic left town today with his wife and child. He didn't want to tell me where they were going for my own protection.

I went home last night and someone had broken into my apartment. Things were tossed about thoroughly and purposefully. It is abundantly clear what was being sought. I wasn't stupid enough to keep my Europa work at home.

And Solo, my cat, was missing. Fuck with me, but *do not* fuck with my cat. He was already pissed at me for being gone to Europa for so long. I would like to stay until Solo comes back, but I get the point that is being made. I've asked a friend to drop by from time to time to see if Solo returns.

As for me, I am going to ground.

Be careful. Someday maybe we'll meet again. If we do, I hope you'll remember me.

Brooke

* * *

PART THREE:

GOING TO GROUND

A gleaming white arc spread like the edge of a sickle across the distant horizon. It was the towering ice cliff above Marble Point, where tectonic forces were slowly pushing one ice shelf up onto another. Annie and Arroyo had been rolling all day and half the night. They were perhaps an hour away now. The brutal ice had shaken loose everything in Drag Queen's cab that wasn't bolted down. Arroyo's back and kidneys hurt from the pounding. He could hear bad squeaks and grinding noises coming from Drag Queen's underchassis. His beloved tractor was being raced to death.

Annie offered to relinquish the controls to Arroyo several times, but he was busy with his iMind. He sent a message to Beverly Pabodie. It would take 45 minutes for the message to reach her inbox on Earth. He told her he would be happy to answer her questions some day, once he had taken care of pressing business on Europa.

He read more of Brooke Applegard's messages. He sent her a simple reply: "Take care until we meet again." But he knew she might have ditched her iMind when she went to ground. It seemed unlikely they would ever see each other again.

Arroyo turned to Annie. He spoke loudly so she could hear him over Drag Queen's screaming turbocharger: "You and Brooke keep in touch."

"We got to know each other out in the field. She's a hoot. Brilliant *and* funny. She asked me to keep an eye on you until your memories came back."

"I hope she's safe."

"She can take care of herself. I got a message from her a couple of weeks ago that was passed through a couple of dummy iMind accounts. She's hiding where no religionist would suspect—western Australia. When the world regains its senses she'll be back. Don't worry about her."

Reading Brooke's messages had been like hearing her voice for Arroyo. He could remember her: tall, athletic, a former college long-distance runner. Chiseled cheek bones, piercing grey eyes, a no-nonsense butch haircut perfect for anyone who spends most of her time wearing a helmet or cold-weather headgear. She always had something funny to say, invariably dry and sarcastic, as is often the case with extremely intelligent people who spend their lifetimes surrounded by others with far lower IQs. She and Arroyo enjoyed gross-out stories, and would try to out-do each other in the galley. Many times others would have to get up with their trays and move to another table.

An alarm went off on the instrument console. "The transmission is hot," Annie said.

Arroyo glanced at the monitor fed by the tractor's rear camera. He could see a long trail of dark spots on the ice receding into the distance behind them. "We're losing fluid. The damage has already been done. Let's just keep rolling." He reached past Annie and shut off the alarm.

He could remember sitting by the hidden crevasse, sipping cocoa. It was drilled and loaded with an orderly grid of charges, ready to blast once their break was over. Derrick Sanders sat beside him, the blasting machine between his legs. Derrick was a cautious blaster and never let the blasting machine get more than an arm's-length away. "Blasting machine" was an ancient term from Terran mining. It was simply a hand-cranked electrical generator that would send a current to a blasting cap attached to the det cord. When the blasting cap detonated, it would trigger the det cord. The det cord would in turn detonate at a rate of 7500 meters per second, in turn setting off the carefully spaced explosive charges. Piercing all of the charges with a hand punch in the extreme cold to thread the det cord through them was a serious physical workout. The explosives were almost as hard as granite at minus 160 degrees C. Some of the younger operators gleefully volunteered to help Derrick with a crevasse shot. Arroyo found no glory in it, and was, in fact, shy of all things that went boom. He helped because—as camp equipment operator—his help was expected and needed.

He tried to step into his memory-self and look for other faces. Two others sat beside Derrick and himself. Arroyo—or his memory-self—turned his head to see who they were.

Lazarus. Yes, Lazarus was there. Herbert Pinkton. Europa's own Queequeg. Brilliant, hard-working, hardened by what he'd seen in Australia. And generous to a fault. Through the reflection of Ganymede in Lazarus' helmet visor Arroyo could make out the mysterious facial tattoo. Arroyo always hoped that Lazarus would finally learn the meaning of the tattoo—and that, perhaps, it told the story of his wild and sad wanderings throughout the solar system.

And beside Lazarus, a younger operator. Abbie Hoffman. No: nicknames were a means of diminishing a person. Arroyo regretted having coined the appellation. His name was Che Feldman. It was the name of a revolutionary. A freedom fighter. Arroyo wished Che Feldman were there now so he could apologize.

The four of them watched in disbelief as four scootmobiles approached along the flagged route from the camp. They could see the BBS camera crew driving alongside the scootmobiles, the suited camera crew riding in the back of the open Mattrack.

"What the fuck?" Arroyo asked.

"I briefed the entire camp this morning about our blasting operation," Derrick said. "They shouldn't be out here."

The four operators jumped up and ran into the middle of the flagged route. Waving their gloved hands over their helmetted heads, they got the attention of the scootmobile operators. It had been tough to get their attention: they were busy mugging for the BBS camera.

"Don't you recall my pre-blast briefing after breakfast?" Derrick asked, when the scootmobiles and Mattrack had pulled to a halt. The exhaust from the engines hung close to the ground and drifted around Arroyo's ankles.

"Sorry," Dr. Zellerhaus said. He straddled the lead scootmobile. "We were just having some fun for the camera crew." Zellerhaus and the other three scootmobile riders wiped ice crystals from their visors.

"Just remember we're going to be opening up this puppy shortly. The blast is scheduled for the top of the hour. Be clear of the area, please."

One of the British camera operators looked down from the back of the Mattrack. "Please don't be a dick," he said.

"I'll leave that to you," Derrick said, waving gaily and turning his back. It had taken Arroyo years to accept certain British ideas of humor. The scootmobiles made a broad turn back toward camp, followed by the Mattrack.

Drag Queen crested a rise in the chaos terrain. Annie slowed down as they took in the view ahead. The tectonic cliff above Marble Point was only a few kilometers away now. Even in the soft light of Ganymede it glowed brilliantly. It rose almost two kilometers into the sky, and Arroyo and Annie had to crane their heads to spy the top of the towering ice cliff. It was impossible for Arroyo, even after fifteen years on Europa, to accurately estimate

Jim Fairchild

heights and distance by eye. There was not enough foreground detail to lend a sense of proportion. It was almost as bad as in Antarctica, where you could drive for days on the polar plateau while mountains seemingly dead ahead never draw nearer.

Finally, as Drag Queen lurched down from the rise, Arroyo could spy a few gear caches, and then the railing that encircled the hatch leading to the subsurface camp. *Marble Point.* He had worked here for a brief few weeks before his second accident.

The cab began to fill with a hot, acrid stench. Annie glimpsed at Arroyo.

"Scorched tranny fluid," he said. "The damage has already been done. Limp her in."

Annie pointed to her right. Far off in the distance, a plume of ice crystals drifted across the surface. The ice was being kicked up by a piece of equipment racing at breakneck speed. "The Kregg Vehicle," she said.

Arroyo squinted. "It's maybe thirty kilometers out. They'll be here in less than two hours."

The blast crew finished their cocoa and walked to the end of the det cord, 150 meters from the hidden crevasse. Drag Queen was parked there, idling, in case someone got cold and needed to climb in to warm up. Derrick set down the blasting machine beside the wire leads to the blasting cap. He got on the camp radio channel to give a five-minute blast warning. "Who wants to be Guest Blaster today?" he asked. Arroyo and Lazarus had done it many times; they knew Che would get a kick out of plunging the handle on the blasting machine. Arroyo and Lazarus leaned back against Drag Queen's tracks while Derrick carefully hooked the leads to the terminals of the machine. He explained the procedure to Che, who eagerly listened. They gave thumbs-ups all around as the second-hand approached the top of the hour. They turned away and covered their visors against the impending concussion and possible flying debris.

Derrick checked the time on his wrist keypad, then counted down from ten. *"...Three. Two. One. Hit it, Brother Che."* Che leaned down on the handle with his chest. Before there was even a sound there was a shock wave that made Arroyo's knees buckle. The shock wave pushed against him as if a stranger had jumped on his back. A geyser of ice particles, dirty with partially combusted explosives, flew into the air. And then came the sound, feeble in Europa's thin atmosphere but still discernable: a muffled CRUMP.

And then the ground shook like an icequake as thousands of tons of ice dropped into the yawning crevasse, plummeting toward the sea two kilometers below.

When the cloud of contaminated ice had slowly drifted and settled, the blasting crew approached the hole. Derrick and Arroyo rode in Drag Queen; Lazarus and Che stood on the deck outside the cab's hatch. Arroyo parked a safe distance from the hole. They climbed out to examine their handiwork. They slipped into climbing harnesses and clipped into ropes anchored to Drag Queen.

"It's a wide one," Derrick said, inching out to the lip and peering over. *"I doubt we can fill this one. We'll want to drag over a plascrete bridge and set it in place after lunch."* Che inched out toward the lip for a look, sliding his safety prussik along the rope.

Arroyo had looked into enough crevasses. He would be the first to admit he had a problem with heights. The scale of crevasses on Europa boggled his mind. In Antarctica, a monster crevasse might be eighty meters deep. On Europa, they could be up to ten kilometers deep, with the black sea often waiting at the bottom. Arroyo stayed close to Drag Queen.

Annie brought Drag Queen to a gentle stop near the hatch

Jim Fairchild

leading down to the camp. "I'll leave it running," she said.

"That's fine," Arroyo said. "But I don't think Drag Queen is going anywhere from here. The transmission is toast."

The radio crackled. *Drag Queen. Drag Queen.* This is the Kregg Vehicle. Do you copy?" Annie and Arroyo looked at each other. It was the voice of Bryon Sturm.

Arroyo reached for the cab mike. He thought about what he wanted to say, then keyed the mike. "This is Drag Queen."

"Arroyo Bronson, this is Bryon Sturm. I'm the new director of the National Science Welfare Foundation. I insist that you stop where you are."

Arroyo laughed. "I know who you are. I know *what* you are. And I know *what* you want. You'll have to come through me to get it." Arroyo hung the mike back on its mount.

"Wow," Annie said, locking her suit gloves in place. "That sounded like something out of one of those ancient Westerns Fran likes to watch."

Arroyo reached for his gloves and helmet. "We don't have much time. We'll do what we can. But I'm afraid things aren't going to end well. Some folks might not live to see Io rise again."

The radio crackled once more. It was Barry Wilton. "Arroyo, this is Barry. We can work this out without anyone getting hurt. We can all live to see another day, my friend."

Annie and Arroyo climbed out of the cab without responding to Barry's entreaty. After a great deal of tugging they lifted the icy hatch to the camp's stairwell. They descended into the darkness.

* * *

They climbed downward by the illumination of their helmet floodlights. The grotto of the Marble Point camp had been sealed for months. Annie explained to Arroyo that Bryon Sturm had

240

ordered the camp shuttered after the accident in which Arroyo was grieviously injured a second time. They moved slowly, feeling their way through the narrow, rime-encrusted passageways. Their helmets cast small, bright puddles of light, but all else was pitch-black.

Arroyo had visited this camp many times over the years before his assignment in July that had ended so badly. He remembered the icy passageway leading from the stairwell to the arched Jamesways. And yet, in the dark, it seemed completely different. He had never thought himself afraid of darkness or of tight places. But he was working to overcome a growing sense of dread.

They moved slowly. The camp's generators had not run in almost five months. The grotto was only a few degrees warmer than Europa's surface. Any metal object—door handles, hinges, electrical switches—could snap with a careless touch at these temperatures. Annie paused when she reached a Jamesway with a stencilled sign on the door: SCIENCE.

She trained her helmet lights at the sign and placed a gloved hand gently against the door handle. She turned back to Arroyo. "How are you doing?"

"I'm breathing," Arroyo said.

"That's always a good thing." Annie pushed the door slowly open.

In a far corner of the otherwise dark Jamesway, Arroyo could see a faint red glow. It came from a cylindrical object about the size of an old 55-gallon drum. It lay on its side, surrounded by instrument consoles. The red glow came from a small light indicating that the backup power source was functioning. "That's the specimen stasis chamber," Annie said. She and Arroyo crept toward it.

Their helmet speakers crackled. It was Bryon Sturm again. "Arroyo, I insist that you halt. You are not authorized to enter the

Jim Fairchild

Marble Point camp." Arroyo and Annie both turned down their helmet speakers.

Annie stood in front of the stasis chamber. Arroyo could see a small viewport on its upper surface. The viewport was the size of a dinner plate. The glass was caked with rime.

"The juvenile Delta is inside of that?" Arroyo asked.

"Roger that." Annie leaned forward and peered into the icy viewport, but saw nothing.

"Was the Delta here when I worked at the camp?" Arroyo asked.

"It had been caught about a week before the accident. Doctor Zellerhaus's group was still celebrating when the accident happened. They thought they were on the verge of writing the biggest chapter in the history of Europa. Maybe they were a little too giddy after their find. You know how beakers can behave when they get excited. You don't remember when they brought up the juvenile from their observation shaft?"

Arroyo stepped beside Annie, trying to remember. He wiped ice crystals from the viewport and squinted inside.

Zellerhaus's group had used a hot-water drill to bore a smooth shaft through the ice down to the sea. Here at Marble Point the ice was two kilometers thick—relatively thin compared to much of Europa's icy crust. As in the group's many previous visits to Marble Point over the years in search of the elusive Deltas, they had lowered a remote submersible equipped with cameras and radar down the shaft. They worked long shifts watching the banks of monitors before the first sightings occurred.

The researchers gasped at the fleeting blurs on their screens. Singly, then in pairs and in large groups, the huge, manta-like creatures raced past in the darkness, then circled, then teased the submersible. It was rare to get a clear glimpse of an entire Delta. They were usually just black blurs against a blacker

242

background. The illumination from the submersible's lights was swallowed by the sea like headlights on wet pavement. In past years, submersibles had been damaged and even destroyed in encounters with the Deltas. But this visit, it was as if the Deltas understood the purpose of the submersible, understood its delicacy, and wanted to be seen. It was if they were at last pulling back a dark shroud to reveal themselves.

Brooke was on duty at the monitors on the tenth day of observation. The rest of the camp could hear her frantic shouts throughout the camp grotto. "Something small," she hollered. "There's a pair of Deltas, and something small is swimming right behind them."

The research team crammed into the Science Jamesway to watch over Brooke's shoulder. After years of observations, this was a monumental breakthrough: a young Delta had at last been glimpsed. The Deltas apparently reproduced. It was one more reason to argue that the Deltas were life as we knew it.

Arroyo could now remember watching the youngster on the monitors with the rest of the camp staff: the tiny, jet-black triangle cavorting in the dark waters beside its fully-grown companions, presumably parents. Its antics reminded Arroyo of a baby sea otter: tight turns, somersaults, back flips. Clearly the little Delta delighted in showing off its swimming prowess. The larger Deltas nudged it closer to the submersible's cameras, as if proud parents at the park showing off their infant.

And then, one morning, the tiny Delta was alone.

It floated just a meter or two in front of the submersible's main camera. It's jet-black, leathery surface rippled slightly. The camp staff watched the tiny Delta for four days, waiting for the mature Deltas to return. With increasing alarm, they realized the juvenile had been left—or even abandoned.

The Zellerhaus group held fierce debates in the galley. The debates became so heated that Arroyo had to occasionally seek

Jim Fairchild

peace and quiet elsewhere. Doctor Zellerhaus and most of his assistants felt that the NSWF's "Protocols on Flora and Fauna" should be strictly followed. No interference in natural processes should be made by humans. If a juvenile creature is abandoned by its parents, that is Nature's way. Humans must not impose their value systems. Humans must not anthropomorphize. The offspring must be left to perish.

Brooke had argued vehemently otherwise. She had suggested that the offspring had been deliberately left beside the submersible. She warned against employing human logic in trying to understand the Delta's actions. Of course, she was doing that herself, although her logic was not that of her colleagues. She considered the "Protocols" deeply flawed and antiquated, a relic of 20th-century Antarctic research. She suggested the mature Deltas had left the juvenile deliberately so that humans could study it and thereby narrow the gap of understanding between man and Delta. What greater gift could the Deltas leave than their own offspring? It would be an abomination—it would be criminal—to abandon it.

Through both Brooke's cool logic and warm passion, she convinced Dr. Zellerhaus and the rest of his team that it was incumbent upon them to rescue the juvenile Delta. They lowered a retrieval net with the submersible; Brooke, working with joysticks in the Science Jamesway, gently extended the net with the submersible's arms. The juvenile Delta made no attempt to shy away. Brooke gently cinched the net around the creature. The stasis chamber was lowered down the shaft on another cable. Its clamshell was opened once it was in the water; Brooke carefully maneuvered the netted creature into the open chamber. The net was released; the tiny Delta settled into the chamber. The clamshell was closed and carefully lifted to the surface.

The stasis chamber was scootmobiled back to camp. Brooke and her hushed companions slid the chamber into the

Science Jamesway on a small sled, then lifted the chamber into its cradle. Power and monitoring cables were connected; after a night-long discussion, the group agreed to administer the pre-stasis drug cocktail that would render the animal comatose. They had to assume that the drug doses should be based on body weight, as with humans. An initial round of sedatives was followed by a percolated infusion of Z-Gas. The tiny creature seemed to respond safely to the dosages. It floated within its stasis chamber while the group argued over what to do with its find.

"What's our plan?" Arroyo asked. Tendrils of frost grew back almost instantly where he'd wiped clear the viewport.

"Brooke sent me instructions via iMind on bringing the juvenile out of stasis. She wants us to return it to the wild before Bryon Sturm has a chance to kill it. You can help by rounding up all of the Zellerhaus group's things. Check in the camp manager's office. There should be a couple of large cases holding their drives, data logs and journals. It should be well-labelled. Haul it topside and load it on a small sled. We need to take it somewhere for safekeeping."

Annie rummaged through the drug cabinet next to the specimen chamber while Arroyo stumbled down the dark passageway. He found the office; inside were two large black cases marked *ZELLERHAUS B-235*. He slid them across the icy plascrete floor. He headed back down the passageway to the mechanic's Jamesway. Inside, five scootmobiles were parked in a neat line. Four had been sitting without their heaters plugged in for five months. They would never start without many hours of pre-warming. For that, the camp's generators would need to be taken out of slumber, a job that took a qualified mechanic a couple of days. The fifth scootmobile had been left plugged into a trickle charger from a long-term storage battery. Arroyo flipped the scootmobile's ignition to the ACC position. Several instrument panel lights lit dimly and flickered. He flipped on the pre-heaters for the engine and drivetrain fluids. If the storage battery still had enough charge, it would still take awhile to get the icy machine warm enough to start. He fought with the icy latch on the service doors to the scootmobile ramp. If the camp had been occupied and pressurized, he would have had to go through the ramp airlock. In the station's current state he could bypass the airlock. The latch to the service doors broke off in his hand; he tossed it aside. He shoved the doors with his shoulder; finally, he kicked them. They opened reluctantly. He dragged the two cases holding the truth about Deltas up the ramp.

When he stepped outside the doors, dragging a case with each arm, he looked around. Something was waiting for him just a couple of meters away.

"*Pegleg*," Arroyo said. "How the Dickens did you get here?"

Arroyo let go of the cases. He leaned toward the Tetra. He could see the old scar where it had been snared in the cable. Its body was caked in fresh rime. Arroyo knew the creature could not have followed Drag Queen from Discovery Bay over the ice. He could only assume that the Tetra had climbed down to the sea and swam to Marble Point, then ascended a crack in the ice. The creature's tetrahedal surfaces pulsated deeply. If it were a Terran mammal, Arroyo would have said it was breathing hard.

Arroyo reached out and tenderly touched Pegleg's apex.

The blast had gone without a hitch. Derrick, Arroyo, Lazarus and Che had driven back to camp for lunch. Afterward, they planned to drag a plascrete bridge section over the chasm. At another table in the galley, the BBS camera crew looked at their handiwork on the small monitor on their camera. They didn't seem to like the lighting of the video they'd shot before lunch. They discussed different camera angles, then sat down with Doctor

Zellerhaus and the rest of his group. The researchers were happy to jump on their scootmobiles one more time for the camera.

Arroyo and Derrick hooked a bridge section to the back of Drag Queen after they were done eating. They dragged it out the spur road to the edge of the hole they'd blasted. Che and Lazarus followed in a tractor equipped with a crane. They climbed out of the tractors to have a face-to-face safety meeting before beginning the bridging operation.

Derrick was a stickler for safety and made sure everyone knew their jobs before starting. The bridge would be lifted by one end and gently "walked" toward the lip of the hole. Then—after the near end was anchored—the high end would be lowered to the crevasse's far edge as the crane was extended. It required a deft hand with the crane. Che was young and eager and had superb common sense and steady hands; he climbed into the cab of the crane tractor. The other three stood nearby while Derrick radioed the camp manager to advise her that bridging operations had begun. The area was now off-limits until Derrick gave the all-clear.

And then a cloud of ice approached. Derrick, Arroyo and Lazarus turned and watched in disbelief. It was the four researchers on their scootmobiles again. The BBS camera crew once more paced them from the Mattrack racing along beside them. For these after-lunch shots an even more festive look had been chosen: the four scootmobilers had tied Halloween masks from the camp's party supplies to their helmet visors. In the lead was Dr. Zellerhaus, wearing a Mad Scientist mask. Behind Zellerhaus came one of his young assistants, Sarah DeMarinis. She wore a Pennywise the Clown mask. The third scootmobile bore Brooke Applegard, sporting a Spider-Man mask. The final scootmobile carried the group's safety advisor, Rob Falsworth. Falsworth wore a Grey Alien mask. Falsworth, a wizened Kiwi mountaineer who held the record for most ascents of Olympus

Jim Fairchild

Mons on Mars, had been coming to Europa for decades. He was in his mid-sixties. This assignment was his last hoorah. Every science group in the field was assigned a mountaineer to advise on safety issues. As the scootmobiles raced up the road, Arroyo wondered why Falsworth was in the rear—and not leading—in a known crevassed area.

"Unbelievable," Derrick muttered. He got on the radio and tried to hail the scootmobilers. They couldn't hear him over the wailing of their machines. Derrick, Arroyo and Lazarus stepped into the road, wildly waving their arms. It was like a re-run of the incident before lunch.

This time, the scootmobilers never saw the three suited figures frantically waving them down. Their vision apparently hampered by their Halloween masks, they raced directly toward the bridging crew. Derrick and Arroyo stepped back at the last second as Zellerhaus raced past. The lead scientist was still waving gaily at the camera crew off to the side.

Lazarus didn't get out of the way soon enough. The second scootmobile clipped Lazarus's right leg, slashing his suit's fabric. Everything was happening at once, but Arroyo could hear the explosive hiss as the emergency sealant cannister in Lazarus' backpack discharged, sealing the hole in his suit. The downside of the emergency sealant was that the aerosol adhesive nearly blinded Lazarus before it was forced through the tear and coagulated into a patch. Lazarus crumpled to the ground, unable to see. The third and fourth scootmobiles flew past. Across the road, the camera crew could see what was happening. The Mattrack driver slammed on his brakes and stopped in time. The camera crew in the back, almost thrown over the cab of the open truck, managed to keep shooting.

As Derrick and Arroyo watched in disbelief, the lead scootmobile sailed over the near lip of the open crevasse. They watched as Zellerhaus seemed to look down into the dark void

248

beneath him and comprehend what was happening. His feet left the scootmobile and he clung to the machine's handlebars; for an endless moment he looked like an ancient superhero flying through the air. The scootmobile climbed upward through the air a meter or two, as if Zellerhaus hoped he could jump the crevasse to the other side.

But it was far too wide. Gravity began to take charge. The scootmobile began to drop downward in a gentle parabola. Then gravity overcame forward momentum with a vengeance. The second scootmobile was already airborne behind him as Zellerhaus plummeted downward, still clinging to the machine. His feet dangled in the air high above him. There was a deafening CRUNCH and a tremor in the ice as Zellerhaus smashed face-first into the far wall of the crevasse somewhere below. The second, then the third, then the fourth scootmobile followed the leader in their shallow parabolic plunges. Arroyo heard the sound of two more impacts.

He ran to the lip of the crevasse. Normally he would have never approached the lip without a harness and rope. Those things didn't cross his mind right now. On the far wall, perhaps five meters down, he could see the marks of three impacts. Scootmobile fluids and already-frozen blood trailed down from them. He could hear pieces of scootmobiles and dislodged ice clattering far down into the echoing bowels of the crevasse. Something stared back at him from the first impact point. He tried to stop shaking enough to focus. It was a face staring at him, surrounded by a frozen spray of blood, like a scarlet blossom. He realized it was the inside of Zellerhaus's Mad Scientist mask, frozen by blood to the ice wall.

Che leapt out of his tractor and ran to Lazarus, stretched on his back on the ice. Derrick ran to Arroyo's side. "Whoever made those blood trails is dead," Derrick said. "It looks like their helmet visors shattered when they face-planted. If the impact

Jim Fairchild

didn't kill them, they would have died from instantaneous decompression."

"I only see three impact points," Arroyo said.

"That leaves a fourth person," Derrick said. "They didn't hit the far wall, but free-fell instead. It's two kilometers to the fucking bottom, Kemo sabe. That person had plenty of time to think about what was happening before they died."

"We don't know for sure if they're dead," Arroyo insisted. "Someone's got to go down there."

Derrick was already on the radio calling Mactown for a medevac. "Mac Ops, Mac Ops. This is Marble Point Camp. We have a life-threatening emergency with multiple casualties. This is not a drill. I repeat, THIS IS NOT A DRILL. All other units keep off this channel. I am requesting flitter support and SAR and EMT personnel ASAP. We will respond to the best of our ability in the meantime and will keep you advised once we can assess casualties."

Che had helped Lazarus into the pressurized cab of the crane tractor so he could remove Lazarus' helmet and clear his eyes. Arroyo jumped into Drag Queen and backed her carefully toward the lip of the crevasse. He leaped back down when the tractor was in position. He unlocked Drag Queen's winch cable and dragged the steel eyelet at the end of the cable toward the chasm.

"I'm going down there," he yelled to Derrick. Derrick paused, then gave Arroyo a reluctant thumbs-up as he gave Mac Ops coordinates for a landing zone. Lazarus, able to see now, stumbled over with Che to help drag the cable into position.

Arroyo knew Drag Queen's cable might not be long enough to reach the bottom of the crevasse. He sent Che to dig through the survival bag strapped to the roof of Drag Queen's cab for a climbing rope. He stepped into a climbing harness, then clipped into the end of the cable. He clipped the winch's handheld

250

control to his suit with a keeper cord. Che handed him the coiled rope; Arroyo pulled out a couple of meters from the coil and tied a hasty figure-eight. He clipped the coiled rope to the end of the cable so it would hang within reach as he descended.

One of the BBS camera crewmen, out of breath, ran up to the crevasse. "Bollocks! That was a gold-standard cock-up. We shot the whole bleeding thing."

"Please don't be a dick," Che said, helping Arroyo do a final safety check on his harness.

When the BBS crew landed on the Mactown flitter pad that evening, its camera's memory stick would be confiscated by Barry Wilton, on orders of Bryon Sturm.

Arroyo eased back over the edge of the crevasse, letting the thin but strong cable take his weight. He looked over his shoulder down into the depths of the chasm. The crevasse's upper reaches were soft with shadow; all he could see were the three bloody blossoms and the etched lines where machine and human parts had slid down the wall. Less than a hundred meters down, the yawning crevasse was overwhelmed by pitch-black darkness. Somewhere down there someone might still be alive. His trembling thumb paused over the winch control.

Somewhere down there, someone might need his help. He tried to swallow, but his mouth was too dry. He closed his eyes. If he had believed in God, this would have been a good time to pray. He continued his descent into the darkness.

Arroyo, standing beside Pegleg, realized that his helmet speaker was still turned down. He turned back up the volume. Someone in the Kregg Vehicle was keying the mike. Arroyo could hear an argument.

Darla Hovenweep's voice came through his helmet speaker. "Arroyo. Arroyo. Answer the radio, please."

Arroyo dragged over a scootmobile sled for the cases

Jim Fairchild

holding the Zellerhaus group's records. As he began to stack the cases on the sled, he answered. "Hello, Darla. This is Arroyo. Have I forgotten to sign some HR paperwork for you?"

He could hear Darla sigh. "Arroyo, you need to stop what you're doing and return this instant to McMurdo with us. Your contract is being terminated for failure to maintain a safe workplace. You've been involved in two fatal accidents, and have been seriously injured twice yourself. The Company considers you a danger to your co-workers. I would refer you to the Safety Training Acknowledgment you recently signed: 'A workplace injury only happens when you fail to meet one or more of your job requirements.' You will be placed in stasis for your return to Earth. Because your contract is voided, you will not receive the customary quarter-pay for your return to your home of record."

Arroyo cinched a cargo strap around the cases. "I guess it's too late to change my mind about that janitor job in Kardashia." He threw another strap over the load for good measure.

"I'm sorry, Arroyo," Darla said primly. "That offer no longer stands."

"Fair enough," Arroyo said, rolling the strap ends and tucking them away. "I'm too old for a career change, anyway. Darla, I hope you aren't wearing your alligator boots right now. It's a long walk back to Mactown."

Arroyo climbed down the scootmobile ramp back into the subsurface camp. He needed to learn more about Annie's plan. Barry Wilton's voice come over the radio. "Hey there, Arroyo. Are you still monitoring?"

"Hello, Barry. I hope you don't have saddlesores from riding all night."

"I'm an old man, Arroyo. My butt is nothing but rawhide and gristle. I just want you to know that I want us all to sort this out peacefully. There's no need for anyone to get hurt."

"Tell me, Barry. How far out from Marble Point do you

252

figure you folks are right now?"

"Shucks. Math was never my strong suit. But I'd guess maybe an hour."

"How come you couldn't commandeer a flitter and fly out?"

"Funny thing about that," Barry said. "Piss-poor prior planning by senior management. The last flitter was being winterized and put to bed when we left. The flitter crews are all scheduled for stasis. I would never presume to question the brilliance of Mr. Sturm, especially since he's sitting right behind me. But it might have been wise to leave the flitter fleet running until all of the NSWF's skulduggery was concluded."

Arroyo winced as the radio mike was apparently pulled from Barry's hand. Bryon Sturm spoke. "Arroyo, the specimen in the stasis chamber is the property of the National Science Welfare Foundation. If you misappropriate it, you are committing theft of government property. I assure you that you will be duly prosecuted."

"Duly noted, *Herr Kommandant*," Arroyo said, stepping through the frosty passageway toward the Science Jamesway. "But the specimen is the property of Europa. I intend to return it to its proper owner." Arroyo turned down the radio again.

In the Science Jamesway, Annie was bent over another scootmobile sled. She had already manhandled the specimen chamber onto the sled and was strapping it down.

"How are you coming?" Arroyo asked, using his iMind for secure comms.

He startled Annie. She stood and faced him. "Bringing a specimen out of stasis should normally be a gradual process entailing 48 hours of observation to monitor the creature's vitals. I've given this little fellow half an hour. We've got to hope for the best."

"It's time for you to fill me in on your plan," Arroyo said.

Jim Fairchild

"Help me drag this sled up the ramp," Annie said. As they both grabbed the haul rope and tugged, Annie explained. It had actually been Brooke's plan. Arroyo needed to return the baby Delta to the sea. And then he needed to disappear into the Back Forty with the Zellerhaus group's records. He needed to go to ground until the attempt to hide the truth about life on Europa had been quashed. It wasn't just the Zellerhaus group's data that needed to be protected. Arroyo—and the changes to his genome—were part of the truth that people like Bryon Sturm wanted to erase.

"Where will I go?" Arroyo asked. The ramp grew steep, the load exhausting, even in low-g.

"Brooke suggested the Pole Station," Annie said. "It's just been evacuated. You'd have it to yourself. The infrastructure has been left on auto-pilot, so you'd have power and heat. There are supply caches all along the route to the Pole. You won't run out of food or fuel getting there. You've made the trip dozens of times before. You could stay at the Pole until sanity returns."

"And when is that?"

"Maybe tomorrow," Annie said. They crested the top of the ramp; Pegleg awaited them. "Maybe five years from now. Maybe the Senate will resolve the budget problem next week and everyone will be brought back out of stasis and go back to work like nothing happened. But then again you might be the last man left standing on Europa."

*　*　*

Arroyo went back down to the mechanic's Jamesway. After several tries he succeeded in getting the scootmobile started. He normally would have let it warm up an hour or two. But he didn't have that luxury. He rode it at a crawl up the ramp. Its oils were still as thick as tar; it bucked and smoked. He might need to put some serious kilometers on it, so he babied it.

He hitched the sled with the specimen chamber to the back of the scootmobile. He told Pegleg he'd be back. He drove slowly in the direction of the shaft the Zellerhaus group had melted for lowering their submersible to the sea. His improving memory was constantly surprising him. He could distinctly remember where the shaft should be.

But it wasn't there. He found only a mound of icy rubble.

"Annie," he said over his iMind. "What happened to the submersible shaft?"

There was a pause. Annie was down below, trying to warm up the camp's mothballed Mattrack. She would need wheels to get back to Mactown. Then she answered: "Bryon Sturm sent Derrick Sanders out here after the camp was closed down. He had Derrick blow up the shaft. The electric winch wouldn't be operable even if the shaft still existed. It was damaged in the explosion, and we don't have a generator running. Sorry. You're going to have to take the baby Delta down to the sea the hard way—down that crevasse by the bridge. You've been down it before. You can do it again."

Arroyo made a gentle turn. He parked the scootmobile and its precious sled-borne cargo behind Drag Queen. He attached the nose of the scootmobile to Drag Queen's hitch with a strap. Then he climbed up into the cab of his beloved old tractor. It had been idling since he and Annie had arrived. The cab was warm. It still reeked of scorched transmission fluid. He knew he could not drive it all the way to the Pole Station. Still, if he was gentle with it— and when had he not been, except the pell-mell race all through the night to get to Marble Point?—Drag Queen might be capable of performing one last task.

He shifted the tractor into gear. There was a long pause, then a grinding and a shrieking as unlubricated gears fought with each other. Then, with a rough lurch, Drag Queen began to inch toward the crevasse out on the spur road. Arroyo could make out the flagging marking the plascrete bridge; then he could make out the wide, black gash of the crevasse beneath. As he got close he made a broad turn so that Drag Queen's rear end faced the crevasse.

Arroyo climbed down and unhitched the idling scootmobile from the tractor. He pulled the scootmobile and sled out of the way of Drag Queen's winch. The winch still had the yellow plastic safety lockout tag that had been put on it by Vinnie Kuzawa at the behest of Barry Wilton. *Safety first*, Arroyo thought, as he ripped off the tag and tossed it to the ice. *Unless it gets in the way of getting the job done.*

He released the winch brake and dragged the end of the cable toward the black maw of the crevasse. He had done precisely the same thing just months ago, in precisely the same place. He was dizzied with *déjà vu*. For a moment he thought he was losing his mind again, like the Monday morning meeting in Stalag 17 when he thought he'd been gone for a month of R&R on Ganymede. But he shook his head and the confusion went away.

His mind had never been clearer. Someone's life had depended upon him the first time he had descended into the dark depths. And now, again, a life depended upon him. It was a simple equation. He had to descend into the dark depths once more.

Arroyo dug into the survival bag on Drag Queen's roof and pulled out his climbing harness, a coil of rope, some nylon webbing and a few carabiners. He stepped into the harness and cinched the buckles. He unstrapped the specimen chamber from the scootmobile sled and gently slid it toward the crevasse lip. He cut a two-meter piece of webbing and tied figure-eights in each end. He clipped one end to the chamber with a carabiner. He clipped the other end to the steel eyelet at the end of the winch cable. As he descended, the chamber would ride below him, so he could guide it through tight passages.

"Arroyo," a voice said inside his helmet. For a moment his mind was already deep down in the darkness, nearing the hidden sea. Then he realized that Barry Wilton was calling him again.

"Go ahead, Barry."

"Arroyo, I can see you on my monitor. It looks like you're getting ready to descend with the baby Delta."

"I'm doing what I have to do, Barry." Arroyo clipped his harness to the end of the winch cable, then ran a quick diagnostic on the handheld winch control.

"I understand that, partner. I just want you to be safe. You're snakebit, Arroyo. You've been the unluckiest darned fellow I've ever met on Europa."

"It's been a pleasure working with you, Barry. Take care of yourself."

"Is Annie Pfleger safe?"

"Yes," Arroyo said. "She's down in the camp trying to get a Mattrack running. She's been my rock."

"They broke the mold when they made Annie."

Arroyo thought of one more thing. "Barry, I understand Vinnie Kuzawa is in the Kregg Vehicle with you."

"That's a big ten-four, Bucko."

"Would you tell Vinnie that I fried Drag Queen's transmission last night? I know he thinks I break things on purpose. Let him know I'm really sorry." Arroyo could hear someone yelling his name on the other end. It was Vinnie.

Arroyo gave Annie a final call on his iMind and asked her to wish him luck. Then he adjusted the tension in the cable and eased the chamber over the edge of the abyss. He leaned back and began the descent.

* * *

He could remember the first time he had descended into the crevasse, searching for a possible survivor of the scootmobile accident. When he looked between his legs on that first descent, he had been peering down into two kilometers of blackness. This time, he knew to focus on the winch control hanging from his suit and on the ice directly in front of his helmet visor. He looked down from time to time to make sure the chamber was descending smoothly. But he knew to focus on the chamber, and no farther.

He could remember looking across to the far wall of the crevasse, where the three scootmobiles had crashed. The impact points had been like bright crimson blossoms. The three blossoms sat atop long vertical stems painted with blood. And then the markings in the ice petered out where flash-frozen corpses began to tumble in low-g freefall. This trip down, he looked for the gruesome blood blossoms. They must have been hidden by a new coat of rime.

He could remember passing shredded pieces of EVA suit still filled with the remnants of people with whom he'd been eating lunch not long before. As the bodies fell, they had careened off razor-sharp ice projections and ledges. The bodies had been turned into shattered fragments of frozen meat. He had passed scootmobile parts hanging from ice nubbins and crushed on ledges. Black oil and cherry-red coolant had sprayed across the icy wall wherever a scootmobile had ricocheted against a ledge.

He could remember these things, and wished he couldn't. His mind was working again, and he wished it didn't.

Arroyo quickly dropped down out of the shadowy upper reaches of the crevasse, and entered total blackness. He switched on his helmet floodlights. Occasionally the wall in front of him was so steep that it overhung. The chamber bearing the baby Delta beneath him began to spin slowly. Arroyo struggled to maintain contact with the wall with the toes of his boots so that he wouldn't spin, too.

That first time down the crevasse he went much too fast. He knew there was at least a slim chance that someone might be alive below him. He nearly beat himself to death as the winch paid out the cable so fast that Derrick later told him the winch brake smoked. He looked for more Halloween masks. As Arroyo dropped lower into the darkness, he had looked all around in the puddle of light cast by his helmet. A couple of hundred meters down he had found a gore-caked Pennywise the Clown mask frozen to a ledge. A glove was next to it, with a severed hand inside. A scootmobile operator's manual sat open beside it, as if the hand were leafing through it for troubleshooting tips. A few hundred meters lower, he spotted something else on another ledge.

It was another gore-covered mask. He prayed—even though he didn't believe in praying—that it wouldn't be a Spider-Man mask. When he drew near, tumbling and bouncing too fast down the wall, he could see that it was the bloody face of a Grey Alien. He felt a wave of relief—and a wave of guilt, too. He still held out hope that Brooke might be alive, far down in the darkness. He would not write her off yet. She was strong, and the universe an infinity of improbabilities, many of which are ultimately probable given enough spins of the wheel.

Arroyo found a perfect speed for the winch and left the controls alone. His previous descent he had frantically adjusted the speed, and soon was bouncing so badly he couldn't hold onto the remote unit. It had been attached by a safety tether to his suit, but he couldn't keep hold of it. He was in control this time.

The crevasse began to narrow. It was now perhaps three meters wide; then two. He guessed he must be at least halfway down. Outside of the puddle of light from his helmet, he was surrounded by pure blackness. It was the very birthplace of silence. The only noise was the occasional squeak of a carabiner

259

as the chamber twisted gently beneath him, and the sound of his own raspy, measured breathing.

The icy walls continued to narrow. Soon, the crevasse was just wide enough for the chamber to slip downward. Arroyo could no longer lean back in his harness without touching the wall behind him. And then his right boot bumped into something. It was a scootmobile, caked with ghostly rime, wedged between the vise-like walls of ice. He slipped past it and continued his descent.

On his first descent, it was here, where the crevasse walls necked down to within a meter of each other, that Arroyo had found the scootmobile perfectly wedged, sitting upright, as if it had been carefully lowered into place. Only the shattered windscreen and a gently twisted ski hinted that it had fallen almost a kilometer-and-a-half. Then he noticed that the paint on one flank of the machine was scraped off down to bare metal. Another hundred meters down, he found the Spider-Man mask. It had come to rest on a narrow ledge. Arroyo had been almost too afraid to look at it. When he found the courage to examine it, he could not find a trace of blood. He refused to give up hope.

Arroyo checked his winch control. The readout indicated that he had descended 1500 meters. He would come to the end of the cable in another 250 meters; then he would have to clip the climbing rope to the cable for the final descent. As he paused to look at the remote, he could hear a hushed sussuration far below. It was like countless whispering voices.

He knew the sound. *It was the sound of the sea.*

Below him, the crevasse began to resemble the narrowing end of a funnel. For most of his descent into the darkness, he could look to his left and his right and see the crevasse stretching seemingly forever. Now, the sides were closing in, too. It was like being forced down an ever-tighter drain. Below him, the specimen chamber slipped through an icy tunnel barely wide enough for it. The slopes all around him were littered with frost-caked bits of battered scootmobile cowlings, engine parts and blocks of ice that had been dislodged in the July accident.

And then, as the sounds of the sea grew louder, the specimen chamber came to rest. Arroyo looked down. He could remember this spot from his first descent. The ice funnel took a zig-zag here; rather than a clean vertical shaft, it made a diagonal traverse several meters before heading straight downward again. He would have to push the chamber through this section before reaching the final straight drop to the sea.

Arroyo landed on his feet atop the chamber. The funnel was too tight to stand beside it; He had to put some slack in the cable and then push the chamber with his feet to get it around the first turn. Mindful that a living being was in the chamber, he pushed gently. The chamber slid forward a few meters into the diagonal section; the slope was just enough that gravity again assisted Arroyo.

Once he was in this diagonal section, Arroyo halted. In the light from his helmet, he remembered this stretch. When he had been here the first time, looking for Brooke, he had been descending far too fast, and ricocheted through the zig-zag like a pinball through an arcade machine. He hadn't been going too fast to glimpse a boot with a shattered tibia protruding from it. Apparently a SAR team had later recovered body parts.

This was the first part of the descent where he couldn't look straight up and at least *imagine* an escape route directly overhead. He suddenly felt trapped. He had to sit a moment, his arms wrapped around his knees, his eyes closed tightly. The claustrophobia didn't go away, but it began to recede a bit. He concentrated on the sound of the sea. The sea was so close now. It was no longer a whisper. He could hear the rhythmic slapping of slush-filled water against the bottom of the icy crust.

Jim Fairchild

Not far now, he thought. *I can do this.*

He pushed the chamber along the sloping floor, peeking around it to see where the passage started to drop again. He could feel the chamber start to tip downward; he pulled it back a few centimeters. He checked his winch control readout. He would run out of cable in a few meters. It was time for the climbing rope.

He dug into his utility pouch and pulled out two carabiners. One promptly slipped from his gloves and skittered down the slope. He could hear it make the turn and then freefall toward the sea. It was still too far down to hear a splash. He dug into his pouch again and pulled out a belay device; he clipped it to the end of the cable with the carabiner. He uncoiled the rope and tied one end to the cable eyelet. He dug for another carabiner, then clipped the other end of the rope to the chamber. He laid neat coils of rope on the ice in front of the chamber. He fed the rope through the belay device. He would be able to lower the chamber down this last vertical stretch, braking its descent. Arroyo checked his knots several times. He had come too far to screw it up now. He unclipped the chamber from the cable leading upward to Drag Queen. The chamber—and the precious life inside—now hung from the rope.

Arroyo had never missed Europa's sky as much as he did now. He would give almost anything for a glimpse of Io or Ganymede. He caught his breath. He tried to see through the viewport on the chamber, but it was iced up. He began to feed rope through the belay device. The chamber slid slowly forward on the incline; then it dropped into the final vertical section. It bounced gently on the rope.

Arroyo, holding the rope tight in the belay device, slid forward until he could glimpse the chamber just below. Now, with his head past the zig-zag, the slapping of waves against ice grew loud. He could feel the ice close around him tremble whenever a big wave broke. As he looked down the shaft past the chamber, he could remember his first descent. He had bounced around this corner at breakneck speed, headfirst, out of control.

And then, far below him, he had seen the faint red glow. He could remember it all.

It was the glow of an EVA suit's wrist keypad. It wouldn't have power unless the suit was intact. And if the suit was intact, someone below him might still be alive. Just a meter or two past the final zig-zag, Arroyo had been brought to an abrupt halt. His harness nearly cut through his waist. He would have to descend the rest of the way by rope. As he hastily uncoiled the rope and clipped it to the cable eyelet, he hollered into his helmet mike, trying to reach anyone below him on the camp radio channel. He got no response.

Arroyo unclipped from the cable and descended on the rope toward the red glow. As he got close, he could see that the glow was bobbing in the slush-filled waters below. His boot dislodged a chunk of ice; it free-fell into the water below.

The glow moved. An arm was waving. A helmet tilted back. Suddenly Arroyo could see a face brightly illuminated by helmet lights.

"It's about damned time," a woman's voice said through his helmet speakers. It was Brooke. She sounded as if she was miffed by a late-arriving bus on her morning commute and nothing more. "I could use a good stiff drink right about now."

Arroyo slid down the rope, stopping just above Brooke. He was out of rope. He had been in a rush; he hadn't managed his rope well, and the final couple of meters had turned into a snarl of spaghetti-like knots in his descender. This was as far as he could go.

Brooke explained that she had bobbed in the slushy water as her suit and life-support backpack slowly caked with ice. Her heat exchanger was apparently iced up, and the inside of her suit

263

was like a sauna. "Not to mention I shat myself while I was falling. What I would do for some air freshener." She had tried to call for help via both radio and iMind, but the signals couldn't reach the surface. She had turned off her radio and helmet lights from time to time to conserve power.

Brooke had seen the two scootmobiles ahead of her go airborne and crash into the far crevasse wall. It was too late for her to stop, but she pulled back on the handlebars enough to keep from smashing into the wall. Instead, she plummeted.

And plummeted. And plummeted. She managed to keep the scootmobile upright as it sailed downward. Then, as the crevasse narrowed, one side of the scootmobile began to drag against a wall of the chasm. Inundated by a shower of ice shards, still bombarded by stray pieces of machinery and bodies that were clattering down all around, she realized that if she shifted her weight slightly, she could dig the side of the scootmobile against one wall as a brake, like the metal edge of a ski. It was a delicate move. She knew the laws of probability were not in her favor. But she had to try.

She glanced hard against a couple of ledges while trying to brake her fall; even though she fell in low-g, she thought at first that she'd broken her back on one of them. The crevasse continued to narrow. Suddenly, both sides of the scootmobile were digging into ice. Then, as smoothly as if she'd planned it, the scootmobile slid to a smooth stop—perfectly upright, wedged between the ice walls as snugly as a cork in an icy bottle. Brooke looked above her. The mouth of the crevasse was too far up to spot. All around her was infinite blackness. A faint, wet breeze wafted upward from the sea like the breath of something huge and horrible and alive and eager to swallow her. If she could just stay put on the wedged scootmobile, rescuers would find her. Eventually.

And then the scootmobile slipped one or two centimeters.

264

That was all it took. Brooke lost her balance. She fell off. She was tumbling downward toward the sea. She put her gloves over her helmet visor to protect it, and tucked her knees upward, not wanting to land on a ledge with legs extended and shatter a femur. She hit the zig-zag and careened through like a tennis ball down a gutter downspout. And then the falling stopped with a gentle splash. She was bobbing in the slushy sea, weightless, stunned but alive. She couldn't believe it.

"I need to get you up to the end of the rope," Arroyo said.

"Tell me something I don't know." Brooke tried to reach up, but her suit was encased in a thick armor of ice. She couldn't raise her arms above her shoulders.

Arroyo struggled at the end of the rope, trying to reach down to her. She was so close. If he untied from the rope, he would plunk into the sea beside her, and both would be doomed. He searched frantically through his utility pouch for a stray piece of webbing, a cargo strap, anything. What he would do for a pair of bootlaces right now.

And then Brooke screamed.

"There's something in the water. It brushed my leg. Get me out of here!" She lost it; she screamed again. Arroyo swivelled in his harness so that he hung head-down, but his extended glove still couldn't reach her.

And then the water around Brooke surged and foamed. She bobbed upward gently like a leaf floating over a tiny stream's ripple. Something in the water was lifting Brooke toward Arroyo. Her ice-caked glove touched Arroyo's outstretched glove. They touched, slipped apart, touched again. Brooke was lifted higher; Arroyo grabbed her above an elbow and held on with one hand. He grabbed a daisy chain clipped to his harness and after a couple of frantic tries clipped it to a d-ring on Brooke's backpack.

She was safe.

Arroyo, still upside-down, watched the foaming waters

subside. "What the fuck was that?"

Brooke was silent. She watched the waters around her settle. "I think a fucking Delta just saved my fucking life. And for some crazy reason I'm suddenly thinking about my mother singing me a nursery rhyme: From the high rooftops, down to the sea, no one's as dear as baby to me."

Arroyo could hear the chamber splash into the water below. The rope went limp; it quivered as the chamber bobbed in the sea. Arroyo attached himself to the rope with prussiks and descended. He just needed to release the baby Delta, and then he could leave this horrible black place forever. He slid down the rope slower than his first visit, avoiding kinks and snarls.

Suddenly Arroyo was weightless in the sea, bobbing beside the chamber. Ice instantly began to cake his suit; his visor defrosters began to work overtime.

The EVA suit was so buoyant that Arroyo didn't have to struggle to stay afloat. He pulled himself to the chamber. The viewport was covered with a film of ice. He wiped it off; peering in, he could glimpse movement: a fleeting glimpse of something pure black. He thought of the grainy black leather of an old family Bible. He thought of a black leather butterfly.

The indicator light on the chamber's portable power pack still glowed red. Arroyo reached with an icy glove to the chamber's keypad. He punched the sequence Annie had given him. He could hear latches smoothly unlock; the clamshell slowly opened on its hydraulic arms.

Purple stasis fluid gushed out into the sea as the chamber drained. Something black and wet and glistening lay in the corrugated bottom of the chamber. It was the size of a seat cushion, a perfect equilateral triangle. It reminded Arroyo of an ancient colonial-era tricorn hat. Seawater began to slosh into the chamber, and it began to ride lower and lower in the waves.

Arroyo had done all he could do; it was up to the baby Delta now.

A wave of seawater splashed over the edge of the open clamshell. The chamber began to sink. Arroyo was about to reach for the Delta when it suddenly quivered, as if shivering from the cold. And then, as Arroyo watched in disbelief, it somersaulted perfectly out of the chamber and splashed into the sea. Arroyo unclipped the chamber from the rope; the chamber sank beneath the waves.

Arroyo struggled against his suit's buoyancy to get his helmet underwater. When he did, he broke out in a smile. The tiny Delta was cavorting in front of him, racing in circles, doing flips. As Arroyo's eyes focused in the murky water, he realized that something huge and black rested just below him. It was an adult Delta, its back pulsating gently. The baby swam a playful lap around it, then paused beside Arroyo.

And then the water began to foam and seethe. Arroyo was lifted upward out of the water on the adult Delta's back. For a moment, as he reached for the dangling rope above him, he had a flash of memory.

It was a winter morning in Duluth. Arroyo was in his bedroom, sitting on the edge of his bed. He couldn't have been more than four years old. His father knelt before him, clumsily clipping Arroyo's bowtie for him. Arroyo was staring past his father's shoulder, mesmerized by the feathery snowflakes drifting slowly downward outside the icy window. His father's breath smelled of cinnamon rolls and coffee. His father struggled with the tie, but Arroyo knew his father would fix it. His father could fix anything. A voice came from the hallway. It was his mother. "You men need to hurry. We'll be late to church, and the roads are going to be nasty." It was a strange memory, but Arroyo realized it must be accurate. He remembered so little about his parents. He had forgotten that they had once been church-goers.

Jim Fairchild

The flash of memory filled him with a warm glow. It had been a lifetime ago that he knew what it felt like to be loved.

He grabbed the dangling rope and began the climb upward.

Arroyo clambered through the zig-zag section before untying from the rope and clipping back into the cable. The hard part was done. Now he would just have to ascend a two-kilometer-deep crevasse and disappear into Europa's Back Forty for a day or two, or perhaps for the rest of his life.

He scraped a sheath of ice off his winch remote. It still looked like it was functional despite the dip in the sea. He pressed the IN key. The cable slowly began to retract; the slack was taken out, and then the cable tugged gently at Arroyo's harness. His boots lifted slowly from the ice. He began to rise. *Slow and steady wins the race*, he thought.

He never looked down. The sea was far below him, the hypnotizing murmur of its waves now just a memory, the sound swallowed by the ice. There was only one direction now: up. He leaned back every minute or so to look upward, hoping to catch a glimpse of the hole through which he'd descended, hoping to catch a glimpse of the sky. He passed the wedged scootmobile.

At last, he could see a tiny patch of light above. It slowly grew from a pinpoint into a jagged slash. He so wanted to stand on the surface of Europa again that he nudged the speed control upward. There was a tug in the cable, and he began to climb faster. He used his boots to steady himself against the wall. The jagged slash grew wider and brighter. A huge weight was lifting from his shoulders. Whatever might await him on the surface, at least he would never have to descend into the bowels of Europa again.

As he stared at the brightening hole above him, he could remember his prior ascent. He didn't need to brush against a Delta or a Tetra or use a dubious Dali Box to remember it. The memory was his own. It came welling upward unbidden, set loose from that closet in his mind that he had kept padlocked for so long. It overwhelmed him, but he knew he had to face it.

Brooke hung from him by the nylon daisy chain. Arroyo had the winch control set to the maximum speed. The winch had been designed to pull huge tractors out of crevasses; pulling two humans in EVA suits was essentially no load at all. He should have backed off on the speed, but he wanted to get the hell out of that cold, dark chasm. As the mouth of the crevasse grew nearer and the sliver of sky grew brighter, Arroyo and Brooke began to bounce wildly. Arroyo could see the cable go slack from time to time and whip wildly above them. He needed to slow down the winch but he couldn't get his gloved hands on the control, bouncing wildly on its keeper cord.

And then there was a horrible jolt as he was yanked over the lip of the crevasse. There was nothing but open sky above him. He was completely out of control, but they were out of the crevasse. Arroyo was on his back, being dragged toward his tractor, the cable whipping in wide arcs across the ice. There was a microsecond's pause as Brooke caught on the crevasse's edge. Then the cable rebounded. The daisy chain connecting him to Brooke broke with an explosive report. Arroyo desperately tried to grab the winch remote. He saw legs of people racing past, trying to grab ahold of Brooke while avoiding the vicious whipping cable. He was being dragged straight toward the winch at an incredible speed. He looked back, and for a fraction of a second was relieved to see that Derrick Sanders had ahold of Brooke before she could slip back into the crevasse. He could see Che Feldman running to Drag Queen, hoping to stop the winch.

The accident only took a few seconds. The winch was spinning so fast that cable began to fly off the spool. A wide arc of cable whipped across the ice between Arroyo and the tractor. He could see Che jump over the cable as it whipped past him. Arroyo grabbed the cable at his waist and swung himself so that he would hit the winch with his feet and not his head.

Another suited figure tried to jump out of the way of the cable. That person's timing wasn't good enough. Just as Arroyo accepted that he was certain to be sucked into the winch, there was a sickening ripping noise. He caught a glimpse as the cable cut Lazarus in two at the waist like a machete through butter. His suit decompressed instantly with a loud explosion; blood geysered high in the air, and was flash-frozen before it tinkled to the ground as scarlet ice pellets.

Arroyo was aware of a tremendous impact as he was sucked into the winch. The impact stunned him. He wasn't aware of pain. He hung from the winch, his shoulders on the ground. He felt embarrassed, and looked back toward the others. He saw Derrick helping Brooke to her feet. Arroyo saw that she was okay; he was overcome with relief.

And then he dropped abruptly to the ice. The impact confused him. When he looked at the winch spool, his severed left leg hung there, still stuffed into a torn piece of his suit, caught in several wraps of cable. He never heard his suit's emergency sealant cannister discharge, although it did its job perfectly. He was slipping into shock. But what he could remember was surreally lucid.

Che had managed to stop the smoking winch. He glanced toward the two bloody piles that had once been his friend Lazarus, and knew that he had to turn his attention to Arroyo. Che knelt over Arroyo and examined the stump where his leg had been. The suit sealant had coagulated around the hip, preventing the suit from losing all of its air. The stump was already flash-frozen; it had stopped bleeding. Che jumped into Drag Queen to find the trauma kit that had been in the cab for years; Arroyo had often used it as a pillow.

Arroyo lay on his back on the ice, staring up into the visor of the dreadlocked young man. It was hard for Arroyo to focus; his own visor was caked with his own frozen blood. "Is Brooke okay?" Arroyo asked.

"She's banged up, but she'll be okay. Derrick's helping her into Drag Queen to get warm."

"I'm so sorry to cause this mess," Arroyo told Che. "You're being so good to me. Thank you so much."

Che was busy shooting morphine into Arroyo's stump. He had to fish deep with the needle to get past the rock-hard frozen flesh and reach tissue that still had circulation. "You're going to make it, Arroyo. I'm going to make sure of it."

"Lazarus?" Arroyo asked, looking toward the two piles of bloodied suit.

"It happened so fast he never knew what hit him," Che said. "I doubt he suffered."

Derrick joined Che now. He looked down into Arroyo's visor and smiled at Arroyo, then patted him on the shoulder. He stood back up and got on his radio. "Mac Ops, Mac Ops. This is Marble Point Incident Commander. I want to give an update on our situation. We've got four confirmed fatalities: three in the crevasse, one on the surface. We have one injured person suffering a traumatic leg amputation. The individual is stabilized but will need medevac ASAP. One of the individuals who fell into the crevasse has been extricated and has non-life-threatening contusions and sprains, but is hypothermic and will need attention. We're still waiting on that flitter. Can you provide an updated ETA?"

Arroyo lay on his back, growing groggy. The morphine didn't do that much for him after so many years of guzzling Trank. He was just exhausted, and wanted to sleep. He looked up into the visors of those surrounding him. Che and Derrick knelt beside him; Che held his gloved hand tightly, telling him over and over *he'd be okay. Derrick looked down at him and said, "Bucko, do you know how much paperwork you've created for me?" He patted Arroyo again on the shoulder.*

Brooke had climbed down from the tractor, concerned about Arroyo. She knelt beside him, too. Arroyo looked up at the faces of the people surrounding him. He knew he was in good hands. Arroyo had thought he was alone in the universe. But he realized these people were his friends. They were so kind to him it made him cry. Their kindness was breaking his heart. He promised himself he would never forget this moment.

And, of course, he *had* forgotten. But, as he slowly clambered up over the lip of the crevasse for the last time and stopped the winch with the remote, he could remember again. *All* of it. *And on his own.* Arroyo stood, his back aching, and brushed off his knees. Above him, Ganymede was reaching its zenith, and all of Europa spread out before him.

* * *

Arroyo climbed out of his harness and let it drop to the ground. He stepped to Drag Queen and carefully wound the last of the cable onto the winch. When he turned, he realized Pegleg was behind him. The creature seemed agitated; it bounced up and down nervously on its three corners. Pegleg had no eyes, but it seemed to Arroyo that the Tetra was watching something.

And then Arroyo could hear the Kregg Vehicle, racing into the camp's flagged perimeter, just a few hundred meters away. Its eight huge wire-mesh tires bounced wildly, kicking up a cloud of ice. Arroyo could see that one of the three-meter-tall tires was shredded and flopping on the rim, showering sparks everywhere.

Arroyo's radio crackled. "Arroyo Bronson, this is Bryon Sturm again. I order you to stop where you are. You're going back with us." Arroyo jumped on the scootmobile he'd left idling before returning the Delta to the sea. He raced across the plascrete bridge to the far side of the crevasse, looking back a couple of times to make sure the sled with the Zellerhaus group's data was safe. When he had the scootmobile parked on the far side of the bridge, he ran back to Pegleg and Drag Queen.

As he climbed up the ladder to the tractor cab, he looked over his shoulder at the Tetra. "Listen, pal. I'm going to make my stand at the far side of the bridge. You're welcome to join me if you want, but I'm afraid some folks are going to get hurt before this day ends. I don't want you to get hurt, too."

Arroyo had to fight with the gear selector to get Drag Queen moving. Smoke billowed out of the tractor's undercarriage as the transmission burned. He made a tight pivot-turn and swung toward the bridge. When he looked ahead, he saw Pegleg had already crossed to the other side, and was sitting impassively beside the idling scootmobile.

Arroyo eased the old tractor across the bridge. The plascrete span flexed and swayed, as it was designed to do; crossing in the tractor felt like driving across a trampoline. Arroyo stared straight ahead at Pegleg as he crossed, determined never to look down into the crevasse again. When he got across to the far side, he pivoted the tractor and parked it so that it blocked the bridge.

He left the tractor idling. When he climbed down, he looked back across the bridge.

The Kregg Vehicle, caked with rime, sat just across the crevasse, belching black exhaust. Judging by the rough idle, Arroyo guessed the Kregg Vehicle may have been ridden too hard all night, too.

Bryon Sturm got on the radio again: "Arroyo, you realize that you've committed multiple criminal offenses on a federal worksite. The officers who are with me are going to take you into custody. You will be flown to Ganymede and will appear before the federal magistrate there to answer for your crimes. Let's do this peacefully."

Arroyo stood between Pegleg and the scootmobile and stared across the crevasse. "Haywood," Arroyo said.

"Who?" Sturm asked.

"Haywood. *Haywood Jablowme.* It's an old joke. Thank you for the offer of a trip to Ganymede. That certainly sounds better than stasis. But I must reluctantly turn down your kind offer. I have some unfinished work. I've been selected, much against my druthers, to help protect the truth about Europa."

Sturm lost his cool. "The truth is what the adults in charge say it is, you silly, inconsequential little fuck. Welcome to the real world. *Grow the fuck up.*"

"*My goodness,*" Arroyo clucked. "Such language."

Barry Wilton's voice came on the radio. "Arroyo, this is Barry. I'm the U.S. Marshal in these here parts." Barry chuckled hoarsely. "*Man.* I've always wanted to say that. Listen, my old friend. There are two armed goons sitting behind me. They reek of bacon and donuts and look like a couple of shopping mall guards. They hate Europa and would gladly shoot you if it got them back to Kardashia and their fat wives and unappreciative kids any faster. Let's chat a spell before anything rash happens."

"I think we both know how this has to end, Barry."

"Let's not get our pantaloons in a bunch. I'm in no rush. I've got nowhere else to go. You and I are kindred spirits, Arroyo. You don't have anywhere else to go, either."

"Hey, Barry. Are you packing that Colt .45 of yours?"

Barry laughed. "Naw, kid. It *did* exist once. But I hid the pieces so many years ago I can't even remember where they all are now. My memory is shot. Too much radiation, pardner. I'm *baked.* Stick a fork in me and call me done."

"Is the grave of Petty Officer Bowers hidden under the

274

Pegasus Ice Runway?"

"Yes," Barry said. "That wasn't my call. I argued against it, but *Herr Oberführer* sitting beside me here insisted it was a convenient way to deal with a piece of inconvenient history."

"So how do we resolve this?" Arroyo asked. "You know I can't let you cross the bridge."

"I don't know," Barry said. "Any thoughts?"

"Believe me, I'm thinking."

"Hold on, kid. Darla Hovenweep wants to speak with you."

"Arroyo, this is Darla. You realize that you have put yourself on the *Do Not Rehire* list by your recent actions."

"Oh, Jeez," Arroyo said. "I've been so busy that it hadn't crossed my mind. Would you kindly put Barry back on the radio?"

"Go ahead, young man," Barry said.

"I understand Vinnie Kuzawa is with you."

"Bryon wanted Animal along for the ride to make sure Drag Queen is decommissioned out here," Barry said.

"Vinnie, this is Arroyo."

"Arroyo, this is Vinnie. What the heck's happening? I thought I was just coming along to bury Drag Queen. These two goons with guns would like to bury *you*."

"Hey, Vinnie. I want you to know that I never purposefully broke equipment."

"I know that, Arroyo. I just liked flipping you shit. You're the only person on Europa who treats me decently. I just want to go back to Mactown and forget about this whole business."

"Take care, Vinnie. Put Barry back on the radio."

"Go ahead, Arroyo."

"Barry, I've strung dynamite under the bridge. It's ready to blow. Don't come near."

"That's classic," Barry said, laughing. "You're still reading those Louis L'Amour novels, aren't you?"

"Yeah. There's no dynamite. I just wanted to say that."

Barry cleared his throat. "There's something else I've always wanted to say: 'As science pushes forward, ignorance and superstition gallop around the flanks and bite science in the rear with big dark teeth.'"

"That's appropriate for the occasion," Arroyo said. "Did you come up with that?"

"It's a quote," Barry said. "From a fellow named Philip José Farmer. One of those old-school science fiction writers. Arroyo, it's been a tremendous pleasure working with you. Safe journeys."

The Kregg Vehicle lurched into gear. It belched a black cloud of exhaust as Barry Wilton floored the accelerator and drove it over the edge of the crevasse. Arroyo ducked as a mushroom cloud of ice flew upward. The ground trembled as the huge machine plummeted downward toward the dark sea.

*   *   *

Arroyo climbed into Drag Queen's cab. It had been an honor to operate the old tractor. It had been offloaded on Europa half a century earlier; it had led the way on many of the pioneering traverses across the Jovian moon. Drag Queen had hauled the first radio telescope to Europa's fledgling Pole Station before Arroyo was born. It was simple, antiquated, lacking all the bells and whistles of the newer models; the younger operators had always made fun of Drag Queen. But it had been built back in the day when designers understood Antoine de Saint-Exupéry's exhortation: *Perfection is finally attained not when there is no longer anything to add but when there is no longer anything to take away.* Arroyo felt sick to his stomach thinking about what he had to do. Drag Queen had been a faithful old steed, and if Arroyo was lucky enough to live to a ripe old age, he knew that when he sat out on his porch in a rocking chair, drooling on himself and leaking into his diaper and dreaming of his grand adventures as a younger man, Drag Queen would always be a central character in those dreams.

Arroyo climbed onto Drag Queen's roof and unstrapped the survival bag. It contained a tent, a sleeping bag and pad, a stove with a couple of liters of fuel, some emergency rations, a spare pair of socks and an old Louis L'Amour paperback. It was just enough to help a person through an unexpected night out on the ice if a tractor broke down. It didn't guarantee a comfortable night; it didn't even guarantee you'd *survive* the night. But it might help.

He dug through the cab and pulled out the first aid and trauma kits, a spotlight, a small tool kit. He tossed all of these things to the ice. He sat in the operator's seat one last time. He looked around for anything else he should take. He spied an ancient dog-eared postcard he'd found in a Kardashia antique shop years ago. It was tucked into a seam in the cab's headliner. He read the card's caption:

WINTER FESTIVAL 1997
SHORE OF LAKE SUPERIOR
DULUTH, MINNESOTA

The ancient postcard was faded and scratched, and even when new the image had been so airbrushed as to be merely an impressionistic spin on reality. But Arroyo had spent countless hours on traverses staring at the photo, trying to imagine himself in the scene, bundled in warm vintage woolen clothes and a plaid Stormy Kromer cap, strolling along the ice-clogged water. He slipped the postcard into his utility pouch.

The gears ground sadly as he pivot-steered the exhausted old tractor so it faced the crevasse. He fought with the gear selector and finally got it into F1—forward first gear. He tapped the hand throttle so that the tractor inched forward at a crawl.

Arroyo climbed quickly through the airlock and scrambled down the ladder. He stood to the side as Drag Queen crept toward the crevasse. The tractor's front counterweights inched out over the abyss; then the engine compartment. When the tractor's center of balance passed the edge of the crevasse, the tractor tipped instantly. It nosedived into the abyss in a cloud of ice particles and transmission smoke. He could hear metal shrieking against ice, then a horrible crash as the tractor hit the Kregg Vehicle. For several seconds Arroyo stood there, listening to equipment parts and dislodged ice clatter down into the abyss.

Then he turned, picked up the things he'd tossed from Drag Queen, and loaded them onto the small sled behind the scootmobile, along with the records from the Zellerhaus group.

Arroyo cinched those last items down with a couple of cargo straps as Pegleg squatted nearby. Arroyo was surrounded by perfect silence. It was a perfect crystalline silence like Arroyo had known on windless days on the polar plateau of Antarctica: a perfect silence that few humans ever experience and would never understand if it were explained to them. You could strain so hard to hear something—*anything*—that you would swear you could hear the tinkling of ice crystals in the air; that you could hear the whispering of spirits that lived within the ice—even, perhaps, that you could hear the awed whispering of the gods who witnessed the moment of the universe's creation.

And then the silence was broken. The uneven idle of a vehicle approached from camp. Arroyo looked up. It was a Mattrack, laying down a low cloud of silver exhaust, pulling up to the far side of the bridge. An airlock door swung open; Annie climbed out and waved.

She hailed Arroyo on the radio. "I take it you're okay?"

Arroyed waved. "As okay as I can be."

Annie walked toward her end of the bridge. "Meet me

halfway. I want to give you a hug before you leave."

"I'm not crossing that fucking bridge again."

Annie started to walk out onto the bridge. She waved with both arms. "Come on, Arroyo. Don't be a pansy."

Arroyo watched the plascrete bridge bounce under Annie's weight. "Don't call me names. I'll have to report you to HR."

Annie got to the middle of the bridge and stopped. She leaned over the edge and peered into the depths, spotting the twisted, smoking wreckage of the Kregg Vehicle and Drag Queen far below. "I think our HR lady is temporarily indisposed." She looked across at Arroyo again. "Get your bony ass over here, Old Man."

Arroyo took a step onto the bridge and tested it. He took another two steps; the bridge began to flex under him. "Forget this," he said, stepping back. "*You* come over *here*."

"Get your butt over here, Arroyo."

Arroyo took another step. He made the mistake of glancing over the rail into the depths of the crevasse. He looked at Annie. She had helped him get his life back. He owed her.

He dropped to all fours and crawled to the middle of the bridge.

"That's the best I can do," he said. "Don't make me look down there." He sat cross-legged in front of Annie.

Annie knelt down in front of Arroyo. She gave him an awkward hug, their helmets clanking together. "I knew you could do it," she said.

"I had to crawl."

"I don't mean crossing the bridge. I mean everything else."

"It wouldn't have happened without your help." Arroyo patted Annie on the shoulder. "What are you going to do now?"

"I'm going to limp that ice-cold Mattrack back toward Mactown. I'm sure more goons will be headed out this way to look for Bryon Sturm and his friends when they miss their next

Jim Fairchild

radio check with Mac Ops. There will be a search-and-rescue party on the way after that. I'll try to link up with the SAR team and not with the goons. I need to turn myself in back in Mactown and hope for mercy. With Sturm gone I imagine Sally Train will be in charge. I have no clue what's been going on with the Senate and the budget in the last couple of days. With Sally in charge maybe everybody can catch a long breath and come up with a better plan than a wholesale evacuation of Europa. And you?"

Arroyo pointed back toward the idling scootmobile and Pegleg. "Another kilometer up this spur road is the intersection with the Pole traverse route. Drag Queen is dead, but I've got the scootmobile and some emergency supplies. It's a little over a thousand kilometers to the Pole, with emergency supply depots every hundred klicks. If the scootmobile runs well, I could make it to the Pole in about ten days, conditions permitting."

"I'm sorry you won't have Drag Queen for the trip."

"The scootmobile is faster and drinks a lot less fuel," Arroyo said. "Of course, it isn't pressurized, and doesn't carry oxygen. So I'm going to have to hope I find adequate oxygen at the emergency depots, along with fuel, food and water."

They hunkered down a moment in silence. Then Annie rose. She patted Arroyo on the helmet. "If anybody can pull this off, you can. We should both go." She extended a gloved hand to help Arroyo get up.

"Thanks," he said. "But I'll leave the way I came." He crawled on his hands and knees back to the scootmobile.

* * *

Arroyo checked the fluids one last time on the scootmobile. The oils and coolant looked good, and the fuel tank had been topped off before the machine had been put in storage. He turned to Pegleg.

"I wish you could come with me," Arroyo said. "But I've got to make tracks. You've been my best friend. Stay safe. Go back to where you belong." The squat Tetra sat silently. Arroyo felt as if he were abandoning a faithful old dog at a highway rest stop.

* * *

Arroyo rode for an hour before taking a break. The icy traverse route was so rough, despite countless passages by tractors pulling heavy loads, that it almost shook his teeth and vertebrae loose. He left the scootmobile idling while he checked the fluids, tightened the straps on the sled load and peed into his catheter. He would have to rely on recycled urine for drinking water until he got to the first depot.

He sat side-saddle on the scootmobile, already exhausted one hour into his journey. He squinted into the distance, trying to spot any of the surface outbuildings at Marble Point, already far behind him. A shimmering Fata Morgana mirage distorted the view; multiple layers of phantom horizons stacked one on top of the other, exaggerating the heights of penitentes in the chaos terrain. They looked like skyscrapers in a postcard of Old Minneapolis. Something caught Arroyo's eye—a hint of movement on the trail behind him.

He squinted harder. Halfway back on the trail, a tiny black triangle seemed to be struggling in his direction. Occasionally the Fata Morgana made the tiny black spot look hundreds of meters tall. Arroyo's heart sank. He had to keep moving. He straddled the machine and rode another hour.

When Arroyo stopped for another break, he looked back down the trail. The tiny black triangle was still there, still moving his way.

Arroyo waited.

*   *   *

Arroyo waited for two hours. He left the scootmobile idling, burning up precious fuel. He jogged laps around the machine. There was only so much heat the suit's life support system could produce when he was sitting still. The black triangle no longer shimmered in the distance. It was closing the gap. Arroyo could see that it paused frequently, taking quick breaks, then moved again.

Just when Arroyo thought he was getting hypothermic, Pegleg ambled up. The creature was caked in rime, as if sweat exuded through unseen pores had frozen on its tough hide. Pegleg slowly sidled to within reach of Arroyo and stopped. The creature's tetrahedral mass seemed to droop and sag. Arroyo could see that it was exhausted.

"Please forgive me for leaving you," Arroyo said, slumped on the scootmobile. "You can come with me. I can't promise that our trip will end well. But we can enjoy each other's company."

For a fleeting moment, Arroyo wished he could turn his back on the journey ahead. His heart was heavy. He just wanted to go back to Earth to find his parents. He just wanted to go back to Earth to find Misty. He wanted to return home and find those whom he loved. He wanted his years of self-imposed exile to be over.

Arroyo had no clue how this journey would end. Perhaps Annie would radio him in a day or two and tell him that it was safe to turn around and come back with the load he was carrying. Perhaps he would have to go all the way to the Pole and hide in the empty station. But at least he had a faithful friend who would always stay at his side.

He reached down to stroke Pegleg's apex.

Arroyo and Misty had spent Christmas Eve in Duluth. His parents were in New Minneapolis for a conference at the Humana Colony. They were ardent humanists; they believed mankind's only hope was through compassion and tolerance for all people. They were driven by a desire to help others lift themselves from the chains of millenia-old ignorance. It was a growing movement, and the Humana Colony was its epicenter.

Arroyo and Misty had enjoyed having the house to themselves. They weren't partyers; they spent the weekend watching ancient movies: "It's A Wonderful Life," "A Christmas Story," "Rudolf the Red-Nosed Reindeer," "Mr. Magoo's Christmas Carol." They were both fascinated with the willful naiveté of pre-Crash culture. The world would never be like that again, but it was a wonderful dream that it once had been.

They had walked down to the lake on Christmas Eve to look at the ice sculptures. The castles, lit from within, filled their hearts with joy. Arroyo cooked them waffles and bacon on Christmas morning. And then they packed the car for a leisurely drive back to New Minneapolis, where they planned to have dinner with both sets of parents. Misty's parents were also attending the Humana Colony conference.

They were about fifty kilometers north of New Minneapolis, cresting a rise on I-35 just outside of Forest Lake, when the first hijacked heavy-lift transport ship streaked down through the sky like a burning comet. It was a tanker, just topped off in Earth orbit, originally bound for the ice mines on Luna. A Thumper had cut the crew's throats and taken control.

That first ship struck the Humana Colony at 1:46 p.m. From fifty kilometers away, Arroyo and Misty were almost blinded by the flash. The car's windshield was cracked by the concussion. Hundreds of thousands of kilograms of rocket propellant and oxidants leveled not just the Humana Colony but much of the city center.

Jim Fairchild

The second ship—a heavy-lift tanker hijacked from an Asian Bloc orbital station—crashed into the already-flattened remains of New Minneapolis seventeen minutes later. Arroyo and Misty were parked on the shoulder of the highway, frantically trying to call their parents, when the second impact occurred. The shock wave knocked them to their knees. The second hijacker succeeded in turning already-mangled rubble into ash.

The twin blasts instantly killed 4,752 people. Hundreds of bodies were apparently vaporized and never found. The toxic cloud drifted eastward over New St. Paul, asphyxiating many hundreds in that city. The survivors of the Twin Cities fled, thousands on foot. The cities—one flattened, one contaminated— would remain uninhabitable for decades.

Arroyo and Misty, stunned, turned around in the highway median and drove back to Duluth. They watched the news all night. The next day, Arroyo tried to hug Misty, but she pulled away. She only spoke a word or two all day. That evening, she went for a walk. Arroyo asked if he could join her. She said she wanted to be alone.

She never came back.

An ice fisherman reported to the police that he had seen a young woman walking out on the ice, dressed inadequately for the cold. When he looked again, she was gone. Her body was found under the ice during spring break-up.

The Humana Colony faded into history. Tuffie Lindblad, the political commentator, insisted that the attack had never happened. His agitprop crockumentary, "Inside Job: The Truth About the Humana Colony," painted the humanists as godless Marxists who staged their own destruction to win over converts. It was Lindblad's most popular film.

Arroyo sighed. He moved a few things around on the sled to make room for Pegleg. He gestured for Pegleg to scoot on back;

he gently wrapped a couple of straps around the Tetra to keep it from falling off when they moved on.

Arroyo wasn't afraid to touch Pegleg any more. There were no more hidden truths to be revealed. If Arroyo ever got the chance to return to Earth, he would not be searching for loved ones. He would be searching for graves.

He would be okay. He knew where he was, and he knew where he had to go, and he knew how to get there. He remembered all the things he had done—both good and bad—and he remembered what still remained to be done. It had been a crazy life so far. And perhaps it wasn't quite over.

Together, he and his friend pressed on. Their first goal, One Ton Depot, should only be a hard day away. It would be all uphill. The scootmobile bounced along on the mercilessly rough ice. Arroyo thought he could hear the engine hiccup and miss from time to time, and the exhaust looked bluer than it should, but he would nurse it along, just as he had nursed Drag Queen for years, until that final headlong race.

He glanced over his shoulder to make sure Pegleg was safe. He half-expected to get a thumbs-up, and chuckled when he didn't. Pegleg rode stoically behind him, safely strapped in place, quickly caked with a layer of ice kicked up by the scootmobile. Pegleg reminded Arroyo of a flocked Christmas tree.

Behind them, Ganymede slipped below the horizon. Ahead, a bright blue star was rising. It beckoned to Arroyo. *Earth.* Arroyo smiled. *The Water Planet*, he thought. He ached to go back. He had seen enough ice. He hadn't seen rain in more than fifteen years. He missed the smell of rain. He missed the sound of rain. He missed the joyous music of streams running full after a spring downpour, on the verge of overflowing their banks. That's how his heart felt right now. But he couldn't quite trust his memory. Until he could get back home, Pegleg would help him remember.

Jim Fairchild

*   *   *